THE KINDRED

by Luke Walker

A HellBound Books Publishing LLC Book

Austin TX

Luke Walker

A HellBound Books LLC
Publication

Cover and art design
By HellBound Books Publishing LLC

www.hellboundbookspublishing.com

Dedication:

This one is for my brother, Mase. For the copy of Lovecraft's stories he left in the toilet when I was a kid, for his collection of 70s horror paperbacks, for letting me watch 80s horror films at least ten years too young, for being my brother.

Acknowledgments:

Thank you to James, Xtina and the HellBound team for once again doing superb work with another of my tales. I am deeply grateful to the late writer James Herbert for answering the letter I sent to him when I was eleven, and a special mention to his novels Domain and '48.
Also thanks to the people who made Threads in 1984. Still the most frightening TV I have ever seen. Thanks go to Dr. Andrew Futte, and Peter Burt at the UK Nuclear Information Service for answering my questions and for being a huge help when it came to certain issues in my book. Any mistakes are, of course, all mine.
And to Rebecca – my kindred heart.

Other Books by Luke Walker

Die Laughing: 2015.
Hometown: 2016.
Dead Sun: 2018.
Ascent: 2018.
The Unredeemed: 2018.
The Mirror Of The Nameless: 2018.
The Day Of The New Gods: 2019.
The Dead Room: 2019.
Pandemonium: 2020

THE KINDRED

Chapter One

Lazarus kicked through a scummy puddle, and the water soaked into the frayed hem of his trousers. The freezing splash barely registered; he ducked back for an instant to avoid the swing of his brother's axe as Dumah attacked the flimsy wood placed over the broken window. A second later, Lazarus smashed his cleaver into the lower section of the doors and split the bottom of an office chair that had been wedged against it on the other side. He tugged the blade free and heard the brittle tinkle of breaking glass above as Candace struck a pane. The volley of their thuds and the metal squealing on decaying wood and already damaged glass rang through the pre-dawn gloom. Hot saliva squirted over his tongue and teeth and he doubled his efforts on the lower section of the entrance to the police station. Dumah lowered his axe and smashed his shoulder into the weakest spot of the entrance. The doors swung inwards before jamming against a jumble of office furniture. In the clatter of collapsing chairs and shelving units long since made rotten by their exposure to the outside air, Candace loosed her raging screams, and the sound spurred Lazarus on. He used his build, slighter than Dumah's, to shoulder the entrance.

The doors broke in two, the upper section tilting over to come free and join the debris coating the floor of the station's reception. Ears ringing, Lazarus still heard a distinct slam from somewhere inside.

Grunting, he pushed at the opening they'd created, and a large hand clamped down on his shoulder.

It was Priest.

"Slow," he whispered, and Lazarus nodded, embarrassed to be taken over by his hunger.

Dumah clambered through the opening and Candace followed immediately with her usual smooth movement despite carrying the cleaver in her sole hand. Lazarus followed his older sister, rapidly shifting to the side so Priest, then little Martha could enter. Inside, each spread across the floor. The echo of the brief crash from a few seconds before remained in Lazarus's ears. He peered to all sides, attempting to locate the source of the sound that had, without question, been a slamming door. While the last of the night offered little moonlight and there would doubtless be no sun breaking through the damaged sky shortly, a few glimmering beams falling through holes in the ceiling meant he could make out the basics of the room.

Mess across the floor; rusting pipes and thin cables in the ceiling, and a long, flat surface stretching from wall to wall. There were a few doorways on his right, but no actual doors. Lazarus followed Priest who led them to an open section of the flat surface, walking as if he knew the police station inside out.

There was little space for them to spread apart on the other side of the desk or table or whatever it had been used before now. Lazarus was pressed close to Candace and he brushed his fingers on her narrow hip that jutted through her heavy coat. She shifted to welcome the pressure for a moment. In front of her, Dumah a step behind Priest; behind Lazarus, Martha with her butcher knife and her breath hot and quick on his forearm where the tattered sleeves of his coat had ridden high.

"Door," Priest whispered and pulled on a handle.

At once, weak light and shadows found the family. Moving as one, they ran into a corridor and took positions against the walls. Only Priest remained in the centre.

Lazarus might have expected burning torches strapped to the walls as they themselves used in their caves. Instead, several *electrical* torches shone upwards and cast ugly shadows. They knew about *electrics* and had seen lights in use before although they knew they were a rarity because of *Batteries*. They were powerful and rare and special. Mary and Martha had a collection of *Batteries* Priest said were useless. They played with them sometimes, the little cylinders rolling over the uneven floor of the caves and tinkling when they collided.

"Not enough space," Candace muttered. "We should go."

"Wait." Priest's voice was no louder than Candace's. Even with the recent huskiness that filled his tone and occasionally edged into pained croaking, their father's strength remained clear.

Lazarus knew what Candace meant. When they came on the attack and hunt for food, they did so in open areas. If they entered buildings, they avoided narrow spaces like this corridor. Not enough room to spread and only two exits: the door at the back and another at the far end, which could well be locked. There were other doors all on the left wall, but Lazarus didn't need to draw closer to them to see the mountains of furniture wedged high on the inside. Whoever had banged the door closed had run to the other end of this corridor, not into any of the side rooms.

He sniffed a few times and caught nothing but the reek of their bodies and the outside dampness. Air streamed through the main entrance and flowed to their backs and brought the suggestion of the new day instead of night.

"Martha," Priest whispered.

The child scampered ahead. The smallest and quickest of them, she shot from side to side of the corridor, making almost no sound thanks to her slight frame. Lazarus tracked her, knowing she moved too fast for anyone to emerge out of the dark and successfully strike her with a knife or a club. Wordlessly, she pointed to the heavy doors closed at the other end.

"Together," Priest told them.

They advanced, passing the fluttering lights and the shadows, their sides and backs against the walls and their steps as light as their breathing. Martha reached the door first, looked back to Priest who nodded.

She grasped the handles; the others shoved themselves flat on the walls while flakes of rusting paint fell. Martha ducked, reducing her already low height to avoid any weapon swung from the other side.

Nothing emerged from the next corridor.

Fewer lights shone although enough illumination was cast to show the opening into what had clearly been an eating area. Its doors were long since removed, revealing the dull gleam of smashed tables. Great holes were punched into the walls, exposing wiring and stained brickwork. There was nothing for them there and nowhere for anyone to hide.

Moving down the corridor, they turned with a bend and faced a set of descending steps; a square of dirty glass let it in next to no moonlight. Lazarus stared at the steps, knowing they had to go down there and knowing the hunt was not in their favour this time. They'd misjudged the layout of the building after studying it from the outside.

Priest backed up a step, his narrow body brushing Dumah's larger shape. Turning on his heel, Lazarus faced the second corridor and froze.

A man, slight and appearing hunched by the weight of his long coat, stood at the door Martha had opened, gripping a small gun.

Lazarus raised his cleaver and a voice emerged from somewhere close.

"If you move, we'll have to kill you, so please stay where you are."

It wasn't the little man with the gun; he hadn't moved his mouth. Worse, his hold on the gun remained steady.

Lazarus didn't need to see the others to know they had also raised their weapons and had shifted away from each other the instant the speaker said his first word.

"I mean it."

It came from the steps.

Three slow paces, the sound hollow and somehow cold, brought a second man into view. Taller than the first and his face lost to the poor light, he also held a gun. While the weapon was not large, Lazarus knew enough about firearms to be sure they couldn't fight against either man and survive. Guns and their bullets were faster than any blade unless you were already within striking distance.

The skinny man in the corridor advanced, the tread of his boots clear and precise. Lazarus and Martha turned to him. Faced with two cleavers, both stained with rust and blood, the man didn't slow, and Lazarus knew the self-defence Priest often advised wasn't an option. This was a killing time.

He heard a tiny mutter from Martha: *"The Jesus."*

Her prayer said, the child drew a step closer to their assailants.

Weapon cold in his hand, Lazarus did the same.

"Please don't do anything," the man in the corridor said.

Lazarus and Martha moved at the same time, smooth and silent apart from the rush of stale air. As Lazarus dropped to his knees to slide at the armed man, he heard Dumah and Candace go for the other one, heard Priest calling for him and everything came down to the swing of his cleaver.

He swiped it at the man's stomach and struck air as the man jumped backwards, crying out. Martha streaked past Lazarus – a sprinting, hunched figure with her knife jutting like a metal finger. Lazarus went from his knees to standing in a second and, while still running, drew his arm back to throw his cleaver level with his head. Candace shouted Dumah's name and the second target roared senseless noise.

"Martha, down," Lazarus cried. Immediately, the girl fell flat on her back, knife raised. And in the instant before Lazarus threw the weapon, the thin man fired.

Plaster and flecks of brick exploded from the wall, striking Lazarus in the side of his chest. The man had backtracked into a relatively illuminated section of the corridor. Fighting for breath, he held the gun with both hands, the barrel darting between Martha prone on the floor and Lazarus's hand gripping his cleaver.

"No closer," the man spat and rubbed his narrow chest.

At Lazarus's back, there was another gunshot and it was thunder compared to the first from the skinny man.

"Dumah." Uncontrolled panic exploded in Candace's voice and sent dread skittering through Lazarus's heart.

Praying to Priest's God – the God he was unsure whether or not he believed in - Lazarus whirled around.

Priest was between the two groups of his children, caught and helpless. Dumah had fallen at the top of the stairs, Candace at his head, Dumah motionless while the second man stood over him, panting and his shotgun held like a battering club.

"Brother," Lazarus cried, trapped in the same manner as his father. Martha on the floor; the guns, and Dumah motionless because the hated men with their weapons had beaten them.

Screaming, Martha was up and racing past Lazarus before he had chance to react. Priest was faster; he ducked and caught the girl, deftly slipping the knife from her small hands and dropping it to the mucky floor. She sobbed, squirming in her father's arms while Lazarus's awareness of the threat and the guns and the ever-present hunger in his belly slipped away on a cool breath where none of it mattered. Some new place safe from the burned sky and ruptured ground.

Somewhere he would feel less than nothing and pain would never touch his family.

Bellowing a shout of rage that made it clear he was uninjured, Dumah shoved a hand up high and fast, fist striking the shotgun to smash it against the wall, the second man reacting with speed to swing the weapon around, barrel striking Dumah's forearm.

The skinny man in the corridor sprinted faster than Lazarus could turn at the sound of his rapid approach and shoved his handgun against Lazarus's head. His yell was high and frightened, but it was not a lie.

"Everyone stop this right now or I kill him."

Chapter Two

Granger stayed perfectly still as Roe herded the people from the stairs and through the opening into the holding cell area where they clumped in a tight group.

"In there." Roe indicated the nearest cell. While the window built into the centre of the door was a smashed hole, the door did lock.

The group stayed where they were.

"Please." Granger said it without any raised volume. "In there and we can talk calmly."

Although his fingers remained on the gun, he made sure he didn't alter the pressure, avoiding any indication he truly registered the weapon.

The eldest of the group—a towering figure who had to be at least sixty—stared at Granger. Light from the candles spread yellow fingers across the man's features, revealing gaunt cheeks, a thin beard along with scars beside his nose. His eyes were dark; the left had a slight lack of focus. He was either half blind or on his way there. And still, Granger knew he needed to be careful. He and Roe – along with Willis and

Patterson who remained against the wall – had captured wild animals.

"Come," the tall man said. Immediately, the group around him—a boy of about fourteen or fifteen, a man perhaps twenty, a black woman five years older, and a child, a *girl*—entered the cell. While it was designed to hold two suspects, its sparse furnishing had been destroyed years ago. Plus, only the lad aged twenty or so had any meat on his bones; the others couldn't hide the leanness of their arms and chests under their many layers of ragged clothing.

"Roe. If you would," Granger muttered.

Roe aimed his gun directly at the leader's face and held it there as Patterson came from the wall to push on the cell door. Metal hinges grating, the heavy barrier slammed into place. Patterson spun the handle for the lock. It bolted; he turned the key jutting from the second, pulled it clear and immediately backed away with his gun raised again.

Only then did Roe let out the volley of coughing he'd obviously been holding in for moments. Spluttering, he turned his back on them, took a few deep breaths and had to let them out in spittle and hacking.

Granger approached the hole in the cell door. "My name is Granger. What is yours?"

"Priest." It was another rasp.

"Your name, not your position."

"Priest."

"Fine. Priest." He pointed to the three men who'd drawn closer together despite the enmity two felt for the third. "Roe. Patterson. Willis. We were—"

"I know what you are," Priest croaked.

"What is that?"

"The men who set the world on fire."

Granger blinked, unsure if he was more surprised by the clear diction coming from a man he wasn't sure could speak in more than grunts, or the loathing layered deep into every word.

"Not quite. We were with the government. *Your* government. Willis was with the police. We were the men who tried to stop the men who. . .set the world on fire."

For all the reaction he gave, Priest might have gone deaf. In his face, Granger saw the reply and could not help but agreeing with it.

You failed.

Granger licked his lips and resisted the urge to wipe them. He knew there was nothing to fear. The prisoners secure; his darling Carolyn safe in one of the offices on the second floor, and a weapon within easy reach.

But still, his heart beat a little too quickly and despite the lack of any real warmth, his throat had become dry in recent minutes.

"Patterson. Could you get some water, please?

He turned from Priest for the first time, dismayed by his relief at doing so, and glanced at Patterson who came close to merging with a cluster of shadows growing from the wall at his back. Black coat, lowered head, and his frame smaller than Roe or Willis, he might have been rooted to the spot.

"Water?"

"Please."

Granger knew they didn't have much left. The boiled water left to cool and stored in the Cresta bottles had to keep them going for the last twenty-five miles to Dover. If it came to it, they'd find a pond and boil the water until the bacteria were destroyed. Of course, they risked absorbing residual radiation but then, that was a cold fact of life these days.

Patterson left them and Granger waited until the noise of his steps faded before speaking again.

"I don't want any violence here. You're in there for our protection because. . .well, we've heard the odd story about you, and it seems like a good idea to keep a door between us."

The figures behind Priest stood as far apart as they could given the limited space. Only Priest remained in full view and his mouth was as still as his eyes.

"We didn't really believe the things we heard. There aren't a lot of people out there and we've not been on the move for long, but the few settlements we did encounter told us to be careful."

Granger moved closer to the cell door and lowered his voice. "We came across a farmhouse a few miles from here. Blood everywhere, the place torn apart. Not one door or window remaining and. . .pieces thrown into the corners of rooms." He said the next word with deliberate emphasis. "Bones."

Priest's face was still.

"We ate well that day."

"Jesus Christ."

That was Willis, nasal voice thick with anger. Granger felt the same and hid the emotion. Long years had passed since he'd needed to play any real political games but now faced with a decent opposition, he wasn't surprised to feel the old skills returning.

He addressed all of them. "A little back and forth, I think. You first. Do you have a home?"

He willed Priest to answer while water dripped in the darkness and hoped he wouldn't have to resort to threats. Blood had dirtied his hands before and while he didn't like it, he saw it as a means to an end.

Perhaps understanding Granger, Priest finally answered.

"We live at the sea. We have a home in the caves."

"You're a fair way inland." He knew why. Pickings for their food must be scarce nearer the coast.

"We do what we have to," Priest replied.

"I'm sure," Granger muttered. "Well, my friends and I have spent a lot of time underground. Bunkers. There are a great many of them down there and we were lucky enough to be in one when the war began. We were also lucky enough to find others when we needed to go on the move. Do you know *bunkers?*"

"Holes in the ground for rats," Priest replied, and Willis laughed in disgust.

"You could say that," Granger said. "Either way, we were in the position to take shelter and we spent a lot of time underground. We came up when we had to; we saw what the bombs had done and we thought that was it. No rule or hope for any kind of decent life. I mean, you've seen the cities, haven't you? All our industries, our businesses, our society burned away. No crops, no farmland, no animals. It's a wasteland, isn't it?"

"It's whatever you make of it."

Granger drew closer to the cell, smelling the reek of the group's dirty bodies. He had to be honest: he and his colleagues were also filthy. Long days since the opportunity of a full body wash. He could only hope for some basic comforts once they reached their destination; some semblance of decent living after so long out in the grave of Britain.

"Tell me, Priest. Do you consider yourself a good man?"

Willis barked his ugly laugh. Granger ignored him.

Priest said nothing.

"You may well be despite the things you've done. I don't see us as black and white. I see shades of grey, Priest. Good men have to do bad things; bad men are sometimes decent. You and your. . .family, you've done wicked things. There's no two ways about that, but I'd be willing to say you're also amenable to other options."

Granger smiled.

"What is your point?" Priest asked.

"I need your help. *We* need your help." Granger stepped as close as he dared to the cell. Find common ground; that was the key. It always had been. So what if the need for gentle politics had burned with the bombs? That didn't mean it was dead.

"Do you know Dover?"

Priest sniffed.

"Dover isn't too far away. It's. . .potential, Priest. They're getting it together again. Trying to get things working. We're going to join them to get stuck in and have some control over our lives, again. That's where you and your family come in. That's why we need your help, you see. You will come with us."

Priest let out a gruff noise, then another. A few seconds passed before Granger realised it was laughter turned harsh and barking by whatever afflicted Priest's throat.

"You are nothing. Your Dover is nothing. Your government. All dead. Your time is dead. It is a ruin because *you* made it one. Your past is dead and the world is not yours. You are memories."

Above, a flurry of running steps struck the corridor, the stairs and the crashing echo bounded over the wet floor.

The shotgun was in Granger's hands in seconds; he whirled on the spot as Roe raised the Browning and Willis ran for the main entrance to the cells. Patterson skidded to a stop, coughing, unable to keep the air in his lungs for more than a moment.

"What is it?" Granger shouted. The dank and the stink of the cells seemed to blossom into flame and its heat was a scouring torch over his skin. Sweat broke out all over his body, turning the new heat back into a freezing coat.

"Patterson. What is it?"

Patterson sucked in a deep breath and his words collapsed. "There are more of them out there."

"What?" Willis yelled it and stomped towards the little room holding its captives.

Granger blocked his way with the shotgun. "Patterson?"

The smaller man lowered his head and he gave his reply to the puddles.

"It's Carolyn."

Something awful was bearing down on him, something he'd always feared and if he didn't hear the words, then it wouldn't ever arrive.

"What?" he whispered and saw the answer on Patterson's face before the man replied.

"She's dead, Granger."

Chapter Three

The instant three of the men ran from the cells towards the stairs, the clatter of their shoes and boots ringing on the old steps, Lazarus studied all sides and angles of the cell holding them prisoner.

The only discernible features came from damage: the exposed pipework of a sink and toilet broken away from the floor; a few pieces of crumbling tile; some holes in the walls that offered no help; rents in the bricks letting in outside air which at least gave them some sense of place. If his guess was right, the exterior wall faced a green space which ran alongside the road into the main section of the town. The front of the building and the doors they'd broken through were at their back and that meant the safety of the woods with all its decayed vegetation and mud sucking at their feet was a matter of minutes away.

Comforted by that, Lazarus double checked for any potential weapons, unsurprised to see none. The men would have made the space clear for the family long before their attempted attack because they'd known all along what Lazarus and the others were planning. Heat flooded his face. They'd been foolish to think every time they hunted it would go in their favour. While they were quick, brave and did not flinch in the face of any danger, there were dangerous people out there. Priest had told them so often enough. Perhaps too often, Lazarus wondered. Maybe the words had become only words without much meaning. If so, that was his own fault. Dumah's, Candace's and the sisters, too. Priest knew the world before the bombs; Candace remembered some of it, but not enough. A dangerous world then; a dangerous world now.

Dismissing the potential of attack for the moment, Lazarus shifted past Dumah to stand beside Priest. Candace held Martha at the rear of the cell and that was good. The girl needed to be kept out of sight for as long as possible from the men. Lazarus knew what some men wanted to do with women and girls. He would die before that happened here in this stinking cell.

Keeping his head aimed towards the lone man, Lazarus shifted his eyes towards Priest who sniffed, nostrils flared.

Permission to speak was given.

"You," Lazarus said to the man who stared at him with naked interest. Also, naked disgust. He could have been watching a new lifeform crawl out of the earth.

Lazarus knew the man's name. He'd paid attention when the leader—Granger—introduced them. He said *Willis* in his mind, getting a feel for the name before storing it.

"What?" Willis said.

"Let us leave and you will live."

There and gone in a heartbeat, surprise crossed Willis's face. Lazarus had seen the same before. While he rarely had reason to speak to strangers, he knew people expected him to grunt or, at best, utter single words. There was power in voices – something that frustrated the mute Dumah painfully.

"Is that right?"

Seemingly not concerned with his lack of weapon, Willis drew closer to the cell door. His boots splashed puddles.

"I let you go now and there's no trouble. Is that what you're saying?"

He had a cold, thick voice that hurt Lazarus's ears. It was the sound of all aggression no matter the words or the situation.

"I tell you what. You *are* trouble. Not only because of what you've done but because of what you are."

Willis drew closer. Lazarus stayed still despite the strong urge to shove a hand through the little window in the door and grab Willis's neck. A fierce tug and Willis's face would be in the square hole.

His fingers trembled. He kept his arm by his side and didn't need to look at Priest to know his father saw and understood. Dumah pressed against Lazarus, eager to come forward. Lazarus pushed back with the slightest pressure and his brother subsided.

Outside the door, Willis stopped. He obviously knew where to stand to be a fraction out of arms' reach. He placed his boots down into puddles. The water, foul-smelling and brown, trickled over a loose section of flooring to pool into a crack.

"Don't get me wrong," he said. "I know how it is. I know about survival. I know what it takes and I know everyone has lost someone, but you people. God. I knew people like you lot back when I was on the Force. Always ready to look out for yourselves even before it all went to shit. Always ready to drop others if it meant you were sorted. You just take it up to the next level, don't you? No growing crops for you; no working on the land out there. No. You just take what you want." He lowered his voice and Lazarus knew it wasn't because he didn't want the other men to hear him if they suddenly returned. It was anger held inside.

"I've done some bad shit to get by, but even I know what's right and what's wrong. Your people killing Carolyn. . . I mean, what the fuck did she do to deserve that? Granger is going to hurt you for that. He'll hurt you a lot." Willis spat. "But he'll keep you alive. For Dover. Worse fucking luck."

Lazarus said nothing because there was nothing to be said. Willis saw him and the others as dirty as the earth or the decomposing body of wild animals mouldering into the fallen leaves and rainwater. For the first time in his life, Lazarus knew he would kill someone for reasons other than to eat. He would kill Willis to take away the hate boiling out of the man's heart.

Above, a door slammed; running steps hammered directly above the cells and then clashed on the steps. A voice called out and Lazarus caught only one word – *'windows'* – from Granger before the steps hit level ground and two of the men returned. Granger and Patterson, guns in hand.

Panting, Granger strode to Willis's side and shouldered him out of the way. Still breathing hard and paying no attention to Patterson who rested on a wall and sucked in each lungful as if it hurt to do so, Granger lifted the shotgun.

Silently, Priest eased Lazarus to the side and approached the cell door.

Chapter Four

I will die today.

For Priest, it had become something of a motto. The first thought upon waking; the dictum before the others stirred in the breeze breaking through cracks and holes in the rocks of their caves. It never brought fear, only regret that he would no longer be with his children and no longer able to keep them alive in the cruel world given to them. Tempering the regret, his love for them and his gratitude to God for giving him the time and strength to keep them together.

He prayed quickly, asking for his children to be protected and to have the strength to continue when he was gone, and kept his face as expressionless as he had during their incarceration in this reeking place.

Granger handed the shotgun to Patterson and took the handgun. He aimed the smaller weapon squarely at Priest's head.

"How many?" he whispered.

Knowing what he was being asked, Priest feigned confusion. If nothing else, he could give Mary more time. The child was doubtless already moving into position and he had faith she would avoid Roe who had clearly been sent to search for her.

"How many?" he repeated. "What do you mean?"

He expected rage. Instead, Granger's reply was as smooth as the worn rocks and pebbles of their caves beside the sea.

"How many outside who've killed my wife."

That was unfortunate but ultimately, it changed little. They were locked in the cell no matter who was dead beyond the building. The only difference it made would be to Granger's head once his patience ran out.

Priest gripped the frame of the hatch. It seemed as if the others on either side of the cell door had retreated miles distant, leaving him with the grieving man. That was fine. These next few moments were their business alone. He knew his children would make no move without indication from him; he had to hope the men who saw Granger as their own father would act in the same way.

"Who are you, Granger?" As ever, speaking hurt. Priest found it less of a bother now. Even if that was because his time was drawing to an end, any relief from the sensation of a dozen knives cutting his throat could only be a blessing.

"Who are you?"

The gun lowered an inch and Granger stared at Priest with blank eyes.

"I will play your game, Priest." He took a slow, deliberate step forward. If his men remained in the background and not in some empty space as Priest now saw them, they made no move to stand beside their leader.

"Who am I? I'm a government man through and through. I'm law and order. Do you remember that? Do you remember your flock? Priest?" He made the title sound like swearing. "Sermons? Weddings?

Funerals? People coming to you for comfort and advice? You must remember your work against the chaos of. . .well, let's be grand, shall we? Over evil. You were that man; I was the same. Our only difference was our boss. The Church for you. Government for me. And now our difference is I still work against the chaos. *You* forgot that a long time ago. I'm working to help things. You're just watching what's left burn."

He roared the last few words and the weapon shook madly. Between the groups, moisture dripped and the dawn slipped sly fingers through a high window, the opening small and still barred.

Granger cleared his throat as if embarrassed by his anger.

"You wouldn't understand us and what we're doing, Priest. The people we know, they're working for good. Down in Dover. Government. Rule. Order. All the things that made England great. *That's* what's happening in Dover. The men fighting to take charge, again, to do some good in the mess out there. You're content to be a part of the mess and forget everything you would have worked against before the bombs."

Priest nodded once. While he had not predicted the exact words, the tone and sentiment had been in his ears before Granger spoke.

"Exactly."

The gun was aimed at his head once more.

Flexing away the stiffness in his fingers, Priest brought his hands to his face and clasped them. Without any sensation of movement, the others were right at his back and his side again, and Granger's men were no more than a few steps distant. And why would they be anywhere else? Two sets facing each other with a locked door between them. The world then.

The world now.

"Tell me right now, Priest. How many more of you are out there?"

Priest swallowed and held his cry of pain inside. On some days, whatever ailed him hurt no more than a sore throat; other days, it was as if the tendons, muscles and meat below the skin had been set alight.

But there was no good to come from worrying about it now as there was nothing to be gained from pretence. Never smoked a day in his life and still, cancer had set up its home deep inside him. To be expected, perhaps. The very air was poison. Not as much as it had been back at the beginning of this harsh new world, but still sick enough.

I would like a final drink. That good Scotch Mrs Milligan bought for my birthday. Yes. That would be welcome right now.

He buried his secret smile at the memory of his housekeeper and her impeccable taste.

"How many more, Priest?"

With regret, he let go of his memories and returned to the ugly present. But not so ugly. His children were by his side and all he could hope for was Lazarus taking charge, becoming their leader – even if the lad privately believed Candace was that leader.

"There it is. Your loss of control." Priest spoke with more ease than recent weeks. "That need, that *control* over us is the past." Priest kept his eyes closed. There was no need to see the man now. "It's what brought us to this point." He lowered his voice. "It's what destroyed everything."

Any reply coming into the cell was utterly unimportant because everything Priest had was in his hands and in the words rushing from his mouth like a waterfall come to spray its chill over the tumours in his throat.

"Lazarus, Dumah, Candace, Martha; go, children, go to Dover and kill them all."

His eyes were closed; his hands clasped in prayer and there was time for a sparking memory of his final Christening a fortnight before the bombs; the beginning of April and a day lit by a welcome sun and turned sharp by a strong wind while he said the old words over the child and the daylight at his back held all the good promises there would ever be now time was short, time was short, time was—

—run out

Praying, Priest's last sensation was his own warm breath on his palms.

He did not hear the shot.

Chapter Five

Candace flung herself to the floor of the cell. Her fingers slipped through the gore splattered over Priest's chest and arms and went no higher because there was almost nothing to reach for.

She screamed; her throat felt as if it had split wide open, but the cry of her voice could have come from miles away. It reached her ears as a breathy whisper: the wind playing through seaweed, maybe.

The gun. Fired so close. Deaf.

She was barely aware her thoughts had reverted to the struggling, animalistic grunting they'd been in the time before Priest found her and brought her back to coherent speech and human thinking. In her shock, she could become the same beast Granger and his men thought they were.

Candace stood. More sounds were returning and all were terrible. Shoved to the back of the cell by Dumah before Willis fired, Martha was nothing but howls. Unable to scream or vent his grief, Dumah was a panting dog while Lazarus had fallen against one of the walls and could do only shake from head to feet.

Candace roared and shoved her hand through the opening in the door. Granger was out of reach. Even so, she splayed her fingers, stabbing them towards his face and unable to bellow any words. She was nothing but her need to kill the man, to sink her fingers into his flesh and bathe in the glory of ripping him into chunks.

"Shut up," Granger shouted. "For God's sake, woman, shut up."

Martha's dog-like howls had collapsed into sobbing. Dumah held the girl and she clung to him as if drowning. Lazarus hadn't moved from the wall or taken his eyes from Priest's remains.

Candace saw them all although she felt like she hadn't moved. Groaning, she covered her mouth and did her best to get a hold on a world spinning over and over. She had nothing solid to grip now that all the shit of her miserable past had smashed its way back into her life. All the hurt and grief of love destroyed and the family belonging to the life she'd lost in the flames; all that returning to wrap its arms around her and crush her into the same ash coating the desolate fields and the cities.

"Priest," she croaked. "Father. Dear Father."

"Father?" That was Willis. He was caught between disgust and amusement. "He was your dad? Hate to tell you this, love, but you're a bit too much dark chocolate for him to be your old man."

"Jesus, Willis." Patterson. His name was Patterson and it didn't matter if Willis repulsed him. He would die at her hand, but not before Granger. They would all die at her one hand.

Candace swiped at her lips and nose, smearing rapidly cooling blood, and flicked the mess through the window hole at Granger.

A few drops struck his chest and hand.

"Christ." He backed away, cursing under his breath, and a sudden hissing broke out of the shadows. At once, Candace knew it, tracked it, *welcomed* it.

The shot fired from the wall near the stairs; the arrow streaking a few feet over the ground because the person who'd crept down into the cells was so small.

It hit Patterson in the arm.

Screaming, he dropped his gun, the clatter of the weapon striking the floor merging with his wailing as he spun and slapped a hand at the arrow which had pierced the top of his bicep, shredding skin and muscle, before smashing into the opposite wall. Red sprayed from the ragged wound, the droplets soaking through Patterson's clutching grasp.

Candace had heard Priest speak of time changing its speed during stressful situations: seconds dragged out to minutes, and minutes become hours or the reverse and everything snapping by in the time it took to blink.

She did not blink.

Roaring, Willis shoved a hand to the interior of his heavy coat and yanked a kitchen knife free while Granger made no sounds as he dived for the gun Patterson dropped. Water splashed at his clumsy movement, then splattered Willis's legs as he raced towards the shadows pooling across the ground by the stairs.

Martha's sister Mary, the child's movement silent and fluid, jumped into the light and swung Dumah's axe at the same time.

The blade struck Willis's hand in the centre, cutting skin and bone with ease. His fingers were broken even before the upper half of his hand hung from the rest by stretching muscle. Candace's joy brought senseless screams to her lips. Behind, Martha did the same while Lazarus yelled Mary's name over and over.

Willis shrieked. He fell to his knees, clutching what remained of his right hand even as red spread rapidly on the dirty ground.

"Jesus fucking Christ, my hand, my fucking hand, ah God, my fucking hand—"

If there were more words, they fell apart into broken sobs.

"Don't."

Granger froze. He was splayed flat, reaching for Patterson's gun, and Candace's heart was a burning ball of flame deep within her chest.

My sister. My child.

Mary stood over Willis, holding Dumah's bloody axe inches above his hanging head.

Granger's fingers moved a fraction.

Mary brought the axe to rest on Willis's hair. Gore dripped from the metal, soaking him while he wept and held his arm against his stomach. Drying blood coated Mary's mouth and chin. More flecked her cheeks. She'd killed Granger's wife, broken into the building and hurt the men in terrible ways. The only thing left was to free her siblings.

Granger froze again. The gun was within his reach but Candace knew he would not be fast enough. It came down to what he valued more: killing Mary, or Willis's life.

This is a standoff, dear Candace, Priest said to her. *And what happens next belongs to all of you.*

Chapter Six

There had been no time for horror for Dumah when Granger shot Priest. Grief had been instant and he drowned in it while Candace grabbed Priest's body. It flooded his chest, robbing him of breath and that was fine because it meant he would soon be with their father, and this filthy place so far from the welcome wind of the sea would be out of reach forever.

But then Mary.

Standing taller than the others, he'd seen over Candace's head when she lunged at the opening in the door. With Martha still clinging to him and his hands in a death-grip around her shoulders, he shoved his way beside Candace to stare out into the open space.

Mary stood over Willis; axe ready to kill. Each inhalation was slow despite her exertion. In contrast, Willis was a panting dog and it seemed like one of Priest's miracles that he hadn't simply fallen over.

Patterson had fallen against the wall, still holding his wounded arm. He stared with white unblinking eyes and Dumah dismissed him as a threat. Granger was the danger; Granger so close to the gun.

Dumah realised Mary was shifting her focus rapidly between him and Granger. She didn't need or want permission. She wanted him to understand.

He nodded at the girl and her attention reverted fully to Granger.

"Lay down," she said.

"What? I—"

"Lay down."

Mary pressed the blade of the axe against Willis's head. He groaned, perhaps so far gone into his torment that he was unaware of the threat. The floor around him was a red flood and the smell of his spilled blood made Dumah's grief a fraction easier to bare. The men had been hurt. Within minutes, they would be hurt so much more.

Granger lay prone on the floor and Dumah knew how frustrated and confused and angry the man had to feel. Weapon so close and the leader of their new enemy dead, but all his plans about to be undone by a little girl.

Dumah grunted and his fingers itched to spill their own share of the blood.

"You," Mary said to Patterson and he whimpered.

"Let them out. Now."

Struggling, Patterson lumbered to his feet and used the wall as support. He hadn't let go of the arrow wound in his arm, and the shocking white of his face was a shining contrast to the red dribbling between his fingers.

"Key. Unlock it."

"I don't have the key. I—"

"*Key,*" Mary shrieked, and the man flinched.

Staggering, he crossed the floor to drop to his knees beside Granger. "Give me the keys," Patterson whispered.

Granger made no move.

"For Christ's sake, *give me the fucking keys.*"

Patterson looked ready to pitch over and Dumah wanted to laugh at that. A small injury and so much noise.

"We can't let them go," Granger muttered. Dumah struggled to hear him. The slight change of Mary's posture told him everything was about to go one way or the other and all he could do was hope his sister was as quick as always.

"It's over." Patterson sounded exhausted. "We let them go or we die."

"They'll kill us," Granger shouted.

Patterson said nothing to that. His resignation and acceptance of that death was as clear as the salty, hot smell of so much blood.

"Keys," Mary said, and it was for the last time.

Granger shifted position, obviously aware of the need for careful movement. He pulled a set of keys from a side pocket and wouldn't look Patterson in the eye as they passed from hand to hand.

"Open the door," Mary said.

Willis tipped to the side, still holding his severed hand. Side-stepping nimbly, Mary swung the axe to his temple and the dripping blade hung over his face. Unconscious, Willis presented no threat. Even so, Dumah was proud to see how closely Mary kept the axe on him.

Tears cleaning the muck on his cheeks before trickling through his patchy beard, Patterson rose and showed the keys to Mary.

"Unlock it," she hissed.

Stumbling and ignoring Granger's commands not to let them out, Patterson advanced on the cell door and Dumah would not let him avert his gaze. Struggling with his left hand while his right hung at his side and his upper half was a bloody mess, Patterson fumbled with the keys. The instant Dumah heard metal meet metal, he shoved his face forward to the opening in the door and clamped his teeth around Patterson's nose.

Patterson's agonised squeal became a nasal whine as Dumah's jagged teeth stabbed his flesh. He tried to pull away; Dumah tightened his hold and skin tore.

"If you move, he'll bite your nose off," Candace said, and Patterson was still. Dumah tasted blood and fresh tears; he felt Patterson's hissed exhalations blowing on his tongue and fought the fiercely strong urge to snap his teeth together.

"What the hell is going on?" Granger cried. "Patterson, what's happening?"

Dumah had limited vision of Granger and the outside area; he trusted Mary to see her threat through the instant Granger stood and he wished for the chance to tear flesh from bodies and to cry Priest's name in his mind as he did so.

"Open the door," Candace told Patterson.

Unable to see properly, his fingers soaked, Patterson whimpered into Dumah's mouth and the heavy door swung outwards. Hinges unused to any great extent for years squealed. So did Patterson when Dumah pulled his mouth clear and they shot out of the cell.

Dumah yanked Patterson and flung him into the little room. Lazarus and Dumah went for Granger, their arms flailing. They collided, dropped and Granger was up and sprinting for the stairs. Without a sound, he jumped for the first step and Mary's axe came for him, spinning end over end to smash into the damaged wall inches from Granger's back.

Lazarus found the gun used to kill Priest and slapped a finger over the trigger.

The three shots went wild, each round blowing tiny holes in the walls and sending broken plaster to the wet floor.

Granger was gone with only the echo of the gunshots and Dumah's wailing as his rage blew away to leave him nothing in the world but anguish.

Chapter Seven

Lazarus did his best to stand straight but swayed on the spot. His vision had become a mixture of blacks and reds, each throbbing shade beating in time with his heart. There were shouts on all sides and none made sense. Words had lost any meaning because. . .because. . .he was back in his past, back as a little boy before Priest found him in the stink of the waste and took him to the dry caves and the soft comfort of his voice and his words. He was long ago and all he knew was the non-stop cold of every day and the gnawing in his empty belly, but then Priest would come and bring warmth. Better than any warmth, he would bring *food*.

Lazarus pitched to his side. Dumah caught him, grasped his shoulders and shook them. He hooted, shook Lazarus again and Candace was on his other side, saying his name.

Lazarus bit his lip, felt the brief hot sting and blinked until his vision returned to normal. Candace and Dumah held him while Mary had placed a knife against Willis's throat and Martha had claimed the axe. While it seemed like hours had passed since they'd burst out of the cell, Lazarus knew it was a matter of seconds.

"Cut his throat," Candace shouted at Mary and Lazarus raised a hand.

"No."

He grabbed Willis by his armpits and dragged him to the cell that had held them prisoner. At the rear of the tiny space, Patterson crouched against the wall. He held his arm and sobbed.

"Please, we didn't want any of this. We didn't—"

Grunting with the effort of shifting the unconscious Willis and not willing to see what had been done to Priest, Lazarus dropped Willis to the floor.

"You can bleed," he told Willis, then glanced at Patterson who cringed into a smaller ball. "You can starve."

Lazarus exited the cell, slammed the door closed and locked it.

"They need to die," Candace whispered.

"They will. Slow."

"*No*. We cut them. We tear their hearts out."

Dumah grunted his agreement, nodding his head furiously. Still unconscious, Willis was a broken lump while Patterson whimpered against the wall. Lazarus had seen terror before but never for more than a second because it was their way to kill fast. There was nothing to be gained from filling someone's last seconds with fear and Priest had always stressed the importance of not torturing anyone before the killing. Now, though, Lazarus relished Patterson's abject horror. He savoured the sight and stink of the man as he might have enjoyed the spurting blood and the tearing flesh.

"No," he said. "Die slow."

Subsiding, Candace held the girls. "The other man?" she asked Mary.

"Hurt him. Up there. He found me near the window. Hurt him and ran down here." Mary looked at Lazarus and he wished he was not the one in charge. It had been Priest's instruction for a long time and there was nothing to be done about it.

"Outside," Mary continued. "A woman pissing. On the roof. Shot her. Asked her about men in here. Killed her." She tapped the bag strapped to her side. "Food."

Granger's wife. There was more killing coming because they had killed his wife but regretting anything would get them nowhere. A terrible idea when everything they needed was in the fields and woods.

Dover.

Priest might have spoken from the locked cell. Lazarus swallowed the smelly air, redolent with blood splashes and the patchy moss growing low on the walls. Priest was dead; their father taken from them and everything that came now was on him.

"Weapons," he shouted and Dumah jogged to the tatty bag Willis had placed on the floor. The axe, knives and cleavers rattled together as he emptied the bag before quickly passing the blades around. Candace checked the gun Lazarus had dropped, flinging it down when he said it was empty.

"Other?" she said, pointing at the shotgun. He shook his head. Guns were alien to them. At least with their own cleavers and knives, they wouldn't harm each other.

"Outside now," Lazarus told them.

He led the way over the broken wall to the steps. Above, soupy light trickled through the high window. Dawn had come and brought yet another lifeless morning of the sun's illumination unable to break through the clouds choked with dirt, laden with the rays Priest told them they must avoid otherwise the cancers would come for them. Daylight travel was always a bad idea; now, there was no choice.

Lazarus tied his scarves around his mouth and nose, sealing as much of his face as possible, and the others followed suit. The material muffling his voice but not the sentiment, he bellowed up to the shadows.

"We are coming. You fight us, you die. We will cut you into pieces. Do you hear us?"

Nothing came back. They were listening, though. Hopefully, scared to move; hopefully, the man Mary had attacked too injured to think about fighting back.

"We kill them." Martha stabbed the air.

Lazarus shook his head. "Dover. We kill *them.* Priest said."

Not waiting for argument, he bounded up the steps, splashing in puddles and giving no mind to the uneven surface. The gloom dispelled the further they ascended, he kept low and moved in a zig-zag. Lazarus focused on the route ahead, still jerking from wall to wall and aware the others would be doing the same. Passing the torches powered by their *Batteries,* he yanked one free without stopping and shone the light ahead to brighten the doors at the end of the corridor. Both were sealed. As they closed in on them, he increased his speed and brought his cleaver high. Behind, Candace unleashed her battle scream. They smashed into the doors and Lazarus swung his cleaver in a pre-emptive strike.

Nothing but the long desk, the dirty floor and the chairs they'd hacked into pieces to get inside. Grey light breaking through the punctured holes in the ceiling and the main entrance from their attack sent tired beams through the darkness. Spread out and moving without speaking, the family struck the weakest spots of the entrance, kicked through the broken wood and glass and raced down the steps of the police station towards the mist obscuring the golf course.

It was only when they hit the weeds and balding patches of grass that Lazarus let his grief free. He sobbed for his father, but he did not slow.

Chapter Eight

"**G**ranger?"

Patterson's cry wanted to emerge as a full-blown scream, but he had enough self-control remaining not to let it. Scream and he would have to admit he was going to die.

All he heard after the echoes of his voice faded was the steady drip of rainwater beyond the cell door.

"Oh, Christ." He ran gentle fingers over his stinging nose. While he couldn't get enough focus to be sure, he doubted the man had broken bone although he had punctured skin with his teeth like daggers. God knew what filth lived in his mouth and all over his tongue. Patterson needed some of their dwindling supply of antibacterial cream and hopefully nothing else. While they had a small stash of penicillin and painkillers, neither might be enough if something horrible had swam in from the big man's saliva.

Gagging at the image and the burning in the centre of his face, Patterson tried to see if the blood had stopped flowing from the arrow wound. His hand, arm and parts of his chest were tacky with it and while he knew most came from his movement rather than a massive injury, he couldn't process that knowledge fully. He knew fire in his arm and nose, and he knew a crippling fear of starving or bleeding to death in the cell with Willis who surely had no more than a short amount of time left.

"Willis?"

The man didn't stir at all. The floor of the cell was splattered with his blood; the air reeked of it, and the only mercy was the terrible injury done to Willis was out of sight. He lay on his front, the wreck of his hand under his stomach, and his face turned far too pale and stained with flecks of red and the black of his stubble.

"Willis, damn it. Wake up."

He could have been addressing a corpse. Probably was.

Patterson's fear broke into outright terror and he staggered to his feet, crying, trying to scream words and unable to form a sentence. Kicking Willis's foot, he tripped and was only saved from falling by his impact on the door. The cold metal bruised his arm even as the blow made his teeth snap together. Groaning, Patterson slapped his palm on the door and bellowed out Granger's name again, then Roe's.

The shout stung his throat. He coughed, inhaled the musk of his sweat and something worse: a bestial stench, an animal panic.

They're dead up there. Those people killed them and have left you and Willis to die down here. Willis first from blood loss and then you from starvation or infection because you know the filth that lives in the air. You know how easily it is for germs to get into cuts and wounds. If hunger and thirst don't kill you, then disease will. Slow. That's what the boy said. You die slow.

"Jesus Christ." Patterson slid down the door. He was buried alive with the dying Willis and soon, there'd be no company but his pain and the full darkness when the candles burned down. Maybe then *she* would come to visit him, his dear daughter Lisa. Perhaps she was lurking out by the stairs, waiting for the cover of night before she'd glide over the floor, not disturbing the rubble or puddles. And if he had the strength by then to lift his head, he would peer up to the window in the door to see her staring down at him. His murdered daughter, whiter than Willis, eyes like black stones and her neck a swollen ball of flesh from the hands that strangled her so long before.

"Willis, wake up. Please wake up."

If Willis was conscious at all, he showed no sign at hearing Patterson's plea.

I never liked you, Willis. Never.

Willis's mouth might have curved in a grin or maybe it was simply down to Patterson's aching eyes.

"Lisa," he breathed and heard slow, careful steps crossing the reception area of the cells.

She's finally come for you.

Mewling, Patterson gripped his wounded arm, struggled to his feet again and whirled around to stare through the hole.

Nothing moved in the open area.

"Lisa?" He said her name clearly and a shape jerked into view from the side of the door, a face bleached like a bone and splashes of scarlet turning the snarling mouth into something monstrous.

Patterson screeched and someone yelled his name.

"Patterson. Calm down."

It was Roe, his voice made as nasal as Patterson's by a blow to his nose.

"Let me out, Roe. Let me fucking out."

Patterson crashed against the door, forgetting the injuries to his arm and his face, wanting nothing more in the world than an open space free from the stink of his own dread and surety he'd been buried alive.

"Back up." Granger shouldered Roe to the side. "Back up, Patterson. The door opens in."

Trying to not sob again, Patterson did as Granger said; a lock turned, then a second and the door scraped on its hinges and the floor as it opened.

"Oh, God. Oh Jesus. My arm, Granger. Willis. My arm."

Babbling, Patterson ran from the cell, spun to see both men dashing to the motionless Willis. It was only then that Patterson registered the short-handled axe Granger held and the flaming torch in Roe's hand.

"Willis," Granger shouted. "Willis, are you there?"

He and Roe crouched beside Willis, their knees and shoes soaking into his blood as they struggled to turn him over. Swearing, groaning, they managed to do so and Granger caught his forearm before the broken hand hit the floor.

Willis stirred and a tremor shook his body.

"Arm flat," Granger yelled.

Roe shoved Willis's arm to the wet floor and Patterson knew what was coming.

He turned his back and hugged himself.

In the cell, Roe's shout – *"do it"* – merged with Granger's wordless yell.

Then a solid thud, the squeal of metal on bone before Roe crying out and the sweet, choking smell of burning flesh as they cauterised the wound.

And Willis's echoing scream.

Chapter Nine

Lazarus was first to move.

He stood and stretched in an effort to ease the tightening of the muscles in his legs. It didn't help; they'd run for too far and while they were used to covering long distances, going from the confines of the cell to sprinting over the golf course and back to the woods had been a struggle.

Resigned to the sensation of teeth clamped on the burn tissue covering his calves and the backs of his thighs, he kicked through piles of twigs and branches, and pissed with his back to the others. Steam spread from the flow and the hiss sounded like whispering. Chilled from more than the new morning's cold, Lazarus finished urinating and crushed twigs and through a few puddles with surfaces of thin ice to return to the group.

They'd risen, the sisters still close together while Dumah and Candace stood apart. Some of the dirt on Dumah's face had been washed clean by his tears. Candace held the stump of her left arm, gripping the elbow, her head limp and her long hair like ropes around her face. Lazarus came as close as he could to her, waved under her nose and got no reaction. Dumah hooted at him and Lazarus could offer no more in reply than a lifeless shrug because despite doing all he could to push everything away, Lazarus felt the same crippling sensation as the others, even the girls who were too young to truly absorb what had happened. It had hit him in the instant the bullet hit Priest and wiped out everything else. Their leader had been taken from them; their guide; their father. Now all they had was the freezing world and the empty miles between this woodland with its creeping threads of mist, and their caves by the sea. And even if they made it to their home, they would have no food. Granger and his men had stolen everything from them.

Lazarus closed his eyes, saw Priest falling to the cell floor and had to open them again. Dumah slumped, his useless mouth unable to let out his grief.

"Lazarus?" Mary whispered and he could give her nothing. He knew they saw him as the thinker of their family; they each had their roles and accepted them gladly. His siblings knew his place; they needed him to take that place.

Lazarus stared straight down to the disturbed earth, the cracks and broken pieces of rock. In his instinctive, unquestioning manner, he repeated a word in his head; one of the last words Priest said before Granger fired his little gun.

Dover.

He faced the others. Candace finally lifted her head. Still holding her stump, she gazed back, unblinking, face slack. She'd been with Priest since the beginning. The man had rescued her as a child only six months older than Lazarus was now; they all knew her story and the life he'd saved her from. They knew it as well as they knew each other. Linked by a wordless moment, Lazarus bowed under the ugly weight of Candace's thoughts. They were lost in the wilds of the country, miles from the safety of their home. Drinking the water from puddles would probably hurt them in ways Granger and his men couldn't dream of, and if they didn't find a river that might be clear from the filth caused by the bombs, they'd be dead within days. All they could do was run and hide, go to ground and lick their wounds.

His sorrow pulsed in time with his heartbeat and in that slow rhythm, Lazarus found something hard he could grip. It would do, whatever it was. He could hold onto his life, his loves, and he could do as he'd been told by his father.

All notions of retreat were rejected. Lazarus said: "South. Dover."

Mary and Martha rose from their crouch, their mucky fingers still linked, their breath coming in quick puffs that steamed through the thin material of their scarves. They knew *south*. Priest had taught them all about directions in case they were ever lost. Directions meant finding their way home, and from where they stood, *south* was the wrong way.

Candace replied simply because she was the one who had to. Dumah couldn't, and it was too much for the children to verbalise.

"Dover belongs to those men. It's their place. You heard what they said."

"I heard what Priest said," Lazarus said.

Dumah grunted and waved his hands: his indication that they needed to move. What had once been a trail was still visible through the fallen trees. It made its way in a curve towards the north, and Dumah pointed that way. Lazarus knew Dumah felt the same as Candace – there was no strength or desire in him to go south. He wanted those men to hurt, to scream, but each of them was beaten and pretending otherwise would get more of them killed.

"We can't go home. Priest wanted us to go south to their place." Lazarus said the word that was alien to his mouth even though the concept had zero meaning. Control over him and his family and their lives. Control he couldn't accept.

"Government."

"You don't know *government*. They did this." She indicated their surroundings of the bent tree trunks and their twisted branches, then pointed to the sky heavy with its murk. Grey hung over them and that was the best they could hope for. Black would replace the grey before long and the sun they knew of but only ever saw as an indistinct beam of dirty white would be blanketed by another night and bring the double blessing of shielding the destroyed countryside from view and decreasing any harmful rays from the sun sliding through the damaged sky. And the same tomorrow and the day after and on into the months ahead.

"They killed everyone. I was there, Lazarus. They burned it all. They burned everybody. They—"

"I was there," Lazarus said as quietly as possible. "I remember."

"You were a child."

"So were you."

They locked eyes, the boy and the woman become siblings even if they shared no blood. Mary and Martha held one another. Lazarus refused to see the children with anything other than his heart because the breaking apart of their little group was here in the gloom and the always cold. With the impasse between Lazarus and Candace come to life with shocking suddenness, everything the sisters knew was ready to blow over and smash into pieces like the cities they'd been told of. Broken windows, broken bricks and all burned by the fires that fell from the sky.

It was Martha who moved first, the older girl slipping from Mary's grip. She licked muck from her lips and staggered over the uneven ground to Lazarus. He still refused to break eye contact from Candace as Martha slipped her little fingers into his.

"Dover," the girl muttered.

Wordlessly, Mary approached.

She joined her sister and Lazarus, taking the boy's free hand. His mind wrapped fingers around the steel in his head. He would hold that steel and he would be grounded by it. Mourning for his father would not bring him to his knees, yet.

"Dover," Mary echoed Martha.

"They'll kill us," Candace said.

"We kill them," Lazarus replied, and the small hands in his tightened their hold in agreement. He turned his attention to Mary.

"What did the woman tell you?"

"Little. Men in the building. You underground."

She relinquished her grip on his fingers and rummaged in her tatty bag. She'd left her crossbow in the cells, Lazarus finally noticed. Without its single arrow, it was little more than a useless weight. Her knife, as stained as always, remained strapped to her skinny leg. She'd given her small axe to Martha at some point.

Mary pulled lumpy meat from her bag, the object grey where it wasn't red. Tendrils hung from it. There'd been no time for Mary to sever unwanted sinew and flesh from the liver and there would be no complaint about that. She had rescued them and brought an offering, a toast to their departed father.

Weeping, Lazarus took the offered organ, brought it to his nose and inhaled the sharp aroma of internal fluid dried into scales on all sides of the liver, and of the tissue itself. While they needed a fire (and how wonderful the scents of hot, cooked meat would be right now), there was no time for that and no dry twigs to build one.

"Priest," Lazarus murmured. He raised the liver towards the dusk of the clouds, offering remembrance, then brought it again to his lips.

A small bite, a fragment so delicious between his jagged teeth and slipping over his tongue. All the heaven Priest told them of here for a fraction of time and belonging to his mouth.

Mary took the organ, whispered Priest's name without any tears and how proud that made him. She chewed, passed it to Martha who did the same and kissed the liver before handing it to Dumah. He wiped dirt and tears around his eyes, sighed and uttered a tired grunt. He bit a larger piece than the others which made Lazarus smile for the first time in days before Candace balanced the liver in her palm.

For several moments, it seemed Candace wouldn't eat. Her eyes were dry as she stared at the organ, its juices making it appear as if her fingers were wounded. She sighed, then bit.

"Dover is next to the sea." Candace smiled although it was not a happy one. Lazarus understood how bitter memories could be and often were. "White cliffs. The door into England." She spat. "They think England still lives."

"We will kill them all." Lazarus turned, the girls turning with him, and walked through the mud. The wet earth sucked at his shoes, clumps disturbed by their passage, splatting on the legs of his jeans. After a moment, they found the pitted pathway and pushed their bodies closer together so all three could walk on the stone. While it was uneven and broken in places, the path was a better surface than the floor of the wood. Lazarus kept his concentration on the route ahead while he listened for movement from behind.

For a long time, he had nothing but the hot touch of the girls' skin on his. Then Martha took a quick look back the way they had walked and when she faced forward and gave Lazarus a brief nod, the boy allowed himself a tiny smile against his grief.

Side by side, they walked through the woods now a graveyard of restless ghosts while Dumah and Candace followed.

Chapter Ten

—those sounds, oh God, those sounds, they mean something, they mean—
They were names.
Names. People. You know them. You live with them and you've—
While they might have been familiar once upon a time, the sounds somewhere above his ears and to the side of his head (or maybe below; directions were as meaningless as sound) were an echoing moan, a drawn-out cry racing towards something that would be a much higher pitch and that ringing bell would last forever.
It's you. You're screaming. You haven't stopped since she since she since she—
But the voice trying to tell him what had happened couldn't be allowed to speak because it would mean knowing the truth behind the sounds. They would have names given back to them and *she* would make sense instead of being a spinning mess powered by that echo growing ever higher and more terrible.

A second, maybe two, of the sky breaking apart and understanding raining through the little gap:

"—not good—"

before the clouds closed over again and the sounds following the two words were muffled, not by a lack of hearing or other noise, but by *colours*.

Red, so much fucking red, sweet Jesus, it's everywhere, it's coming out of me, oh God, she did this that little bitch bitch bitch with her axe she's got a fucking axe she's cut me my hand Christ my hand—

Willis smashed through the sky. Dazzling yellow flooded his eyes without blinding him, and understanding of everything and everyone detonated inside that yellow. Raging, swinging his arm that ended in a massive wrap of bloody bandages, he tried to push away from the mattress he knew Granger and Carolyn used and managed to yell a single word.

Bitch.

"Get him down, for God's sake." That was Roe, shoving him, yelling to Patterson who had his own bandages; the wraps covering his scant bicep. That was right. The girl had shot him first. She'd fired a goddamned *arrow* at him from her makeshift crossbow, then come running with her axe.

They got him flat on his back again. Willis stared up at Roe, Patterson and there was Granger swooping in from the side, and their skulls oozed into each other's without a sound. Strands of hair, skin, bone, cartilage and veins slid into an indistinguishable mess. One staring eye glared down at Willis while he tried to scream. Before he could, a melting nose ran over the orb, followed by a long flow of cheek, then a chin turning over and over. In seconds, there was nothing human above him and nothing he recognised of the men he'd lived beside for so long, only a sea of merged hair and flesh with bones become soft like mud pooling into a squashed abomination. And all of it without a single sound which was the only blessing he could take as he finally loosed his scream. No crunch of snapping bone; no hellish shrieks from the agony the three men had to be experiencing. His own screams were more than enough to wipe out everything else as a section of what could have been neck dangled like glue, a dark brown cluster of linked hair sprouting fingers and bearing down on his mouth.

Black.

Willis flings his body into the darkness, his screams a fading cry somewhere at his back. The torture of his severed hand falls with the noise, leaving him with a silky comfort while he spins upside down, drifting as peacefully as a rock at the far ends of space. Maybe that is where he is now. He has become a chunk of ancient stone, lost in the big black, and there are worse things to be if that is the case. Worse places to be. At least out here in the nothing with only memories for company, he has lost his pain and the horrendous creature his colleagues have become.

He tries to say their names and has forgotten them. Instead, he speaks the names of the dead, those left behind while he survived. Each name brings a quick pulse of white light, and in that light, there are faces.

The faces of corpses brought back to life.

A dead place breathing again.

Willis walks the corridors of the bunker, the first *bunker. His home immediately after the bombs fell when all he knew was a crippling panic he had to hide because of what he was. The police officer running from the streets and fighting, pushing, beating, kicking and killing his way through the animal driven insane by terror as it shoved and kicked its way into the entrance for the Tube station. It didn't matter that the animal was hundreds of individual people screaming for help, begging for mercy, pissing themselves. It was one beast he had to destroy to get down to the tunnels and he'd beaten bodies, stabbed, pummelled and kicked until he was through the melee and sprinting down the stairs with a thousand others coming at his back.*

Happy to let those memories of recent times sleep again, Willis tries doors, and all are locked. It seems the offices and dormitories are sealed from him, so he walks on soundlessly and realises the dead people he saw in the flashing lights are at his side, nodding in greeting, asking how he is, telling him yet another meeting is planned for seven in the evening. Willis says their names—Culver, Dealey, Brennan and there is Herbert coming from the next junction—and tells them he's glad to see them. They laugh, tell him he's an odd one but they're glad to have a copper down here and he remembers the reek of piss as people lost control on his way down to the tunnels. He remembers the screams he caused before the howling sirens died and he put on a final burst of desperate speed in the seconds before the world ended.

Again, the memories fade because he sees another dead face. It belongs to the figure seated at one of the tables in the canteen, Patterson beside her. Lisa. She hugs her chest, appearing cold in her thin cardigan even though the generators are working smoothly to produce power and heat, and the fluorescent lighting overhead makes her pale skin appear translucent. He can see inside her to all the places that make her a woman and he wants those places. Yes, he does. There's no point in lying, no need to hide it from himself. Lies are useless given the state of things. All they have is the truth and his truth is wanting the girl Patterson smuggled into the complex.

She shifts position, moving from facing her father to staring straight at Willis and the distance between them, the rows of straight tables and hard chairs built into the floor, and the growing crowd are faraway and long ago because he sees her.

The bitch.

Grinning, the child wearing Lisa's body raises her axe and shakes it. Blood—his blood—flies from the blade to spatter on the table and across her face.

Still offering her smile of wicked triumph, the girl licks her lips with obscene eagerness, and he runs for her, mouth opening to roar his loathing at her. It is no good – the world of his past is fading, fading, fading.

Willis is left with his own piece of space with no stars to light his way, no way home and nothing do to but float and seethe in unending fury.

The girl did this to me. The girl did this to me.

The girl.

Chapter Eleven

Wincing in anticipation of the burst of expected pain, Patterson ran his fingers over the dressing covering his arm. While it ached like a bad tooth (the memory of a removal he'd had to endure a few years before stayed with him), the gentle touch didn't bring any fresh discomfort. Roe had said he'd been lucky; the arrow had skimmed the muscle and flesh rather than piercing his bicep deeply. The words were little comfort with the memory of the few seconds everything went wrong blurring into images and sounds on top of each other.

The hiss like a furious cat coming from the cells exit; the confusion and the spinning thought *what the hell is that noise* and pain drilling through his arm. Then Willis screeching about his hand, his fucking hand, and all the blood stinking, choking in his nose and mouth.

Fumbling with the bottle and refusing to ask for assistance, Patterson dropped three pills onto the table and swallowed them one after the other with a mouthful of sterilised water, grimacing at the taste of the chalky pills and flat water.

It wouldn't take long for the morphine-based painkiller to kick in. All he had to do in the meantime was wait and pretend the morning hadn't happened.

He watched the candles burn. While he had no real idea of the time, it was probably gone midnight. Bizarrely, the whole ugly business with Carolyn and the people who'd hurt them to such an extent was almost twenty-four hours ago. Since then, they'd licked their wounds, tended to the unconscious Willis, and Granger had said next to nothing about his murdered wife.

Taking another sip of the hated water, Patterson crossed the corridor to the office they used as a makeshift rest for Willis. More candles burned here but did little to dispel the night. Roe and Granger were hunched shapes; Roe at Willis's side on a stained mattress, and Granger resting on the opposite wall. The window they'd bordered up with chunks of broken chair was an ugly square above his head but at least the wind could only get in through the doorless entrance.

"How is he?" Patterson asked.

"Sleeping," Roe replied and cleared his throat a few times.

At least he wasn't coughing, Patterson thought. Sooner or later, they would need to discuss whatever ailment afflicted Roe. Not now, though.

Patterson sat on Willis's other side and did his best to forget the sweet smell of the flesh they'd cauterised down in the cell.

How you screamed, Willis. I didn't know you could make a noise like that.

If there was any positive to their drastic action, it was in knowing they'd done all they could to fight any infection in Willis's stump. That, and the fact he'd passed out straightaway, blown into unconsciousness by his torture.

Patterson addressed the other men without looking at either and wondered while he spoke if Granger was actually awake or was he dreaming of his late wife as Patterson dreamed of his daughter.

"Is there a plan?"

Roe shifted but said nothing. He held a crumpled road atlas, kept to hand since London. The pages were torn, yellowing. Even so, they'd welcomed it on the long walk away from the capital.

"We go to Dover." Proving he was awake, Granger spoke in a flat tone. "That was always the plan. It doesn't change now."

Roe offered Patterson a brief shrug. Unbidden, Patterson saw Granger from the morning, sprinting from the cells and bounding towards the steps back up to the first floor of the station. Their leader for so long running away with his tail between his legs; Granger beaten by a child who'd come out of the shadows with her crossbow and axe.

There'd been no mention or conversation about Granger's desertion and Patterson found he had little wish to bring it up now. Granger might have been the one in charge ever since their coup so long before, but he was not a superman. Anyone would flee when faced with such a terrible threat.

He left you and Willis to die.

Patterson found it easy to dismiss the voice. There were no heroes now. All they had was their survival.

He returned his attention to Willis who hadn't moved. The man's face, lit by the three candles on a shelf above, had become waxy and somehow tight. He reminded Patterson of the clothes dummies he used to see in shop windows.

Liz liked C&A the best, didn't she? Or Marks if she wanted to treat herself while you just nodded and said yes, dear.

"He's finished," Patterson said. He wanted there to be a better way, a *cleaner* way of stating the obvious. "He needs what we can't give him. Proper medical care. We're miles away from even the possibility of that and it's only the case *if* anyone in Dover can help him and *if* anyone there doesn't want to shoot us on the spot."

"Shut up," Roe muttered, and it came out a croak. "We can't just leave him to die."

"I—"

"You've never liked him, have you?" Roe said.

There was no energy in Patterson to lie. "No. Not really. Have you?"

Roe held a hand over his mouth as he coughed.

Peace again while the candles flickered and night weighed against the holes in the station's roof. While out in the big nowhere of an England none of them knew, killers walked with their axes and cleavers.

Granger rose stiffly, suggesting he'd been in one position for a long time. He brushed dirt from his trousers and coat and stood at the foot of Willis's mattress.

"He comes with us. We're a team, aren't we, Patterson?"

He spoke in the same flat tone as a moment before and Patterson heard no threat or hint of forced agreement.

"Are we?" he replied and stood.

"Jesus, will you stop causing trouble, Patterson?" Roe said. "You know it's true. We can't survive alone. We'd be torn apart by people like those. . ." The term emerged for the first time. It sounded equally ridiculous and terrible. *"Cannibals.* We're not young men, anymore, and we're not equipped for the mess out there unless we stay together."

It was probably the most he'd said in days and certainly the most he'd managed without breaking into a coughing, wheezing mess.

Patterson felt Granger's unblinking appraisal and refused to look away from Roe who'd jammed his hands into his coat pockets and shivered in the depths of his coat. After another moment, Granger leaned close to Willis's face and said his name.

Willis didn't stir. His cheeks and forehead white like old cream; his lips a bloodless line. All around the watching men, the temperature close to freezing and one, two, three or four in the morning stretching as far ahead as Patterson could imagine.

"I've checked this." Roe tapped the atlas. "The A2 isn't far. Most direct route."

Granger shook his head. "They've gone the other way." He pointed to the wall as if it wasn't there and he could gesture to the outside world and its quiet. "They went across the golf course and to the woods. They'll get to the A257 and follow that. They'll keep to the fields, but they'll use the road as a guide."

"How do you know for sure?" Patterson muttered and knew the answer. Granger didn't, but he wasn't going to doubt his statements. He never did.

"We're going to Dover, Willis." Granger stood straight and spoke with a firm control. "All of us."

He turned and crossed to the entrance. Patterson called after him.

"Harris should never have made it back to us."

Granger kept moving. It was as if Patterson hadn't spoken.

A timid voice spoke up inside Patterson. *Why are you still with him?*

Like Granger a second before, he didn't reply.

Chapter Twelve

Despite her aching legs and tender feet, Martha volunteered to go with Lazarus when her brother said he was leaving the house they'd taken to examine the immediate area. Lazarus was her brother and their leader. She would stick by his side even if the road they'd followed from the woods and surrounding area offered little more than a house beside the one they'd chosen and two more opposite. They were on the outskirts of a town and towns meant people. People meant danger.

After six hours of constant walking, they'd headed away from the exposed fields when they'd spied a few buildings to the west. A brief exploration of the house offered few prizes: a coat Candace took although it hung down to her knees, the remnants of kitchen chairs they could use as firewood with a bit of luck, and a mattress still on one of the beds. While damp had soured the material, the ceiling in that room was whole which meant no rain water or mist had soaked it. The bed would do for shared rest while she and Lazarus searched for either food or weapons.

They fell in pace with each other, leaving the houses behind, sticking close to the right-hand side where a low rock wall was gradually being swallowed by weeds and bracken. The morning's mist had faded by the early afternoon; four hours later, the light was easing. Night would be on them soon, come to bring its wind and struggle to sleep with non-stop thoughts of what they'd done to Priest.

"He's with the Jesus," Martha whispered to herself rather than Lazarus. Even so, he replied.

"Yes, he is."

"You don't believe he is," Martha said.

Lazarus said nothing. In the silence between them, Martha found it didn't matter if Lazarus believed Priest was with the Jesus or not. She did. That was almost enough.

They walked on, her question forming, coming to her mouth and easing away because asking it was a terrible thing and she didn't like terrible things. She liked the warmth of their caves when their bellies were full. On the move with enough daylight remaining to make her bow her head and keep her scarf tight around her face while the soles of her shoes were thin enough to let her feet feel the pebbles scattered on the ground, Martha knew they were right in the middle of a terrible thing. Her few weapons against it were having Lazarus so close and knowing the night she was used to travelling through would take the last of the grey light soon.

"Speak," Lazarus said without looking at her. Martha smiled and the chilly air stung the sections of her gums where her teeth were stunted.

"Priest. Did it hurt him?"

"No. I believe that. It was quick." Lazarus brought his fingers against his thumb sharply like a snapping mouth. "Quick," he repeated.

Content with his answer for the moment, Martha said nothing more. They continued with the low wall at their side while the light faded. To their left, a field sloped towards the motorway a mile away, the land and its trees reduced to hunched figures blasted by the winds. They knew of motorways but tended to avoid them. Most were still choked with useless vehicles. Bodies long since picked clean of flesh by birds or animals were mouldering lumps in and around some of the cars even after so long.

They reached a junction a few minutes later. Lazarus gestured to the right hand turning; they took it and closed in on a few more houses. The town—whatever its name—grew out of the fields another two or three miles away. Martha knew without asking they would not draw much closer to it.

"Do you wish you had killed that man?" she asked Lazarus. "The one Mary hurt? Or the other one?"

"We kill for food and to save each other," he replied. "You know we don't kill for anything else. Priest said so."

She struggled to verbalise her thoughts as well as the intent behind them. "Kill them now. Maybe save each other later," Martha murmured, unsure if that was exactly what she meant.

Surprising her, Lazarus nodded in clear agreement. "True. But we kill for defence, Martha."

"We're going to Dover to kill."

"We kill there because Priest said so."

She could tell his own reply wasn't enough for him and wondered if it was for her, either. Kill the men in the police station and do so for what they had done to Priest. Kill Dover because Priest said so and because

Dover had made the world of the open land haunted by the wind and everything frozen and bloody and covered with ash.

There'd rarely been reason for Martha to think deeply of her situation or to question life. Aware the issue needed more knowledge than she possessed and more adult consideration, she decided to let it go for now and see their journey through. For Priest.

A comfortable stillness between them, they walked on and Martha pulled the sides of her coat tighter together. She had a thin rope around it to keep it closed and another around the waist of her trousers; both kept her secure and blocked the wind from her skin. Even so, whatever slight warmth there had been in the afternoon while they crossed stunted grass and pushed through the low hanging branches was rapidly fading.

A cry rang out, the sound difficult to pinpoint although instinct told her it came from straight ahead where the road passed between more houses, not a one whole or untouched by damage.

Without the need for instruction or debate, Martha and Lazarus sprinted to the front gardens of the houses on their right, reached squat hedges and hunkered down.

The cry came again. Fear. Hurting. Female.

Peering through the tiny gaps between the leaves of the hedges, Martha waited and held her butcher knife.

She did not have to wait for long.

Chapter Thirteen

Scanning the shadows for the slightest movement, Lazarus dismissed the chance of the screams coming from any of the houses directly opposite. Two were little more than scorched rubble; a van had been driven into the ground floor of the third, turning the front into shattered brick and glass. None were suitable shelter.

Which meant the screamer was out on the road.

He shifted position a fraction and Martha did the same, their attention focused on the pavement and road while the last of what passed for daylight trickled away.

Hunched over, a man lurched from the centre of the road towards the left side and back again, his zig-zagging movement suggesting either sickness or confusion. Neither was the case: Lazarus realised the bag he dragged behind was a woman, barely conscious. Her clothes had been torn and shredded, exposing the gleaming marble of her skin, red and raw where it wasn't a shining white. Emaciated, gagged and powerless, she'd been reduced to meat by her captor.

They drew closer to a direct line from Lazarus's and Martha's view, the man grunting with effort and the woman too exhausted to scream behind the gag while gravel drew scratches and grazes down her back.

Lazarus knew what was happening. Priest had told them of crimes and of terrible things done by terrible people. Killing to survive was not a crime; killing for violence was. The same applied to hurting people because you could. *Rape* was one of the evillest crimes, Priest told them while they sat in a close group and the fire sent its flickering light over the walls of the cave. Men would hurt women and girls and such men, worse than animals, deserved no understanding. The Jesus may one day pity those men. Priest would not.

Neither would Lazarus.

The captive woman came to, bent her free leg and kicked out hard. Her foot thudded against the man's lower back, causing him to stumble and bellow behind his scarves. She landed another blow, this one weaker than the first and he pounded his fist into her face. She lay flat after the third blow, face turned towards Martha and Lazarus.

Her skin could have been red for her entire life; there was no white left.

Lazarus lowered his mouth to Martha's ear, whispered and the girl nodded. Seconds later, she ran to the next garden and kept going, head down and arms by her sides. She was a soundless burst of air, vanishing from his eyeline within seconds.

Lazarus emerged from the hedges. The man had dragged the woman to the garden of the house with the overturned van at its front. Any shattered glass or demolished pieces of the vehicle were apparently not his concern. Nor was the cold or the exposed area. Perhaps he thought the incoming night was close enough, Lazarus decided as he moved from the grass. Perhaps he was simply an unthinking animal.

Standing over the prone woman, the man threw his knife down. It struck the grass with a muted thud. Grunting and paying no mind to her muffled screams, he crouched over her and yanked at her ruined clothing.

Then stopped.

He'd seen Martha.

The child had crossed further ahead and was coming back on herself, walking towards the rapist and his victim with her hands behind her back, crying and shaking as she advanced.

"Help me. Food. Need food. Food."

Lazarus raised his axe.

"Food. Dying. Need food."

Still straddling his victim, the rapist shouted to Martha, his growling voice as ugly as his actions.

"Come here."

It was an order, not a suggestion, and Lazarus knew the man saw Martha as a prize. Ten-year-old girl or adult woman, it made no difference to creatures like him.

This is justified, Priest murmured. *In the eyes of the Jesus, you are allowed to do this, Lazarus.*

A disturbing thought flickered and died in a heartbeat

(I want to do this anyway)

and Lazarus bent his knees.

Still crying, Martha closed in on the rapist. The woman on the grass had shifted. One hand with several broken fingers reached for Martha, and she cried out against the gag. It was a warning. Lazarus silently thanked the woman for her attempt to save

Martha; the man shouted for Martha to come closer and reached for his knife without taking his attention from the girl.

Lazarus launched.

He took huge steps, jumping forward the instant his feet struck the ground, and Martha screamed that she was starving, she needed food, *please food, please food now, please.*

The rapist found the handle of his knife; the woman saw Lazarus closing in and her eyes were two staring balls. Her attacker, still focused on Martha, did not notice.

Lazarus swung his axe while still running.

The blade buried itself in the rear of the man's skull, breaking bone and brain with ease. He jerked forward, shaking. Blood sprayed from the wound as Lazarus slammed his foot on the man's back and yanked the axe free. Pitching to the side, his hand opening and closing in a mad spasm on his knife, the man gurgled and reached his claw-like fingers to his mouth.

He tipped off the woman; he made a peculiar sound somewhere between a human word and a bestial grunt, and the sour reek of shit stung Lazarus's nose.

He hefted the axe and held it squarely over the rapist's head. Trapped behind her gag, the woman wailed. Martha covered the last few feet, long knife growing from her hands like another finger.

Lazarus slammed the axe into the man's forehead while Martha dove for the grass and the woman. Blade struck neck, severing her carotid artery with ease.

Gazing at the dead man, Lazarus made no move to shield himself from the spray of blood pumping from the woman Martha had killed.

The red rain coated his face with a welcome heat.

Chapter Fourteen

The dark didn't bother Dumah even if it made hunting for supplies that much more difficult. Finding any useful objects by touch was not hard and his sense of location was finely developed. Being unable to talk did not give him any edge over the others; it simply meant he had no choice but to listen and see.

A quick perusal of the house before Lazarus and Mary left brought up a few items they could use and after watching his siblings until they were out of sight, he'd indicated to Candace and Mary he would have a second look in the bedrooms. Being alone with his grief was more of a reason to do so, and they'd known it. Caught in a mix of emotions – gratitude, a deep physical tiredness and a sorrow that went far beyond his body – Dumah shifted through the mess in the bedrooms, finding nothing they could use other than potentially taking the destroyed furniture as kindling for the fire Candace had said she would build. He kicked through a shattered set of drawers and stood at the window. A section of glass remained hanging from the frame and a lone curtain, heavy with mildew and mould, flapped near his face. Absently, he pushed it away, then wiped his hand on the sill.

The rear of the house faced a sea of flattened fields, the grass and meadows keeping their secrets in the night. They'd crossed the land more to the side of the houses rather than their backs and leaning through the ruined opening to peer that way brought an image of Priest in the police station. There was as much comfort from the picture as there was anguish. Dumah hooted and cried for a moment while the icy breeze played over his face and the exposed skin of his neck.

Father, he thought and could manage no more. He gripped the frame, tiny shards of glass pricking his fingers, the pain welcome, *deserved* because Priest was gone while he remained.

"Dumah?"

Blinking rapidly, Dumah turned and made out Mary's silhouette, the girl slight in the mouth of the bedroom door. He wiped his hands on his coat and joined her. They held one another, Mary's little head swallowed by his greater build and for a moment, their shared grief needed no words.

Eventually, the girl pulled away. "Candace made a fire."

Dumah hooted again, indicating his pleasure. Cold was unavoidable, but none of them liked it.

They both took handfuls of the wrecked chest and joined Candace in a room at the back of the house. She and Mary had dragged a few items of furniture to the patio doors while he'd been upstairs, sealing the juddering illumination cast by the flames from view. The broken windows acted as vents, sucking out the smoke, combating the heat but not winning.

"There," Candace said, gesturing for them to dump their salvaged kindling in a pile she had already made. The three sat close to each other. Flames crackled and spit. Candace held her hand to the heat while Dumah gazed into it, lulled by the gentle sound and warmth. Motionless for a few moments, Mary stirred and Dumah knew what she would say before a word was uttered.

"Dover," Mary whispered.

"We don't need to talk of it," Candace replied. Dumah saw instruction in her eyes. The fan of reds and oranges from the fire illuminated her pupils. He offered her a quick shrug; the movement meant for her alone but also seen by Mary. That amused him. She might have been small and the youngest of them all, but she was also quick.

"We do," she said. "I want to know. . .I want to know what is it."

Candace seemed as if she wouldn't answer. Dumah had seen the look on her face before and understood it. She never mentioned the past and there were issues about her even now that were an unknown business for him. Eight years as brother and sister and he had never once given a second thought to their different skins. Candace was his blood but if she kept some doors of her heart locked, that was up to her.

She turned her hand over the flames, fingers spread, and Dumah thought of cooking meat. His stomach rumbled gently and Mary grasped his fingers.

"It's close," Candace said to the fire. "We can be there in two days, I think. We stay near the road. We follow it from the grass. We reach the town."

"What is it?" Mary asked again.

"The end of the country. Sea after it. It looks out to the world. Everything else out there, all the other countries who sent the bombs and who men here sent more bombs to, they're out there beyond Dover. After the sea. Lands and hills and woods. The stories Priest read to you. Everywhere beyond our country, that is those stories." She lowered her hand. "The men who hurt us, their friends in Dover, they are like the men who killed everything. Government. Rule. All the old world that burned everything, it's there in Dover. They'll do it again if we let them." She stared at Mary, a rage like the surface of a still river flowing with her words. "We kill them all, Mary. We don't let them burn us. We burn them."

Still holding Dumah's hand, Mary gripped Candace's fingers. "I like that," she said. "We burn them, and we go to those other places after the sea."

Eyes drawn again to the fire, Dumah pictured the soft stillness of their caves while Priest read from his collection of old books, voice melodic and strong without being raised, and the sisters at his side listening intently to tales of lives and places from which they had been born far removed.

With a simple longing, Dumah wished for those nights back again.

Candace sniffed abruptly. "Food."

Dumah kept his eyes on the fire and listened to Lazarus and Martha approach while he inhaled the good scents of meat still fresh.

Thank you for this meal, Priest. Thank you, Father.

A smile in the shadows and in the dance of the flames. *You are welcome, my son.*

Chapter Fifteen

"**D**id you bring any fags?" Roe asked, already knowing the answer. Patterson shook his head and his focus remained on the motorway. The flat surface, free from decaying vehicles with their slashed tyres and siphoned fuel, seemed much wider than he'd expected despite being only two lanes across. Probably because of the farmland at either side and the lack of fences. Roe had studied the wide green turned brown by lack of cultivation, watching for the slightest movement. He'd seen nothing but trembling weeds near the road, and curved elms further out. The more he thought about it, the more the term *farmland* seemed like a bad joke.

He took a quick look behind. Granger remained beside Willis, walking close to the injured man and presumably with a one-sided conversation kept up to ensure Willis didn't lose concentration and pass out. How he was still upright, Roe didn't want to consider. Willis had always been a strange one – powered more by bitterness at his lot in life than anything laudable. There had to be something hard as steel inside him to keep him on his feet. Willpower and painkillers could only do so much.

They continued their steady pace, hands in pockets even with gloves on; scarves and hats secure, and the frosty air eager to slip into any tears and holes in their coats. Roe thought it might be early May although he couldn't be sure. Not that it really mattered. Every day was winter; the seasons and months no longer cared for what they should be doing.

They'd slowed after leaving the carriageway and trudging down a steep embankment before reaching half a mile of a windswept grass verge. Now they were on level ground, their collective pace had increased, and Roe found his chest and throat tightening as a result.

"Anyway, smoking is bad for us. Don't you remember?" he said and adjusted the backpack he carried, the wrapped blankets bulging between the broken zip. Granger had another pack while Patterson carried a smaller bag of their tinned food.

"So is drinking."

"True." Roe considered while he did his best to not cough or wheeze while he spoke. "I'd kill for a pint, though."

Patterson's tired laugh might have been his first for weeks. He hunched his shoulders and Roe envied him being able to do so. The backpack he carried, while essential, pressed hard against his lower back and turned his shoulders into a constant dull ache.

"Going to the pub. That's a memory," he said.

"A pint of bitter and a bag of nuts. I could do that." Roe's mouth watered. He barely registered it and willingly became lost in the memory of gone days: the delicious aroma of welcome scents mixing; the cigarette smoke swirling in the soft light streaming through half-open windows; the good yeasty tang of a freshly poured pint; the rustle of a newspaper and the tap of a coin or a wedding ring on the bar while the landlord filled a glass.

More. The crunch of a few peanuts and the salt on his tongue. The slight sag in the cushioning of the seats, worn and thin against his backside. The jangle of a few seconds of tinny music from the fruit machine as it paid out, then the clatter of ten pence pieces raining into the groove at the bottom. And swimming in it all, a life of normal things.

Tears were pointless, now. They had been for a long time. Even so, his voice shook a fraction when he spoke again.

"Those nuts. Behind the bar. Remember those? Always a blonde on the packaging with her top off."

Patterson nodded, focused on their route. A tiny sliver of sunshine—actual *sunshine*—broke through the seemingly solid sky, lighting the ground with a tiny flicker of gold. It was gone before either man had chance to speak and Roe held onto the image with as much strength as he could manage.

They walked without speaking, drawing close to a slip road. Beyond it, elm trees dotted wasteground, then a handful of houses in varying states of decay stood a quarter of a mile distant.

"Roe?" Patterson said quietly.

Roe glanced at his colleague. "Yes?"

"Do you really want us to stick together?" He asked his question without any force, presumably to avoid the slim chance of his words carrying back to Granger.

"For God's sake, why are you—"

"We're out on here based on information from a dying boy, following the lead of a man who—"

"Who what?" Roe asked and Patterson took a moment to reply.

"Who *was* a leader. In the old days. But now, he's no more important than we are. He's nothing to all this out here. None of us are. We could go our own way. Be our own men, but instead, we're still together through what? Habit? Fear of anything else?"

"We wouldn't survive apart," Roe muttered. "It's been too long for us all together."

"That's how he thinks. That's how he wants us to think because it means we don't question what he wants to do. My God, Roe. We're on a journey to find a family of *cannibals* who already hurt us. And then what? Take them to Dover to prove we can stop people like that? That we're better and stronger than them? Even if Harris was right with anything he said, why would Dealey want to help so long after what we did? We're dead to him. We kicked him out. We stole his command of the bunker and we gave him up to the country after it had been burned to the ground. Harris was a walking corpse when he came back; the chances of anything he said being true are close to zero, but *if* Dealey is in Dover, he'll kill us as soon as he has chance."

He swallowed air repeatedly, the cold stinging his throat.

"Our lives are at stake, Roe. What's more important than that?"

"Some things, maybe," Roe replied and pictured a child's face. Lisa. Small for her age. Looked more like fifteen than eighteen. And what had it done to Patterson to know he had failed to protect her? What would he say if Roe told him finding and stopping the cannibals would go some tiny way to making whatever they had left a little better? That it would take some of the shit out of the world? They couldn't undo what had been done to Patterson's daughter or

Granger's wife, but they could do their bit to ensure the same didn't happen to another's loved one.

He thinks he cares about that, but he's forgotten how to. All he knows now is staying alive as punishment for what happened to Lisa. Willis is kept going by his anger. Patterson stays on his feet so he can hurt. He doesn't want to make anything right because then he won't suffer as much.

"Just think about it," Patterson said. "But not for long."

Unwilling to travel too deeply into any of his thoughts, Roe went for an escape route as they drew close to the houses. "How's your arm?"

Patterson bent it at the elbow. He'd checked the bandage wrapped around it before sliding into his coat. Despite the fire of the injury, it had been a skimming wound. Thankfully, the damage done to his nose was superficial and several liberal splashes of antiseptic ointment had hopefully killed any germs from that man's mouth.

"Just dandy," he replied. "How's your cough?"

"Cough?"

"My God, man. You can't think we hadn't noticed. You've sounded like you're on forty a day for the last two weeks. What is it? Asthma? Are you developing flu?" Patterson studied him. "You're pale but no more than usual."

"I don't know what it is." Roe dragged out his next words from somewhere deep below and found uttering them to be an odd relief. "I've been coughing blood for a few days."

Patterson nodded and his sigh was almost lost to the wind. "I've had similar. I—" He broke off and cleared his throat. Roe looked behind again. Granger and Willis were a good fifty feet back and the distance was growing owing to Willis's walk being more of a shuffle.

"Blood," Patterson muttered. "I've. . .had blood."

He'd paled in the last few moments and his lips were pressed tightly together enough to have almost disappeared. The growth of stubble coating his chin and cheeks stood out in dark dots.

"Front or back?" Roe asked the ground.

Another pause before Patterson replied. "Back."

"I'm sorry." Roe had nothing else. He had never classed Patterson as a friend any more than he had with Granger or Willis, but after knowing him for close to twenty years and a decade of their hellish life, they were as close they could be. Which is why, he suddenly realised, he always reacted so violently when Patterson made it clear they should go their separate ways. As tragic as it might be, they were all each other had left.

"Sorry?" Patterson repeated the word as if it was new. "That's not what's important now, Roe. Chances are neither of us have a lot of time which is why this idea and this plan. . .It's why this whole thing is pointless. We are nothing and soon, we'll be less than that."

Silence between the two men. Even the tread of their boots seemed to have faded away from Roe, taking the steady murmur of the wind with it as the afternoon drew closer to dusk and the clouds were like coal ready to fall to the ground.

Am I dead already?

"Roe. Patterson."

Roe jumped, then stumbled. Granger's shout from behind could have been a reply to his question, an assurance but a comfort that he was still alive.

"Those houses," Granger called. Beside him, Willis's head hung limp and the white of his bandaged wrist was turning a faint red as blood broke through the wound.

"We rest there," Granger shouted.

"Of course, boss," Patterson whispered and marched ahead of Roe who could only watch the other man walk on and wish they hadn't said a word to each other.

Chapter Sixteen

Candace consulted her interior clock and then the starless sky. Dawn probably four or five hours ahead – for what it was worth. Abandoning their original plan of leaving the house as soon as full night fell for waiting until later in case they encountered anyone connected to those Lazarus and Martha had killed, they'd departed several hours later. Walking for another two at a slow, careful pace had brought them past a few more scattered buildings, none of which offered much of anything useful after a brief exploration, then a widening road with a pastoral landscape. The distant smell of algae wafted in from the grass. There would be a river nearby and their plan was to leave the road when it linked with the motorway, and travel cross country again. They could find shelter in trees, build a small fire and boil water from the river.

Pitching her voice low, she said Dumah's name and offered him her knife. He took it, axe in the other, and Candace pulled a birch tree twig from inside her coat. Rubbing it on her teeth and gums, she cleaned the last traces of skin and kidney, licking them and remembering the delicious warmth of the fresh organ. They'd eaten well thanks to Lazarus and Martha, and buried the bones in the rear garden. Loose soil, cold and crumbling under the fingers, had been enough of a cover to hide their presence. Wild dogs would probably find their leavings, but that couldn't be helped.

"Can I?" Martha reached a hand to Candace's twig.

Candace wiped it on her leg and passed it to Martha who proceeded to clean her teeth. They knew about hygiene and the risk of disease. Priest had often said they should care for their bodies as they cared for one another. Injuries could be mended, but germs could not be beaten. *Clean body, clean soul.*

But thinking of Priest was no good for her. While she wanted anger, Candace could only work her way to sorrow tinged with a numbness she knew would not possess for long. Deep pain would take its place and be with her for the long years ahead.

She let out a sigh heavy with tears and sensed Lazarus looking back at her. He had led them without being asked to since they left the house and slowed as he turned her way.

"I am all right," she murmured. "Keep going."

Mary and Martha drew to close to her sides, both with a free hand as their knives were strapped to their skinny legs. Wordlessly, they held her hips and brushed the stump of her left arm on Martha's hair, and let her fingers stroke Mary's forehead. Dumah hooted, offering her the cleaver.

"Will you hold it for me?" she asked him.

He nodded, smiling, and wrapped his gloved fingers around the handle of her tool.

"How far?" Mary asked Lazarus.

"One more mile. Houses ahead. Town. We go to the fields before then. We keep the road at our side."

With childish amusement, Mary asked another question. "How long to Dover?"

Lazarus looked again to Candace and she pictured the sole image she had of the town: cliffs, white and chalky, and the end of the country staring out across the water to Europe. England, so proud. England, so sure of itself and now nothing more than ash while those cliffs would remain white but no longer proud because pride belonged to the time before the bombs. And it should stay that way no matter what that man Granger and his dogs might think of her and her brothers and sisters.

Candace realised she had twisted her mouth into a snarl and closed it. If bothered, Lazarus didn't show it.

"Two days," she said. "Quicker by road all the way, but we stick to the woods and grass, yes?"

"Yes," Lazarus replied.

Seemingly satisfied with the answer, Mary was quiet. They walked on. The clouds drifted, each one miles across and merging with others to form a blanket cover. In patches, holes were visible. The stars were winking eyes made blurry by distance and an atmosphere still choked with dirt blown up from the earth.

From their left and somewhere in the grass verge, a voice spoke. Each of them turned as one, their knives and axes raised, Dumah shoving Candace's cleaver towards her.

"I have sight on you. You move, I shoot."

The speaker's voice was muffled, whether by coverings over their mouth or a physical condition, Candace couldn't be sure. Breath held to avoid noise, she rapidly scanned the nearest section of the field and saw nothing but the line of the hedgerows, jagged and uneven, forming a weak barrier between road and grass.

"You know guns?" The speaker sounded as if their tongue was too large for their mouth. By the sounds, they were unused to speech. "I have gun. Sight on it. Five of you. Axe, knives. Put them all down."

Dumah growled and raised his axe level with his head.

"Axe Man. Don't move."

Dumah growled again and made no move to lower his weapon.

Hush from the grass. No advancing step crushing weeds and pebbles.

Head still, Candace checked over the others. Mary and Martha with their knives up. Martha sniffing, each inhalation a tiny puff. Dumah, tall and proud and ready to kill. Eager to. Lazarus half-turned to the right and his left leg pivoted to the other side of the road.

Lazarus's hand clasping the squat torch with its weak flame, his fingers splayed wide open and pointing to the land on their left.

Candace understood. *Run. Separate. Meet.*

Even if the children hadn't seen his subtle movement and indication, they would react the instant any of the others moved. Candace estimated they would be swallowed by the darkness over the grass in under two seconds. None would run in a straight line; none would be a target even if their mystery assailant genuinely did have a working gun with a device attached enabling him to see well enough to shoot.

Then he called again out of the night and Candace's hope died.

"You with light. I see you pointing. No running. Drop your knives. Now."

They could have been statues and he shouted, voice clearer through obvious effort and his youth betrayed by the tremor.

"I see you. Tall man. Black coat. Girls. Long hair. Boy. Big coat. Black woman. Curly hair. Hat. One arm. I see you."

It was over. Pretence would get them killed.

The sisters trembled, their anger making their bodies shake. Dumah panted and Candace saw how tightly he gripped his beloved axe. Jutting from his fingerless gloves, his fingers were like the Dover cliffs she remembered from a previous life.

And Lazarus was without fear or fury. He was resigned.

"Drop weapons."

A boy in the darkness and they could do nothing to save themselves.

Lazarus was first to drop his knife. The smash as it hit the ground turned something over in Candace's stomach and the numbness she'd walked with since their escape from Granger faded.

Rage took its place.

Chapter Seventeen

The boy kept at their backs as they followed the straight road towards the town he'd said was called Netherton. While Lazarus hadn't had chance to get a decent look at the youth as the night gradually gave way to a sickly shade too thin to be called purple, he'd seen enough. The gun, the boy's firm grip on it; his layers of various coats all untorn or marked; his frame lean rather than deathly skinny. He'd be quick to react whether the gun had any bullets and Lazarus could not take the risk. With his bare hands and their weapons taken from the ground to be placed in the bag the boy kept at his side, Lazarus was no threat.

The youth told them to walk side by a side and to keep close together. Without any choice, they did so, and Lazarus knew it felt as unnatural to the others as it did to him. Keep apart when outside. A matter of fact they'd known for years and it was no help to them now.

The boy had them walk for well over two miles without saying a word and only spoke when the feeble dawn fell towards grey morning and the town was that much more visible.

"I am George."

You will die, Lazarus thought and bared his teeth at the road unfolding ahead of them. More houses were visible at either side, clumps of brick and gardens thick with weeds and brambles while the wind made the wild mess hiss. Crashed into fences and jutting from a dyke, rusting vehicles were misshapen monsters lurking at the corner of Lazarus's eye. He avoided looking after a few moments, frightened by the old relics.

Netherton revealed more of itself: yet another cluster of wrecks cut into uneven pieces; roofs either missing completely or crushed inwards to create holes; rough chunks spreading over the sides of the ruins where windows had been once but were now jagged openings, letting in the wind and rain. While Lazarus had little idea of the true scale of cities compared to towns, he had the idea the settlement they were approaching wasn't one of the country's larger territories. Priest had told them stories of cathedrals and ancient places of learning and books written by people dust and bones for centuries. Nothing along those lines grew beyond the wild grass or the motorway.

You need to avoid the towns.

Lazarus knew Priest told him the truth. He also knew there was nothing to be done when they had a gun at their back.

"I am George," the boy repeated and Dumah growled.

Apparently unperturbed, George spoke in a low voice that still carried and caused puffs of steam to jet from his mouth and nose.

"I'm not a monster. All that back there, that was pretending."

Lazarus turned as he walked. George kept several paces behind and moved smoothly. He smiled when he saw Lazarus's expression.

"I speak well, don't I? I did that on purpose. People. . .they're like animals. One-word sentences. Not me. I like to talk. So, I do."

Let him say whatever he wants. Think, boy. Think about where you are and where you are going. How long to get there?

He estimated another twenty minutes although it depended exactly where their captor would take them. If luck was on their side, it wouldn't be far from open land. While buildings and streets offered places to hide, they also meant more people. More danger.

Lazarus squeezed his hands into fists, frustration threatening to block out coherent thinking. While there was no point in wishing they'd kept to the coast and not come inland for food, he couldn't help knowing Dumah had been right when he'd made it clear their plan was foolish. He also knew Priest would have been quietly disappointed in Lazarus's childish thinking. Fifteen was old enough to know regret was pointless. All he could do now was take any opportunity that came to get all of them to safety.

George spoke again. "I know this isn't the best start for us, but I don't think we're different. Not really. You've lost people, haven't you? I can tell. I had the same when they dropped the bombs. My mum and dad. I had two brothers. Don't really remember them, though. They were older than me." His voice dropped into a flatter tone, possibly through the pain of the old memory. "I remember my mum and dad, but I can't see them." He tapped the side of his head. "Their faces. . .I think of their faces and I just see them burning. I know that's what happened. It's what happened to everyone, isn't it? Still." He sounded as if he'd brightened. Lazarus didn't look back. There was a creeping sense of things not being right. The closest comparison he could make was as if the road surface had suddenly become softer, like a muddy puddle, while appearing solid.

"None of that matters much, now. We're still here. I'm still here. You're still here. We. . .keep going, don't we?"

Facing ahead, Lazarus saw Candace and Dumah glancing his way. They'd noticed it, too: George slipping between night and day, darkness and light, and doing it within seconds.

Lazarus blinked twice. *Yes.* Their awareness noticed, Dumah and Candace looked away from him.

"Four years old. I was by myself like you were at some point, I bet. I hid. I stayed in our house even though a lot of it had been. . ." George made a strange sound that began with a whistle descending in notes before blowing out a harsh puff.

"Rubble. I stayed in the rubble. I ate rats. There were a lot of them, and they were easy to hit with bricks. Then some men found me. Took me. We went out of the city and I thought they'd saved me. They hadn't."

George went on, each word falling out flat. Lazarus wished for the boy to weep, but there were no tears. Maybe his story was too old for him or maybe it had happened to a different George. They were the old days and they belonged there.

He spoke of the things that had been done to him by the men, the scavengers, his language basic and somehow childish. One day while they slept beside a river and after however many months of the abuse and existing on the bare minimum of sustenance, he'd stabbed one of the men in the eyes with a piece of broken glass he'd secreted in a coat pocket for weeks. He fled while the blinded man shrieked for the others. More by luck than anything else, the child found a way out of the city and fled into miles of a wood with its dead leaves and the wind blowing its icy breath. Exhausted after long weeks of surviving on pond water, insects, leaves and the occasional rat, he'd made his way to the edges of a city, one called Cambridge. There, he'd been taken in by a new group and thought he was again prisoner of men who would rape and beat him. Instead, he'd been told if he found food, he could join them in their search of the villages and other towns for food or survivors, the collective of men, women and children always travelling and working their way across the country because there was no point in staying in one place for long – never enough food to feed the starving in a single location. And now here they were. His role was to keep an eye out for those who came wandering, to bring them to the school where they all lived for today, tomorrow and the weeks ahead until the food ran out and they moved on once again.

George finished. More life had crept back into his voice as he neared the end of his tale which brought Lazarus no comfort. Granger and the men in the police station had been dangerous because they still believed in dead things. George was dangerous because he was caught between those dead things and his life.

Eventually, Lazarus knew, being trapped in that place would mean George's death. It was an understanding that added a new emotion to how he felt about the boy only slightly younger than himself who'd taken them prisoner.

Pity.

Chapter Eighteen

Estimating the others were behind about a mile in the detached house, Granger squatted and unfurled the road atlas over the cracked ground. He traced his finger across the lines, refusing to see them as anything other than a guide to a destination. Villages and towns and the lives they'd contained all spreading on the pages in the sickly dawn light were of no use to him.

"The A257," he muttered and peered across the desolate meadows to a few B-roads where the dawn's mist clung to the tarmac and hedgerows. He'd given Roe's precious atlas a look that only pretended to be cursory before snatching it from Roe. If he stayed on the motorway, he couldn't get lost. Worst came to worst, he could find his way back to South Calcott without too much effort.

But that wasn't going to happen. *Dover* was going to happen once they found the bastards who'd come into his life with their knives and their stink. Find them, take them and get to a known place where he could be. . .he could be. . .

Be himself again instead of this man in the middle of nowhere.

Granger checked the B-roads a final time, fighting the wish to walk there instead of the motorway, and folded the map. He knew the others, Patterson especially, wanted to take the A2 but that would be a mistake. The cannibals would be scurrying this way, eager to get to Dover and follow their leader's instructions, unaware they were following a less direct route. They knew woodlands and farms. They crept along like insects afraid of the light and knew nothing of motorways.

Granger realised he was snarling at the air and got moving again. His destination lay ahead while Roe, Patterson and the barely conscious Willis were behind, resting in the house they'd taken the night before when Willis had quite clearly been minutes from collapse after hours of cross-country walking. Roe and Patterson had not put up much argument when he'd told them he was going ahead a way to see what was what while Willis continued to sleep. He couldn't begrudge them that. They weren't young men, anymore. Not one would see forty again or even fifty. While they'd done more walking in the last six months that at any other point in their lives, constant exposure to the grave of the country dragged spirits down into the mud.

Faint movement brushed the corner of his eye. There was no surprise at seeing Carolyn walking by his side. He'd known she wouldn't remain in the police station now the main doors were wrecked, and the entire building was exposed to the elements. It'd simply been a matter of time before she joined him on the journey south.

What are you doing out here? she asked, each word beating in time with his steps.

"Looking for the people who killed you." She'd sounded slightly disappointed with him and he was immediately put on the back foot. Granger tried to relax. Going on the defensive was no way to start a conversation.

Why? What good will it do? I'm dead. They're gone. Go back to the others and let this go.

Granger blew out a tired sigh. He knew Roe and Patterson felt the same, even if Roe hid it. Learning Carolyn agreed with them threatened to shake his surety his plan was the best way ahead.

"Sweetheart, you have to understand, this *needs* to happen. Those people, the things they've done. . .the things they did to you. . .it can't be allowed. I know I can't undo it or make things right, again, but I *can* stop them from making this world worse."

She was quiet for a moment, her journey beside him also soundless. A sliver of rationality tried to speak up and tell Granger his wife could not be talking to him; he was talking to himself and nothing more. He cut it off without knowing what he thought below his waking mind.

Stop them for me or yourself?

"I—"

Carolyn was gone. He gazed at the space she'd filled, seeing only the ground slipping from black to grey as the morning sun attempted and failed to burn away the clouds. His staring eye took in the farmland, the grass patchy and discoloured. Beyond that, a country exposed: farms, suburban streets and Britain's great cities all ticking away to the moment their histories and times were consumed by the rain and wild weeds.

You need to go back to the others. The thought was his alone which made it easier to ignore. Granger walked on, arms tucked to his sides, fingers holding nothing but his gloves. Twenty minutes later, he saw the skyline of a town in the distance. Probably only a market town judging by the lack of a cathedral or any buildings larger than secondary schools. It seemed unlikely the cannibals would have headed that way despite their horrible appetites. Their priority would be getting to Dover as quickly as possible which meant crossing fields and skirting the narrow rivers bisecting them.

They need to eat, though, he thought and inwardly cringed.

Ahead, two houses stood on both sides of the road, the houses relatively free from damage possibly due to their isolated location. Granger walked on and saw a darting shape crossing through front gardens, the figure small and pale in the gathering gloom and the fog creeping in. It didn't take Granger much longer to realise it was a child.

The movement stopped near a wall of spiky hedges at the border of one of the gardens. He kept his focus on the area as he closed in, looking for the slightest indication the child had fled, hoping he presented no suggestion of threat. Clearing his throat and keeping his hands in view, he called out.

"I won't hurt you. I'm not dangerous."

If the child did remain beside the hedge, they could have been invisible. Granger said nothing more until he estimated he was fifteen running steps from the garden and eased down into a squat.

"I have food. Would you like some?"

With slow care, he reached for the smaller bag he'd taken from Roe and unzipped it, eyes always on the spot beside the hedges. Easing out a can of baked beans and a tin opener, Granger held the can so the torn and faded label could be seen from the garden, then cursed. What good was a label for a child that doubtless couldn't read?

"Beans," he called. "Do you know beans?"

He placed the can on the road and opened it while keeping his attention on the garden and the shadows around the hedges. Standing, he winced at the strain of his knees before backing away.

No movement in the garden. Granger wondered if he'd either imagined it or if there had been someone there, perhaps they'd been able to sneak into the rear of the homes without his noticing.

"I have more food," he called and kept any doubt out of his voice. The wind gusted against his face before scudding out to the fields. The grass shivered and muttered.

What are you doing out here?

He couldn't tell whether the voice belonged to Carolyn or was his own.

"Food for your help."

There. A slight shifting of white in the shadows. A hand?

"Have you seen people here?"

It occurred to him that he and the others hadn't encountered anyone on the journey from South Calcott. Maybe that wasn't surprising considering they'd crossed five or so miles of the English nowhere. Skirting abandoned villages and with only a few market towns in the distance, they hadn't been likely to meet anyone on the road. Even so, an uneasy disquiet nicked him.

"New people? A tall man. Two girls. A boy. A woman? You tell me and I give you more food."

He took a second can of beans from the bag. They couldn't afford to give away their meagre stash of supplies, not with an injured man slowing down their approach to Dover, but Granger knew it was necessary to give a little to get a little. Always the case and especially so in this brave, new world. Besides, there'd be food in Dover. Dealey would have supplies, organisation. He'd known how to take care of people and a bad situation. It was why he had made a good leader.

Until you kicked him out.

That was Carolyn, more amused than accusatory. He resisted the urge to look around and check if she was in sight, again.

Another slight movement close to the hedge and a child slid into view. Barely five years old, stunted, hunched over and no protection from the day – their face was uncovered as were their hands. Their only safety net from the elements was a tattered coat and a pair of too large shoes. A second child, two or three years older, crept out of the shadows in the garden. Both sniffed eagerly. They saw the opened tin of beans and grunted.

Granger stayed motionless. He and the others had encountered wild children on their journey out of London and into the surrounding counties although never as close as this. Once, he'd left the camp they'd made overnight near the River and crept into the greenery to urinate. A girl, aged about seven, had stepped into view from behind a few old oaks and Granger had eased his Browning from his coat pocket. She'd fled in an instant. He knew he could reach for the gun if the two children made any violent movement, but it would mean no information from them, no help.

"New people?" he called. "You tell me." He shook the second tin. "More food for you."

The children looked at one another. The youngest squatted as if about to defecate and Granger winced. The girl—he *thought* she was female—dug a hand into the earth below the hedge, scooped up soggy dirt and smeared her cheeks. Mud mixed with the dirt already marking her before crumbling back to ground. Hooting like an owl, the second child cradled her right arm against her narrow chest and held the elbow, forearm obscured.

"Yes," Granger said. They were on the right track. "Where?"

The elder child made a strange clacking sound, tongue slapping the roof of her mouth. She gagged as if about to vomit and jabbed a finger towards the fading skyline of the town. Clearly struggling, she choked out a noise.

"Skull."

Skull? What in God's name does that mean?

"Skull."

She said it a second time, adding more force to the grunt, and pointed to the town again.

Skull? A place? Does she mean a cemetery?

His lack of understanding was obvious; she gave a weak howl and tried a third time, adding more of a drawn-out, higher pitch to the middle of the word. Madly, it sounded to Granger like a noise a dog might make if their owner told them to speak.

"Skooool."

"School," he whispered.

He placed the second tin down, opened it quickly and turned without giving the children another look. Moments later, their happy hooting followed him. He increased his speed to a trot, heading back the way he'd come while the mist sliding over the land on either side of the road seemed to solidify like a growing wall, brick by brick of white ready to collapse and bury everything.

Chapter Nineteen

As another still morning arrived, George directed them towards the perimeter of a park. Its flowerbeds and hedges had died and sunk back into the earth; the outline of small football pitch was lost to the clumping grass, and the swings and a slide in the play area were little more than rust.

"Other side of here," George said.

They crossed through the grass and reached narrow streets of terraced houses, each damaged by fire, that in turn opened to the town's high street. George took them north along a path between a football pitch and more smoke-damaged terraces. It seemed unlikely to Candace that the bombs had fallen here which meant the fires and the broken buildings were down to events in the aftermath. Food riots. Looting. Men like the ones who'd raped George as a boy. The collapse of everything. She had enough memories of the time and had no wish to be reminded of them so starkly.

George cleared his throat and spoke in his normal tone. He'd again become a calm, rational youth and Candace wondered if he heard himself when he alternated between that and the child broken by what he'd lived through.

"You're all very quiet. I like talking. I got it from the books. There was a library in the school. We had to burn most of the books to keep warm, but I read them first. I knew about books before the bombs and I remembered I liked them, so I read a lot. Then we burned them. Most people don't say much just like you lot. Some people can't talk. They're the worst."

Dumah turned back and eyed George who blinked. He laughed a moment later.

"I don't mean can't talk like they don't have a mouth or anything. I mean they never learned. What happened to you? Have you got a tumour in your mouth? I saw that once. Big as his face in the end. He choked on it."

"He has no tongue," Candace said, already tired of the boy despite the short time they'd spent together. She needed to think about what was coming. Without their weapons, they were weaker, but they weren't beaten. Given the chance, she'd show the boy what a woman with one arm and no knife could do.

Two captors in the space of a day was two too many. Granger and his foolish friends had been a relic of before; hurting them and making their escape had been a matter of time, not luck.

"Really?" George whistled. "What happened?"

"Ask him," Candace muttered. George laughed, high and innocent.

The path turned towards a school playing field. Beyond it, a two-storey building with one side formed of many windows was a cracked and ash-covered relic. Outside it, a dozen people were either engaged in physical work or simply collapsed on the hard ground, dead or sleeping.

"We live there," George said. "All together."

Those outside the school able to move were attempting to smash up what Candace eventually realised were doors. They had no axes to do the jobs. Instead, they struck bricks and a few metal poles on the doors with tired blows. Their arms like twigs were not suited for their work in the slightest.

"You have nobody stronger for this?" Candace asked.

"They do it for food. Make firewood. Get given food by the others."

They crossed grass, and dew soaked into Candace's shoes. She ignored the discomfort and appraised the windows in the buildings, surprised to notice most were whole below the layers of muck. Men, women and a few children peered outside, others lurking in doorways. Dawn had broken during the last few minutes; while the last of the night had slipped away, morning did little to dispel the shadows. The family was used to seeing in poor light; Candace made out at least fifteen sets of eyes appraising her and the others.

One of the workers outside the school dropped, blood dribbling from cuts and grazes on their fingers. Cawing like a dying bird, they crawled towards a doorway that would offer shelter from the cold. The trail of their blood was an uneven scribble on the paving and even after watching them for several moments, Candace could not guess at their gender. Their emaciated state and stinking rags for clothes hid it as well as full dark might.

A word from long before swam through Candace's mind and she pushed it away in faint disgust.

Auschwitz.

A word from long ago and faraway. It had no place here, so she wouldn't think of it.

She couldn't take her eyes from the trail on the paving until she dug her jagged nails into her palms; the sting was slight but worked as a distraction from the creeping dread of the people, closer to death than life, and their pathetic attempts at creating firewood. They'd encountered several places like this one before. Settlements. A collective of people attempting to stay alive while they starved. While there were still lone survivors out in the empty places, most seemed to want to live with others. Perhaps it made their dying easier.

George took them from the last of the grass to a flat section of ground. Candace realised they were facing the rear of the school and the middle section was an assembly hall. He ran his gloved fingers on the steps of one of the slides as if caressing it, and a man emerged from the school's main entrance. While the windows were smeared with dirt and filthy rainwater, they offered enough of a glimpse inside for her to make out few people. Not for a minute did she believe the faces she'd seen on the second floor were the only ones inside. Not in a building this size.

A door swung open, creaking on its old hinges, and a man emerged, his body clad in a heavy coat and woollen gloves. He held a small knife. It took Candace a glance of less than a second to note that while the blade was short, it was freshly sharpened. A knife for a killing blow in an eye or a neck. The man's eyes were visible along with a red nose. A tight scarf obscured the rest of his face but didn't muffle his voice.

"Who is it?"

"George. I found people."

For a moment, Candace wondered if the man might be blind. Then his cool gaze tracked from Lazarus and Dumah to her. He grinned and her stomach clenched.

"Weapons?" he asked.

"Knives, axe, cleavers."

"Good. Inside."

He backed up through the open doors and George muttered for them to go inside. Keeping their customary few feet apart, they did so, entering a foyer. Directly opposite, an open-plan office had been cleared of furniture and the walls stripped bare. Three burning torches, much the same as the ones in the cells of the police station miles away, illuminated the surroundings and sent mad shadows skittering over the dirty floor. More people, all keeping well back, watched from open doors.

They were led down a short corridor, passing classrooms now makeshift shelters where cushions and filthy blankets acted as beds, and what had been a gym but now appeared to be a surgery. They had a few seconds to see smears of blood soaking the floor, bags of material tied with string and tables covered with long blades. A short look but long enough to understand. Amputating limbs and hacking away diseased flesh was a part of life.

The hallway ended in the wide space seen from outside: the assembly hall. While it had once been a place for children to sing, it was now a stinking hole. Jumbles of overturned furniture had been thrown below the wall of windows that overlooked the play area and grass they'd crossed; holes had been dug into the plaster and brickwork, and broken debris covered the floor. Candace counted four metal canisters crammed with broken wood from doors and some spindly branches. The containers were fires. Probably for warmth rather than cooking. There was little meat to cook unless you were ready to kill to eat. Crouched against the wall opposite the windows, Candace counted four men, all carrying bats of some kind. Each was perfectly still. The shadows draped over their bodies, presumably acting as a shield from sight for those not used to looking for a threat.

"Stop," George muttered.

They halted and Candace knew without looking at the others that as much distance as they could manage separated them.

"Where are you from?" the man asked, pulling his scarf lower to reveal an unkempt beard, the hair matted with sweat and dirt.

They remained silent.

"Bag down," he said to George who dropped the bag of their weapons beside the remains of a grand piano. Its top and a side section had been removed, revealing its inner workings. George appeared smaller and younger than he had during their long walk out of the town's outskirts.

"Where are you from?" the man asked again. He spoke thickly, sounding a lot like George's pretend-voice. Chances were he had an infection of some kind in his mouth, or the tumour George had mentioned.

Nobody replied. Beard Man nodded as if they'd answered, stepped closer and threw a punch. It struck Lazarus on the cheek. He stumbled but stayed upright. Dumah reached for the man, fingers opening and closing as if he could feel skin on his nails. He didn't make a sound. Neither did Mary or Martha, and Candace let herself have a moment of pride. Lazarus bared his teeth and gazed at the man who showed his own teeth, all brown and broken, in a grin. He spluttered laughter and the stink of his breath assaulted Candace's nose. Seemingly knowing when the initial pain had begun to decrease, the man punched Lazarus again in the same place. The boy rocked on his feet, red squirting from his lips. He spat it at Beard Man's feet.

The fist flew at his face a third time.

"Stop."

The man paused at Candace's word, lowered his hand and studied her. He took particular notice of her missing arm and she refused to lower her eyes.

"From the sea. We live near the sea," she said.

"Long way from the sea now."

"We came for food."

"You find any?"

"Dead animals. Cows. Sheep."

"You have any food with you?"

"No."

Candace didn't dare look at the sisters. The wrapped skin and leftovers from the two people Lazarus and Martha found while exploring were safely hidden in Mary's coat. The cold had so far kept them from going bad, but being indoors would put an end to that. And if the man should search the girls, the truth would be known in seconds.

"What can you offer us?" Beard Man asked.

Candace again refused to lower her head. She understood the meaning perfectly. It was the only way men like this knew how to be. Same before the bombs; same after the bombs. Always men like this who took what they thought was theirs to take.

Dumah advanced, hands held into fists. The men lurking at the edges of the hall burst from the gloom, armed with bats and clubs. Dumah charged them, bellowing. He brought a hand up in a quick jab, struck a chin, ducked and spun to throw a second punch. That one caught another man in the throat. Immediately, Dumah opened his hand wide, grasped and pulled on the man's larynx. Choking, the man fell, reaching for his wounded throat as he hit the floor and layers of dust exploded upwards. The third smashed his bat into Dumah's side, and the fourth brought his down against the back of Dumah's knee. Dropping, Dumah managed another punch, this one weaker than the others, and connected with a stomach. A bat came down again, smashing his back. He hit the floor, squirming.

Beard Man grasped Candace's hand, yanked her from the others and marched her towards a door behind the long counter. She twisted, looking back to Lazarus and the sisters. Martha nodded and Candace was taken from them as Dumah tried to cry out and the sound collapsed into a wheezing cough.

Beyond the hall, another corridor, this one turning in an L-shape. He marched her that way, passing rooms without doors, the windows covered with tatty curtains and the darkness hiding those unconscious or sleeping on the floor. Pained moans flowed out of several of the rooms, a sexless voice begging for food over and over until the sound of their steps drowned it out. Stains marked the walls in smears and there was no need for a close inspection to know the mess came from blood. Same with the occasional glimpse of it on the floor. People had died in this building. Many people over many years. Their bodies had been dragged from the classrooms, their fluids leaking from their corpses as they were removed. They were not her concern. Her family's lives were everything in this stinking, unlit hole.

At the end of the corridor, he told her to open a set of glass doors and take the next left. He'd brought her to what had probably been an art studio – an open space with spacious windows lining three sides. Curtains blanketed each one. A dozen candles flickered on the floor below the windows. Cushions and pillows, all discoloured, lay in clumps along with a few blankets.

The moment he pushed her towards a bundle of cushions, Candace gave up on any hope of getting through her situation untouched. Spinning on her ankle to face Beard Man as he shoved a dinner chair against the door and eyed her, she had to admit the chance of escape had died the moment George came out of the night with his gun.

She itched to cut his throat almost as much as she wanted that for this man.

"What's your name?" He licked his lips and it rasped through his hair.

"Candace." Withholding the information seemed pointless. He would beat her whether she told him or not.

"That's a nice name. Unusual."

"It means *princess.*"

He giggled like an amused child. "I've had a lot of princesses in here." A quick flick of his hand, pointing at her stump.

"How did you lose it?"

"Infection. A break. Cut it off."

She'd never told the lie before, never had reason to. In a way she rarely thought of too deeply, Candace knew others in her position would not like to think of what she'd had to do with her arm; they'd block out the memory in case it made them scream as she'd screamed when it'd been sawed off at the elbow. Instead of blocking the image of that night in the freeze of the winter and the mad light cast from Dumah's wavering torch, Candace clung to it. It made her who she was. It made them all who they were, and nobody could ever take that away.

A truth hidden inside a lie and all she'd give him. What she'd had done to her arm, what she'd welcomed done, was her business and that of Lazarus, Dumah and the sisters. It was not for this filthy man.

That is your name now. You are Filth.

Filth licked his lips again and she understood.

He came for her, hands swinging. She dropped below the impacts, taking them on her head and neck, eyes remaining open to see his spinning shadow on the ground. Grunting, Filth pulled back and fumbled at his trousers, yanking them open to reveal the stink of an unwashed body. Candace didn't recoil. She smelled much the same from her own skin and that of her siblings for a long time. He yanked her hair and shoved her towards his crotch where she tasted warm flesh reeking of sweat. Soft flesh.

Filth grunted again, pulled her by the hair and took hold of himself. His fist worked to no avail. Bellowing, he punched her in the face, the same strong blow he'd given Lazarus, and knocked her to the cushions. When she struggled around and found her sight again, he'd tied his trousers with his frayed rope and stared down at her.

"You tell nobody," he whispered.

"I tell nobody."

"I can kill you whenever I like."

"I know."

"I can kill your friends. The girls. I tear them open."

"I know."

Filth took another length of rope from a nearby shelf and approached her. Knowing she had no choice, Candace let him tie her hand to a stone-cold water pipe, then do the same to her ankles. The scratchy material irritated her skin; she ached for fresh air—no matter its chill—to walk through.

"Scream," he said. "Scream like I'm fucking you."

Eyes on his, she did, wailing, crying, pleading for him to stop. While she'd had no cause to do so in the past (even after the terrible weeks following the bombs and before Priest found her cowering in the broken remains of a hospital in Lincoln), she knew what was required. Candace understood men who weren't her siblings. Demons, not men. So, she gave him what he wanted and when he told her to shut up, she finished with whimpering, then closed her mouth.

Marching around the room, Filth blew out all bar one of the candles, turning the studio into night and making his shape close to indistinguishable. Not blinking, Candace watched his outline stride to the doors and yank at a sheet nailed to their top. It unfurled, blocking the glass panels and robbing the room of what little illumination made it inside from the corridor.

"You touch this door and I'll make the little ones scream like that. For real."

"I know."

He left her, the unlocked door out of reach while she lay on the cushions. Her stomach growled. Her body throbbed from head to toe. She tasted blood and rubbed the tip of her tongue around a tooth made loose by his beating.

Her mind, quick as always, sank into her anger and she let it.

Anger had saved her for a decade, and it would save her again.

Chapter Twenty

Dumah tore a tiny piece of his shirt free and dabbed at the cut he'd dug into his bicep with his thumb nail. The stream of blood hadn't been enough for the children, but at least it had been something. George, again armed with his rifle that let him see in the dark, returned a few hours after locking them in a storage cupboard and brought a bottle of stale water, but no food. Dumah knew eating could wait – at least for a short time. His stomach was well-trained and would not give him discomfort for a while yet. Mary and Martha, on the other hand, needed sustenance. Growing children always did.

"Clean it," Lazarus muttered and Dumah nodded. He spat on the piece of his shirt and wiped it on the clotting wound. A dozen other small scars marked his arm above the elbow, and each had healed without issue.

They'd dozed without sleeping fully, listening for approaching steps outside the door. Noise had been constant: querulous voices begging for help and food, the occasional cry of women being hurt in ways Dumah didn't want to imagine, along with hammering on doors and old chairs – presumably to make more kindling for fires. Whatever was happening in the school, he knew the place was not a family like his own. Togetherness was outside. There was nothing whole about the people in the school.

He'd held the sisters close while they slept fitfully and Lazarus curled into a ball beside the armchair, trying not to think of Candace somewhere else with the terrible man, wishing Priest remained with them because their father would have a plan. All Dumah had was sorrow things had brought them here.

When his body clock told him it was close to noon, steps approached in the corridor and the key turned. Knowing they would face at least one gun, Dumah made no move to attack as the door opened. He pushed Mary and Martha to his back, noting Lazarus stood with his hands splayed. The boy was ready.

His rifle aimed into the storage cupboard, George stood beside a skinny man who wore a thick hat pulled low, and a padded jacket. The man held a dirty bag and a burning wooden torch. The shaking flame offered some warmth and a dancing yellow light.

"Food and water," George said, and the man slid the bag across the floor into the cupboard. A bottle clinked. "Beef."

They knew *beef* and didn't care for it much. Human flesh had so many more flavours, more richness. Still, Dumah knew they would have to eat whatever was offered.

He shook and Martha squeezed his hand.

"You have a choice," George said. His voice was higher than the day before. Nerves. That was worse than aggression. Dumah knew aggression meant violence which was fine. He understood violence.

Nerves meant the boy didn't know how they were going to react to whatever he said next.

Like Lazarus, Dumah bent his knees, the movement quick enough to pass detection. There was no need to check if Mary and Martha had copied him.

"We go looking for food or water we can boil or anything we can burn. We find it, we keep it. All of us. Nobody shares here. If you find something, it's yours. If you don't find anything. . ." He shrugged. "You don't eat or drink or stay warm."

"Why did you bring us here?" Lazarus asked.

"I had to," George replied. "For. . ."

"Woman." The man beside him sounded as if he had a mouthful of broken teeth. "Bring woman here. Girls eventually."

Dumah understood. He trembled, furious and sickened. Behind, the sisters pressed harder to his back.

"He gives woman. Is useful," the man said and grinned. His teeth were as Dumah had pictured – jagged and smashed. His tongue poked between the shards, slimy pink hiding between the grey mess.

"Like I said, you have a choice. You can look for food or anything you can take out there or you stay here with nothing. I know how you feel. I felt the same when I find the people, but it was better than being alone. That's why I stayed. I had somewhere. I had those books. I learned words and how to speak. It was better. . .better than anything else out there."

George trailed off and his rifle shook. While Dumah wanted to hold onto his fury that this child bringing them here and handing Candace to that man, a ghost of understanding crept closer.

He knew about *out there*. In the freeze and the choking air, the destroyed buildings that offered no shelter, the hospitals and schools and shops reduced to burned bricks and broken glass. He knew about all of it from the cities laid to waste to the exposed countryside where so little grew, and the ponds and rivers were ripe with germs that would rot your insides if you took a drink without boiling the water. Dumah knew the endless silence broken only by the tread of his boots on rubble or the sly voice of the wind. That was *out there,* and George was right. There was nothing worse.

Except his sister handed to the stinking rat of a man.

Dumah advanced. Without hesitation, George brought the rifle round to bear on his chest.

"Please," the boy said. "I know how you feel, but you have to understand. Your friend is with him. You hurt me and he will hurt her after he's finished. He will hurt her a lot. If you scavenge like everyone else, you friend is safe."

The torch crackled; the red and orange of the flame merged, and the fire trembled as a breeze blown through a hole in the ceiling caught it. Somewhere else, a fresh round of hammering broke it. Following each blow, an agonised cry for water, please God give me some water, please God.

Dumah slid closer to George. His vision had narrowed down to a beam focused squarely on the boy's face and the shadow cast by the other man's torch; his fury beat in time with his heart and the hammering that could have been coming from the far end of the world. He was still only when Lazarus placed a firm hand on his wrist.

"No, Dumah. *No.* "

Dumah met Lazarus's eyes and for a moment, he saw his father looking back at him.

A hot body squirmed past Dumah, slipping against him and the wall.

"*You* did it," Mary shouted. "*You* gave Candace to him."

Dumah and Lazarus reached for her; she was already running straight for the corridor and George was swinging his rifle away from Dumah to aim squarely at Mary's face.

Chapter Twenty-One

Patterson knew the others thought the watch he wore was an affectation, a relic from the old days that he couldn't bear to lose for some stupid reason. Tapping the useless device with a nail, he understood why they felt that way. It hadn't kept accurate time in at least six years and was stuck at twenty to three. The tiny digit for the date read nine and he'd lost track of how near that was to the correct date within a matter of weeks of the battery dying. Still, he wouldn't remove the watch. It was his and his alone. So what if he could only tell the time by the light and the dark? Glancing around, he estimated it to be perhaps nine AM. Either way, their first night away from South Calcott was over. Morning had broken.

Hallelujah, he thought sourly.

His suggestion they move on before dawn had been studiously ignored. He knew Granger wanted to get moving again minutes after his return to the house in which they'd set up camp and not for the same reasons as Patterson. Granger wanted to track down the killers as quickly as possible; Patterson had wanted to lay low and minimize the chances of bumping into anyone. Night seemed the best plan to him, but Granger made them wait. Willis doped up again and their dwindling supplies of food and water packed away, they'd taken to the road once again. And now here they were – trekking through the silence for no reason that made sense to Patterson, and the town Granger said was Netherton rapidly approaching. If nothing else, a slight increase in the temperature had burned away the fog, leaving the land exposed.

Patterson would have preferred the shielding fog.

They stood in the centre of the single lane road, Willis with his head hanging, his chest rattling and the side of his face pale like bad milk. Roe kept close to Willis despite obviously not wanting to be anywhere near him. Wordlessly, Granger held the binoculars to Patterson who took them. He might have been the baldest member of their group and possessed the least physical strength; older fart he might have been compared to Roe and Willis, but he still had near perfect vision.

He raised the binoculars to his eyes and scanned the town.

It was much as he had expected, much as the few others they'd skirted around on the long journey away from London towards Canterbury. Wildfires, riots and other bursts of mindless violence had torn the town apart. While it was doubtful the bombs' effects had reached a small market town in Kent, one never knew. The last thing he wanted to do was get too close to the damage caused by the bombs; journeying out of the capital and seeing the smaller scale effects further afield had been more than enough for the rest of his life.

Doing his best to block out those thoughts as well as the ghosts of his conversation with Roe the day before, Patterson shifted on the spot and studied the figures in the distance.

Skinny, shuffling bodies with their heads hanging down; arms and legs like sticks, their movement awkward as they kept their attention on the ground, the split pavements and the gardens. Whatever they were doing, it involved looking for something. And as with any survivors now, the *something* was always food, water or makeshift firewood.

"There are a quite a few of them," Patterson said, still looking. "No weapons I can see. They're all on the lookout for food. Grass, rats. There won't be more than that."

"Our friends?" Granger asked softly and Willis, in his semi-conscious state, let out a tired groan.

"Not that I can see," Patterson replied.

"We find somewhere in the town to get a good look from." Granger adjusted his backpack and their few remaining bottles of water clanked together. "We keep a lookout for a couple of hours and if there's no joy, we go and find our friends. Most likely in a school."

His scarf had worked loose while he spoke. Keeping his eyes on Patterson, he tightened it and adjusted the straps of his pack. "Are we ready to continue?"

Patterson knew Granger had somehow heard the conversation he and Roe had shared the day before. While that was impossible given the fact Granger had been far behind, it remained true. He knew Patterson was probably dying and he knew any semblance of togetherness they shared was a sham.

Don't be ridiculous. How could he possibly know that?

The short answer was he couldn't.

Except he did.

"To find our new friends?" Patterson asked. He saw the land at Granger's back with his peripheral vision; fields so open, so spacious, and the dirty brown of the countryside beginning to pale below a weak mist.

"Absolutely," Patterson replied. He smiled – or at least, he opened his mouth and showed Granger his teeth. Walking ahead a few steps of the others, he kept his back ramrod straight and his buttocks clenched. Roe's eyes were all over him; he felt that as strongly as he felt the hard ground below his old shoes. Roe, thinking about whatever was wrong with Patterson's insides and wondering how much time might pass before that wrong thing became Patterson's last thing.

Wondering which of us will fall first? Patterson thought. Roe's constant cough and spitting up blood could mean a lot of issues, all unhealthy, some fatal.

There was nothing to be gained from thinking about any of that business. One foot in front of the other with Roe's focus on him. He had that to deal with. Granger murmured words of encouragement to Willis, telling him they didn't have far to go before the chance to rest and hot food. Lies, in other words. Patterson grimaced and a particularly cold gust of wind blowing in from their right made him bare his teeth at the morning.

Collective conversation impossible, the men headed further along with the countryside rolling alongside the narrow motorway, land turned grey by decay and the weighty sky. Roe trotted for a moment to walk beside Patterson but said nothing. They closed in on the distinct edge of the town – a curving road lined with squat trees on one side and what might have once been cottages but were now scorched piles of rubble. Oddly, the low hedges bordering the front gardens from the road seemed untouched if somewhat wild. Patterson took another look through the binoculars as they came to a junction. The fog he'd noticed a few minutes before was no thicker although it had drifted closer to their position. Patterson found it easy to imagine simply bolting from the others and letting the white take him. While it was too thin to act as much of a cover, the idea remained tempting. Sprint into it and walk across the county to wherever the hell he fancied. He knew he'd be dead within days without the protection of a group, but then if he did have something terribly wrong inside, then time wasn't really an issue.

"Penny for your thoughts." It was Roe at his side and Patterson jumped. Roe watched him intently, eyebrows raised.

"Not worth that much," Patterson said and managed a smile. He couldn't tell whether it felt real let alone looked it. He also couldn't work up the energy to care.

Sudden movement hit his vision, a blur of a falling shape as Willis collapsed to sprawl.

"Quickly," Granger yelled and hooked his fingers under Willis's armpits to drag him to the grass verge. Roe shrugged off his pack; the three manhandled Willis, Patterson doing his best not to inhale the reek of Willis's unwashed body and the aroma of cooked meat still clinging to his wounded arm. Grunting, puffing and pain sinking teeth into Patterson's lower back, they managed to cart Willis to the soft grass and Roe crouched behind him to keep him upright.

"Willis? Stay awake." Granger slapped Willis's cheeks. The sound of the blow snapped through the cold, hollow and flat. Willis's head lolled as if he was drunk; saliva bubbled between his lips before dripping to his chest. Granger jerked his hand clear at the last moment, grimacing.

Patterson had been squatting at Willis's feet. He stood, knees protesting.

"He's dying." The words were out before he could stop them. He found he didn't really care. "He's dying and we all know there's nothing we can do for him."

Roe also stood and jabbed a finger at Patterson. "Jesus Christ. Will you for once think of others? What are you suggesting? We just leave him to die? Well, there's no chance of that. We've been together too long for that. It's. . .unthinkable."

Roe's brief outburst seemed to fizzle out. He kept his hands in his pockets and Patterson knew it was to hide their shaking. He knew something else.

Roe was terrified of being alone. He didn't care for Willis any more than Patterson did. But he'd rather keep a man whom he had no love for alive than risk the slightest chance of being on his own.

Granger showed no reaction to the shouts above his head. He supported Willis by the shoulders, shaking him, cajoling him to wake up while Willis dribbled, and the fog drew closer. Patterson spoke with deliberate care, addressing his words to Granger's back.

"He is dead."

As if powered by a sudden electric current, Willis's head snapped back and his mouth open. Eyes staring, utterly aware; tongue jutting to taste the air and its grey meat like a worm between his teeth, he said a single word.

"Her."

Willis tipped to the side and even Granger couldn't stop him falling.

Chapter Twenty-Two

Lazarus hadn't let go of Mary's hand since grabbing her at the last second before she ran into George's rifle and although he suspected she would rather walk ahead; he did not relinquish his grip. Her slim fingers linked with his, the scratchy material of their old gloves together and Mary seconds from death.

But he wouldn't think of that. Not without losing control.

They were twenty minutes' walk from the school: a slow journey through a few long streets alternating between cleared spaces and half-crushed vehicles robbed of any useful parts. George had brought them down a narrow gap between terraced houses to a park that ended at a lengthy woodland. Bunches of oaks still grew on the park, their trunks solid and thick even if many of their branches had been snapped free. At least a dozen people from the school had reached the grass ahead of them; most had fallen to chew on the blades or lick the dew. Lazarus counted four sitting at the foot of the oaks, nibbling on leaves. The tiny pieces of green held between fingers no thicker than stems offered no sustenance, but they still ate.

"This is what I told you about," George said. He'd turned back to them and kept the rifle lowered. For most of the route, he'd walked ahead, apparently unconcerned about the risk of attack. Candace remained in the school, prisoner of the stinking man. There'd been no further need to point out the risk of harm to her if they hurt George or didn't do what he said.

"There's a river beyond the woods. A bridge across it. Then a meadow. I've heard some horses have set up home there. It's only been a couple of days so hopefully they're still there. You're lucky you came this way now. A week later and there'd be nothing for you."

Lazarus looked beyond George again. Three of the grass eaters lay prone, either unconscious or resting. He could make out the ankle of one where their trouser legs had ridden high. White like stone on the beach polished by the waves. Thin like a twig about to snap. There was no life here. Even the breeze had died.

"Horses?" he muttered.

Apparently taking Lazarus's disgust at the idea of eating horse, George covered the slight distance between them and ignored Dumah's warning growl to back away. With an almost imperceptible increase of pressure between their linked hands, Lazarus gave his own warning to Mary.

Don't move.

On Mary's other side, Martha edged forward and twisted so her narrow shoulder and chest shielded Mary as much as she could manage.

"There's nothing in the town, but they still look. We've cleared it out. The last good stuff was a stash of tins in a TV shop." He paused, eyeing them and Lazarus had no urge to ask what a *TV shop* was. George went on.

"I found a nest of rats in a Wimpy last month. Big ones. They lasted me for a week but there's nothing else there. That's why we come out this way and why I'm giving you a go for your first scavenge. Horse or starve."

Seemingly unperturbed by their lack of a reply, George marched to the grass, crushing a path through it. The faint fog that had formed about an hour before spread tendrils over the front gardens of houses and towards the far side of the park.

"We follow," Lazarus said and walked. Mary tugged on his hand.

"Candace." She said the name gently, but it still carried to George. He glanced back and Lazarus deliberately kept his eyes on the boy as he replied to Mary.

"She is fine."

"She is," George agreed. "She'll be looked after." He paused. "I know you hate me, and I know you want to get away from here, but you'll see my side of this eventually."

It was rare for Lazarus to speak with such precise emphasis. While none of them were talkative, he still understood the power of words and used them when they fit.

"No," he replied. "We won't."

George said nothing more until they were halfway across the grass, their steps kicking and breaking the strands heavy with dew. Trees jutted upwards; their branches jagged. A man and a woman—at least, Lazarus thought they were male and female; it was almost impossible to tell the gender of the skeletal bodies dressed in filthy coats and scarves—had fallen between the trunks, wrapped around one another as if eager for sleep.

He didn't think they were going to sleep.

"You speak well," George said, voice raised because he hadn't turned back. "That's surprising. Before I found the books in the school library, I sounded like them." He gestured loosely towards the shuffling, crawling bodies. "Like dogs. So how did you learn to speak?"

Dumah raised his hands, fingers splayed at George's back. Lazarus shook his head and Dumah lowered his hands although his anger didn't leave his face.

"Priest read us stories," Martha said softly. "From his old books. Lots of stories."

George looked over his shoulder, nodding as if he knew who Priest was. "Stories are good. I told myself stories when I was by myself, so I wasn't alone. Then when we came here, I stole the books and hid them until we had to burn them. I—"

Lazarus said: "We don't care about you or your life."

Lips pressed tightly together, George looked away and strode on over the grass, dampness soaking the lower half of his trousers as it did with Lazarus and Dumah. The sisters, so much shorter, had wet knees but both walked without complaint. As they neared the shrubs growing wild at the border of the two fields, Lazarus looked back. Another dozen people from the school were scattered around the pavements, some dragging sticks, a few holding broken bricks presumably to beat any rats they found. Several cars and a few vans, each overturned or rammed into its neighbour, blocked the road. The houses, all scorched by old flames and most missing either their roofs or fronts, were like broken teeth and he longed for the sight of their clear beach, spacious, free, *theirs.*

Soon, he promised himself.

"We go through the woods and we get to those horses. Like I said, it's horse or starve. You think you have a choice now, but you'll see how it is. There are no friends here. There's no sharing. I only gave your friend to that man to help myself. It isn't nice but that's how it is. I know you can try and kill me for that at any point, but if you go back without me, your friend will suffer for it." George tapped the rifle against his narrow thigh. "Do you understand me? You help yourself here. Nobody else." Apparently not satisfied with their refusal to acknowledge him, he lifted the gun and stabbed it towards the figures either prone on the field or desperately attempting to gain nourishment from leaves and tree bark. "Do you see anyone helping each other here? No, you don't."

Mary pulled clear of her brother.

"What are you doing?" George asked.

"Helping people."

With that, she raced away from the group, skinny legs pumping and little fists raised as she closed in on the nearest copse and the three figures unconscious amongst the trunks.

"Mary," Lazarus shouted, equally desperate to keep her by his side as he was for her not to help the people. *Help* meant killing and they could not show George who they were. Not yet. He broke into a jog after while Dumah hooted in panic. A second later, Martha sprinted past Lazarus, crying Mary's name. Ignoring George's yells to come back, Lazarus increased his pace, closing in on the girls as Mary skidded to a halt beside the oaks.

A flurry of bangs, the sound made slightly tinny by distance, broke. Screams answered the noise. Lazarus slowed, trying to look in all directions, sniffing, staring. A figure running from the pavement suddenly threw their arms out, a spreading red stain flooding their face.

Lazarus understood and bellowed the word to the children in front and to Dumah at his back.

"Guns."

He dropped, his ears smashed by terrified screams and more gunfire.

Chapter Twenty-Three

Candace listened.

The building never dropped into full peace; there was a constant background of low moans, the occasional scream, dragging steps and random banging. As the hours wore on and the discomfort in her hand chained to the pipes became numbness, the noise grew in frequency, and more voices punctuated the hammering and steps. Filth hadn't told her anything of how the school operated which didn't matter. She could guess. While they'd encountered many villages and settlements over the years, there had always been a sense of togetherness in those places, no matter how small or weak. Here was different. The boy George had given her to Filth because she was a woman, because a man like Filth had only one use for women, because it would mean a reward for George. It didn't really matter that Filth could not use her for his disgusting wants. He could appear to and that made him seem strong to the other weak creatures here. That was all these people knew – weakness dressed up as strength.

Filth had made several attempts to rape her, failing each time. Candace had endured his sweaty stink and fingers like wood on her arms as she endured the volley of punches that came after his attacks. She had little in the world outside of her family and her place in it. Her body was purely her own; what she chose to do with it was her business and nobody else's. That had been proven when they cut off her arm, when she'd told them to. Her flesh and bones and skin did not belong to Filth to use and hurt. For that if nothing else, he deserved death at her hand.

We don't kill for revenge, Candace, Priest whispered close to her ear.

No, we don't, she replied. *But we do kill to make things right, Father.*

He was silent at that and in his quiet, she heard soft agreement.

A shout beyond the door; a grating of wood on the floor and fresh light trickling through the crack between door and frame as it was inched open. Candace had pulled herself into the ball he expected. She had a glimpse of the corridor, the window opposite her room opening to what she thought was the front of the school's grounds although the muck on the glass made it too difficult to be sure.

He kicked the door closed, lit a few candles and crossed his arms over his chest. Shadows marked his face.

"You hungry?" he asked.

Candace shook her head. She was and exceedingly so, but not for anything this man might offer her.

"No?" He sounded honestly surprised. "Everyone hungry. Always. Hungry, dying, dead."

Scratching at his cheek made tiny flakes of skin fall like white ash and Candace had a flash of a memory: the ash after the bombs falling without a sound, dropping like snow.

"We have all here. Hungry. Dying. Dead. We throw the dead ones out. We wait for the dying to be dead and we let the hungry find their food. You are none of them."

He crossed to her in three quick steps, crouched and couldn't quite cover his grimace. Hand unseen in the shadows of her mid-section and clothing, Candace eased her fingers from her stump and splayed them.

"Hungry. Dead. Dying," he whispered.

With an inward scream, Candace willed her sleeping fingers to move. While a tiny tremor worked its way from her wrist into the palm, that was all she managed.

"No good to me," he said.

"I could be."

He laughed and the stink of it made her want to gag. "Liar. You want to kill me."

Candace remained still; fully aware he wanted a reaction.

"Don't you?"

His fist moved, a blur coming for her face.

She refused to try ducking it.

An explosion boomed below her eye and across her cheek. It formed a void for a second before pain consumed the emptiness. Candace ate the pain and smiled. He studied her curiously.

"Want to stay alive." She nodded at her chained hand.

"No good to me. No use." He brought his face an inch from hers as if about to kiss. The reek of sweat, dirt and disease assaulted her nose, but she showed no sign.

"My hand," she said.

By some miracle, she managed to spread her fingers a little. He looked at her palm, then back to her face.

"Hand," she said again, hoping his stunted intelligence was enough to take her meaning.

A smile slid over his face. "You want to live?"

"I want to live," she whispered and made it as broken as he expected.

Snorting his giggle, Filth fumbled for the key in his coat pocket and unlocked the handcuffs. Candace dropped her hand to the dirty floor.

Filth pocketed the key and reached for his belt.

Make him believe, child, Priest muttered.

Mouth trembling, Candace lifted her hand. The flesh and muscle below her elbow were waking up, a chorus of stinging voices gathering strength. Filth loosened his belt and reached for his broken zip. With his free hand, he yanked her wrist and bent her fingers into a circle.

Pulled her towards his crotch.

She gripped his limp penis, swallowed the need to spit at him and, for a count of twenty, let him pull and push on her forearm while strength returned to her fingers.

Now, child.

She slid out of his grasp, found a hanging testicle and squeezed with all her strength.

Filth roared, swung a fist which she ducked, bringing her mouth to his throat at the same time. Her teeth broke skin with ease, cutting into the flesh as he cried out and hammered at the sides of her skull. Taking the blows, dismissing them, Candace clamped her mouth over the wound, tasting blood and his stink, then yanked her head to the side in a speeding tug.

Filth howled, struck her again and she shoved her teeth back to the wound, widening it, chewing as she bit deeper, giving no thought to the hot flood coating her face and boiling over her tongue. She found muscle and sinew, shredded them even as he pummelled at her, his voice wet and gargling. Candace, vision turned red, pulled back and shoved her head upwards, hard. The top of her skull struck his chin, snapping him backwards. Another explosion detonated, no more important than the first a few moments before. Gore spluttering from his mouth and pumping from the hole in his throat, Filth came for her again which she had banked on. Moving with the speed she'd honed over her life with Priest, Candace rammed her index finger to his right eye.

The nail, filed into a claw, pierced the orb. He drew breath to shriek and Candace slammed her palm against his mouth, silencing the scream. He managed to get a hand up and threw another punch. It slammed against her cheek. She rocked with the blow, lessening it, and ignored the bloom of fire that cooked half of her head. Candace let go of his mouth and pummelled him in the throat. His scream fell apart into a choking cough.

Grasping the oily grease and dirt of his wild beard, she slammed his head into the floor and blood burst from his nose to merge with the liquid still jetting from his savaged throat. She heard at least one tooth snap, then his screams muffled by the floor. Panting and aware her advantage was in her speed against his greater strength, Candace straddled the top of his back to avoid his flailing fists, yanked his head up and went for his other eye, nail sinking into the cornea. Hot liquid soaking her hand, she slammed his face down. Blinded, barely able to breathe, Filth made a last effort to save himself. He bent double and shoved a hand up to Candace's hair, grasping the long strands to pull her loose. Riding him, Candace pulled free from his fingers, shoved her face to the side of his neck and clamped her teeth over his skin a second time.

She bit.

The delicious tang of squirting blood struck her teeth, tongue and lips. Chewing frantically, she tore into him again, ravaging muscle and flesh, opening another hole and swallowing even as she kept her thigh muscles clenched against his arms and shoulders.

Face against the floor, Filth made a noise that wanted to be a shout but failed utterly. A second noise was little more than a child's whimper.

Candace pulled away from him, her heart become thunder, and her mouth alive with blood hotter than any burning torch. She sucked her teeth, found a piece of torn skin and swallowed it.

Mouth to his ear, she whispered: "Now you're dying."

She slid clear of him, watched for a few moments and saw no movement. Red continued to pump from the wounds in his neck and his battered mouth and nose. If the bastard had any life left, it wasn't enough to power him.

Candace took a few deep breaths, swallowing the stinking air and blood still warm and splendid over her mouth.

Then she charged at the door.

Chapter Twenty-Four

Roe finished his inventory of their bags and waited until Granger turned away from the bedroom window. He peered over Granger's shoulder towards the town centre—such as it was with its handful of pubs, a Littlewoods, a Wimpey and a BHS all smashed down into crumbling bricks and broken glass—where half a dozen shuffling people studied the pavements and road with desperation born of starvation.

"Another day. *Maybe,*" Roe said. "After that, we'll have to find food on the way. Water is the bigger issue. We can go without food for longer than water."

"Dover is close," Granger replied.

"Do you see us actually on our way to Dover?" Roe yelled, surprising himself as much as he knew he surprised Granger. Raising his voice wasn't Roe's style. Nor was questioning their plan. That was Patterson's job, and as much as Roe often felt like the compliant one, the man who said next to nothing let alone *yes, Granger,* some of Patterson's not so private doubts had wormed their way into his head.

Granger turned his back on Roe and lifted his binoculars back to his eyes.

They'd taken an end terrace on a side road from the high street after noticing that a second-floor window overlooked what was probably the main route in and out of the town. By then, Roe and Patterson would have chosen any available building to get some rest from carrying the unconscious Willis between them.

There were no sounds from the other bedroom where Willis lay on a single bed and Patterson kept watch at the park opposite the front of the building. Wind blew through holes in the walls, bringing more cold with it, and the remnants of a shredded curtain hung heavy with mould from a frame rusted to the wall. Little furniture remained in the room; anything that would burn had been smashed into pieces and used as kindling.

"Why not just keep running? Why join with anyone here?" Roe's questions broke apart at the end when he struggled not to cough. He wheezed the last two words and struggled to swallow through a throat that felt no larger than a fifty pence coin.

If Granger noticed, he showed no indication.

"You heard their *father.* Their priest. He told them to go to Dover. They do everything he says, but they still need to do what they do. They can't help themselves. Once they're done, they'll keep going. Their order was Dover. Dover is where they're going."

"Sounds familiar," Roe murmured and didn't care that it was a Patterson statement and a Patterson tone.

"I am not your father, Roe. I am not in charge of you. You are free to go wherever and whenever you like." Granger's voice remained soft and silky. Roe had heard the tone long ago: their coup in the bunker, the splintering of the group, of men who'd known each other and worked together for years before the bombs.

Roe turned to face Granger full on and briefly wondered if Patterson was listening from the other bedroom. "I can go? Really? Where, Granger? What's out there for a man alone?"

Granger was silent.

"What about Willis?" Roe asked, lowering his voice.

"What about him?" Granger replied. He sounded drugged and Roe was utterly sure Granger genuinely wasn't with him. He was *out there* in a dead England, walking with the corpse of his wife for company across the countryside and through rivers flooded with disease and poison.

Roe's temper, closer to the surface for longer than he wanted to admit, rose. He felt it, blood ascending from chest into his throat, into his face, the liquid bubbling.

"He is dying," he said, teeth clenched.

Granger's reply was staggering in its denial. "No, isn't."

"He is, damn it." Roe roared it. "He's got blood poisoning. Any idiot can see that and even if he didn't, he needs bed rest. My God, she cut off his hand. She chopped it off with an *axe,* and we're marching across country on the say-so of a boy who was barely able to spell his own name. We're going after killers, Granger. People who eat people. Not for fun or because they can but to eat them. We're trying to stop them and get to whatever the hell is waiting for us in Dover and Willis is a dead man walking." His throat had shrunk from a fifty pence piece to a penny, but still he barked out the rest of his rage.

"Gentlemen."

Patterson's call sounded from across the hallway, somehow managing to sound bored and urgent at the same time.

"What is it?" Granger shouted.

"You might like to see who's outside."

Granger broke into a run, bouncing off the doorframe and bearing down on the other bedroom like a missile. Roe followed.

Patterson stood at the hole of the window; coat collar up to meet his scarf. He spoke without turning to either man coming across the floor.

"Our new friends are here," he said.

Roe pulled the handgun free, heard a step crunching on the mess of the floor and tried to turn.

He was too slow.

Willis's fist struck him in the side of his head much harder than Granger's blow, and the gun was yanked from his grip. He went down in a mess of waving arms and shouts, had a flash of Willis lumbering for the door, then caught the thunder of the man's mad descent on the stairs.

Groaning, Roe reached for Patterson's hand as Granger ran for the hallway and stairs.

"What the hell is he playing at?" he coughed.

Downstairs.

A crash as a door smashed open.

Then gunfire.

Chapter Twenty-Five

There was no fear. There were only his sisters.

Dumah streaked over the field, crossed an overgrown path in and closed in on Mary and Martha.

More gunfire, each sound a hollow bang. More shrieks of all-consuming panic. None of the noise mattered to Dumah.

Martha, behind Mary by ten seconds and ahead of Lazarus by five, dropped to the grass. Dumah howled, already scanning the soggy green around Martha for splashes of red.

It was clear.

The child shifted to look back at her approaching brothers, eyes staring, and Dumah howled again. Ahead, Mary smacked into one of the oaks and clung low to the trunk. Still sprinting, Lazarus ducked, grabbed Martha and ran on without stumbling, his larger body acting as a shield. Dumah changed course to run in a zig-zag, saw the others cluster at the oak, and looked back. George was a vanishing shape at the border of the park, the boy scuttling out of sight instead of coming after them or returning fire on whoever was shooting.

Head down, Dumah tucked his arms at his sides and jumped another narrow path to crash into the grass and churned up earth of a flowerbed while Lazarus frantically waved him on.

Another two shots, shrieks and milling shapes at the corner of his eyes as those who could move ran for cover. Throat bursting, Dumah dove the last few feet and hit wet grass. Mary and Martha were all over him, crying, calling his name and they were silent only when he raised his hand and snapped it shut.

Spacing apart was out of the question; there simply wasn't enough concealment offered by the oak unless they went for a cluster of them nearby. Body pressed against the trunk while Lazarus held the sisters, Dumah peered around the tree.

Half a dozen bodies lay on the grass, the green around them wet with red, fog too thin to offer much cover of the bodies. Another two had fallen on the road, and a few more staggered over the grass, desperately seeking cover. Scanning the pavements and houses beyond the rusting cars, Dumah saw the men, the big one with a gun barely able to keep upright as he tried to aim across the park again while the others jumped on him from the back and the sides. All four went down in a heap, and their yells drifted towards the trees.

If you see them, they can see you.

Dumah pulled back, grateful to see Lazarus also peering at the houses; he wouldn't have to attempt to signal the danger they were in now the men from the police station had tracked them here. Priest, killed by those men and they were here, again. So close. So easy to sink his axe into their heads. But of course, their tools were back at the school with the dirty beast who had stolen Candace.

Dumah growled deep in his throat and punched the tree.

"Listen. We need Candace. We need together." Lazarus spoke rapidly, not looking at them. "Dumah. Take the sisters back to the school. That way." He pointed to their right where the side of the park ended at broken railings. "Do what you have to. Get her out. We find each other after."

Dumah whipped his head back and forth, fighting tears.

"Yes," Lazarus hissed. "Now. They're not looking for us. The man with the gun, they stopped him. I go for them now. You go for Candace. Right now."

Lazarus shot away from the oak, low and fast. Mary and Martha grasped Dumah's hands and it was only then that he realised he had failed to stop his tears. They ran through the dirt on cheeks and he furiously blinked them away.

"Candace," Martha whispered.

"We go low," Mary said.

Dumah shook his head and pulled the girls to his sides. Combined, they were a fair weight, but he had held them close many times. Without complaint, they linked their arms around his back and Dumah looked around the edges of the trunk again. Lazarus slid fast towards the road while the men were still struggling with the shooter.

Priest, Dumah thought and didn't know if it was a plea to his departed father or a prayer to the Jesus.

Clutching the children, he raced for the side of the park and the railing, boots kicking through the grass and his chest turning into a flame within seconds. He upped his speed, sprinting in the same zig-zag that had taken him from the boy George.

They hadn't made it to the railings before another round of shots crashed out.

Chapter Twenty-Six

Fighting the need to swallow a deep lungful of air, Lazarus crawled to several trees and crouched there. Looking back the way he'd come, he saw Dumah vaulting the railings. He was out of sight a moment later and no longer in range of the shots. Lazarus sent love after his brother and the sisters, hoping they'd get to Candace without trouble.

Panting, he pulled his scarf from his neck to let the chill brush him and dry some of his sweat, then peered through the brambles entwining around the lower half of the trunks. The men had brought the shooter down a second time, and Lazarus could only make out a jerking leg, a waving arm rather than their faces. It was enough. Priest's killers come for the rest of the family and one of them out of control because. . .

He wants you all alive. Him. Granger. Wants to take you to his government and give you to them. In Dover.

Lazarus snarled and clawed at the trunk. Bark scraped loose under his long fingernails and he shook it free.

"Lazarus?"

He jerked around at the sound of his name. Mary skulked through the grass much as he had. Shocked into inaction for a few seconds, he could only watch her advance. Then reaction flooded in. He dove, crashed down and pulled her close.

"Mary? What is happening?"

"They shot again. We fell. Dumah up. He got Martha. I came back for you. They shot at you."

She was near tears and Lazarus would not have her weeping for his near death or for believing she had angered him. Scooping her up, he kissed her cheek and smelled the combined stink of their filthy bodies. Without speaking, he promised her the chance to wash in the sea soon.

The one Mary had injured stood against a garden wall, supported by the old bricks while another man—Lazarus knew their names and he whispered *Patterson*—held a handgun on him. Willis's head was limp. Red stained the wrappings around his stump and although Lazarus couldn't be sure, he thought the wound might have opened again. He hoped so.

Roe and the bastard Granger stood on the road, Roe's face a white hole while he nudged the dead with a boot and looked like he might soon vomit. Granger scanned the park for movement, and Lazarus's frustration threatened to boil over. His father's killer seconds away and nothing but the patchy fog, grass and lifeless cars between them.

"Wait," Mary whispered, and Lazarus subsided. He nodded at the child, wishing she had remained with Dumah but still glad to have her at his side.

The wounded were still, their deaths come for them. Lazarus counted five bodies between the old cars, and another three on the pavement. Willis's bullets had struck heads, backs and chests, blowing out bone, exposing innards to the day.

Roe backed away to the pavement outside the houses they'd clearly been hiding inside while Granger appraised the park a final time. As he turned his back, Lazarus caught his voice as he called to his men. Most of the words were lost, but he heard one.

School.

There was some shouted conversation. Patterson didn't want to be left alone with Willis; Roe needed a break while Granger ignored all of it. He held the shotgun, handed another small gun to Roe and pointed to the east.

School. Going there to find us.

Caught in an impossible situation, Lazarus could do nothing but watch Granger march back to the road and sidle between the cars while Roe followed with obvious reluctance. Within a minute, they were gone, leaving Patterson with his gun on Willis while Willis might as well have been asleep for all the movement he made.

Lazarus put his mouth to Mary's ear. "Two men gone. Two there. The one you hurt and smaller man. They have a gun. You stay and I go through the cars. Behind them. Kill them."

"Together," she muttered when he pulled away.

Lazarus shook his head. "You stay here."

Her mouth closed firmly and her frown made her appear younger. In other circumstances, he might have found it funny.

From across the road, one of the remaining men uttered a high-pitched cry and Lazarus knew immediately which one was dying and which was the killer.

Chapter Twenty-Seven

Candace hit the weak doors which flew open, a hinge breaking. Her momentum took her out and across the corridor, feet skidding through rainwater puddles. At the last second, she stopped herself from crashing into the opposite wall and saw running shapes advancing fast. The man and the girl passed a window, the smears of dirt on the pane casting patterns on their faces and on the unconscious figure the man dragged with him.

Dumah and Martha.

Candace screamed, the joy in her heart too great to be contained by her chest. Martha crashed against her legs, the girl sobbing, and Candace's tears falling into the wild mess of Martha's hair.

Yelling his wordless noise, each hoot an exclamation of happiness, Dumah shoved the spindly figure he'd dragged from somewhere to the floor and kicked him in the face. Blood and broken teeth struck the wall and bounced off Dumah's boot, and the man tried to squeal through the mess of his face. The noise became a choking cough and more of his blood sprayed low over the wall.

Candace embraced her brother and sister, wishing to have her amputated arm back if only to be able to hold them both with equal strength.

"He told us you were here." Martha gestured at the man, dead or unconscious – Candace didn't know or care. "Told us you were prisoner. Told us that's what happens here."

"The others?" Candace checked both ends of the corridor. Nobody in sight which meant little. The building was rammed with the those not yet dead and those seconds from their end. It reeked of them.

"Out there." Martha spoke quickly, telling Candace what had occurred in the park: the shooting, the panic and the men who'd hurt them miles away come back again. Knowing that Granger had tracked them this far was no surprise for Candace. It had taken barely a few minutes in his company to see what sort of man he was. He'd call it his duty or job, but his plan was simple revenge.

"Mary couldn't let Lazarus go alone. She had to go with him," Martha said, and Candace nodded.

"She will be fine. They both will. We trust them to each other and to Priest."

"And to the Jesus," Martha replied. Candace avoided Dumah's eyes, aware he trusted her, Mary, Candace and Lazarus but that was the extent of his faith.

"And to the Jesus," Candace echoed.

Dumah grunted and touched the bruising and blood on Candace's face. He and Martha had seen inside the room; looking again, Martha said:

"He hurt you?"

"Not as much as I hurt him." Candace licked the sprayed blood around her mouth; it was cooling but still tasted delicious. Running, she returned to the room and grabbed their bag of weapons from where Filth had left it in one of the corners, then handed the bag to Dumah. He hummed his happiness and pulled the blades free. Having her cleaver back in her hand was a deep joy for Candace. It made her whole again.

"We don't kill for violence." She lifted the cleaver. "We kill to protect ourselves. We will do that, and we will find our brother and our sister."

Martha raised her butcher knife. She smiled, and in the cool morning light, her pinched face and skin the colour of curdled milk was beautiful to Candace.

Dumah tapped his axe on the wall, chipping at the plaster and apparently pleased at the sight of it flaking like dead skin. From somewhere, new screams broke out, weak. The sound of a woman being hurt in ways only a woman could be hurt. Candace wished for Filth to be alive so she could kill him again.

Mixed with the screams, shouts in the distance. The uneven thud of running steps.

"Together," Candace said.

They moved down the corridor, Dumah and Candace sliding along both walls while Martha kept her head down and scuttled between them, never keeping still, a foot between them as they kept their sides close to either wall. Passing open doors to classrooms become makeshift shelters or stinking pits, they didn't look inside or pay any attention to the weak cries for food from the mostly unilluminated rooms. The smell followed their backs, a reek of bodies moments from death. Filth told Candace they threw out the corpses; the stench suggested they had not been overly concerned with doing so. He'd told the truth about another issue: the dying were left to their dying.

The corridor turned to the right, more classroom doors on one side, featureless wall on the other. The screams of the brutalised woman were no longer audible. Shaken by them and her own experiences more than she would have thought possible, Candace hissed her disgust with the building and the men who lived in it. She pointed straight ahead as a few voices wafted from somewhere close, pleading for help. Within seconds, they died, and she murmured to Dumah and Martha.

"We came in down there. The big room."

There was no need to elaborate. They would leave the way the way they came in and they would kill anyone in the way.

Outside, a few quick bangs crashed out. They froze. More bangs, the noise muffled by walls and windows, but still audible. Gunshots. Then screams.

Screams outside.

Screams inside.

Giving up any efforts to stay hidden or be quiet, Dumah, Martha and Candace sprinted down the corridor, their shoes and boots kicking up dust and cracked pieces of flooring while the screams continued. They skidded on a puddle, Martha seconds from falling until she grabbed hold of Candace's hip. Digging her nails into Candace's coat, she righted herself. One of the girl's brittle nails snapped. Martha made no sound.

Running straight on, they smashed through the doors to the cafeteria, the three hitting a mass panic rather than the fight Candace had expected. On all sides, the skeletal people who populated the building were frantically attempting to shift broken tables and splintered chairs to the windows, their bodies too weak and malnourished to succeed, resulting in the wrecked furniture simply being pushed end to end which shrank the available space for the bodies and left the upper half of the long windows exposed. Outside, the gunfire had ceased but the panic and fear remained in non-stop shrieks and the spinning shadows cast by the few people able to run doing so in all directions. At the doors beyond the panicking crowd, men struggled to push a piano to the entrance, thumping the few keys as they moved, creating a discordant, grating noise above the babble of voices and shouts.

Candace made her decision within seconds. They'd be trapped if they stayed as would every person in the room.

"Out." She pointed to the far doors where the men were close to placing the piano into position. On all sides, people staggered back and forth, coughing and choking. Several had collapsed and were kicked by those still able to move. Dumah picked up Martha as he had in the park and they went for the doors, kicking their way over the exhausted, dodging others and bearing down on the men and the only way out. The piano struck the doors and one of the men, his body a shaking mess soaked with sweat from the effort of sealing the room, fell away, his feet tangled.

Dropping Martha who landed lightly, Dumah took hold of the man's head and ran with him to the wall. Skull struck stone; bone cracked, and hot blood splashed over Dumah's hand. He hit the man against the wall again, then again, two rapid beats. Dropping him, he spun around and ran for Candace who clung to another man's back, her nails at his throat as she whirled with him, blood streaming from the cuts she'd dung into his skin. Dumah yanked hold of the man's shoulders mid-spin; Candace let go of his neck but remained clinging on to his back and rode him as

Dumah brought the man's head down and his own knee up.

Bone and cartilage snapped. Candace dropped clear and the man fell, blood bubbling from his ruined mouth and the hot liquid pooling into his throat. His back arched. A flailing hand struck Martha's knee and she swung her knife down without pause. Blade sliced skin, opening a deep wound in his palm and his hand dropped.

"We move this and we go," Candace yelled.

Dumah nodded his agreement and took hold of the end of the piano. He shoved; wet fingers unable to find a grip. It slid an inch but no more. At the other end, Candace put her shoulder on the side of the instrument and pushed with her lesser weight. Pressure pushed back and she screamed her frustration while Martha ran to Dumah's side, shouting she would help. Blinking away sweat, Candace saw advancing figures, a few clutching bats. Behind them, half a dozen others followed.

Dumah wasted no time. Hooting, he went for the nearest men, fists swinging as they swung their bats.

A single gunshot struck the piano.

Candace whirled around, already knowing who had fired.

Chapter Twenty-Eight

It seemed to Patterson that sound departed with Roe and Granger. He watched until their shapes vanished in the fog and between the overturned cars. The moment his colleagues faded from view, he felt as if he had stopped – or at least any sound had faded from the world to leave him on the pavement outside the house that had been their temporary shelter while Willis was probably so far into unconsciousness that it may as well have been called death.

Patterson cleared his throat a few times if only to hear something human. While the noise was weak, it was still his and he was still there.

Wonderful. And where is that precisely? A million miles from anywhere or anything you know.

He studied the bodies, the fog encroaching over the grass. Whoever they were, Willis had killed them without thought. Patterson amended that: there *had* been thought, but it was the thinking of a man driven insane with pain. Willis had probably seen the cannibals coming out of the walls even before he'd fired randomly at anonymous people dying of starvation and exposure.

Patterson nudged Willis's foot and it was like tapping on a rock.

"Willis? Are you there?"

Willis remained in the same position as he'd slid down the wall – knees pulled up, head down and left hand cradling the stump of his right. The bandages around the wound were stained with dirt, grit and old blood. On the million to one chance Willis made it to Dover (and if there was anyone there to help them), he would need a healthy dose of antibiotics to stave off any infection. Even then, Patterson didn't rate Willis's chances.

It was safe to say Willis was a dead man walking, no more alive than the poor bastards he'd shot. And Patterson knew the same applied to the rest of them if they continued with Granger's foolish plan to go to Dover and seek help from a man they'd betrayed.

It's over. It's all over. Go your own way, for God's sake. You've thought it often enough. What the hell is stopping you?

Go his own way? And do what exactly? Try and find a new home? Search for other survivors willing to take him in?

The reply came back without fanfare.

Why not?

"Willis?" he said, pitching his voice low. His stomach was a tight ball that had little to do with his non-stop hunger.

"On the move, Willis." The words were a feather on his lips.

Patterson swallowed the air, doing his best to avoid thinking of any residual radiation and sure it had been washed out of the atmosphere in the last decade.

We stay away from the cities, from the blast areas, we'll be fine.

Almost believing himself, he pocketed the Browning, tested the weight of one of the packs Granger and Roe had dumped on the pavement, and decided freshly boiled water was more important than food.

The bottles clanged together when he lifted the bag from the ground and, grunting, slid the tattered straps over his shoulders. Scarf pulled up around his mouth and nose, the bag already sending aches up and down his spine, Patterson relished the untouched joy of a decision made, a plan formed as thin as it might be. He was his own man; any link the four of them had shared was long since lost, and he knew Roe would eventually see it for the farce it was.

Patterson shifted position, turning as he addressed Willis for the last time.

"Bye, Willis."

Except Willis wasn't sitting on the road and he was no longer holding his ruined arm. He was coming up, a rippling, slow form no different to a swimmer breaking for the surface, and Patterson tried to yell anything; it didn't matter what emerged from his mouth as long as he made some strong protest against Willis clearly still alive and the kitchen knife in his hand a dull slice of silver turned cold like snow by the thickening mist.

Patterson's cry blew out of his mouth at the same time as blood splashed from his stomach to soak his crotch, his legs and shoes and Willis's remaining hand. He registered a sudden jerking movement; the knife cut deeper, twisting inside him, *oh dear God, it's inside me, I can feel it inside me.*

Something in his gut popped and he could smell his own shit; he could smell the disease, the whatever was wrong with him and dripped blood into his stool. Mouth wide open, he tried to howl and succeeded only in coughing gore into Willis's face.

All the colours of the world were fading, losing their urgency to be replaced by a cooling white far removed from the murk of the fog. Even the red coating Willis's cheeks and nose had become pink, its pallor robbed by the fire of his belly and the sickening reek of his waste. He managed to raise a hand he no longer knew as his own and trailed his fingers down the side of Willis's head. Willis continued to turn the knife, opening the wound wider to let more blood free. Innards pulsed in the jagged hole, and while the agony was fading, the freezing air that should never be able to touch Patterson so deeply, so *intimately*, was almost worse than any pain.

Willis's mouth was opening, revealing the grey of his tongue and his teeth flecked with pink. And the pink was Patterson's blood. Willis made a noise Patterson couldn't quite identify although it sounded familiar. Willis repeated himself, a single sound, two syllables. A name.

With the last of his ability to think, Patterson echoed the name.

"Lisa."

He saw his daughter's face for a few seconds, the pretty girl overlapping Willis's features, and Willis spoke with Lisa's mouth.

"Wasn't me, Patterson. It wasn't me."

Willis pulled Patterson close, the knife still penetrating Patterson's mid-section to the handle.

Willis said another name and punched the knife and his fingers into Patterson's stomach.

A white light detonated behind Patterson's eyes.

When it went out, it took everything with it and he went into the black with the knowledge of what had

been done to his daughter, cursing the final name
Willis said as the black closed in.

Chapter Twenty-Nine

Granger a step ahead of Roe, they passed a lone swing, the chains tangled in an impossible knot, and several lumbering figures emerged from behind a wall of low bushes. All were clad in muddy and sweat-soaked clothes, and all were lucky to still be on their feet given their physical state and near starvation. They held no makeshift weapons and it took Granger less than a second to decide they weren't a threat.

"Go," he shouted and waved the shotgun.

Whether or not they understood English, they recognised the chance of escape and eagerly took it. Sticking close together, they made their way towards the playing field and whatever shelter they might be lucky enough to find beyond. Granger dismissed them from his mind and studied Roe.

Willis's blow back in the house had struck Roe in the nose; blood had finally stopped streaming. His upper lip was a red smear and the look of a dazed cow hadn't left his eyes. He breathed too quickly, each inhalation a rasp, and Granger had to admit to a certain irony: Willis would have been a better man for a situation such as this.

"Roe, I need you to focus, all right?" Granger pointed at the building on the other side of the playground.

Roe wiped his mouth and a little of the stupid cow went out of his eyes. Not all of it, but Granger would take what he could.

"Remember. Don't waste bullets. Fire only when necessary, but don't blink if they challenge us in there. *We're* in charge of this; they need to know that."

Dismissing the man as he had the straggling survivors a moment ago, Granger advanced on the main section of the building. A wall of windows overlooked the play area and while the light of the miserable day wasn't in their favour, he knew they'd group in the largest open room which would be the assembly hall.

From inside, the single sharp crack of a gunshot was followed immediately by screams, bellowed voices and the thud of people bashing into the broken furniture they'd attempted to use as a cover along the windows.

Ducking, the men ran for a set of doors near to the windows. The entrance to the centre of the school was missing glass in the two windows although what appeared to be a cabinet had been shoved against it on the inside. Doing his best not to pant, Granger stood to the left of the doors; Roe smacked against the wall to right, gasping. Around the school grounds, all was still.

"Inside," Granger shouted. "You people. Can you hear me?"

The storm inside the school subsided when Granger called through the damaged doors. There'd been no second shot. Standing against the wall,

Granger played back their mad dash after the bang. No glass had broken; the shot hadn't come out of the window. He focused on listening for the slightest sound and heard a few sneaking steps beyond the door. Hoping none of the family had been injured or killed, he listened while Roe covered his mouth and nose.

"We've no problem with any of you." Granger kept his finger half an inch from the trigger of the shotgun. He couldn't afford to waste any shots or to shoot to injure. Roe wasn't a dangerous man even if his life was on the line. Granger knew he could only rely on himself.

"We're not here for anyone other than the new people. The killers who've come to you. They're dangerous and if you're sheltering them, you are in more danger than you realise. Give them to us and we'll be on our way."

All he heard was Roe struggling to quieten his ragged gasps.

"We don't wish you any harm. If you give those people to us, we'll leave you in peace."

His sole reply was in the wind as it skimmed over scabby grass.

Granger raised the shotgun and saw Roe do the same with the Browning, albeit with no enthusiasm.

"Remember," Granger whispered. "Don't waste any shots. I've got two. You've got six. It's them or us."

Roe's face was an expressionless mask. But his gun remained up and ready.

Granger shifted position, taking a step away from the entrance and aiming the shotgun squarely at it. The instant before he squeezed the trigger, a woman screamed inside the building, voice catching in her throat as if she wasn't used to speech.

"No. Shoot. No. Shoot."

No shoot, Granger realised and kept the tiny pressure on the shotgun's trigger. Browning held in both hands, Roe did the same. Furniture scraped on the floor, a babble of voices coming with the noise, and the cabinet shook against the entrance as it was dragged to the side. Someone reached through the holes of the windows, grabbed the crumbling frame and pulled it open to reveal half a dozen emaciated figures, cowering and stinking of decaying bodies.

"Jesus Christ." Roe backed up. Granger held his ground and kept the shotgun aimed into the entrance.

"You have any weapons?" he called.

A man, possibly aged about thirty although it was next to impossible to say for sure, hesitantly raised a thick branch while a girl no older than seventeen held a blunt dinner knife. Granger didn't bother telling them to lower the pitiful attempts at defence. The people here knew what guns were and they knew when they were beaten.

"You have the new people in there? The killers?"

"People," the girl with the knife croaked. She'd been the one to tell them not to shoot; Granger recognised the dog-like growl of her voice.

"Inside," she added and backed away.

There was nowhere for anyone to hide; an open corridor and the few shadows outnumbered by the beams of daylight—weak as it might be—sliding through holes in the walls and the roof.

"Are you with me?" he whispered to Roe.

"I'm here," Roe said, the reply made nasal by the blow to his face. Granger allowed a moment of regret over the man Willis had become thanks to his terrible injury. They'd need to deal with him somehow when this was over. For now, though, he had cannibals to recapture.

For Dover.

For himself.

For what they'd done to Carolyn.

"Out of our way," he shouted and the starving people immediately scattered, spindly legs taking them to the sides of the corridor and towards a large set of double doors that opened to the centre of the school. The girl with the knife lurched to the opening, reaching for it and freezing when Granger called for her to stop.

Side by side, weapons still raised, Granger and Roe crossed the corridor, their boots tracking through layers of dirt and grit. Somewhere, querulous moans rang out: the cries of the dying and the damned. There was nothing to be done for them. Granger shut his ears to the weak wails and motioned for the woman to back away. He hefted the gun to aim at the middle of the doors while Roe turned in a slow circle, tracking the few people who hadn't already scattered to the far side of the school. Above the alcove between the cafeteria and the corridor, a hole in the roof let the day spill in, and the floor below the opening was awash with puddle water, broken plaster and stains Granger didn't want to see.

No sounds beyond the double doors. It was if they opened to a void.

"Ready?" he asked Roe.

"Ready."

Without pausing to think, Granger booted the doors square in the centre. They flew open, revealing a floor clear of furniture because, by the looks, it had all been shoved against the windows that overlooked the school's play area and field. Clustered in small groups, more of the wretched people who'd set up home in the building stood beside the overturned tables, some whimpering. The big man from the cannibals stood alone while the coloured woman with only one arm kneeled on the floor in the centre of the cafeteria.

Behind her, a small figure dressed in an oversized coat that did little to disguise their slight frame. A heavy hat and the scarf around the lower half of their face obscured most of their features. Even so, it was clear they were young. Perhaps still a teen. More importantly, they held a battered rifle with a telescopic sight, the barrel pressed against the back of the black woman's head.

Granger advanced two steps, eyes darting in all directions. Where the hell were the others? The boy, Lazarus, and the two girls? Especially the one who'd hurt Willis to such a terrible extent?

The door on the right hadn't swung open as far as the one on the left.

Hoping Roe would be able to react without command, Granger smashed the right-hand door with all his strength and dashed into the cafeteria. Across the floor, the man who couldn't speak let out a helpless noise of rage and the assembled bodies by the windows screeched. The door struck a small object, rebounded and Granger brought his shotgun to bear on the child with the knife who'd been hiding there.

"Drop it or I shoot you," he told her.

The girl glared at him, eyes the same colour as the muck spread over her small face, the butcher knife a growth between her fingers. Roe stood close to Granger, thankfully facing the other way. The man might not have been as impetuous as Willis, but he had his uses.

The child opened her fist without breaking his gaze or without seeming to move her hand. The knife clattered to the floor.

"By the window with the others," he muttered and tracked her as she crossed to the attempted barrier. For the few seconds it took her to reach the mess and the bodies, she did not once look away from him or blink. Her eyes were doll's eyes and a cold that had nothing do with the broken walls and crumbling brickwork brushed over Granger.

He returned his attention to the coloured woman kneeling on the ground and the figure behind her with their rifle. Neither had altered their position while he'd dealt with the girl, and the big man without a tongue—Dumah, Granger remembered—raised his fists towards Granger as if he could reach him.

"Where are the others?" Granger asked Candace. It was more important to know where they were than directing his first question at the gunman.

It wasn't Candace who answered. It was the child.

"Gone for your friends outside the house. Skinny man and one hand man." She grinned. "The one Mary cut. Gone for them. They will die."

"Shut up," Roe bellowed and Granger signalled for him to quieten. Dismissing the girl and unconcerned with Dumah—there was no danger from a man without a weapon especially when he was a good fifteen feet away—Granger focused on Candace and her captor.

"Hello. I appreciate your guarding her, but there's no need now we're here. Lower the gun and we'll take them off your hands."

The slightest flicker of Candace's gaze as she looked Granger in the eye. A brief look but long enough for him to see her mixture of exasperation and frustration. No fear, though. Not of him or the figure with the rifle.

"You want the woman?"

The voice rather than the question shocked Granger. This was a boy, not a youth or a man. He was facing a child with a gun.

Dear God. What is this place?

The boy—and that was exactly the correct term—slid his scarf down to reveal a chin free from stubble or a firm jawline.

"You want her? Well, then we have a problem. Because so do I."

Chapter Thirty

As the wounded man tried to scream again but could only manage a wavering groan, Mary tugged on Lazarus's arm a second time.

"I go," she repeated. "Distract him."

Lazarus kept his eyes on the scene across the road.

"Lazarus." Mary's thin fingers formed a tight grip on his wrist.

"Go," he replied. "Stay out of sight. Move fast."

She was gone like a moment of sunshine, sprinting for the maze of cars, head down and arms tucked to her sides. Lazarus watched the two men on the pavement close enough to kiss, one-handed man then pushing the other away, dropping him and revealing the gore soaking his hand, forearm and coat. Any silver of the knife he'd used to kill his friend had become as red as his hand, and thick droplets oozed from the blade and his fingers along with a long string of intestine. The man flung it, then wiped the remainder on his chest, marking himself. Clots dropped to the pavement beside the dead one, and the sound of the impact was muffled by the fog.

Wishing for even a small piece of glass from one of the broken car windows, Lazarus could only hope Mary found a weapon. He shifted into a ready crouch. Willis was on the move, kitchen knife still held firmly while he kept the stump of his other one at his side. He avoided the tight cluster of the cars by jumping onto the rear of one, clambered to the roof and hopped to the next. His boots crashed on the old metal and more blood dribbled from the knife. Standing tall and alert, he peered at the murk on all sides. Lazarus realised how Willis had managed to fool the one he'd killed and probably the other two. He was injured, but he was also a ruthless beast.

There was no time for Lazarus to regret underestimating Willis and to agreeing to Mary acting as a decoy. Even now, she would be coming through the cars, sliding under them, crawling on the road, assuming Willis was a desperate, dying wreck. Dying he might be, but he was an alert, thinking monster.

He will kill her the first chance he gets.

Lazarus didn't know if the thought belonged to Priest or was his own. It didn't matter.

Willis jumped to a third car, stumbled but stayed on his feet. "Come on, them," he yelled and cackled. "Fucking have a go. I fucked up little shits like you back in the day. Every fucking day. And I tell you what."

A fourth jump, a fourth thud of heavy boots on a car roof. He swayed, left arm waving. Now he was closer, Lazarus made out the flecks of blood splashed over his face and drying in his hair. His hand was red like fire.

"I tell you what," he said again. "I loved every minute of that."

Lazarus sent a mental command for Mary to strike now and slice at Willis's ankle with a piece of glass.

He knew it wasn't possible. By taking the roofs instead of keeping to the ground, Willis was a few inches above Mary's reach.

"So, let's have a talk. Me and you. Right fucking now."

Willis launched from the car roof, crashed to the pavement and rolled, still laughing even though the impact had clearly been heavy and jarring. The little gun spilled out of his grasp and the blood from the stabbed man was black on the ground. Coughing and still laughing, Willis made it to his knees and Lazarus flew.

Without a sound, he streaked between the trees and saw a mirroring shape burst from between two overturned cars: Mary with a dagger of broken glass in her hand, the shard held high.

Darting, Willis went for the gun as Lazarus hit the pavement, bringing both fists towards Willis's head, and Mary swung the glass and Lazarus saw at the last second that he hadn't been fast enough.

Willis grabbed the gun and pulled the trigger as he swung around to face Mary. The shot blew a hole in a car door inches from her head and Willis's bellow was healthy and hellishly strong.

"You move, she dies."

Chapter Thirty-One

Helpless, unable to make a move, Dumah could have wept with impotent frustration. So close to three people he wanted to kill for their threats and violence to his family and not a thing he could do.

Although Granger and Roe had been inside the school for less than two minutes, they'd ordered all the people caught between the two sides to stand near the windows; Roe kept out of Dumah's reach and made sure the handgun remained aimed at his head while, in a low voice unlike his usual sure tone, Granger told Martha to stand a few feet from the school people. Without a choice, she did so, marked from the others by her place on the floor.

And that left George with his gun on Candace, and Candace clearly enraged by another captor in this awful building with its dead and dying.

Dumah estimated there were eight running steps between him and George. Maybe a couple less to Roe and while Dumah knew he was fast, he wouldn't be faster than a gun. Furious, he watched Granger advance while Roe remained still, handgun ready. Across the floor, Martha's small body thrummed with energy and her hands were the same as Dumah's: desperate for the cold metal of a cleaver or an axe.

"We didn't want any of this." Granger sounded calm and Dumah didn't think that was much of an act. Granger believed in his precious law and order; that had got him this far and would see his plan through to its ugly end.

Dumah shifted position a fraction, body aimed towards Roe rather than Candace and her captor.

"We don't like violence or threats and I genuinely wish none of this had happened. The man who hurt your people, he's gone now. He wasn't well. He's been hurt and it affected him."

If anyone understood, they weren't showing it.

Granger pointed at Candace. "We have come for her and the others with her. That man, the girl and another, and a boy."

Dumah let out a furious hoot, unable to hold it inside. Granger glanced at him. Dismissed him.

"What say you?" Granger asked. While he still didn't smile, a light crossed his face, an illusion of togetherness.

George muttered a reply.

"Sorry? What was that?" Granger asked,

The boy leaned closer, head above Candace's.

"I said, she's mine."

Granger said nothing and George spoke again.

"The others are gone. Outside. Dead for all I know. Your mate might have killed them." The boy giggled. Dumah heard nothing of the relaxed friendliness George had presented to them in the night or while appearing to regret their imprisonment. The whole thing had been an act, a pretence of a child refusing to become the same as those with whom he was forced to share shelter and his life. In his own small way, he was worse than any of them, the ones who left others to starve or the bearded man who'd taken Candace as if she was nothing. All the speech and the regret over what life was, all a lie.

George worse than Granger. Dumah ached to kill the child. Even Priest's silent admonishment close to his side couldn't stop that ache.

"What was his name? Lazarus? And the other girl. The sister of that one over there. Shame. I liked them."

He bumped his crotch on the back of Candace's head. Dumah's anger pulsed with his heart: fast and deep. He roared and George yelled to him.

"Stay there or she's dead."

Dumah did his best to stay focused on Roe despite George's terrible words. Candace could look after herself. Roe was his goal, but still, the hunger for flesh in his mouth.

"You can have him," George said and nodded in Dumah's direction. "The others if they're out there. Fuck them. I don't care. Take the girls, too. She stays with me." Sickeningly, his voice hitched. "He said I could have her when he was done. He said bring her to me and you get her afterwards."

Still motionless, Granger said nothing and Dumah felt a new fury, a rage beyond what he knew of the world. It could have come from the old days he barely remembered, or from the years when the sun shone all the time and there were no monsters walking the land.

He took his eyes off Roe for a moment, studying Granger's face while everything slowed down as it always did in the seconds before killing. In that perfect quiet, he understood a new and terrible thing.

The family and Granger had similarities that went deep into the blood and bone of their bodies. Further.

Into their hearts where no threat or death could ever reach and turn out their own light.

They were both killers and they were both survivors.

Granger spoke. "Very well."

George pressed his lower half against Candace's head a second time and opened his mouth.

Granger's expression changed: all the life that kept him on his feet collapsed. Dumah bellowed Candace's name in his chest and that was all he had time for.

Granger dropped to one knee, the shotgun extending from his chest, and Candace shoved herself towards the ground. The boy and Granger fired at the same time.

The shotgun blast struck George in the stomach, his own shot going wild as Candace hit the floor. Blood streamed from the side of her head, soaking her hair. Groaning, she managed to make it to her knees and looked at Dumah with dazed eyes. He hooted, desperate to take hold of his wounded sister. The shot had grazed her skull, opening a wound and turning her face into a gore-streaked mess. If she'd been a fraction slower diving for the floor, it would have taken off her head.

Advancing from the shadows and carrying a chunk of broken chair, Martha scuttled forward. Roe swung towards her.

"Don't move," he yelled and the gun danced between Martha and Dumah still powerless to cover the distance between himself and Roe.

On the floor, George squirmed. He pressed against his exploded stomach. Striding around in a rapid, disjointed pattern, Granger raged at George and at the huddled bodies across the floor.

"You are filth," Granger bellowed. "All of you. Filth. You deserve nothing but your deaths. You should have had those deaths a long time ago." His anger turned his voice into a shriek. *"It should have been all of you when the bombs fell. You should have burned."*

Raging, spitting, he booted George in the chest. The boy tried to curl into a ball and Granger booted him again, connecting solidly with George's forehead and the boy turned over. Granger kicked again while Dumah watched, feeling nothing for the child. He had proved what he was.

Granger continued his attack and as he'd understood the other man a moment before, Dumah did so again. It didn't matter that George was already dead. Granger would kick and he would curse the boy on the floor who thought he could take bodies for his own sick pleasure. He would turn the grinning face into mush and he would wipe out everything that had been done in the school.

Still on her knees, her skin turned darker by her blood, hair matted into clumps, Candace raised her head.

Met Dumah's eyes.

He nodded.

Cutting across the floor like the shot that blew a hole in George, Dumah bore down on Roe as Martha zig-zagged from the window.

Roe managed to fire once and the shot struck the ceiling. Dumah crashed into him, knocking the Browning to the floor and grabbing his neck. Swinging her snapped chair leg, Martha bashed it into the back of Roe's knees. He collapsed, fingers spasmodically curling and uncurling as Dumah clamped his fingers around Roe's neck. Blood bubbled between Roe's lips and he managed to make the sound of a dying bird even as Dumah's pressure increased.

On her feet, Candace went for Granger who turned at the last second. Candace's arm struck the shotgun which dropped to the floor. She raked nails down Granger's cheek, missing his eye by an inch, and Martha sprinted towards Granger's back, chair leg held like a spear. Screaming, Granger swung a punch, hit air and swung again. He managed to land a weak blow against Candace's chest but it wasn't enough to shake her free. He tripped, crashed down and Candace scrambled up his body to straddle his chest and wrap her fingers around his neck. Taking his ineffectual blows against her arms, she tightened her hold. Spit burst between his lips and she screamed her joy. Dumah echoed it and Martha lunged with her chair leg. Purely by luck, Granger side-stepped in his attempt to shake Candace free, and the chair leg flew to the floor several feet away. Spluttering, his face bleeding, Granger grabbed Candace's arms around his neck and slammed his head backwards. The blow wasn't enough to dislodge her, but Dumah still saw his sister's hold ease a degree. Crying out like a wounded dog, Granger smashed an elbow into Candace's face. She fell, dropping onto Martha. Granger kicked at them, boot striking Martha in the chest and knocking the girl flat.

Still shouting, Granger spun and aimed at Dumah. He pulled the shotgun's trigger and got nothing but a flat click.

Dumah bellowed his savage happiness and something in his head flipped over, his surroundings spinning with the wild movement in the centre of his skull. Vision became a multi-layered pattern; his eyes were all the unbroken windows that had filled buildings in the past and he saw in clear streams through each one. He saw through Roe's eyes, through Granger's. He knew their minds and it was all wonderful, all terrible, all more than his voiceless mouth could take.

Dumah roared negation, roared heaven and hell, and still the spinning revolution taking his head into everything and everywhere turned over, faster, faster.

Roe's face was turning black.

Roe's vision detonated with noiseless pools, each one welcome because it was a way out, an exit from a life he loathed, trapped with men he no longer knew.

And all he had to do was dive deeper into the pools flooding his eyes.

Granger's face was on fire; blood filled his mouth and the shotgun in his hands was utterly useless; the man screaming as Candace and Martha attempted to rise and both able to do little more than pant and bleed.

Metal at Granger's foot.

"Roe." Granger booted George's knife towards Roe and grabbed hold of Candace. He slammed his hands on her shoulders, yanked her up and threw her over the floor. She rolled, crashing into the few people left at the window. Two fell. She spun over, panting as she stared across the room, head a ball of sticky blood.

And still Dumah saw inside their minds, through their eyes.

Unaware of anything outside his rapidly fading vision, Roe's nails dug deep into the layer of muck, blood dribbling between his lips and the light from the windows descending into a shrinking hole.

Granger's shout of Roe's name from a few seconds before reached Roe and meant nothing. How could it when it was a word from another life when there'd be others in the world and a job to go to and houses, the parks near his home where he'd liked to walk on the occasional day off from the City and all the suits and men and their decisions and the growing tension between the Soviets and the Americans?

How could his name mean a damn thing when put against all the dead things he was seconds from joining, seconds from being made welcome by those dead things? And wouldn't that be wonderful? To be away from the freezing days, the black of the nights and the weeping heart locked in his chest?

Roe's twitching fingers hit the cool blade Granger had kicked over the floor.

Touch.

Reaction.

Blood oozed from his mouth and nose, the light at the window now smaller than a pinprick, Roe's fingers lunged along the blade, found the metal and closed over it.

As the last of the light winked out, he plunged the knife into Dumah's forearm.

Hissing, Dumah let go and Roe pitched forward, retching through the pain that drove out all other thought. He jacknifed on the ground, inhaling, exhaling, blood splattering around his face. Knife still growing from his arm and the spreading red worth no more important than the barrage of senses and vision invading his mind, Dumah went for Roe. He lurched forwards, gore splattering from the wound in his arm and there were no thoughts other than killing this man, then Granger.

From somewhere faraway, a door banged.

"Dumah."

Candace.

Her shout. Her agony. Her voice always soft, always as welcome as any of the others and not only because he couldn't give them his. How he loved them to speak. How he loved them all.

Dumah came to a stop, searching through the now full dark for sight of Candace, to know why she had screamed his name with such desperation. He would go to her. He would think the words that couldn't come to his useless mouth and she would know he was well. Then they would find Lazarus and take the children in their arms and they would eat. They would cross the miles of barren land, keeping away from what was left of the wiped-out cities and horrible towns like this one, and the meadows would take them to the cliffs, then the beach, then the caves and their home of tunnels and stone.

He saw it all and he held the image in his head so Candace would know what he saw because she always knew.

Blood from his arm where the terrible man had stabbed him with his own knife. Blood not stopping and more pain, growing pain, *all the pain.*

And all the blood boiling over in his chest where the gunshot had been the banging door and opened him and let the air spread its cold towards his still beating heart.

A heart slowing. Slowing. Slowing.

Stopping.

Dumah died with Candace's name in his silent mouth.

Chapter Thirty-Two

Somehow, he was on his feet. Somehow, he wasn't dead.

Roe stared at the man he'd shot, watching with detachment as Dumah dropped. And detachment wasn't the word.

Dislocation.

He'd been removed from the school, from the agonies of his battered body. While he still possessed vision and hearing, both senses were outside his head; both reported the facts like a news report on the television. Perhaps he was watching the Six O'Clock News while Alison made dinner for him and the boys. But that was a joke because when was he ever home in time for dinner around the table with his family?

He was still in the school populated by its dying people and his hand remained outstretched with the Browning clasped between his fingers.

Roe tried to speak but what felt like a noose around his throat choked off any words, leaving him with nothing but blood at the back of his mouth and wheezing like a boiling kettle moments before it broke down.

Martha screeched and raced across the floor to her fallen brother, paying no mind to the guns. Moving faster than seemed possible given the bullet graze in the side of her head, Candace caught the child before she reached Dumah, spun and dropped to her knees. She kept her one hand on the girl's back, pressing their bodies together while Martha howled into Candace's neck and Dumah remained dead.

Wiping at the weeping wound on his face where Candace had dragged her nails down his cheek, Granger stood beside Roe, the shotgun limp. Roe's eyes reported the fact that none of the few people who remained at the window had tried for an attack or to flee. Instead, they crouched on the floor, entwined with their hands and arms and stench.

He processed the information and had no idea what to do with it.

"Roe?" Granger muttered. "Are you okay?"

Roe croaked. It was the noise of an injured bird.

"Him or you, Roe. You were dying. I would be, too. Him or you."

The same croak, the same utter lack of sense.

Candace rose, still clutching Martha to her bosom, the child's weight slight enough for Candace to support with only one arm. The shot that killed the boy had grazed her skull, opening a wound through her hair. Blood splattered her ear, cheek and soaked her neck.

But Roe saw nothing but her eyes.

They were nailed to his. Everything melted away, floor, walls and the outside world trickling down a drain in so much muck and sludge and leaving Roe in some plain white space where he knew nothing but vision and his damnation in the black woman's eyes.

"We didn't want this," Granger told Candace and her attention remained squarely on Roe. Granger continued as if she was paying him any mind. "We really didn't no matter how hard you may find that to believe. But this place. . .this place and these people." He waved the shotgun at the window and a woman whimpered. "This is what we're dealing with and it's why we have to be as we are. You'll see that eventually."

He turned away and nudged George's body with the toe of his boot. Roe heard something squelch, and again, it could have been a report on the telly's news. Moira Stuart or Jan Leeming with her calm tone detailing some horrible crime in a faraway land that had nothing to do with Britain or the Home Office and nothing to do with his wife and children burning, burning, burning; everything slipping into a grating drone and that drone was his family screaming forever, the sound slowed down so it would last with him always.

He sobbed once and the fire in his throat flared high. Candace was a clothes shop dummy, no movement at all in her face; loathing that went beyond human filling her unblinking eyes while the girl continued to weep over her lost brother.

"We get the others and we get out of here," Granger muttered. "We deal with Willis later. Let's just move." He sighed, weary and flat. Absently, Roe wondered if he'd ever heard Granger sound tired.

"This place is done," Granger said.

Roe remained staring at Candace but his head and his heart saw the swings and slide of the play area; they saw the field he and Granger had crossed on the way from the suburban streets and the bodies fallen at Willis's hand.

Your friend is right, Candace said in his head. *This is done. And so are you.*

Roe nodded.

Chapter Thirty-Three

The pain.

The fucking pain.

Willis had known next to nothing else for days. Weeks, maybe. Any sense of time had gone out the window in the same instant the little bitch had swung her axe at him and he'd heard it right in the middle of his skull—the squeal of metal on bone. For probably less than a second, blinding shock had taken hold on any other sensation. Then the pain came, destroying shock, time, thinking, himself.

And that was all he'd known.

The others had finished what the girl started and hacked away the last of the tendons and bone keeping his shattered hand to his forearm; he knew that without having the slightest memory of it. A mix of voices, shouting and panicked; heat in his body like an oven; spinning light from their torches on the walls and always a sensation of falling into darkness thicker and deeper than any sea.

That same sensation even when reality crashed back down, crushing his head. They were on the move, walking, the day sharp and stinging like the thousand bees living in the space where his hand had been. The shelter of the police station far behind and any familiarity or sense of being in his place no matter how small the station had been compared to working in the Met long gone. He had one foot in front of the other, the wet earth and the hard road, the sobbing anguish of his severed hand and the pills the others shoved into the dry tomb of his mouth a hard lump in his throat before they did their thing and the pain moved an inch to the side of his head.

Falling into darkness all the way, all the time. A stone dropping down a never-ending well and any light he remembered from the past now a tiny pinprick miles above.

Then Patterson's voice muffled and distant as if they were having a long-distance telephone conversation, coming with a second's delay along a thousand miles of lines trailing on the sea bed.

There they are.

And he'd woken, brought back to the world and the deep burning in the meat of his arm. There'd been no need to look at his skin to know it was blood poisoning. Despite whatever precautions and treatment Granger and the others had given him, infection had set up home inside him and would quickly spread. Even if they made it to Dover, he had next to no chance and so there was only one thing to do as he stared at Patterson's back and replayed the words the man called to the next room.

Kill her.

The seconds after launching out of the chair, bashing Patterson to the floor and grabbing the gun from Roe and running to the door belonged to another life. He had let go of that life because all the shooting meant here he was, the Browning aimed squarely at the child's head while she lay flat on the road.

Kill her.

He'd fired several times at the stinking bodies. Probably just three rounds left. That bastard Granger would have taken the other Browning and both shotguns. No matter. A squeeze of the trigger and the little witch who'd hurt him so profoundly would be dead. One less animal in the world, one less creature that could have been human but was so far away from it.

He knew the boy was close but might as well have been on the far side of the park where the trees bordered it. The boy might be fast, but no way could he get to Willis's back before Willis blew the girl's head into bloody chunks. There'd been no sound from behind since he'd ordered the kid to stop.

Willis tasted blood on his teeth. Patterson's blood. Or maybe he was bleeding in his mouth. It could have been during his struggle with Patterson or the jump from the last car to the ground; he had no idea. Sucking the liquid back, he rested it on his tongue and then spat. Red flecked on the girl's head and back. She was motionless, eyes staring across the road. Willis prodded her hair with the gun. Still nothing. He could have been nudging a stone.

"Up," he croaked.

She showed no sign of understanding let alone doing as he demanded.

Willis spat more blood at her and risked a look away from her to the boy inches from the edge of the grass. He'd frozen seconds from leaping, reaching for Willis.

"You okay there?" Willis asked, grinning. "Don't worry. I'll get to you in a minute."

He returned his attention to the girl on the ground and pressed the gun as hard as he could into the side of her head.

"Get. The. Fuck. Up."

Easing the weapon away, he kept it on her as she pulled her legs up into a crouch, then stood, now facing away from him, her back like a dismissal. He gaped at her, shocked by the little bitch's arrogance.

"Turn." He had to spit again and the thought that he might have done more than bite his tongue tried to speak up. He wouldn't let it. "Around."

The child did so, but slowly, revealing the upper half of her face, the rest obscured by a scarf. Her clothing of padded jacket and gloves did little to hide the fact she was severely underweight: legs like sticks, eyes two sunken pits, and those eyes. . .

Judging him.

Dismissing him.

Willis aimed the gun squarely at her face.

She slid a step closer to him.

"Enough." Willis altered his aim, the gun pointing at her narrow chest. "I mean it, girl."

She paused and he wondered if the gun was a threat to her or if she'd placed herself where she wanted to be. Sweat made the hair on the back of his neck prickle and the bees were alive in his stump, stinging their poison deep into his exposed nerve endings and flesh turned crispy.

"You." He had to spit again. "Boy. Think you can move faster than I can pull this trigger?"

No answer.

"What about you, girl? Jump me before I blow you in half?"

Still nothing but her eyes and her judgement of him an irrelevance. It almost made him want to laugh just as it infuriated him.

"All right." He addressed the girl. "You have three seconds to move next to him. Your *brother.*" He deliberately made the term sound like an insult. "Don't move and I'll hurt you." He lowered his aim to land it on her knees. "You won't die fast; you'll just bleed and suffer on the ground. Your choice."

The slightest change came over her eyes. The dismissal remained, but was now mixed with curiosity. She could have been looking at a new species of insect and Willis bit back a tired laugh.

"Up to you. Right. One, two—"

"Mary." It was the boy, uttering one word with no urgency or panic.

The girl walked in a curve around Willis. He tracked her with the weapon and focused his aim where her shoulder met his hip. A boy no older than sixteen and a girl of about ten. Jesus Christ. The worst threat he'd faced since they'd clambered up out of the last bunker and it was a couple of poxy kids.

Kid who cut your fucking hand off.

That woke more of the bees. He ground his teeth, sinking his bite into the pain and daring it to try and undo him while the children appraised him.

From somewhere, gunfire roared. Made weak by distance and the wind blowing away from

They're at war. Granger. He's. . .

Willis didn't possess the strength to complete the thought. His work with Roe and Granger was over for now. They might meet again, but he doubted it. As for Patterson, that had been a shitty thing, but necessary. Patterson had never been a full member of their team; he'd never wanted to see anything through, happier instead to live in the misery of his life burned to a crisp and his failure to keep his pretty daughter alive. Fuck Patterson. And for that matter, fuck Roe and Granger. Willis knew he didn't have a lot of time left, but what he did have, he intended to put to good use. Let Granger and Roe do what they needed with the people from the school and the other members of this foul family. Let them get to the new government in Dover. He had his own plan and it involved moving right now.

Willis hissed at them to walk, directing them through the overturned bodies to the end of the wrecked cars and back to the pavement outside the houses where weeds grew wild and tall through the cracks in the ground. Their steps were hollow and cold while the stinging in Willis's stump grew to a crackling fire and his throat ached in a way that made him want to vomit. He was infected. He was a rotting pile of meat still upright and he would only get worse.

But not until he was finished. Not until he was as close to a home as he could be.

"Walk," he whispered to their backs, not caring if they heard him. Not caring about anything other than what he could do with the hours or days he had left. They followed the path between houses, their boots and shoes tracking old leaves and dislodging pieces of broken rubble, before they emerged a few minutes from the town's centre. Across the road, terraced cottages were without their roofs, the frames of each home crumbling. A loose beam hung over a front door, swinging with monotonous rhythm.

The siblings stopped, backs to him, and he smiled. His face and teeth ached. He made the smile grow.

"North," he said. "We're going north. Home again." He had to laugh and it emerged as a choking snort. "Home to see your dad one more time."

Chapter Thirty-Four

The men secured Martha's hands together with a piece of ragged rope they took from the school people, Granger tying her wrists while Roe stood at her back with his gun at her head. He hadn't been able to look at Candace who'd been ordered to stand several feet away, the wind making the hem of her long coat flap at her shins and gusting through the holes, new and old, in the assembly hall's walls. They'd tied a wrap around the wound in her head, sealing the scrape from the bullet. It felt like nails had been driven into her skull and she didn't care in the least. She'd tried to focus on what they were doing to her and Martha but couldn't unsee Dumah falling to the floor, his mouth open, his eyes unaware of what had happened. And the man, Roe, gun still aimed at the space Dumah occupied, his mouth open and stupid, his face slack like someone had cut the muscles under his skin.

Dumah.

He was behind her now; they were a mile or more away from the school. Fields on one side, broken and burned trees on the other with the wind making the crispy leaves crackle. She'd caught a brief discussion between the men: Roe telling Granger the A2 would bring them to Dover faster; Granger muttering Willis would be on that road so they would stick to the A257. Minutes after, they followed a sloping path from a narrower road surrounded by the wrecks of houses and this huge space rolled ahead.

A2. A257. Roads. Names. Said like they meant a thing to Candace. And it was so hard for anything to mean anything now.

Priest, gone. Dumah, gone. Lazarus and Mary somewhere miles behind, maybe dead, maybe not. And it didn't matter that Roe had managed to meet her gaze as they departed the school, clearly registering his death in her eyes. She could kill them all and it wouldn't bring back Priest or Dumah.

There'd been no sign of Lazarus or Mary near the houses; only bodies with their gunshot wounds, and the skinny man, Patterson, knifed in the stomach and his body resting against a wall. Granger and Roe had said little when they spied his corpse apart from Roe's growling mutter of *Willis*. Patterson had gone into the house, emerging with a second shotgun and a handful of bullets which Granger had loaded into his weapon. They'd taken the backpacks, shouldering whatever they contained while the day trickled by in its cold indifference to the deceased and the violence.

All that behind them because here was the open road that would take them to Dover.

Their steps echoing flatly on the tarmac, they walked for at least an hour, nobody speaking, Candace unable to see either men or get an idea what they might be thinking. Eventually, Martha stood straight and walked without support. She held her tied hands over her stomach, focus fixed firmly on the route uncurling ahead. As much as Candace wanted to speak to the girl, tell her things would be well, she couldn't. Even without the men and their guns at their backs, she couldn't lie. Things might be well if the family could find one another and make it back to some semblance of the life they knew and loved; until then, all they had was each other in this quiet piece of the land.

Something about that thought niggled at Candace; she seized on it immediately.

The utter lack of people.

While it was true they were away from villages and far from the ruined towns, there were still no signs of a hiding population. The school and its wretched inhabitants were miles behind and it now felt as if they'd walked to the end of the world, leaving all other survivors far away.

Her stomach growled, reminding her it had been a long time since their last meal. Ignoring their captors for a moment, she and Martha needed to eat – a much more difficult issue given the lack of food out here in the unknown country.

Thinking of food seemed insulting after so much loss. Even so, her body needed fuel and another rumble sounded from her mid-section.

"We'll eat soon," Granger muttered. While she caught a jollity to his tone, Candace knew it was put on. The events at the school and his own loss had hurt him. Good in a way because it might weaken him. Bad in another because loss made people dangerous.

"We need a rest," he added. "And. . .food."

Candace came to a stop. Unbidden, Martha did the same. Candace addressed Granger without turning to face him.

"We disgust you."

Silence at her back save for Roe's slight wheeze. Then Granger skirted around her, shotgun ready. He strode several paces ahead and faced them. Candace didn't need to see Roe to know the injured, sick man had levelled his own weapon at her head. She saw it in Granger's eyes.

"Disgust me? You believe that?" Granger asked and the worst part was his honest curiosity.

"It is true," she replied, aware men like Granger were always surprised when she or one of the others spoke in clear sentences.

"I won't lie," Granger said. "You absolutely sicken me."

"Why?" Martha asked. Behind, there was a clear shifting on the spot as Roe altered his aim to Martha before jerking back to Candace. That was also interesting. Candace noted it, held it inside her blank face and answered her sister.

"Because he thinks we're demons."

"Because you *are*," Granger said. He appeared almost relieved as if the words were a weight he'd been carrying for long miles. Candace supposed that was true.

She smiled, and while it hurt to feel anything but misery, the smile was genuine.

"Men." She pointed at him and briefly wished to have her missing arm and hand so she could point at Roe at the same time. "You men. You burned the world down. You killed them all. You are wicked. We are survivors. We kill to eat. You kill. You killed the child. The boy."

Granger nodded, making no attempt to deny what she'd said.

"I did kill the boy. I killed him because he was like you. He saw no value in life. He would have taken you, used you, hurt you. I saved you from that and I saved God knows how many other women from the same. The world is a better place without the boy in it." He came closer, shotgun still high. "Killing is horrible, but when one is faced with a thing like that boy, it is the only option. You and your family have options. You kill to eat, but you don't have to. There is food out there. Meat if you want it. You kill because of what you are. Animals."

Candace closed her mouth. Convincing Granger he was wrong was a pointless battle. But still, he wouldn't shut up.

"I know I've done bad things. So has Roe. Willis did terrible things even before the bombs. My wife. . ." He seemed to lose his thoughts for a few seconds; Candace watched him struggle, watched light and dark war behind his eyes. Eventually, a grey shade coated his face and turned the brown of his pupils into a watery soup.

"My wife was one of the good ones." He glanced to his side and nodded. Candace saw nothing near him which didn't matter. He did. The world was full of ghosts in any case.

"She was better than me. Better than any of us. Patterson wasn't far behind even if he wasn't a strong man. He knew right from wrong and now he's dead. He's—"

"Shut up," Roe moaned. "Will you please shut up?"

Each word was a rattle in his throat. He could have been speaking through a mouthful of gravel. With slow care, Candace turned in a half-circle and faced him while Martha remained focused on the now silent Granger.

"I will kill you," Candace said to Roe.

His contemplation of her was whole and strong. "I know."

She faced Granger again. "You will die in blood."

While he didn't answer, she saw his answer swimming in the grey of his eyes.

I know.

With a slight wave of the shotgun, he signalled for them to walk on. Martha and Candace did so while the afternoon drew closer to evening, while the patchy mist slid between branches and dampened the landscape beside the parkway, while the only company they kept as they walked was their ghosts.

Chapter Thirty-Five

Willis ordered them to tramp over the fields instead of sticking to the road and while he could only croak his words instead of speaking clearly, Lazarus knew he couldn't risk going for the man. Weakened he might have been, sickened by the germs invading his body thanks to Mary, Lazarus still had no chance of succeeding in an attack when Willis carried his shotgun. All Lazarus could do was obey the command to keep going and hope the uneven land would eventually take Willis's attention while his obvious pain robbed him of his focus. Time wasn't on his side, though. The road might have been a quicker route away from the small town falling behind, but Willis apparently knew his directions and kept them moving through battered hedges separating each field from its neighbour. They'd be back into the big nowhere soon enough, any houses or settlements out of sight.

Lazarus couldn't think about that. It would do no good. Get Mary away, run to the others and escape back to their old life. *That* was what he had to do.

"You." Willis grunted the word. He sounded as if his throat had been sanded raw. Lazarus caught a look at Willis's arm soon after they left the town, the coat sleeve ridden high to expose the tell-tale signs of infection. Angry red lines snaked out of the dirty wrapping around his forearm, the skin pulsing. Lazarus knew about germs and infection; Priest taught them how to take care of themselves. *Blood poisoning.* That was what would kill Willis. But that didn't mean he was unable to cause some more hurt before he died.

"You." He said it again. "Boy."

Lazarus glanced around without breaking his stride. Willis had told them to ditch their scarves once they were on the grass. Let the wind get to their faces and hopefully blow away their stink. Lazarus supposed they were lucky he let them keep their coats.

"Your name," Willis said.

"Lazarus."

He gave his name to the day, letting the air take it where it would. The white bleaching out of the light, the spreading grass, each blade soaked and still, and the trees sheltering no birds, they were all welcome to his name. Willis was not.

"Like the Bible," Willis said.

"Like the Bible," Lazarus echoed.

"How come you were named from the Bible?" Willis asked, and Lazarus sensed him mentally answer his own question.

Priest. Lazarus kept that name in his heart. It didn't belong to the day anymore.

"He was a real Priest?" Willis said. "A *real* one? Well. Imagine that."

He sounded like he was grinning, showing his teeth in a dog's snarl. Lazarus managed to look at his sister without moving his head. Like him, she faced ahead and offered a quick, secret smile.

"Tell me something, Lazarus," Willis said. He paused while they crested a slight rise, mud sucking at their boots. They were nearing a road that wasn't much more than a brown line.

"Tell me your story and I'll tell you mine. If you like. I mean, you're not related. Anyone can see that. I don't need to be a copper to know that. You know what I mean?" Willis laughed and it was as jagged as broken glass. "You. White. Your *sister* here. White. The other girl. White. Big man who didn't say much. . .what was his name?"

Lazarus didn't reply. If Dumah was here, they'd have a chance together against Willis. As it was, Lazarus could only be grateful his brother had run with Martha for Candace. They'd be safe together.

"Anyway. He was white. But your other sister. One armed bird. Black as the ace of spades, son, so you tell me how the fuck you lot are family?"

Lazarus rarely thought about his past. Gone days were dead days and had nothing he could use now. The sneer in Willis's tone held some ugly magic; it brought the life before Priest and the family closer and that could only be an ache he didn't need or want.

"Priest and Candace met first," he said. Saying their names was a help and while their lives were no business of anyone else's, he found he didn't mind letting Willis hear it. "Months after it." He gestured to the surrounding countryside, all the land a corpse. "He kept her alive. Food. Water. Shelter. I found Dumah in a house. A broken building. Essex." The name of the county meant next to nothing. He only knew it because Priest had told him long ago that a person's home should never be forgotten. "He gave me his last rat. We shared it."

"Touching," Willis muttered.

"Priest found us." Lazarus brushed a hand on Mary's shoulder, feeling the jutting bone even under the padding of her sweaters and coat. "We found the sisters in the trees. Almost dead. We saved them. We were together."

Willis laughed. "Very nice. Very cosy. So, what's the deal with your names? Lazarus? You die or something? Come back to life?"

"Yes," Lazarus replied and had no need to say anything more. Let the man make of it what he would.

Willis paused. When he spoke again, his aggression was a little more forced than before. "What about the girls?"

"My sisters," Lazarus replied.

"Okay." Now Willis sounded annoyed as well as aggressive. Lazarus's brief answers were needling him for some reason. Lazarus kept his awareness of this tool secret. A quick look at Mary told him she had noticed the same.

"Candace? What kind of name is that? Even for a wog, that's strange."

Wog meant nothing to Lazarus; the obvious insult did. He bristled, exhaled through his teeth and replied to Willis.

"Princess."

"Princess?" Willis was alternating between aggravated and amused. More importantly, he sounded alert. Their long trek and his injury weren't weakening him. If anything, the opposite was true. He lived on violence, and with all the control over his situation meaning he could indulge in the threat of violence, he was feeding on both.

"Didn't know many wog princesses back in my day. Just shoplifters and pros, really." Coughing, he cleared his throat. "I was on the Force. You know about the Force? No. Course you don't. What am I thinking?" He sighed, the ugly reminiscing an act Lazarus did not believe in the slightest. Willis was a present threat.

"Five years. Would have been more if the war hadn't happened. I'd have gone right up the ranks. I showed them what I could do when it kicked off in Brixton. Same over at Broadwater Farm. Remember that one?" He giggled. "They only kept me down because they didn't like me, but so what? I got results. That's what it's all about, right? Getting the job done. Bollocks to those fuckers who couldn't understand that."

Mary was smiling, her mocking judgement of Willis powering the grin. Lazarus couldn't help but to return her smile. The man was dangerous but he was also weak and stupid – two factors which might make him more dangerous or easier to kill.

"None of that government shit for me," he went on. "Home Office shit. Patterson had his place there. Same with Granger and Roe at the Foreign Office. I ended up down in the bunker by accident." Willis trailed off for a moment. "Or luck." He snorted. "And now here we are out in the great nothing. Just me and you two animals. Granger and Roe, they can have what they want. Their government. They're welcome to try for that. Me, I'm happy with you two to keep me company."

Ten minutes later, they were on the motorway, their muddy footprints marking the ground and the inclining road. The woods they'd travelled through after fleeing the police station were thin and patchy but would soon grow to the cover they'd used. Some of the town's remaining buildings were in sight although there was little to focus upon. Lazarus had seen more than enough crumbling roofs and stains of fire damage to last the rest of his life. He kept an eye out for anything he might be able to grab and use as a weapon: a sturdy branch broken free from a trunk; a discarded knife; broken glass. Even a large stone would be a help. There was nothing but leaves, pebbles and the town approaching below the last of the weak sunlight.

Trudging on, the shelter of the growing woods fell out of reach and fields rolled into the hedges that formed the side of the golf course. And opposite the course, the police station where it had started to go wrong in so many awful ways. Willis stayed quiet until they closed in on the building, their boots and trousers soaked with earth.

"Inside."

He coughed and Lazarus heard deep sickness in the noise. He wished for Willis to collapse. Instead, Willis repeated himself.

"Inside."

Shouldering half the ruined doors aside, Mary behind him, Lazarus entered the shadows filling the station reception, ready to make a move for any of the debris on the ground when Willis clicked on a small torch. He managed to cradle the light and the shotgun, resting the weapon on his stump despite the pain it must have caused. Blandly, Lazarus stared at the man, noting the sickly pale shade to his face, his clenched jaw and the muck coating the bandages around his stump.

"Don't think about it, son. I'm not in the mood."

Lazarus moved on, stopping beside the long reception desk. Had it really been such a short time since they'd fled this place, sick with fear and anger and grief? That escape could have happened years before, not days.

"Downstairs. Like before." The light from Willis's little torch trailed over Lazarus's head, darted around Mary before settling between them.

"No," Mary said.

Willis cackled. "Oh, girl. You make me laugh. You really do. Now walk before I make your brother scream."

"It is fine." Lazarus slid his hand into Mary's tied fingers, not caring if Willis told him to let go. She relaxed at his touch and nodded.

Side by side, they followed the corridor with its broken walls and roof towards the next set of doors and Lazarus swallowed the foul aroma of decay. He knew the smell of a dead body; this was the stench of rotting. Granger's wife, somewhere in the building, exposed to the elements. And Priest, down below, rainwater dribbling onto this corpse and spreading the muck over the hard ground.

Down the steps and closer to the stink of the moist walls and the body they'd left to rot in the cell. The doors remained wide open, the metal and the broken hole in its centre ice-cold, dripping wet. Mary's grip on Lazarus's hand was fiercely tight. He increased his own pressure. Priest's body was lost to the poor light, but the smell filled everything as did the horrible memory of their father with the hole in his head falling to the floor of the cell and the crashing echo of Granger's shout hammering into Lazarus's skull.

"In there," Willis said.

They wouldn't give him any satisfaction or joy; they would walk together. Hand in hand, Lazarus and Mary crossed towards the entrance, Lazarus a step ahead of his sister.

Light spun madly; a savage tug ran up Lazarus's arm, jarring his shoulder. He spun, unable to stop Willis. The man had shoved the gun under his armpit and grabbed Mary by the hair. Moving with a terrible speed Lazarus wouldn't have believed possible, he threw her to the opposite corner where she smashed into the wall. The second he let her go, Willis ran at Lazarus who was yelling, madly eager to spill Willis's blood.

Willis crashed into Lazarus and his heavier weight sent Lazarus flying, arms spinning. He struck his head on the top of cell door and dropped to his knees. Willis kicked him in the chest, knocking air from Lazarus's lungs and spilling him to the filthy floor. Gasping, croaking, Lazarus attempted to stand, made it to his knees and pitched over. Crawling, grabbing the flaking wall, he rose and fell on the solid door as Willis slammed it closed and spun the lock. He whirled around and caught the barrel of the gun as he let it fall from his armpit. Mary had risen but clearly couldn't come at him. She'd made it to her knees; her head hung limp and she swayed. Willis yanked on the key in the cell door, securing it before backing backed away.

"Mary," Lazarus whispered and his legs failed him again. He slid down the door, doing all he could not to see Priest's crumpled body. He had fallen inches from the corpse and the stink went beyond any horrible smell. It was the reek of grief and it wrapped itself around Lazarus's pounding head.

Outside the cell, Willis's voice carried. "Up. Right now."

Unable to see what was happening, Lazarus could only call his sister's name again and try to stand again. He heard their boots kicking through puddles, Willis's panting, saw the beam of torch light spin over the walls before vanishing when a door banged closed at the far end of the cells.

For less than a minute, there was only his own gasps sucking in and pushing out the grief-stink.

Then Mary's screams began.

Chapter Thirty-Six

The motorways and A-roads were behind. They were between open country and lanes become little more than tracks, and that was just fine with Granger. They'd re-join the A257 again soon enough. While he would never admit it to Roe, being so exposed to the sky while they walked down the motorway had taken more out of him than he liked to think about. Carolyn had strolled beside him for a time and he'd spoken to her in his head, but she hadn't answered any of his questions. It seemed she'd become a watcher and a witness rather than a guide.

Granger estimated the time was about four in the afternoon. Maybe closer to five. There was no need to study the sky to know that. Full dark soon. Another night out in the open. With any luck, it would be their last. Dover could not be much further ahead.

Roe drew closer to him as he chewed his thoughts and Granger kept his awareness of the other man secret. Roe hadn't spoken since his brief outburst miles back which could have as easily been down to the damage done to his throat as it was his emotional state.

"Willis," Roe said after a moment. A few steps ahead, Candace and the girl walked close enough together for the child's arm to rub on Candace's hip.

"What about him?" Granger replied, watching their prisoners.

"Do you think he's dead?"

With uncharacteristic bluntness, Roe's question was out, solid like the ground beneath their feet. Granger welcomed it.

"Possibly. If not, he soon will be. And if we meet again, then we deal with him. He was ill, Roe. We can't blame him too much for losing it."

"We're not going to find him and take him with us?"

"No. There's no point."

They covered another quarter of a mile, the ground rising and falling slightly. Granger was thinking about how much further they could travel before needing to rest and make a fire when Roe spoke again.

"You still believe Dover is the best plan, don't you?"

He said it without anger, only a bone-deep exhaustion. On Granger's other side, Carolyn looked up from her appraisal of the ground and grinned. Granger had to look away from his wife. While he'd seen her smile plenty of times, he'd never seen her grin.

"Best or not, it the only plan. We—"

"It's shit, Granger." Still with the tiredness, the words more than a croak but still not normal speech. "Harris told us nothing. This is all on the say-so of a dying boy who—"

Granger punched Roe on the side of his chin, the blow not as hard as it could have been. Even so, a lightning bolt flashed inside Granger's knuckles and through his palm. He bared his teeth at Roe, aware the woman and the girl had turned back and almost dismissing them from his attention.

Roe rocked with the smack, shook his head and stared at Granger. Save for the area Granger hit, his face had sunk into the colour of fresh snow. Around his chin, blood rushing to the surface made the skin scarlet.

"Dealey may be there," he said. "But he was not happy to see Harris. What makes you think he will be happy to see you? Or me?"

It's a good question, darling. Carolyn sounded like she was still grinning and the last thing in the world Granger wanted to know was whether or not that was true.

"Dealey did not hurt Harris." Granger faced Candace and Martha, the coloured woman with her missing arm; the child nothing but skin and bones, and both with his death in their eyes.

"They did. Or people like them did. That's what they do, Roe. They hurt people because they can and because they want to. It's who they are now. They killed Harris."

For the first time in weeks, a few drops of rain fell, warm against the chilly day. They lasted no more than ten seconds before dying. The breeze, dancing over the countryside they'd crossed to get to the road, brought a fresh wave of cold.

"Who is Harris?" Candace asked lightly and Granger answered before Roe could.

"He was one of us. He was young. Quick. Healthy. He went ahead to scout the area and see what was out there." Granger used his old talent, one he hadn't brought out since the days of ministers and meetings, and addressed Candace and Martha at the same time. "He was our friend."

Roe stirred. "Looks like we've all lost friends."

It was the child, not Candace, who answered him. "We lost our brother and our father."

Tears might have been expected. Instead, the girl said her piece like a robot and Granger flashed back to a film his nephew James had been desperate to see. Some violent American thing about killer robots and time travel with a bloke who had a silly name.

James, gone now. The same with Granger's sister Rachel, her husband William. Everybody from friend to family to colleague nothing but earth and dust.

Grief made his heart crack and he knew Carolyn at his side shared the secret he'd kept for ten years.

I wish it, too, darling, but then if I had died back then and our family had lived with you in the bunkers, where would they be now? They'd be as dead as I am right now. They'd be ghosts. Just like me.

Inwardly, he howled his hurt but showed nothing to his colleague or the sisters.

"Everyone has lost someone," he murmured.

Martha spat at his feet and turned her back on him. Saying nothing, Candace also turned away and they walked on in silence.

They moved single file between a cluster of cars, stepped over a broken bundle of metal and reached a relatively clear area. Granger told them to stop; the group halted and he turned in a circle.

Five or six cars on either side, the road under the vehicles stained with burn marks still not faded despite the years; a few long slivers of glass from windscreens lying here and there while further out, the open land on their right rising in an embankment towards what had been a farm. A few of the buildings remained. On the other side of the road, trees with their bare but still thick branches encroached towards the tarmac. The sunlight had no chance of illuminating the murk on the wood's floor meaning it appeared as if black water had risen from the ground to drown roots and weeds.

Candace had slid closer to Martha in the second while he'd had his back to them. Roe, the fool, had also been giving the land a once over instead of watching them. They faced him now, expressions bland.

"It's not far now," Granger said to nobody in particular. "Twelve miles. Maybe a little more." For a moment, he kept his eyes on Candace's face, signalling to her that he'd noticed her sly movement.

"It'd be quicker going across country," Roe said.

"Perhaps, but we know where we stand with the road. Onwards." Granger gestured with the shotgun that they should move ahead.

Within a short distance, the wrecks became more spread out although the signs of fire damage were clearer in the melted windscreens and twisted cars. It was easy to see the blast from the nuclear fireballs consuming every vehicle attempting to outrun it, but that hadn't happened here. There'd been a straightforward crash somewhere ahead, vehicle after vehicle smashing into each other; petrol splashing, a tiny spark, the detonation consuming cars, vans and the tangled mess of a coach. Granger's eyesight remained strong; the coach had melted into a lorry, forming a surreal creation of too many wheels and windows sunk inwards as if they had been made of oil. The fire had ignited each car, vehicles in turn going up in flame and the knock-on effect turning the road into a conflagration.

They reached another clear section and Roe drew further away from the woman. She saw it and Granger saw her.

She made no move other than to keep walking forward. As for the girl, she was like a statue come to life. There'd been no emotion on her face whenever Granger studied her, and in her slight frame and calm, she could have been as dead as the people back in the school.

"Candace, isn't it?" he said.

"Yes."

"It's a nice name."

She said nothing.

"Where is it from?" Granger asked. "It's not English."

The delicate and deliberate implication that Candace was also not English hung between them.

"The Bible."

"Is it?"

He didn't manage to hide his surprise and had to wonder if that surprise was more to do with the woman knowing the Bible or the name being Biblical.

"Did your priest give you that name?"

She halted. At once, Martha did the same. Roe reacted faster than Granger expected, Browning level with Candace in a second.

"Priest," Candace said. "His name was *Priest.*"

Despite the several feet between them and the weapon in his hand, Granger struggled not to take a step away. The idea of the time this woman and the others had spent in a world like a grave placed gentle fingers on his heart and he did his best to shake them off. At his side, Carolyn kept quiet which was worth little. She pressed back on his chest, eager for him to truly see things as Candace did. With a mental shove, he pushed it all away but still couldn't quite lose the mental picture of Candace with her one arm surviving the endless days of winter while the waves hissed as they broke on the beach where she and her siblings had set up home.

"Priest," Granger said. "Of course."

She made no move to walk on. Her lips had parted slightly, revealing the edges of her teeth and he couldn't help but to wonder how sharp those teeth might be as they dug into his skin.

"Shall we go on?" he asked and increased the pressure on the trigger. The little piece of metal was ice-cold even through his glove.

Her eyes flickered and it wasn't until a moment later that he realised she'd shifted her observation to the shotgun and back again.

"Of course," she muttered and gave him the slightest of mocking bows.

It quickly became clear they could go no further without altering their angle: at least twenty cars had smashed together, crushing those in the centre of the wreck, knocking others to their sides and snapping doors completely free. The passenger door hung loose from a Transit van, a single rusting hinge keeping it attached. The breeze played with it, pushing and pulling and the noise of the regular beat like a clock chipping away at the seconds of the day. It set Granger's teeth on edge and made him want to lift the shotgun despite there being nothing at which to aim.

"I don't think we can get through this," Roe said. His voice was returning to normal even if his breathing remained ragged.

Granger studied the surrounding area. Grass sloped in a fairly steep incline to what he thought had been farmland. Opposite, scrubland ended at trees and the woodland matched the line of the road, the trunks rising higher further into the distance. While he didn't fancy the ascent to the level farmland, it was preferable to the blockage ahead or keeping too close to the woods. He wanted to see the land exposed in all directions.

If the land is exposed, then you are exposed, Carolyn whispered.

"Good point," he muttered and Roe glanced his way, presumably thinking it was a delayed reply to his own comment. Granger blushed and nodded at the farmland.

"Up there." He said it clearly for Candace and Martha and they moved as one, neither appearing to pay him any mind.

"Seems we're going cross country after all," Roe said.

Granger paused, replaying the words and scanning for mocking even as he asked himself why it mattered.

Because this is all you have.

He didn't know if he'd replied to his own question or if the answer belonged to Carolyn. She'd faded from the corners of his vision; grey soup grew from her arms instead of hands and he had the idea she no longer possessed much of a lower half. Perhaps she was weakening the further they drew away from her body – a thought he knew was senseless but one he believed might well be true.

A hollow ache made his chest pound.

I never wanted to lose you, Carolyn.

If she did comment, it was a nothing more than a sigh of the wind.

He had to take hold of things. Had to stay together. Had to survive this body of a country devoid of a heart or flowing blood or any air left in its lungs. Do that, make it to Dover and hand over the creatures that had terrorised so many. Prove what he still was to Dealey and start again.

That was all there was to it.

"After you, ladies."

Candace shifted towards the grass, Martha at her side, and the sleeve of Candace's coat flapped around her stump. Granger waited until they were on the grass and trudging upwards before speaking again.

"What happened to your arm?"

He expected a curt reply at most. Instead, Candace surprised him again.

"Priest cut it off a long time ago."

"Why?" Granger puffed as quietly as possible, not wanting to let any of them know he found the ascent a struggle.

"So we could eat."

Granger came to an abrupt stop and stared up at Candace's back. Open-mouthed, he waited for her to elaborate. She said nothing more and simply walked to the top of the embankment where Martha stood at her side and Roe held the Browning, face much paler than usual.

For the first time, Granger realised he had vastly underestimated the people who'd attacked the police station back in South Calcott. While the stories and rumours he and his men had picked up from the few survivors they'd met on the way south had been as detailed as they were horrific, he hadn't believed them all the way down. Even after the events days before when they'd been in the cells, he hadn't accepted what he was dealing with. Now that knowledge was right in front of his face and there was no way of getting away from it.

Cannibals. A family. A woman who would willingly let a man sever her arm to feed that family, presumably eating her own skin, muscle and flesh in order to stay alive. Had it been in their caves, lit with the weak light of a spluttering torch while the sea air slid in and out of cracks in the rocks and the salty moistness stuck to their clothing?

Had she screamed as he cut? Had they cauterised the wound much as he, Roe and Patterson had with Willis? Had the air stunk of cooking flesh?

Had the children, the two little girls, licked their lips in hideous anticipation?

My God. My dear God.

He had to let it go and keep his mind on their present, not nauseated supposition.

"Move on," Granger said. "We'll stick to the field but keep the road at our side. Let's go."

The group crossed the grass with the wet earth clinging to their shoes and boots. Their passage slowed, Granger kept the tarmac and smashed cars in his peripheral vision and occasionally glanced at the farm buildings away to their left. Fences bordering land were broken, the wood either salvaged or smashed to rot in the grass. Hedges grew haphazardly. The spiky brambles spread and hung low in some places while in others, they were a sickly grey instead of green.

The ground dipped sharply, the descent and flatter land affording a view of the farm, the road less blocked with wrecks, and the trees of the wood growing densely together. At the same time, the grass grew taller, the strands brushing their shins and trailing dew on their trousers.

"Back to the road?" Roe asked and gestured at the wrecks.

Gunfire streaked over the farmland and the echo had no time to fade before Candace yanked Martha to the ground.

Chapter Thirty-Seven

A grip like steel clasped Martha's ankle and yanked. She kicked backwards, struck an arm and came free from Roe's grasp. Another shot blasted the land like a clap of thunder. She squirmed forward, closing in on Candace who reached for her, then rolled upwards, hand already a fist.

"Bitch." The cry came from behind Martha: Roe bellowing it as Candace swung at him. Martha turned over, pulling her knees up, and saw Candace strike Roe in the mouth. Blood squirted from his lips and he fell back, crying out.

"Get your heads down." That was Granger. He'd slid down the slope a few feet, dropping the shotgun as he fell, yelling for all of them to duck while more gunshots exploded overhead. Martha reached the side of Candace's head and hissed at her.

"Gun."

Candace looked back to where Roe had found his weapon and was bringing it round to bear on them.

"No," Candace said.

Grunting from below as Granger tried to come back up the slope without lifting his body from the incline. The sky a spinning sheet. The deep hurt of knowing Dumah was not with them to put his fist into the mouths of these men and pull on their tongues and teeth until they shrieked and his hand was a puddle of red.

"Up," Candace whispered and Martha grasped her sister's strong arm, rising with her as Roe yelled for them to get down or he'd shoot and Granger screamed Roe's name.

Side by side, Candace and Martha stood in full view of any shooter. A few hundred feet away, the farmhouse was the only possible shelter and the only location someone could fire from without being seen.

Martha understood the speeding run of Candace's thoughts.

Woods or farm?

Granger and Roe wouldn't be able to rise and shoot, not without offering their slow, stupid bodies as targets.

And if the shooter was aiming at all of them?

Then they'd die but at least they would die hand in hand and attempting to live, not at the hands of these men.

Woods or farm?

Martha decided for both of them.

She gripped Candace's fingers, pulled and ran. Seconds later, they parted, a gap between them while they sprinted in a loose pattern and Granger roared for them to stop, to come back and the air whistled past their ears.

They fled from the men with their guns, Martha asking the Jesus for protection and his love while their feet on the ground was as much thunder as the gunfire that could blow them into pieces at any second.

Chapter Thirty-Eight

Somehow, Roe had made it ahead of Granger when they bolted from the farmland and the gunfire. Even while they skirted the abandoned and useless vehicles, every second promising more shots aimed at their heads, he'd managed to run several steps in front, going at an undignified shuffle between cars until he hit the grass and then raced for the cover of the treeline. Pretending he wasn't out of breath, Granger followed and knocked branches aside to move further into the woods. Several feet of undergrowth and sloping between their backs and the road, he slid to a stop and called Roe's name. Roe looked back, still struggling onwards, and bashed into a wide elm. He leaned on it, panting, shaking.

"Far enough," Granger said and broke already crumbling foliage as he approached Roe. Although less than two minutes had elapsed since the first shot cracked through the late afternoon, it already felt much later. What little sunlight there was failed to break through the cover of the merging branches high overhead and while there wasn't much in the way of leaves to act as a shield from the sky, the woods were older than he'd imagined. Hundreds of ancient ash trees, bowed but not broken by the damage done to the environment, kept the surrounding area pregnant with gloom.

Granger looked back the way they'd run, seeing the clear signs of their track through the green and dirt. Their packs were out of sight and he had to hope they could get back to their diminishing supplies of food and water. If not, they wouldn't make it. It was as simple as that.

He drew a few breaths, each one sharp in his chest, and took steps towards the grass and the farmland.

"Where are you going?" Roe cried and had to cough hard.

"Our supplies. We won't make it to Dover without them."

Roe coughed again and when he spoke, whatever illness affected his lungs seemed to have vanished.

"Fuck Dover."

Granger turned back to Roe, facing the man he'd known for more years than he could remember. A lifetime of politics, decisions, choices made and lives lost and saved from those choices. Roe, the quiet man; Roe, the man of the background who'd somehow survived the dog eat dog world of their jobs by always keeping his head down.

Roe. One of the few to make it through a country on fire. A world set alight. And while countless others Granger had known in his old life were now ash, Roe had kept going by being the man he'd always been.

Quiet. In control.

Control, Granger thought and no word had ever sounded so meaningless.

He made no move towards Roe and kept a poker face. Around them, the last of the afternoon died, letting in the evening and all its biting teeth to the woods. Out on the road, there'd still be another ten minutes of daylight and that light might as well have belonged to a memory.

"We are doing this, Roe." Granger spoke as if addressing a frightened dog. "It's all we have. Dover. Dealey. A life with government. And to get that, we take them—" He stabbed the shotgun towards the road. "We take them and we prove who we are and what we can still do. Old men we might be, Roe, but we are still who we were. We know what's best and we do that for everyone. Always have, Roe."

Roe cleared his throat which became a coughing fit. Bent double, he spat and coughed again. Granger stayed where he was, waiting for the storm to pass. When Roe stood straight again, he saw the splatters of red staining the milk-white of Roe's chin.

"For God's sake, Roe. Look at you. You're coughing up blood but you're still here. Still standing. And you can be helped just as you're helping others. Dover—"

"Dover?" Roe interrupted and spat again. The spittle stuck weeds. "You think Dover is anything? Patterson was right. It's nothing. We are nothing, Granger. Not anymore."

"Patterson never cared." More of the weak light had faded. In a minute or two, Granger would be addressing a silhouette. "Not even a little bit. Willis was never interested in anything except what he wanted. You and I, Roe, we're different. We keep going. Willis, he was powered by anger and hate. Patterson was built on regret. I always knew that. Even before the bunkers and. . .what happened with his daughter. He lived to punish himself, but you and I, we know what's best so *we keep going.*"

Roe crushed leaves as Granger had a moment ago. He stopped when two steps separated them.

"Patterson knew it was all pointless," he muttered. "And Willis was a monster. Willis made Patterson who he was and—"

"No, he didn't."

The faint emphasis Granger put on his second word was barely discernible but it was enough.

There was a moment that could have been less than a second or longer than a century; he didn't know which or care in the slightest. Everything he possessed was in their little patch of woodland with the dying daylight and all of Roe's understanding in the jerking movement of his gun coming up to shake as he aimed at Granger's chest.

"You did it," Roe croaked. *"You."*

Granger said the name he had not uttered in almost ten years. "Lisa."

He kept his shotgun at his side, waiting to see what Roe would do.

Waiting to see if Roe would punish him for his wicked crime so long before.

Chapter Thirty-Nine

Martha's small fingers clinging to Candace's sole hand, they raced away from Granger and Roe. The farm buildings drew closer with every second, Candace convinced gunfire would come from ahead or behind.

Her throat and lungs burned. They ran on, Martha needing no encouragement to move faster and Candace unable to give it. Every breath was fire. Even so, she increased her speed, the child at her side doing the same. Dirty green whipped by, grey light turning into pulsing beats. They shot over a destroyed fence, hit gravel and the main door to the farmhouse flew open.

An old woman, horribly skinny, emerged. Despite her frailty, she held a rifle with surety and strength.

"In," she cried in a crow's caw.

There was no chance of running anywhere else with Granger behind. Candace and Martha pounded over tiny stones and weeds and bore down on the house's entrance. The woman stood aside at the last second, her rifle still aimed the way they'd run. Seconds from the house, Candace pushed Martha to her back and raced into the building. The instant they were both inside, she yanked Martha to her side. Moving with surprising grace and speed, the woman sprung through the door and yanked it shut.

"Help me lock it," she shouted and tried to slide a heavy bolt across the top of the door while not dropping the weapon.

Not wanting to let go of Martha, Candace pulled the girl with her. She grabbed the bolt and realised the woman still held it. Their skin touched.

Both women pushed and the bolt slid smoothly.

"Down there, too." The woman pointed with a shaking finger to the bottom of the door. Martha slammed the second bolt into place.

"Good. That'll help. Keep away from the windows."

Barrel of the weapon aimed at the floor and one gnarled finger close to the trigger, the woman pressed against the wall beside the door. A window, whole but coated in smeary dirt, let in light.

"Nothing. They'll come, though. They always do." She appraised Candace and Martha. Candace tried to stifle her gasps and failed. Giving up on the attempt, Candace inhaled deeply, let it out and took another. Martha mimicked her and the woman smiled.

A few small holes had been cut into the wall and while they let in bursts of cold air, they also acted as spyholes. Ignoring them for the moment, the elderly woman lifted binoculars from a battered table and held them to her eyes as she looked through the mucky glass.

"They're on the move. Going to the woods by the looks. Two of them, yes?"

"Two men," Martha said and Candace recognised the hunger in the tone.

"Two men," the woman echoed. "Into the woods. They'll hide there."

She waited another moment before pulling away and standing. "I don't need to know your life story. I see men with guns walking with a woman and a girl and I know what's what. I watched you for long enough."

Seeing Candace's frown, she pointed to the ceiling. "Up there. With these." She waved her binoculars. "I have a good view for miles around. Not that there's usually much to see but the odd dying sheep or the birds." She smiled and it was more like a grimace.

"I see men with guns walking with a woman and a child and I. . ." She sighed. It trembled in her throat before she rejected any potential upset or tears. "They'll come and we'll deal with them."

"You saved us," Candace said and thought of Priest.

"I suppose I did. My name's Joanna."

An instant of loose memories and emotions passed through Candace, the sensation almost completely alien. It was –

Before.

A lifetime ago. A world outside this one and it all belonged to someone she no longer knew; a name and a life before –

"Candace." She whispered her name, owning it as much as she had for close to ten years.

"That's nice." If Joanna noticed any pause, she hid it. "What's yours?" she asked Martha.

The girl said nothing, instead moving closer to Candace and entwining their fingers. Candace let Martha pretend to be too shy to speak, willing her not to act without instruction. She eyed Joanna's gun, uncomfortably reminded of the boy George back at the school. Like Joanna, he'd held a rifle with a sight jutting from the top of the weapon. Hers was clearly more advanced than his although it still showed signs of damage: a crack in the sight and a spiderweb thin crack running down the barrel. Candace wasn't fast enough to hide her appraisal from Joanna.

"It's old but it's got some life left in it," she said and grimaced. "I'm not the best shot in the world, but the sight helps. Not many bullets left, either, but let's just keep that between us, eh?"

Moving closer to the little window and wincing with the few steps, she held the binoculars to her face again, giving Candace a second to study the interior of the farmhouse.

Dark. Stone. Heavy beams. A wide fireplace devoid of any flame. A dozen ornaments and old photos decorating it. Another window at the far end of the room and a second in the kitchen, both sealed with broken chunks of wood. Two tatty armchairs, their feet and arms frayed as if clawed by a cat. A wide dinner table and a mixture of chairs around it. Stairs in the corner with little visible beyond the third step.

Taking it all in without moving her head, Candace noted the second door which presumably opened to the rear of the property. A set of rusting keys jutted from the lock.

"I've been here for a long time. This is my place." Joanna spoke while still peering towards the woods. "Don't see a lot of people. Not out here. I have a few animals. Two chickens. A cow whose best years are behind her. They give me what I need and I use that to exchange for what I can. It's best part of a day's walk to the nearest people. They don't want me with them and I'm not leaving my house so we just make our trades and leave it at that."

Seemingly satisfied Granger and Roe were not about to launch an attack, she lowered the binoculars and studied Candace.

"It's ugly. Everywhere. Men like that with their guns. They take what they want and they don't care about who gets hurt. It's all they know they how to do. Before the bombs, after the bombs. It's all the same to them."

For no reason she knew, Candace said: "Dover."

Joanna pursed her lips and placed the binoculars on the table. "Dover? You were going there?"

Candace nodded once and wished to be faraway from Joanna's calm eyes, friendly and a deep brown. Even with her advanced age, she had a strength in her face. Lines and wrinkles, skin and bones – none of it mattered. Her eyes were aware and thinking.

"Well, don't. Dover is. . . it's not the town it used to be. I know it's not far from here." She glanced at the window as if she saw across the quiet miles to the edge of the country. "But it's not a town for anyone, now. Stay away from it."

She tightened her threadbare coat. "We'll make a fire in a few minutes. I don't like to make smoke but your gentlemen friends know we're here so it makes no odds." Joanna addressed Martha again. "Would you like a fire?"

Martha nodded and her index finger stole to her mouth where she sucked on the tip. Prickly cold crept over the back of Candace's neck at the sight.

"Good." Joanna crouched, hissing at the strain on her knees. "Now. What's your name?"

"Hungry," Martha replied.

Joanna blinked, then her mouth parted. For the first time in what could have been months or years, she laughed.

Candace did not laugh.

Chapter Forty

Lazarus's awareness had been reduced to three points.

The night falling through the windows lit by two candles near the cell entrance and how it pressed against his eyes as if wanting to get inside his skull.

The terrible smell of Priest's body on the floor.

Mary's screams from the other end of the cells.

Unable to battle against any of it, Lazarus crouched close to the door and gripped it. The mossy stink from the walls made each breath taste foul. He ran nails down the hard surface and imagined stabbing through it to the open space beyond, pulling it from its frame and hurling the door into the opposite wall.

More screams, so close and so far out of reach. No words in Mary's pain, no muttering voice from Willis. Whatever he was doing to the child, he was doing so without speaking or yelling. Perhaps to hear her better or perhaps because he didn't have the strength to speak.

Lazarus had to hope for the latter as much as he hoped the man would drop down dead right now.

Mary screeched like an animal being torn in two.

Heat brushed Lazarus's cheeks. He was crying and there was no way to stop the tears because there was no way of stopping his sister's torment. Barely aware of his own movement, he rocked back and forth, still with a palm pressed on the door and swallowing the moss-smell dripping down the walls to the stagnant puddles and Priest's remains. Lazarus sank into himself, chasing a darkness far below where no tears or screams would reach him, but not a total darkness. Something lived below, a tiny spark of a fire come to warm his skin and bones from the non-stop chill of every day.

"Mary."

Nothing.

Lazarus said her name again, dry throat catching on the word.

Willis had not killed her. Lazarus was sure of it. While the man obviously didn't have a lot of time remaining, he would want to make the most of it. That meant Mary suffering, not dead.

"Mary."

Lazarus bellowed it, jumped to his feet and gripped the broken hole in the centre of the door that had once held a panel of glass. He tried to shake it and succeeded only in making the hinges squeal and sending flakes of rust pattering to the puddles on the floor. Fresh tears fell. He tasted them and the dirt around his mouth, and the salt stung the cracks in his tongue.

Head bowed, Lazarus wept.

When the gloom from a few moments before returned, the small fire burning deep below his mind, he sank towards it if only to escape the screams that were coming again before long. Drawing closer to the spark, he realised something wonderful and terrible.

The fire was Priest.

Lazarus knew it before he fell all the way down into the hole of his mind, the dance of the flames spreading wider, growing brighter the further he fell, the closer he came to its reds and yellows.

Priest, down there and waiting for him.

There was no fear as he dropped, no need for panic as he spread his arms and opened his mouth to feel and taste the fire. It struck his fingers and he closed them in a death grip, the burning solid in his fists, the fire like sunlight slipping down his throat to burn him from the inside.

Lazarus opened his eyes. The fire was out and in its place was Priest. They gazed at each other, the white on all sides still calming. More than calming, the featureless surroundings took away all emotion and that could only be a good thing. Otherwise, Lazarus thought he might sob until he dried into a piece of stone. Priest, here. Priest, the man within touching distance.

"You are in trouble, Lazarus," Priest said.

"I know."

"No. You don't. Not completely." Priest had rarely shouted at Lazarus or any of the others and that had not changed now he was dead. Instead, he spoke firmly despite the growl in his voice. *Growths,* he'd called them. Growths in his throat pressing on his words before they came out of his mouth.

"The man who is hurting Mary will hurt her for as long as he can. Then he'll kill you. He's dying so he has no fear. Only those who have something to hope for are scared. His hope is long gone and so will yours if you don't kill him first."

"How?" There was still no panic or grief Lazarus could get a grip upon. Maybe it would have been better had he been able to hurt. He'd wept for Priest, and those tears had eventually sunk inside to heat his chest. Now, he wanted to rage at Priest for dying, for leaving them alone when everything no longer made any sense.

Instead of answering the question, Priest spoke without opening his mouth. Images Lazarus didn't fully understand or recognise swam on all sides and even as he tried to focus on one, his eyes were moving to the next, then moving again.

Light, so much light and not all of it from the sun. Where there was an insane degree of sunshine (probably more than Lazarus had seen since he was a tiny child), there was also beams of white shooting from the fronts of cars, actual *moving* cars that looked the same as all the wrecks and burned chunks of metals he'd encountered in the towns they'd raided. Cars and larger vehicles full of people sitting together, and everything moving at speeds that seemed too fast to be real.

The people, so many people, more people than could surely fit in the world. They walked on pavements, in pleasant parks; they filled houses unmarked by fire, windows unbroken, and their gardens tidy and healthy. People all around, smiling people with their clothing unsoiled by mud or blood; no tears and rips in their coats and sweaters letting in the cold air.

And around the people and the streets and buildings, sunlight and illumination from ceilings merged into one sun on the earth that brightened every inch of the world.

It was a light Lazarus knew. A memory from his earliest days tremored between his hands, too slight for him to hold. He saw the ghost of an image—a car on a twisting road, dozens of others moving in the same direction, others coming from the opposite way while Lazarus's eye tried to stick with the particular car, the red one with the shining roof and clean windows he liked to look out of from the back seat, watching the familiar and welcome streets of his home passing by as they went from. . .

From. . .

Home.

It was gone and the faces of the two people in the front, the man and the pretty woman, went with it, just another car in the flow, the non-stop movement and the eternity of the sun becoming a hell.

All the light he'd marvelled at blossomed into a blinding whiteness a thousand times brighter than the surroundings he shared with Priest, and his eyes had no chance against it. Instead, they consumed every mote of the white, always hungry for more and more. He couldn't scream because he had no mouth; he was only his eyes staring into the sun that lived on the surface of the world and high above it at the same time.

I remember.

"I know you do."

Lazarus blinked. He hadn't spoken but Priest had replied all the same. The white and the world from before were gone, leaving him in the same position. Priest traced a pattern in the air. For a moment, his finger caught on sunlight shining from nothing and Lazarus saw the suggestion of a face, there and gone in the time it took him to say a name.

"Dumah."

"Dumah is dead."

The flat statement brought hurt but it was a hurt that belonged to someone else. They described it to Lazarus: a story of another's memory and no matter how much it had caused them agony, all he had was his imagination of it.

"No." The automatic reply was the only one Lazarus could give.

"The man in charge. Granger. He and his friend killed him. He has Candace and Martha and he will kill them eventually."

"No."

Something was happening to the surrounding white. A darkening, a weak grey in places. At the same time, the pain from a moment before snuck closer and became more his own rather than a second-hand sensation. Even as it was welcome to feel something, it was a horrible, creeping flood of dirty water drowning his feet, now up to his shins, higher, higher.

"No."

Tears exploded, and the emotions that had either been taken from him or been left outside before he came to Priest returned in a detonation. He was buried alive in grief and loss.

No Dumah no not Dumah not Dumah as well I can't I can't please no Dumah come back to us come back come—

The embers of a dying fire were right in front of him, then below because he was rising. Lazarus floated, his body weightless. Priest was gone; only the spark and occasional splutter of flame from the fire shone. The white had vanished with Priest. Black above and on every side had taken their place.

You are kin. You are survivors and you will survive. Go to the new government; go to the men in Dover and show them who you are.

No, please. I can't without you. Dumah. Please bring him back.

Priest's voice right in Lazarus's ear: "He is gone, my son, and so am I, but you can use me. Use me, Lazarus."

The embers were little more than pinpricks, and what was left of the fire brought no warmth. All Lazarus knew was the familiar chill of exposed flesh meeting unbroken air.

His arse on the rock-hard floor. His hands like ice. The awful stink of his body, the moisture on the walls, the stiffening corpse beside him. With him.

Lazarus listened. If Willis was anywhere near, he made no sound. Lazarus had to be believe the man was resting from his torture of Mary, sleeping now in a room up in the hallway. Lazarus mouthed his sister's name and could do no more for her. Not until he killed Willis.

He rubbed his hands together until he generated some warmth, then used the light of the candles to bring his fingers to the wounds in Priest's palms.

No palms. Just holes and stumps and broken pieces of loose bone and all of it covered in flesh turned hard from the cold and the inescapable fact of Priest no longer being their father but now as dead as anyone else in the world.

Lazarus set to work on Priest's fingers.

It took some time.

But eventually, the little cell echoed for a second with the crack of a bone snapping free.

Chapter Forty-One

Perhaps it was the middle of the night or perhaps dawn would come in the next half an hour. Roe couldn't tell either way and found he didn't particularly care. All he knew was his watch could have been going on for an hour or five. Time had ceased to exist while the last of the embers in their fire went from glowing red to a fading glimmer, and the fog, creeping from field to road to woods with sly speed, found every hole in his coat and every thin fibre in the scarf encasing his mouth and nose. Shifting position did little to alleviate the chill. As his movement was the only sound other than Granger's weak snores and occasional grunts, he was better off keeping still. Arms wrapped around his narrow chest, gloved hands shoved tight under his armpits, Roe stared at the surrounding night and wondered if anyone was staring back at him. Ordinarily, the thought would have been terrifying, but it appeared he'd gone beyond fear. Now the image of staring eyes belonging to a motionless figure who'd be happy to see him stabbed to death was a mere curiosity. Maybe he'd see them advance through the trees, a shadowy shape clutching a knife, their feet making no sound as they came like a ghost and the branches parted for them.

Come on if you're coming.

Granger let out another of his rumbling grunts.

Roe's mouth curled in what would have been a smile back in his past but now felt like a twitch.

Back in the past. Yes. Absolutely. Back when he'd known who he was and what his life was. A life of his house in Surrey, and his wife Alison and their boys. A perfect middle-class life on the surface of things; a cold disaster underneath. He lived in the office most of the week, returning home for the occasional meal and a few hours of telly with Kelvin and Marcus made uncomfortable by knowing they would much rather be out with their friends. Alison said she understood his work although he'd often suspected she had a lover in the City. If that was true, then so be it. He wasn't thrilled about the idea or the occasional mental image of her with another man, the two of them in a doubtless swanky hotel, but he could understand his wife if she had. He had his job and all that came with it especially as the business between the Soviets and the Yanks rapidly went tits up. Alison would have needed something he could not give her.

Alison. I am sorry. I really am.

There was little point in apologising to a memory. She wouldn't even be a body now. The first of the bombs would have seen to that—turning his wife into nothing just as it did the same to the world of his past. Nice house, the cars, the suits, the office and all the business conducted there with the PM and the military men and every piece of that life vaporised. In the void leftover, he'd been trapped where time jumped from a day in April to right now in the woods while he watched and hoped for his death.

He was a time traveller, ejected from his known years to this one. And how long was it, really? An entire decade? That seemed right but it could be more. He'd honestly lost track. A needle jumping on a record; a car skidding on ice and coming off the road; a blacked-out night from one of his long-ago days at Cambridge when drinking was a fact of life. He'd been thrown forward in time, a man from the past lost in a future become his hellish present.

Roe rose and his knees cracked. Soggy ground sucking at his boots, he turned around and made out Granger close to the ashes of the fire. He'd curled into a ball and pulled the collar of his coat up to the scarf covering his lower face.

Roe stared at the motionless man, aware of the night's cold as an abstract thing. The same with the shotgun he held.

Everything a waste. The words were in his head again, full of sorrow and a tired anger.

Roe raised the shotgun and aimed it at Granger's head. One round left. It was all he needed.

"I wasn't a bad man." The sibilant was a snake's hiss. "I really wasn't. I wanted to do good things; I wanted the best for people. I know people said we were all the same and they couldn't trust us, but I really tried, Granger. I did. But you. . . you were all about yourself. You never. . ."

If there was anything else to be said aloud, it trailed off into the smoke that oozed from his mouth and nose to merge with the fog. The night made his throat tickle, or maybe it was more blood threatening to spill over his lips the next time he coughed.

The same mad time that had transported him from his own place to whatever world this was slowed to a halt. He didn't breathe. He didn't blink. There was no need for either because he'd left his body holding the gun on Granger and he existed outside all of it. In his nothing-place, Roe saw his finger tighten on the trigger.

Everything went away and a memory took its place, or rather the fading outline of a memory: the family room with the curtains drawn against the afternoon sun, turning the space and most of the back of the house into a sauna; Alison at his side and a rare time he could spend at home, Kelvin and Marcus laying on the floor and the TV on, a film the boys had begged him to get from the video shop. *The Goonies.* The screen showing the adventures of a gang of American kids; pirates and danger and family of criminals and the boys coming together to save the day and their town while Roe watched his children watch the film and felt the good, clean weight of Alison against his arm and smelled the late summer sun baking their home.

Roe wept for his wife and sons and for the man he'd been once upon a time. He wept for being as weak as Granger had always thought him to be; he wept for his present and for what Granger had done to that poor girl back at the beginning of their hell.

Fear.

It was a new voice in his head. Oddly, it sounded more like Granger's wife Carolyn than his own voice or even Alison's. He cocked his head, held the shotgun on Granger and listened.

Fear, Roe. That's what kept you going. It's what kept you on your feet for so long. Patterson wanted his punishment; Willis was just too stupid to know when to stop and you're too scared of what comes after to do anything about your life.

"I should have died." There was no agreement other than the scratch of the few leaves brushing on each other. Down on the ground, Granger snored once and that was it. Beside him, his shotgun merged with the floor of the woods and was almost lost from sight.

"You were always in charge." Roe wanted to shout it at the sleeping man. Instead, he barely heard his own voice. "Your rule. Your law and order." He snorted in derision, the ugly noise shockingly loud in the woods. Again, the leaves rustled.

"That's what keeps you going while I'm just a coward."

His index finger tightened on the trigger. A fraction increase of pressure and the woods would echo for miles with the crash of his shot.

He couldn't do it. Fear, his old favourite friend, stilled his hand. Fear of seeing Granger's head detonate and fear of becoming a new man. While there was no doubt Granger deserved to die for what he had done to Patterson's daughter, Roe was not the man to bring that punishment down.

Time started again. Roe eased his finger from the trigger. His hand cramped and he held his hand beside his hip in a clenched fist, his left fingers wrapped around the barrel of the shotgun.

Granger snorted. For a spinning moment, Roe thought Granger would wake and there would be less than a second to get his cramping fingers back to the trigger. Instead, Granger settled and lay still. It was only then that Roe tasted the wild electricity in his spit and registered the cramp in his bowels.

The pain in his fist finally easing, Roe carefully transferred the gun to his other hand, kept the barrel hanging towards the ground and thought of Granger's firm voice hours earlier, detailing his crime without embellishment or excuse. He'd known what he was;

he'd known it was a terrible thing and all he had to offer was his weakness of being a younger man.

Roe spat what little saliva he had near Granger's head and Granger stirred for a few seconds, grumbling nonsense, before settling again.

Roe turned his back on Granger, faced the impenetrable fog in which he'd imagined eyes staring back at him and wondered what would kill him first. Exposure. Some random person out in the countryside who'd stab him literally for the clothes on his back. Or the lung cancer eating him up.

Roe walked into the white swirling between the trees and welcomed it as it welcomed him.

Chapter Forty-Two

Managing the keys and the thin torch in one hand was a struggle, but Willis was nothing if not adaptable. Plus, he didn't need to take the Browning from his coat pocket while Mary was unconscious on the shitty mattress that had been stinking and rotting in the cell for a decade.

He pulled on the cell door, shutting it with gentle care, then fumbled with the keys to lock it. Peering through the glass in its centre, he made out nothing but darkness like a wall and shone the torch through it. In the second before the weak beam found Mary on the bunk, he expected the girl to be inches from his face, mouth open in a terrible snarl and her lips and teeth streaked with blood.

No such thing. She was where he'd left her, curled into a small ball, clutching her right hand. Willis studied his remaining hand, wondering if he'd gone too far with the kid. Blood on his coat sleeve; blood on his legs; blood in his nose and swimming in the stinking air.

Killing her was one thing; cutting off a finger was another.

Can't take it back now.

He tested the handle and satisfied she had no way out, he walked towards the boy in the cell at the other end, stopping when dizziness turned his vision into a rolling, spinning wave and nausea spread through his stomach. A white flash went off behind his eyes, bringing a burst of clarity.

Dying. You are dying.

Willis bit his lip until the pain made the nausea less of an issue and blinked again and again. While he was cold deep into his bones, he felt a little clearer and spat to the puddles until the last of the sickness left his belly.

Dying. There was no getting away from that. While he didn't feel any fear, there was a frozen anger at being killed by a child, an inhuman child to boot. He'd considered death and all its glories for a long time. Even before the bombs, Willis had known he'd die in a way that mattered. Saving others; taking out an almost unstoppable threat; leading the men through some final danger before they reached the safety of Dover.

But this shit.

This shit was not fair. Not right. Not for him.

He groaned. Negation changed fuck all. He was still burning up, still with his arm a sick throb from stump to shoulder, and still with the horrible pulsing red radiating up from where his hand used to be. All the painkillers and fresh bandages in the world wouldn't change that.

"Fuck," he whispered and it made his throat want to weep. It felt like sweat had managed to coat every millimetre of his skin, turning his body into a clammy piece of meat that managed to be the heat of a sun at the same time it was the exposed land made frosty by a winter moon.

I don't have any time left.

The reply was immediate.

So, kill them now.

The Browning seemed to weigh much more than usual in his coat pocket; the gun was cold on his hip even through the thinning material. That was okay. It meant the weapon was close to hand.

Hand that's a good one what fucking hand?

He sniggered, not caring that he wasn't sure why did so, and stumbled on a loose section of flooring and bashed into the side wall. He laughed again. Not bothering to check the floor, he made it to even ground, splashed through puddles and coughed out the reek of the fungus growing in corners as well as the horrible smell of his feverish body.

"Lazarus," he whispered and tapped on the cell holding the boy prisoner. If the kid was still conscious, he wasn't saying much.

"Fucker." Willis bared his teeth at the door and pulled the handgun free. Levelling it at the little opening in the door while still carrying the torch and keys proved difficult, the movement not helped by the sweat dribbling into his eyes or the dance of his vision.

"You awake in there, son?" he called and attempted to shine the torch through the opening. He came within seconds of dropping torch, gun and keys and pressed the lot to his belly for a moment.

He needed a better shot. A clear shot.

Grinning, spit on his tongue doing little to alleviate his thirst, Willis clamped the torch between his teeth and used the illumination as a guide to stab the key into the lock while still holding the Browning.

Locks clanked.

Biting the torch and swinging the beam towards the opening door, Willis brought the gun up.

The movement of the door went from a glide to a shove and the last of his thinking mind shrieked

he's coming shoot him shoot him jesus christ

and Willis fired as a darting movement sped towards his face. He turned at the last second, felt a horrendous stinging, *scraping* enter his throat and his mouth was awash with blood.

He managed to lift his injured arm, smashed his elbow into Lazarus's chest and knocked the boy backwards. Choking, Willis flung his full weight on the door and it swung closed as Lazarus jumped at the other side. Willis heard the boy cry out at the fierce impact. Hand slick, throat feeling as it was full of wasps, Willis slammed his fingers on the keys and turned.

Locks clanked again as Lazarus bashed into the door and shoved a hand through the opening. Nails tore at Willis's face, missing his eyes by a fraction. Blood poured from his mouth; he tripped and went down to the wet ground, jarring his hand and tipping to his side. Above, Lazarus screamed through the opening in the door, howling for Mary, cursing Willis while all Willis could do was bleed and focus the last of his strength on the sight of the furthest cell door.

The one keeping the girl from him.

Willis began to crawl.

Chapter Forty-Three

They were talking in low voices, Candace and the old woman. Joanna. That was her name. The first part of the name was its own; the end was like Martha's but not Mary's. She missed her sister in a way that made her chest hurt, but listening to their soft conversation a short distance away helped to take her mind from the separation of her family. At no point before the events in the school had Martha believed she and Candace wouldn't be back with Mary, Dumah and Lazarus soon. Now Dumah was gone to the same place as Priest and one of the bad men had taken Mary and Lazarus. They'd be together again soon, though. She knew that as well as she knew who she was and that Candace was probably aware Martha was pretending to sleep. Even so, she stayed curled into a ball on the sofa, her ears on their voices and the gentle crackle of the fire Joanna had lit.

"You are both healthy," Joanna said. "You and the girl. That is strange. Good, but strange."

Martha listened for how Candace replied with more focus than on the exact words. A lot could be given away in a person's tone and manner. It was a strange concept to her child's mind but one which Priest had been firm on teaching her and Mary.

"We hide," Candace murmured. "In caves. We don't drink dirty water or eat the trees. The bombs, they. . .made them diseased."

"Yes." Joanna sounded as if she was nodding. "All of it out there is filthy. You two are lucky not to be badly hurt. That graze in your head, it should be fine if you keep it covered. Even a small cut can get infected these days." She laughed gently. "Then there's the radiation to worry about but I think that's mostly gone from the air now. Doesn't stop sickness or poor health, of course. My eyes are fine, would you believe, but my stomach hurts more every day. I urinate blood sometimes. You are a lucky woman even if you are missing an arm."

Martha sensed Candace shift in her chair, uncomfortable with the mention of a matter that belonged only to them and their brothers.

"You see people?" Candace asked. "They come here?"

"Rarely." Joanna sounded like the idea of other people made her uncomfortable and Martha understood that. "There was a village not too faraway although *village* is probably pushing it. Twenty people. Thirty, perhaps. They had little in the way of food and supplies. Mostly stuff they'd taken from the towns near Calcott. I'd give them eggs or a chicken; they'd give me something in exchange. All gone now, though."

"Why?" Candace asked and there was nothing in reply. Along with the fire, Joanna had lit three candles and placed them on the table. Martha opened a single eye, studying Candace and the old woman in the flickering light. The orange shine bounced off a mirror over the cold fireplace and made the shadows of the table and chairs into giant pools.

Eventually, Joanna answered Candace with a quiet, reflective tone.

"I don't know what happened. I went there a month after my last visit. This was. . .three months ago. There was nobody there, just bloodstains on walls." Joanna sounded matter of fact but only on the surface. "There wasn't enough blood for everyone there to have been hurt or died." She spoke in a softer tone. Still, her words carried to Martha. "A lot of blood, but not enough. Some were killed; others ran, I think."

"Where was this?" Candace whispered and Martha knew. She remembered the place if not its name. Names weren't important.

"Six miles away. Seven, maybe. South from here."

Their raid on the village had been quick, an attack hours before dawn and their knives and axes finding men and women and children in their beds. Metal struck heads and limbs, hacked at flesh and bone while screams and shrieks merged into one hellish note. Some had fought back but not many and not for long. Dumah had smashed skulls together and used someone's head to break a window in the house used as a refuge by four boys. The children had fled into the fields where Mary and Martha waited for them. The whole attack had lasted a matter of minutes. Several men had escaped into the surrounding land; Priest said to let them go and Martha had surprised herself by wondering if their father was right to do so. Others would hear of the attack which might make further raids more difficult. Seeing her doubt, Priest had said they fought on their terms which didn't involve running blindly into the night. Martha had said she was sorry to which Priest laughed and said no apology was needed. They'd eaten well and taken food back to the cliffs where Mary and Martha heard all the details of the raid information readying them for the next attack. But of course, the food hadn't lasted. It never did.

"Candace?"

Martha watched Joanna's hand rest lightly on Candace's. Despite the night, Joanna looked as if she radiated as much heat as the little fire. Martha wondered if the warmth came from the woman's cancers, the sickness generating warmth from eating away at all the goodness inside Joanna's organs. Martha knew all about tumours and the promise of death. Priest had suffered with them in his throat and chest along with his bad eye. Cancer was life; she knew that and so there was no sorrow for the old woman who had let them into her home.

Candace said: "I think we passed an empty village. With the men."

"Probably you did."

Martha risked opening both eyes. She didn't know why she wanted Candace and the old woman to believe she was asleep; the instinct she never questioned told her to and that was enough.

In the little light cast by the candles on the table, the two women were close together, and the fire sent their shadows high up the wall to merge into a single pool. Martha had a profile view of Joanna. The woman's mouth opened in a grimace, the movement echoed in the change in her tone.

"Those men who had you prisoner. It wouldn't surprise me if what happened in that village was down to them. Animals, all of them. They destroyed the world and they'd do it again given half a chance. Life isn't anything to them. Anyone who isn't with them is worth nothing. They'd have killed you and the girl eventually but not before. . ." She trailed off for a moment and Martha had need to hear the missing words. She'd known for as long as she could remember what men could do. She and Mary had seen it happen before Priest came to them and while they'd been spared that particular horror, she knew exactly what Joanna was talking about.

"Animals." Joanna's voice grew softer. "Each and every one of them."

"They are," Candace muttered.

Out of nowhere, Martha thought of Priest's last moments and the police cells echoing with the gunshots and the screams. The sudden sting of tears made her close her eyes for a few seconds. When she opened them again, Joanna had moved. She had her back to the sofa to face the boarded-up window and Candace had lowered her head, appearing uncharacteristically weak.

"They won't leave without trying to get you. You know that," Joanna said.

Candace lifted her head and Martha closed her eyes again. It wasn't lying to Candace to pretend she slept. It was. . .necessary even if she had idea no why.

"I know," Candace said and Martha opened one eye again. Joanna had shifted closer to the fire, warming her hands, while Candace kept her head down at the window where the night was becoming the sickly grey of morning.

"I don't have a great deal in the way of weapons. Just the gun and a few knives, but it could be enough if we were lucky," Joanna said.

"You want to kill them?" Candace asked.

"I don't like it. Never have, but. . ." Joanna sighed. "Life isn't what it used to be, is it? We all get bloody at some point." She rubbed a finger below her eyes in a quick slashing motion and it took Martha a second to realise the older woman had wiped away a few tears.

"Out there, it's all gone, but it can't be the same everywhere. I often think that." Joanna's ire was gone for now. In its place, a regret Martha was too young to fully understand. There was something else; a suggestion behind Joanna's tone she recognised but couldn't name. While she'd never heard the word *wistful* before, she had known the emotion when she'd been younger and they'd all been in the caves, the fire lit, bellies full of meat and the air redolent with the smell of blood from whoever they'd killed.

"I think sometimes if I were younger, I could go out further. All the way up the country to Scotland. Out into the wilds. The Highlands. Or across country to Wales. Out to the countryside there. I know it's spacious and open around here, but it's still close to what's left of the cities and towns. They're all rubble these days, but there are people there. People like the men who held you. I want to be away from that."

Candace murmured a reply Martha didn't catch. Neither did Joanna.

"What was that?" she asked and Martha suddenly felt cold.

Candace held her stump, a movement Martha knew she made when she was unsure or angry. She repeated herself a little louder.

"You could come with us."

Martha came within seconds of hissing her shock. She bit her tongue hard enough to taste a few drops of blood. Swallowing the salty taste, she stared at her sister, desperate to understand. Candace, Lazarus, Dumah, Mary and poor dead Priest – that was her family, not this old woman in her house so tiny under the blanket of the sky. They belonged to the caves and the millions of pebbles and stones on the sand just as much as they belonged to each other. Out here was nothing but the hunt for food, not for other members of their family because there were no other members of their family.

In the quiet after Candace's hesitant statement, a piece of Martha's childhood went to sleep and something that might one day grow into maturity woke. She knew what people like Granger and his friends thought of her and the others, and she knew they'd come together in a way that was not babies and birth. If the thing that made no sense actually happened and they gained another member of their family, would it be so different to how Priest had brought her and Mary into the arms of Candace, Lazarus and Dumah?

"I appreciate it," Joanna replied after what felt like hours of nothing. "But I can't. I'm unwell, dear. I'm not the girl I was. I can only walk for an hour before I'm ready to collapse and it's a long way to any safety. This is my house. It's my shelter and it will stay that way as long as I stay here."

"I understand," Candace said.

"I have to admit to being tempted, though." Joanna laughed with honest warmth, and Martha felt a brief of burst of affection for her, the sensation caught between pleasure and pain.

"I keep myself to myself," Joanna went on. "And doing that somewhere with no threat would be something special. I tell you, Candace. I've often thought about what happened to the rest of the world after the war. I'd like to find out. I'd go if I could. To the coast and find a small boat."

Watching Joanna, Martha wondered if the woman was still in the cottage or if she'd become lost in her own head. That was insanity. Martha knew people like the boy in the school were part of insanity. It meant a locked room in your mind where all the fear and bad things were trapped. That boy George being nice one second and then wanting to take Candace from them for the same reason as all men hurt women, he was insanity. So was Granger. And the other man. The big one Mary hurt in the cells. All of them insanity because they'd gone into their secret rooms and let the bad out. If Joanna was opening the door into her own room, even momentarily, they were in trouble.

Joanna went on. "Find a boat. Cross the sea and leave all this behind. The world is a big place, after all. I'd walk over all of it. Mountains, forests, ponds and rivers. I'd swim and walk and run. I'd find somewhere secret away from any cities." She wiped her eyes again. "Somewhere where I could see the sky. Somewhere with green and clean water. I'd get away from this place and people like those men out there and I'd stay in the sunlight."

On the sofa, Martha wanted to shake, to let the tremors rolling through her stomach fly into her arms and legs. Joanna was still talking, describing the land beyond the sea, the magic place where all was peaceful and warm. No mist or poison in the air in that new country. The world of spells. The realm of magic where the sun shone and any wind was warm and soft. Somewhere all the hunger went away.

Her world. Hers and the others because it had been given to them.

The need to shake died. She had control. She knew what needed to be done.

Martha was up and off the sofa in a second, bare feet gentle on the stone floor as she ran across the room. Martha's shadow was a misshapen stream; the flames in the grate were a merry jig and Candace was peering through the window, back to Joanna as the woman still went on about owning the land given to Martha by Priest.

Three seconds after leaving the sofa, she stood behind Joanna, long knife gripped in both hands and the blade aimed at Joanna's neck.

Candace began to turn and Martha shoved the knife forward.

It missed the prominent knobs of Joanna's spine but cut through flesh and scrawny muscle with ease. Joanna managed to stand for a moment before collapsing, hand reaching for her throat as her lower half went into spasms and her feet smashed against the floor in a mad beat. Blood pooled from the exit wound the knife had plugged until she fell, dislodging it. As the liquid spread into a puddle and turned her final noises into a mix of gagging and the thud of her feet on the floor, Candace dropped to Joanna's chest, slammed her weight on the woman, grabbed Joanna's head by a fistful of hair and yanked it around with a movement as sharp as it was smooth.

Joanna's neck broke, the momentary snap louder than the feet and the choking. Candace let go of the woman's head; it bounced on the floor, her eyes staring towards the door and the end of the knife scratching the wood below her body. Martha tugged on the knife, twisting it to ease it free. It cut tendons and muscle, grated on bone and popped clear. The tip dribbled blood. Martha wiped it on her hand.

"Why?" Candace asked.

Martha studied the body. Feeling as if it was a separate entity, her stomach rumbled.

Why. The one-word question with a million answers that all came down to nights from a year, two years, three or four behind. Martha had no real sense of time and while she knew was she'd been eight years old, the age meant little. Days became months; months became years. Time was simply a collection of the same day, and every year was its own long day.

At some point in the past, there'd been the caves on the beach and sheltering in those caves. The burning fire and her small tongue working at stringy pieces of meat stuck to her teeth; the meat of her tongue clever enough not to nick itself on each sharp tooth. Mary was beside her and Priest was behind them, long arms encasing her and her sister while he looked over their shoulders to the book he'd placed on the mossy rock.

He'd read them the stories in the book while they took it in turns to turn the pages swollen with sea air. Priest told them about people in the old days, the princes and princesses; the giants residing in the sky and the dragons who slept in the forests far beyond the sea outside their caves. While a story each night meant the few books Priest kept in his bags were done within a short time, Mary and Martha had insisted their father started again and he'd done so, low voice bringing a new land to life and promising them the stories belonged to that land beyond everything they knew.

Martha did her best to explain her memories and her thoughts. While her vocabulary had developed thanks to Priest as well as the others being sure to involve both girls in their conversations, the girl lacked the skills to fully explain what she felt and could only sum it up in a mutter.

"It's our world out there. Not hers."

Candace said nothing for a moment. Then: "You should not have done that, Martha."

Martha looked up at her sister and tried to process what she'd been told.

She couldn't do it.

Chapter Forty-Four

The floor of the cells was an ocean and the last door in the row was the other end of that giant sea. Willis would swim that ocean; even the blood flowing in a waterfall from his throat and pouring from his mouth wouldn't stop him. Everything turning grey wouldn't stop him. The only thing in the world he wanted was at the other end of the ocean of the floor.

Liquid splattered his knees and it took a moment's dazed thought to realise it was *his* blood soaking his trousers and turning his coat into a tacky mess; *his* blood pumping between his fingers and striking the wall; *his* blood jetting out of his body and bringing him closer to death with each passing second.

Devils had found him and while they'd come in the shape of children, they were still devils.

Sobbing, vision a shaking blur, Willis took another step. Then another. Somehow, he'd managed to keep hold of his little torch between his teeth, and the illumination was a dance of sickly yellow. It spun across the walls in a mad pattern and turned the grey doors into capering shadows. He made a strange noise that made him think of an injured bird and stumbled around to face Lazarus's cell. It remained securely locked. The boy continued to hammer and scream at the barrier, then punch through the opening in its centre. Willis tried to yell at the kid, to tell him his little plan had failed and Willis would not die from any poxy stab wound in his throat. He wanted to say the kid was an animal for violating his father's body like that even if some distant, spinning part of Willis's soul could understand such a desperate move. Appreciate it, as well, in some way he didn't recognise as belonging to his morals.

Pulling the torch from his mouth and not giving a fuck about the cold or dirty feel of it as he clasped the device close to his ragged throat, he shuffled away from Lazarus's cell. From far away, the boy screamed at him and shouted the girl's name. The noise was unimportant. The boy could wail and scream until he ran out of air. He would die and so would the little bitch. The only regret for Willis was in knowing he would die before either of them. So be it, though. They deserved nothing less and so did he after the things he'd done. Or allowed to be done.

Another step, his shoe slipping through blood and his centre of balance threatening to spill him to the rock-hard floor where he'd drown in the puddles of rain water and blood. At the last second, he righted himself and managed a grin.

Not dead yet.

He said it aloud and the shock at his weak voice was a dull surprise from faraway; maybe even as a far out of reach as the entrance to the police station and the outside world.

On. Further. On.

The boy had fallen silent, or maybe it was because sight was a narrow beam with darkness pressing in from the sides. Smell and taste were nothing but blood.

After what could have been hours, Willis staggered to the last door and immediately crashed against the wall. His knees buckled; his back pressed on the stone and he hung there, suspended between dropping and staying upright. Aware in the dimming light of his mind that if he went down, he would never move again, Willis let out a wet groan and coughed gore. It struck the floor at his feet and the beam of his vision collapsed into a closing hole.

He had seconds left.

Moving on the willpower that had kept him going for longer than he could remember, Willis slid forward. Feet kicking against each other, he staggered right to the cell door and hammered his fist on the slick metal.

Mary stood in the middle of the cell, the space devoid of furniture, cradling the hand he'd mutilated. Her bloodstains were black marks all over her coat and trousers. They could have been scorches from some terrible fire and in the burning meat of his head, Willis fancied he heard the crackle of a fire streaking over the countryside. He let go of his throat and focused the torch as well as he could on her.

Mary made no move as he appraised her and tried to speak. Words were out of the question; time had become a drain and the swirling red water was him falling into it. And still, the rumble of the fire grew louder. At any second, it would finish cooking the streets and parks of this little nowhere town and then it would come for the buildings, come to blacken them down to their bones. And if he was still there when the fire knocked on the door to the station, he would burn and burn and burn.

Willis managed a smile at the thought and shoved his hand to the small window in the door, showing Mary the keys to her cell.

Everything grew darker and the sole remaining colour was the white of her little face, the white becoming grey. Then beyond the black pressing in from the sides, the distant thunder of the bombs.

They're falling again.

But, no, they couldn't. They *could not.* The war had happened. The bombs, the fire, the country turned to so much terrible heat.

With his thundering heart, Willis heard the fire coming. He heard himself say the girl's name as he wrapped his fingers around the keys that would free her.

He went down and the flames burst through the ruined entrance to the station, streaked through the building and down the stairs to smash into the cells before his body hit the floor.

Chapter Forty-Five

Later, Granger would wonder what woke him. Whether it was the sneaking fog soaking into his clothes or the gradual increase in light against his eyes as white hung low on all sides.

He would prefer to think he'd simply known Roe was gone.

Flat on his back, he stared straight up to the roof of the woods, two dozen branches growing together and forming a mostly unbroken cover from the sky. White glimmered through it in places while closer to the ground, soupy dawn light on the trunks and vegetation failed to do much to banish the fog.

"Roe," Granger said and had no idea if he meant it as a statement or a question.

Sleeping bag crinkling around his body, he rolled over towards their small fire which had died hours before. On the other side of the pile, there was a log, crumbling and stinking of rot. Roe had used it as a perch for his share of the watch overnight. There might have been an impression of his boots on the earth, but that was it. Granger was alone.

He slithered out of the bag, head aching as if he had a hangover, and stood ramrod straight.

"Roe?" He said the name again and it was definitely a question. Questions were all he had and that was worse than any physical injury. Questions belonged to others, not to him.

He crossed to the log, kicking through the leaves, and ran his fingers over the cool surface. Flakes broke off under his touch. The smell of the old wood stuck to his nose. Still resting on the trunk, he studied the immediate area, able to discern a few of the trees around the little clearing they'd used as a base. With the fog like a fallen cloud stuck to the ground, it seemed even smaller than the night before – as if the branches and trunks had closed in while he slept and while Roe abandoned him.

"Roe."

Granger roared the name, his throat burning with the yell and spots dancing in front of his eyes. Something small, maybe a field mouse, scarpered from nearby undergrowth. The long weeds and bushes shook. Granger held his breath, watching for the slightest movement and pretending he didn't feel watched by someone he couldn't see.

Watched was not the right word. He was *appraised.*

"Come on." He held the shotgun like a club, ready to swing his weapon. Stillness returned to the woods, but Granger refused to relax. He was utterly alone for the first time in longer than he could remember and certainly for as long as he'd been part of the post-war world. No Willis, Patterson, Roe or Carolyn. He was his own man with nothing to show for the life given to him by the death of his old one.

A lonely man in a dead place with eyes watching. Lots of eyes. Thousands.

Cold from his toes in his old, battered boots to his hair matted with sweat under his hat, Granger felt countless ghosts watching him, each spectre somehow out of his direct eyeline no matter where he looked or how fast he turned his head. They were here, come to see the one living man in their woods, and what would he do when they eventually grew tired of looking and pushed their way between the old trunks and through the tangled shrubs that hadn't seen healthy sunlight in over a decade?

"Let's see you," he muttered. Somehow, he'd altered his hold on the shotgun and grasped it properly. He aimed in front, slowly revolving so he could track the gaps between the nearest trees and be ready for the first of them to appear.

Dover, darling.

Carolyn hadn't spoken in hours, nor made any appearance since they'd been on the road. While she remained out of sight now, her voice whispered between his eyes and brought him back to his body.

Dover. His destination for so long; the last piece of order left in this blasted country. The ancient town guarding England, watching for invasion across the sea and keeping the nation from harm for as long as there had been a nation to protect.

"Dover?"

It was a nonsense term, a place where all the mad things lived and anything that made sense had been stolen from it. He had nothing left because he had nobody left. Not even weak, foolish Roe who couldn't stand up for himself or punish a wicked man for a wicked deed.

"That's right. You told him." Furtively, Granger looked around. Nothing to see but endless trees and still with the weight of hundreds of eyes crawling over him.

Told Roe. Told him the story. Went back in time to the events after the bombs when there'd been nothing in the bunker but panic and disorder. Standing in the cool air, panting as if he'd sprinted to this spot, Granger had enough self-awareness to understand what he had done so long before, but that changed nothing. It still felt like the memory of another man, and the previous night's conversation while Roe kept the shotgun aimed at his chest could have been nothing but imagination. It was probably for the best that it became imagination. He wouldn't pretend it had been anything other than a horrible act but there was some good in every situation, and in this case, he'd become a better man by doing a bad thing. He'd gained himself; he'd learned how to be in charge and they'd all needed that.

So that had to be worth something.

Dover.

The word was an anchor in his head; it brought him back to land and smashed aside all the memories of the night before and the moments in the bunker.

He gathered up the few items they'd removed from their packs – the empty cans of beans, the almost finished squash bottle of water and the tatty sleeping bag – and took a few moments to hide any signs of their camp while trying to not think about his options. It was no good. Granger knew he'd never been good at believing his own lies because doing so was for men who didn't know what they wanted. That wasn't him.

Sleeping bag folded and stuffed deep into the backpack and the leaves kicked over the fire, he stood on the trail they'd taken to the clearing, running the tips of his fingers on the barrel of the gun. Cold.

Warmth was another place. Perhaps he should find that other place and live out his life there.

Granger sobbed once without closing his eyes and saw a flicker of tiny movement – a rapid discolouration of grey against the fog. At the same time, Carolyn spoke beside his ear.

Dover, sweetheart. Dealey is there. It's time for you to take your place with him. Harris shouldn't have died for nothing. Use the information he brought back to you and go to Dealey. The two of you can make amends and you can show him what sort of man you are when you give him the woman and the girl. You can show him who you've always been.

"Carolyn. My love. I'm sorry."

What do you have to apologise for, darling? Not a thing.

He did, though. Lisa, for one. Carolyn's death for another. And probably a dozen other things.

But he couldn't say them aloud.

Whatever had moved through the trees was gone – if there'd been anything there in the first place. Probably just a shadow cast by the high branches. The wind had picked up in the last few moments and the wood was a creaking animal.

His fingers were wrapped around the small gun, and it no longer felt like ice. It felt as hot as the head of a match, the flame ready to grow into a miniature sun falling out of the sky at a great and terrible speed.

The sun raining to the earth, a ball of vibrant red and orange and yellow streaking over town, field, lake and mountain, and all that fire warming him on a new morning.

"I'll go to Dover," he muttered to the woods. "The woman and the girl. With me. Nobody else."

He giggled and wanted to shake from toe to skull. Shake and shiver his excitement all over.

Carolyn spoke again and it was not a breath beside his ear or a whisper between the leaves.

It was a musing, crawling growl right at his back.

"Kill them all."

Chapter Forty-Six

Lazarus had called repeatedly to his sister, telling her they would be all right. Her sole replies had been gentle sobbing, a sound he did his best to block from his ears if only to try and think.

Think and do his best to believe they would not die in the decaying building, left to starve with Priest's body.

Again, he paced around the cell, stepping across Priest's corpse and running his fingernails over the bricks of the walls. His hope was to find a loose one he could break free and maybe use as a club on the door. While the walls were slick and the bricks crumbled in places, all were solidly packed together. The cells, like the rest of the station, had been built to last. Even if the windows were broken and the walls were damaged in places throughout, it would outlast him and Mary.

No.

Lazarus studied Priest's remains and the damage he'd done to the man's hand to turn it into a weapon.

He'd served them in life; he'd helped Lazarus in death, but he offered nothing more. Lazarus crouched and kissed Priest's shoulder, not minding the smell. Standing again, he crossed to the rear wall, dug his fingers into grooves in the bricks and tried to climb to the slash of a window an inch under the ceiling. He had no chance.

Fighting his fatal resignation, Lazarus returned to the door, poked his fingers through the opening to feel the free air beyond and then gripped the sides of the hatch. Shaking it, he begged the hinges to break free. While they squealed against the brick, they held firm. Tears of frustration finally broke free, each drop hot and furious.

The day would soon be over; another one buried and a new night come to them while they were trapped in their holes, left to die by a man who didn't believe in mercy. He'd thought they were animals or even the monsters from the books Priest used to read to the sisters. He'd believed they didn't deserve as quick a death as Lazarus and the family gave to their food. Suffering wasn't necessary, and Willis giving both to them proved who the real monster was.

"Lazarus." Mary sounded as if she'd stopped crying and that was worse than her tears. It meant she'd lost her fear. If that was true, she'd also lost her hope they would make it out and back to the others.

"I'm here," he shouted into the last of the spluttering light cast by the candles. He stared at the nearest flame for too long and its imprint remained on his eyes even when he blinked repeatedly and tried to focus on the wall opposite his cell. It was like trying to see to the other end of an ocean. He poked his mouth and nose through the hatch, sniffing. No fresh air; no unnoticed exit down here. The only way out was back to the first floor and through the reception area to the same doors that had led them to Granger, to Priest's murder.

And how he wished those doors had been impenetrable those few nights ago. They could have retreated to the safe woods unlit by stars or the moon. While hunger would have torn at their bellies, hungry was better than what had happened to them from the second they'd smashed their way into the station.

Lazarus licked sweat from his knuckles. While there was some brightness falling through the high window, it was too little to shine through to the floor beyond his prison. The area between the cell doors and the opening to the stairs was rapidly becoming a secret where anything might hide.

Lazarus attempted to shake off his scrambling panic and called to Mary again. "You have any tools, sister?"

It was a stupid question and he knew it. If Mary possessed anything useful, they would no longer be prisoners.

"No, brother," she shouted without judgement of him or his question.

Frustrated tears wanted to spill. Lazarus ran the jagged nail of his index finger down the scant flesh of his forearm. While he spilled no blood, the momentary needling fought the childish need to weep.

"We're trapped, aren't we?" Mary's voice did not waver in the least.

She deserved the truth. Lies were for others. Be honest, Priest told them. Trust one another. Love one another.

"Yes." The word hurt his mouth as if he'd been struck. "I am sorry."

"Don't be."

Although there was no way she could have moved, Mary's voice still sounded like it came from much further away than it should. Or maybe he was the one who was removed from the cell with Priest. Perhaps they were falling away from one another at the end.

Never.

Lazarus clamped his hands on the door again, fingers spreading over the grime. He closed his eyes and held Mary's face in his mind. They weren't together which didn't matter. They would leave the building and the incoming night together.

"Sister."

He knew he'd shouted it. All the same, it could have been a whisper.

"Brother."

Mary's reply right beside him, not yelled or screamed, but spoken into his ear by his smiling sister.

"We'll go together, sister. We'll leave."

"Leave. We'll—

leave, we'll leave together, my brother, my Lazarus.

I'm sorry I didn't save you. I'm sorry he hurt you. I'm sorry I didn't protect you.

You did, brother.

Lazarus thought he might be crying but didn't know for sure. It was outside his body and so it belonged to another world.

Are you ready, sister?

I'm ready, brother.

It will not hurt. There is no pain.

No pain, brother. No pain for us.

Child she might have been, but Mary was a giant to him at that moment. Quick, brave and owning nothing but love. She, along with Martha, was the best of them.

Lazarus felt Priest standing close, their father nodding his encouragement, his blessing given freely while the final candle died and the murky shine of late afternoon died in the cell window.

Bite your wrist, sister. Bite through the skin. Bite through the blood. Bite into the blood and keep biting into the blue lines. Keep biting.

I will bite, brother. Will you bite?

I will bite. I will come with you. We will go together.

Their words fell away and that was fine. They'd link their bloody fingers and they would walk over the grass of the courtyard as the sun finally broke free of the weighty clouds and did all it could to lay warmth on the land.

Out to the meadows where Dumah and Priest waited for them and they would talk together back to the sea and cliffs and they would wait for the day Candace and Martha would join them to make their family whole again.

Lazarus brought his wrist to his mouth, teeth and tongue resting on the scant flesh. His pulse thrummed against his lips, the promise of his lifeblood flowing so very close to his mouth. One bite would join him with that flow, and the way out would open before them.

Stop.

It was a mutter from the from the ghosting light of the cell entrance where a shadow slipped in and out of the floor.

The stream of Lazarus's blood flowed against his lips, ready to flood into his mouth and all he had to do was use his teeth as he'd used them so many times before.

I can help you.

Every candle was a cooling stump, the wax already solidifying now the flames were gone. Lazarus had the horrible feeling that if he reached through the hatch in the door, he'd touch a rock-hard surface within an inch because he was now buried in the cell.

A spark lit the black, died before flaring a second time. It was a match held high, the tiny beacon coming closer. It lowered a few inches, brightening the figure who held it. Although he'd seen their face for a short time, Lazarus recognised it. Before he had chance to let out his swirl of emotions, the figure spoke and the flame crept towards their fingers.

"I can help you. Both of you."

Mary.

Her name rising into his mouth and the worst terror of his life rising with it.

"Mary, don't do it, don't bite, don't bite."

Silence from Mary's cell.

Chapter Forty-Seven

There had been little conversation between them since the moments after Joanna's killing. Candace lacked the energy to question or berate Martha further and she knew the girl saw no need for debate – she'd made that much clear when she'd explained in a slow, considered way that she had killed the old woman to keep her from what didn't belong to her. The peace of the world beyond the sea would be theirs alone. It was in the stories given to her and Mary by Priest: so many free spaces with no danger or threat to anyone Martha cared for. All they had to do was make it there and they could live forever in the fields and meadows, and that meant keeping it from people like Joanna.

Candace had done her best to process Martha's logic, dismayed the child believed in such things when she was old enough to know Priest's tales had not been real. At nine, Mary could afford another few months of make-believe, but Martha was the elder of the sisters. Staring at Martha and taking in her lack of comprehension that killing Joanna had been wrong, she'd known the stories were not the big issue. Priest was. Always Priest. Martha had lost her father and her brother; she would keep either of them alive by any means possible.

Unsure if she believed any of it, Candace rifled through drawers and the few cupboards in the kitchen to salvage whatever they could take as supplies and told Martha to sit beside the front wall to keep watch through one of the spyholes. Dawn had arrived a few minutes before which changed little. Vision would still go no further than the pebbles and the tatty grass, Candace knew. She spilled the contents of a drawer to her feet and kicked at the mess. Nothing she could use in the yellowing paper, broken ornaments and photographs with their torn edges.

She hissed. Everything was out of her hands. They were separated; home was completely out of reach and the millions of lives before the bombs were sliding over her feet in the form of pictures of people dead for years and scribbled notes that belonged to a woman who'd saved them from a lonely death in a town she had never seen but already loathed.

Time passing in a surging stream and each twist of the current sending her further away from Lazarus and Mary, her brother and sister who might have been as dead as Priest and Dumah.

No. They are alive. The man would keep them alive.

The terrible man. Willis. He would not kill them. He would want them alive so he could hurt them. Candace had to believe that because she had nothing else.

Martha left the wall and crouched beside the body. Candace heard the child's movement and tried to pretend she hadn't because she knew what it meant.

Pretence didn't stop her mouth from watering. It'd been so long since food and that was exactly what they had on the floor thanks to Martha.

Reaching for a few steak knives, she paused, caught between a disturbing thought and the need to get moving.

Had she ever known the name of any of their meals?

There was little need to think any further. The answer was a firm no. Meals were meals; food was food, and names didn't come into it.

The grating of metal on bone broke her concentration.

Martha had brought an axe down on Joanna's head, shattering the skull in the centre of the woman's forehead and creating a deep wound. Blood ran from the hole, pooling to the floor. Grunting, Martha smashed the axe into Joanna's throat, the single blow all that was required to sever the head. Axe blade wedged into the wooden floor and lines of blood streaming towards the door, the body gave up its interior scents. Martha bent her head towards the ruined skull, mouth opening.

"No." Candace marched from the kitchen and stabbed a finger at Joanna's skull. "No, Martha. No brain. Never the brain."

"I want to know what she knows. I want her stories."

"No. Arms."

Chastised and plainly aware she deserved it (*never eat the brain*, Priest told them long ago. *You'll sicken and die)*, Martha struggled with the axe handle, yanked it from the floor and brought it down squarely on Joanna's shoulder. Metal squealed as it hit wood again. The arm broke free from the body. Martha offered the dripping weapon to Candace who nodded to tell the girl she'd done the right thing, and cut the other arm free.

Not wanting to look at Joanna's eyes, aware both were open and staring, Candace dropped the axe, picked up the two arms and carried the limbs to the kitchen. Both trailed splashes of blood on the floor and the salty aroma made Candace's tongue and teeth itch with hunger. Using a cleaver, she cut them into smaller pieces and bagged them. It meant they would have heavier luggage now Dumah was not with them to carry baggage, but there was no choice. They needed to eat.

Cleaver still in hand, she turned back to Martha who'd leaned into Joanna's decapitated body. Within seconds, she'd ripped into the inner flesh of the woman's throat and swallowed still warm chunks. Blood splashed her face, into her nostrils and she grinned up at Candace who advanced, cleaver still in hand.

Audible through the half a dozen spyholes, stones crunched together.

Martha went for the axe and slid over the floor to the wall. Eye to the spyhole, she whispered to Candace.

"Man. Their father."

Granger. Come for us.

"Fast," Candace hissed.

The straps of the bags over her shoulders and the wet limbs dripping their fluid down her coat, she kicked at the logs in the fire. They rolled clear, fell to the floor and one brushed against the table. The other came to a stop before reaching the sofa. Candace booted it to the seat. In seconds, smoke wafted up. The legs of the table smouldered. Candace knocked another log free. Out of time to mind the heat or the sparks, she kicked it to the chairs which caught light in seconds.

She moved for the rear door and jerked to a halt when she saw Martha at the body again, mouth deep into the neck.

"Martha. Fast. Now."

She said it too loudly and dropped to the floor as soon as the words were out of the mouth.

The window nearest the front door blew in. Shards of glass and scorched pieces of curtain rained to the floor wet with blood, and another shot smashed a hole in the door. The fire Candace had set as a diversion to cover their escape had grown, the two burning objects a single blaze while the cottage filled with choking smoke. Outside air flowed in through the destroyed window and ruined door, the oxygen feeding the flames and turning the fire into a roaring animal.

Giving up all attempts to be silent, Candace screamed Martha's name and hated herself for the fury at Martha delaying them through raw hunger. Martha grabbed the axe and lunged for the door.

"No."

Candace spun Martha around by the wrist and threw her into the kitchen. Madly, less than five seconds had passed since the first shot but that was enough time for the smoke to render them close to blind and starve them of breathable air.

"Back door," Candace said.

Staggering, they ran for it and a third shot came through the remains of the front entrance. Using her body to push the child through the little kitchen and coughing as she bellowed at Martha to open the door, Candace heard rather than saw the impact as they hit the exit. The old wood rattled, opened a tiny amount to let in fresh air but that was all. Something on the outside blocked it.

Furious, Candace kicked at the lower half of the frame. It shook again and bounced off whatever was outside.

They were trapped.

She tried to shout for Martha to stay close and couldn't get enough pure air even with the blown in entrance. Thankfully, the girl understood all the same and crowded close to Candace's side.

Back door blocked; front an open mouth blowing on the flames, and the window at the other end of the cottage unreachable beyond the fire.

Trapped.

Which left one option.

Fight.

Candace dropped to Martha's height, axe in her fist and the bag with the severed legs a weight on her back.

"Kill him," she whispered.

They dashed over the floor, furnishings aflame and the fire a deafening thunder on all sides. The heat scorched their exposed skin, dried the spit in their mouths and sent speeding orange fingers reaching for them as they raced for the door.

Keeping their heads low and their weapons high, Candace and Martha smashed through the wrecked entrance into the sweet freeze of the fog-filled night. Breathing was heaven even as the need to cough until her throat bled filled Candace's chest. Ignoring it, she spun around, searching for their attackers while Martha ran several steps away.

"Down on the grass now."

The shout broke over the crackling fire, the man's location impossible to narrow down.

Candace swung her knife through the air, cutting nothing but smoke and creating a slight hiss. Martha, panting, crouched and darted around, axe swinging.

"Down, now."

A wave of smoke parted and Candace blinked tears away. The need to cough was huge; she settled for hissing and spitting. Somewhere in the swirling smoke, Martha did the same and screeched Granger's name. A section of the roof collapsed, sending a flow of black booming out of the windows and knocking aside every other sound for a moment. Candace ran further out to the rocks and scrubby grass, still blinking tears and sucking in the stink of her sweat-soaked body mixed with the fire. Little feet pounded behind her as Martha closed in, and there he stood, tall and thin and smiling. Granger.

He held his gun with both hands, making no move to back up despite there being only eight or nine running steps between them. Martha skidded beside Candace for a heartbeat and went for him, axe spinning, the girl a speeding burst of energy.

Every single thought vanished from Candace's head. Moving on pure instinct, she flew at her sister, knife falling from her hand, dispassionate eye tracking the axe even as she watched Granger shift the aim of his little gun to bear down on Martha's head while the cottage became a piece of burning hell.

Chapter Forty-Eight

Roe didn't dare approach closer to the cell door or raise his voice. Doing so felt like he'd be shouting in a church or a cemetery – which he supposed South Calcott Police Station now was.

"I'm here to help you," he whispered again and shifted his weight from foot to foot which did nothing to alleviate the strain in his thigh and calf muscles. The march back to the station had taken him along empty roads and over uneven land with only his memory and interior compass as a guide through the mist. The food in his pack was almost done; *he* was almost done. Once his last bottle of water was empty, he thought it would just be a matter of time. Or the boy might decide to open his throat: revenge for what had been done to his father. Either way, it would almost be a relief to be off his feet and get some rest from the trek back to South Calcott and the police station.

His hands twisted and rolled over his stomach. It wasn't any indication of a leader, but then he'd never claimed to be the man in charge. Not in a previous life and not in this new mess of one.

Trapped in the cell, Lazarus stared at Roe through the hatch, making no attempt to shield his eyes from the small torch. The entire area was in shadow save for the shaking light. While dawn was not far away, none of its light dropped through the few windows above. Night seemed to want to hold the minutes and hours with a terrible grip.

Not moving his eyes, Lazarus called through the opening.

"Mary?"

He'd shouted the name several times, each one heavy with fear and barely withheld panic. His final yell held a weak resignation as if he knew there would never be an answer.

Standing out of arms' reach of the cell, Roe inhaled the terrible reek of a decomposing body along with the fresher stench of Willis's corpse. Put with both, dirt, sweat and despair.

"Brother?"

It was hesitant, unsure, but alive.

Lazarus froze for a moment, hope widening his eyes while the cold light of fear remained in their centres.

"Mary? Are you hurt?" he shouted.

"No, I'm—"

"Do nothing. Stay still, sister."

"Yes, brother."

Lazarus held the lower edge of the hatch and edged as close to it as he could. His nails were as black as the ground; dirt inked his skinny forearms, and the shadows growing out of the cell walls seemed to be as much a part of his body as his opening mouth and his teeth like broken stones.

"Leave her alone."

The light left him for a second to spin towards Mary's cell. It returned to his face as Roe advanced, still holding his torch. Only a single step, but still movement.

"I can help you."

Lazarus said nothing.

Roe moved another step and winced at the bolting pain stabbing the soles of his feet. His boots splashed on a puddle, the sound unclean. The air was unclean. It was creeping into his diseased lungs and throat and would cling to his chest like the mould growing all around him.

"I can help you," he said again, sweating freely. "But you have to promise me there will be no violence."

He kept the gun at his side. As Lazarus had obviously fought the need to vent his fury, Roe struggled against the command to raise the weapon. He was trapped with people less than human and all he had as protection were a few bullets.

"I want to kill you." Lazarus's fingers tightened around the grids of the doors and tiny pieces of flaking metal scrapped loose.

"I know. I understand. I am not. . . I am not with them, anymore. Granger. Willis. I am alone and I want to help you."

"Why?"

"Because there is nothing left." Roe spoke and felt a weight slide away. The secret fear he'd kept locked in his heart was out of his mouth and instead of any crushing fatalism it could have brought, it meant freedom. There *was* nothing left which meant letting go of the life he'd brought out of the past. Voicing that fear and admitting its truth might mean his death soon, but he had no real fear of that.

Boots squelching, he approached the cell, stood within arm's reach of Lazarus and raised the shotgun.

The boy's face remained impassive and his eyes held on Roe's.

Neither blinked.

Roe shifted the weapon around so the barrel faced his chest.

"Take it."

Somewhere, water dripped into a puddle, and the reek of stale air and mould on the walls pulsed in time with the drops.

Lazarus took the gun and slid it through the hatch. He spun it around, found the trigger and held it on Roe's face. Roe guessed while the boy had limited knowledge of firearms, he knew what the trigger did and his finger pressed on it with the slightest pressure.

His desire was obvious: Roe on the ground with his head blown into pieces.

Kill the man and he killed his sister. They'd be buried alive again.

"Unlock it," he said and it was a growl.

Roe made no move to do so. Instead, he swallowed the sour smell of the nearest body. It made his stomach turn and he felt a kind of sorry hilarity. So little food in his belly meant next to nothing to vomit. A joke even Granger would have laughed at, the humourless bastard.

"Your father. Priest. A good man? He taught you honesty? The value of truth?"

There was a snatched second in which he saw Lazarus's heart break, the cannibal and killer turned back into the boy he was. Brothers and sisters who killed to live, to eat, and this boy not yet sixteen close to weeping.

Roe saw through Lazarus's eyes and found he understood the boy in a way that would not have been possible had he remained with Granger.

One of the men who'd hurt them so badly understanding Priest so well after such a short time; this man who was Lazarus's only chance to free his sister and find the others.

This man who should be a corpse in the dirty puddles if anything made sense.

"Why come here?" Lazarus asked.

Roe's reply was immediate because it was all he had and it was utterly true. "You didn't deserve what Willis was going to do. And I don't care if I die."

Lazarus kept his poker face and Roe had to wonder why the boy would believe him. Watching, waiting, he saw Lazarus cock his head as if he'd heard something. Then:

"I won't kill you," Lazarus said. "I promise."

Aware it could mean his death, unable to care, Roe brought the key he'd taken from Willis's cooling body and stabbed it into the lock.

A final look at Lazarus and he turned the key.

Bolts turned and the door eased open.

Gun in his hand, Lazarus crept out of the dungeon, stood an inch from Roe who remained utterly still, and held a flat palm up. Wordlessly, Roe placed the key in Lazarus's hand.

Lazarus studied the gun for a moment, sniffing the man without looking at him. Roe waited, aware what would come next and ready for it.

With the slightest movement, Lazarus raised the gun, aiming it at Roe's face. Roe kept his torch on Lazarus, the beam low down so the boy could see. There was fear, but not terror. His struggle through the densely packed trees and foul vegetation, every step taking him further from the life he knew and understood with only some vague plan of returning to the police station as his company – terror had been left behind the moment he stood up and walked away from Granger.

Lazarus lowered his hand. Skidding over the wet stones, he ran to the other end of the cells, calling Mary's name, calling for her as Roe spun the beam of his torch after the boy to light the way. Mary called back to her brother; she cried for him and when he unlocked her cell door, she ran for him and they were joined again, brother and sister while Roe remained still and shone his torch on them. When they turned to him, he knew without any interior debate what was coming next.

Eating.

Chapter Forty-Nine

Granger shifted the position of his trigger finger when Candace fell on the girl, her weight and size acting as a shield. They were within kicking distance which meant he was within reaching distance. Despite the threat, Granger made no move to retreat and kept the shotgun aimed downwards. They might notice his finger half an inch from the trigger; if so, it would be back in place before either could make their move. The plan for Dover had been all the family but he would not risk his life for that. One was better than none; none was better than either Candace or the child sinking their teeth into his skin.

Panting, Candace pulled the girl off the ground, Martha's slight frame no problem even with Candace's missing arm. The coloured woman eyed him with flat hate while the girl was a hissing valve. The fire in the house roared on and it was only luck that kept the waves of smoke from blowing in their direction.

"Hello," he said and their expressions didn't alter. "Good to see you again."

Still nothing. He had to admire that.

"Who was in the house? Who fired at me?"

Candace spoke, voice croaking, full of smoke.

"A woman. Old. Her house for years. She saw you with. . ." She mimed holding binoculars.

"A woman? Is she dead?"

They needed to get moving and sharpish, too. They were thirty or forty feet from a raging fire, the air stinking of smoke, the land where the house had stood for decades already blackening and the flames turning their location into a beacon. Dover was close enough for him to taste the sea but he had to know what threats he was dealing with especially now he was alone.

"Dead." Martha coughed out black strings of saliva.

"I killed her," Candace said. Granger nodded, suspecting as much. He dismissed the matter.

"Okay. Listen. You're going to crawl away from me until I say stop. Then you're going to keep your backs to me. There'll be no trouble from either of you and no pretending you don't know what I want you to do. I know you understand me perfectly. You're clever girls. You know I'm in charge. So crawl, ladies. Bums in the air. Crawl."

Without argument, they did so, backsides raised, both scrawny to the point of skeletal, their fists digging through the pebbles and then the surrounding green. He called for them to stop when they were a few feet into the grass. The house was finally burning itself out. Give it half an hour and there'd been nothing left for the flames to eat. Give it a week and the place would be just another destroyed wreck with the rain, mist and wind playing in the rooms and making the house ready for the weeds to grow eventually.

Cradling the shotgun, Granger fished in his coat pocket and withdrew his piece of tatty rope. While it wasn't long, it would do the job.

"Girl." He shouted it and remembered her name. "Martha." Granger threw the rope to her back. She didn't flinch when it thudded at her feet.

Able again to hold the shotgun and keep a finger near the trigger, Granger marched across the stones and stood on the grass.

"Remember what I said. No pretence. I'm not in the mood. You know what I want you to do."

"Do it, Martha," Candace murmured.

The child shifted, picked up the rope and began tying her wrists together while studying the last of the flames. Granger watched for any sign she had left the knots easy to break. The bonds weren't perfect but they would have to do. No way was he getting any closer than necessary to the girl, and Candace was no help with her sole hand.

"Right. That's lovely." Granger wanted to check the surrounding countryside for any signs of approaching threat. Just because they'd seen next to nobody out here, that didn't mean there weren't watchers in the woods or scouts from Dover.

The two at his feet had to be his focus, though.

"Candace." Her name was pleasant in his mouth. It tasted like a piece of exotic chocolate. "You'll need food. Go in the house and get some."

She whipped her head around to stare at him. There was no hiding her shock and that was pleasing. She wasn't in charge of their situation and maybe that was beginning to sink in.

"Food," he said again as if it was an inconsequential matter. "We have a little way to go yet but you still need to eat." Granger kept his tone level, pretending to them but not to himself that the whole idea didn't make him nauseous.

Moving as if her entire body hurt, Candace stood. Wafting smoke continued to drift out to the farmland, most of the black blown to the east. By the sounds of the quietening crackle, the fire still burning inside was more or less done.

"You may think I'm joking but I am really not. You and the girl need your sustenance; I appreciate that. God knows when you last got any so I'm giving you the chance to rectify that. Just bear in mind you shouldn't try anything I won't like. No weapons. No escape attempts. Not while she remains with me." Granger nodded at Martha. You've got to the count of sixty to get in there and do whatever you need to do."

She simply stared at him.

"One, two, three, four, five –"

Running in a lumbering lurch, Candace wasted no time in saying anything to him or to the child. She covered the drive and grass to the collapsed building, hand and forearm covering her mouth and nose, kicked a section of loose door aside and vanished inside.

Granger fell silent, no longer counting. On the ground, facing away from him, Martha was motionless and he said nothing to her although for a moment, he wondered if he was misjudging the girl. Child or not, she'd proved she was as dangerous as a wild dog.

Coughing, eyes streaming, Candace lunged out of the farmhouse. She held her sole hand to her stomach, cradling it. Granger watched her stagger back to them, grimly fascinated by what she was holding and equally disgusted by his curiosity.

Candace doubled over when she reached them, retching. Her clothing, her skin, her hair all reeked of smoke and when she managed to stand straight, her eyes were red and watering.

"Done?" Granger asked quietly.

She nodded.

"Good. Now I'm not stupid, Candace. You might have found a weapon in there. You very probably did, but if you try using it, I'll kill Martha. Ideally, I want both of you in Dover, but one will be enough to show the people what the outside world is like and what it takes to survive." Abruptly, he was close to exhausted and had to wonder when he'd last eaten. It was all well and good telling cannibals to fuel their bodies; he was in the same boat.

Granger's stomach rolled in a lazy spin.

"No lies. No pretence. We're going to my people in Dover and I fully expect you to try to kill them, but you'll fail. You're done. The best thing is for you to appreciate being together now." He considered his next words carefully. "For what it's worth, I loathe what you are. I think you're foul, but I understand family. I do understand that. When it comes to the time, I will kill you both in an instant."

Candace's mouth shifted and it took Granger a moment to realise she was smiling without a single degree of warmth or humour.

"Let's go," he said and tapped the shotgun's barrel.

The sisters a few steps ahead, they walked away from the smouldering farmhouse and the smoke scudding over the empty land.

Chapter Fifty

Telling Mary to keep a look out in all directions as well as she could, Lazarus directed the group towards the wafting smoke become soft and grey due to the mist. Briefly, Roe wondered if the boy knew which way to go and realised his doubt was pointless. While the wind spun the smoke in all directions, their route was clear in the few waving leaves and the flapping of the longer strands of grass. The wind blew from the east; they headed south, and the smoke already in his mouth and nose rose in a straight line.

A decade of growing up in the natural world made Lazarus just as much of a tracker as a dog might be out here.

Occasionally spitting and not liking the rattle deep in his chest, Roe walked parallel with Lazarus, keen to keep distance between them. The grass ended at a narrow dyke, the water a dirty brown fit for nothing. Lazarus paused, frowning for no more than two seconds. He put his blank mask back on when Roe appraised him. No words were spoken and none were needed. Roe had seen the girl's reactions and speech slow a fraction since they'd left the station. A search of Willis's pockets had given them half a pack of painkillers; Mary had swallowed three and the painkillers were doing their job. All well and good, but it meant the chances were good she'd fall in if she tried to jump to the opposite embankment, and Lazarus clearly couldn't manage his axe, the gun and his sister.

"I can jump." Mary swayed. Not a lot but enough.

Roe pointed at the dyke and wheezed for a moment.

"It won't be comfortable, but we'll dry out," he said when he caught his breath.

He waited for Lazarus to reply, understanding the boy's thoughts and appreciating them. He made no offer to take the gun or the knife and short-handled axe they'd found in the room Willis had set up as his base. They eyed one another while the wind flung the cold in all directions and the smoke from the burning building merged with the clouds overhead. The fog was growing thicker; it would obscure all but the immediate land and the smoke within half an hour at most. Mary swayed again. Her injury put with the walk in the frosty morning was obviously taking what little energy she had.

"Through the water," Lazarus said and Mary nodded. She moved ahead before he finished speaking.

Stifling a sigh, Roe slid down towards the brackish water, grimacing at its stench. While he didn't want to investigate closely, it smelled as if an animal had died close by and its bones mouldered in the dyke. The distinct reek of excrement was also in his nose and he tried not to wonder how far it might have travelled in the sluggish flow.

He flexed the thin muscles of his thighs and shins, backed up to get a running start and dashed forward. Launching at the edge of the grass, he sailed over the brown water and had a second to marvel at the air parting around his face and body in a way he hadn't known since the days of his childhood. Crashing to the other embankment, he went down on one knee and slapped a hand into the soft earth to keep his balance. Slightly more out of breath than he liked, Roe faced the others. Lazarus held Mary with one arm cradling her. He held the axe in his other hand while she gripped the kitchen knife, blade pointing to the ground. They whispered to each other and Roe had a brief wish to know what they shared. Then Lazarus ran.

In a smoother motion than Roe, he cleared the water, struck the slope and overbalanced immediately.

Without any thought, Roe reached for the boy and grabbed a handful of Mary's clothing. Her arm tightened around Lazarus's neck; his feet skidded on a soggy patch of grass and the three slid towards the dyke. Groaning with the weight of their bodies, Roe used his left leg as an anchor and fought for a better grip. For another second, they continued their descent. Lazarus did the same as Roe with his leg and found firmer ground. They halted, Roe's fists bunched with Mary's coat and Lazarus's scarf. Roe puffed hard, his heart hammering. Blinking, he realised the freezing sensation on his chin and lips came from Mary's knife. She'd swung it up the instant he went for them and it was only her realisation he was attempting to help them that had stopped her from cutting into his face.

She could kill me at any second.

There was no surprise in the thought, no real dismay. He was in the lifeless wilds of England with killers and his continued existence was purely down to them.

Lazarus's face was rapidly turning red but the boy made no move to remove Roe's hand from the scarf strangling him. Roe relaxed his grip, fingers splayed. Mary's knife remained on his mouth and he tried not to think about the pieces of skin that might still be on the blade's teeth.

"Are we all right?" he whispered as well as he could without moving his lips.

"Mary," Lazarus croaked and swallowed the crisp air. He gulped a second time and Roe did the same as quietly as he could. The cold felt good in his mouth. Mary pulled the knife clear of Roe's face. A line of blood from the weapon and from a cut in his lower lip trickled through his stubble.

"Are we all right?" Roe asked again and Lazarus nodded.

Roe took his hands from them, flexing his stiffening fingers, and walked up a few steps before stopping to hack burning coughs. Lazarus followed. Only when they were clear of the slope and the dirty water did he lower Mary to the grass. Roe stood straight, still wheezing, tasting salt and heat, body a dozen or more separate aches. The air, cooler than earlier, clung to his exposed skin and felt as if it was corroding his clothes and then skin to get to his bones. He caught Mary peering up to her brother, eyes asking a question.

"Everyone okay?" Roe asked and thought he might know what the girl was thinking if not asking. By saving them from the shitty water, he'd become something more than an enemy to her. To Mary, people who weren't her brothers or sister were probably only either food or a threat. He had to hope she had the mental capacity to consider a third option.

"Everyone okay," Lazarus said and it was a firm statement.

Crossing the land with little in the way of natural cover, they moved at speed, Mary studying the surrounding earth for any movement. Ten minutes later, they closed in on the building turned to a now fading bonfire. The last of the smoke flowed from the collapsed roof and innards of the house, the black fog wafting towards the sky. It took no more than a minute's appraisal to see the damage done to the windows and door that had nothing to do with fire. Or the splashes staining the pebbles of the drive around the house.

Lazarus passed the axe and knife to Mary and crept forward with the Browning while Mary skittered to the exterior wall of the cottage and ducked below the blown in window. Roe, weaponless and exposed, could only watch. There were no voices inside, no Granger yelling at them to lower their blades and gun. He'd been here, though. He'd done this.

Lazarus crept over the stones, each step careful and light while Roe relaxed as much as he could. Granger was gone. Little comfort, perhaps, but something at least. He followed Lazarus, jerking to a halt when the boy raised a fist. His heart had jumped from a relatively normal beat to a drumroll.

Then he saw what Lazarus had seen.

A shape on the ground in the doorway. It had merged with the floor and ash until he dared approach and revealed itself to be a body. *Some* of a body, he noted. Cooked and shrivelled, it was missing an arm, a leg and its head.

Creeping behind Lazarus, Roe's empty stomach pulsed like an irregular heartbeat and the only reason he didn't vomit was down to a lack of food.

Aware he would likely be killed if the body should prove to be the black woman, Roe murmured to Lazarus.

"Is it. . .?"

"No." Lazarus let out a soft whistle and Mary jogged to him, now making no attempt to be silent. "Hand," Lazarus said.

Momentarily, Roe thought he might have misheard the boy. Then he understood. Unlike Candace, the scorched body possessed its left arm.

You did this on purpose, didn't you? Roe thought at Granger. The left arm still intact on the corpse; the corpse left in view. It was a message.

"Check?" Mary asked Lazarus. He nodded.

Knife jutting forward, the girl trotted to the doorway and the body. Roe wanted to tell her to be careful and was distantly surprised Lazarus hadn't said the same. With the same bitter realisation he'd felt about his hollow stomach, he realised he was still looking at the two of them as if they were from his world, his time. *Careful* was a state of mind for them, not something they turned on and off.

Close to the cottage entrance, Mary poked her knife into the body's trunk. It cut through the cooked meat before meeting the sternum. She pulled it through and traced the tip of the blade around a small bump beside the wound she'd made. Roe winced. Breasts, once. Now, melted skin and muscle sliding together into a mound.

A woman. Not Candace. Which meant Candace was still alive.

Blinking away a few tears, Mary returned to Lazarus. "It's a woman," she told him.

"Not Candace," he whispered. "Remember that."

Roe risked advancing to them, faltering slightly when Mary glanced his way. He really had been close to an uneventful death here in the smoke and dying warmth of the fire. The girl would have split his head open without a thought if Candace lay in the doorway.

"We know where they're going," he reminded them.

"Your Dover," Lazarus said.

"To the new government. To the law."

Lazarus faced him and Roe flinched.

"Why? Your government. Your order. Why does this matter to Granger?"

"Because it's all he has. It's all he's ever had. He lives for it. Always did." Roe knew they wouldn't understand the background and found he was too tired and hurting to care. Let them hear it.

"We were important men. We were safe from all this." He gestured to the surrounding farmland where no animals grazed and no crops grew. The fog and the damp were becoming stronger, the soft white welcome in a way because it helped to cover the scarred land.

"Underground in the bunkers. We thought we could keep things going from down there. A man in charge. Dealey. He was near the Prime Minister." They didn't know the term. Again, he cared nothing for the fact. "High up. More important than any of us, but he and Granger wanted different things. Granger wanted direct action, for us to go to the other bunkers, find more survivors and get things going again straightaway. We had no radio contact with them so we couldn't know who was out there which was why Dealey said to wait and see. He was cautious. Scared, I think, but he was in charge so that's what we did. For a while."

The memories of the days and months after the bombs were close. They pressed their fingers over his chest, making each already difficult breath that much harder. Soon, he would smell the cold, clinical aroma of the steel corridors and the vents. He would hear the echoing tap from every step and he would squint against the harsh lights glaring from the ceilings of each room.

"Eventually, it all fell apart. Granger led a coup against Dealey." Roe laughed, caught more in memory than present. "A very English coup. No blood. No violence. Granger simply got into the weapons storage and took over. Rounded up those who didn't agree with his idea of going back to the city and taking over whatever was left. If that meant killing survivors or the diseased, he said it had to be done so we could then have something for ourselves and the people in the other bunkers. Dealey had no time for violence. We split into the two groups; Dealey and his people were asked to leave. He and Granger shook hands before they went out to the tunnels and we never saw them again."

Roe blinked a few times. His chest had not ached during his memories and his soft words. The throb in his lungs and throat returned to join the animal sinking claws deep into his feet and leg muscles. He watched Lazarus for any reaction.

"Now he wants to take you to Dover and hand you over because he thinks he can prove he's still a man of decisions and action. He stops you from hurting anyone and he shows everyone he's got what it takes to make the world a better place."

"Why there?" Lazarus asked.

"He thinks Dealey has set up some law and order in Dover because that was one of the plans when we were underground. There were key places we thought would escape the worst of the blasts because of their locations and the geography. Dealey said they would head there before he took his people. We left that bunker a few weeks later and travelled underground to the nearest other one. Then the next. Then the next. Then the next. We took what we wanted and we. . .killed them. We killed anyone who tried to stop us taking what we wanted. Now here we are."

His last sentence collapsed into a broken croak before he finished speaking.

Lazarus stepped closer to Roe while Mary watched them. Roe waited for the boy to shoot him. After all, he was no more use to them.

"I know why Priest told us to go to your Dover." Lazarus smiled, exposing sharp and broken teeth. "We kill all of them."

There was nothing else to be said. Setting out cross-country, they left the house and its anonymous body to its smoke and its dying heat.

Chapter Fifty-One

The moment the few twigs were alight with enough strength to warm them against the afternoon, Granger wordlessly undid the bag of body parts they'd taken from the woman in the cottage and withdrew the head.

Splashes of red stained the cheeks and coated the mouth which hung open. Its eyes had rolled over to reveal whites now turned grey, and tendrils of dangling sinew and muscle hung from the ruined neck like string.

Disgust seemed to have faded into nothing and all Granger had in its place was the knowledge everything was a tool and could be used. That included the head of the woman from the cottage.

He knew how he would appear to Roe if his colleague had bothered to stay with him. Roe, in his quiet way, would say Granger was breaking down, losing his self-control. But so what if that was true? His wife murdered by cannibals, and a battle to survive the same cannibals so he would finally, *finally* find some peace and the chance of a new life with men who understood him. Roe wouldn't appreciate that. Carolyn would, but she had left him too. Perhaps she lurked in the woods miles behind, haunting the abandoned paths where people had once walked their dogs.

Granger held a shiver inside and tossed the head to Candace and Martha. It rolled to a stop near the child's feet and the fire light made the dull blood marking the cheeks shine as if it were fresh again.

"Are you hungry?" Granger asked. He heard his question and wondered if he felt as curious as he sounded. He wasn't sure of anything anymore. "It must be lunchtime by now."

Candace and Martha made no move even though Candace's single hand was unbound. The tatty piece of rope around Martha's wrists held her secure. Both were as still as the spiky bushes dividing the field from the next one.

"You must be." Fascinated, Granger watched them, waiting for the slightest movement. "How long has it been since you last ate?"

Candace hissed at him, sounding for all the world like a snake. He blinked, then smiled.

"I'm hungry. You must be as well. Plenty of food to go around. Soup for me. The head for you. I eat what I eat. You do the same."

There was an almost imperceptible shift in Candace's posture—a straightening in her posture and a lifting of her head.

The girl did the same, eyes firmly on Granger and not on the head within arm's reach.

Sighing in disappointment, Granger sifted through another bag and withdrew a battered tin of tomato soup and a bowl. Despite a few cracks and chips, the bowl was serviceable. He set about preparing his soup over the little fire. Within five minutes, the strong scent drifted over the grass and masked the smell of the earth. On all sides, the fog covered the grassland and turned the motorway no more than a dozen paces from where they sat into an undefined line. He ate, slurping the soup and keeping a watch on Candace and Martha. The woman's black cheeks put with the hood of her coat almost made her float with the smoke from the fire. For the first time since waking to discover Roe had abandoned him, the thought of that betrayal left Granger.

She could have been pretty once upon a time, Granger thought and winked at Candace.

She simply stared at him. He ate more soup and then said: "At the farmhouse. Why did you kill that woman?"

Her only physical reaction was a leisurely blink.

"Tell me," Granger said and resisted the urge to tap the shotgun.

"You know what we are. You know what we do," Candace replied eventually while Martha stared at nothing. Her pinched face seemed even smaller and thinner than usual.

The child spoke in a tired voice. "You think we're evil."

Granger held a shiver inside. *Tired* was too weak a term. Martha could have been an old lady with her life winding down instead of a girl who hadn't yet reached puberty.

"I did," he replied, relieved he sounded normal. "But now I think you're survivors." He switched his attention back to Candace. "Am I right? Is that what you are?"

"Call us what you want," she said.

Not taking her eyes from his, Candace shifted forward and grasped the head.

Granger lowered his spoon and watched.

Candace lifted the head and handed it to Martha. The child turned it over and around, frowning as she appraised it.

Candace and Granger stared at one another while Martha's fingers prodded the flaking pieces of burned skin, nails sinking into the baked meat of the face.

The swirling smoke merged with the fog and the quiet world.

Martha brought the head to her mouth and sank her broken teeth into the cheek. Flesh tore, broke free and hung from her lips. She sucked it up, chewing, swallowing and shoving her mouth back to the head.

More skin ripped, splitting as it pulled away from the face.

Granger fought the need to turn away or at least close his eyes. Sickened, fascinated and furious such a filthy act could be carried out as if it was the easiest thing in the world, he watched.

Martha's teeth and lips found a strip of skin that opened into a wound exposing the stumps of teeth. The girl eagerly sucked at the hole, her probing tongue flicking over the lump that had been a tongue and was now a small mound melted into the gums.

Opposite each other while the fire burned and Martha ate, Granger and Candace continued to stare at one another. "Remember, Martha," she said. "Don't eat the brain."

"I know." Martha's reply was muffled by the torn flesh between her teeth.

Jesus Christ.

The movement close to unfelt, Granger tilted his head in a brief nod and forced down another mouthful of soup. It tasted of nothing and he thought that was probably for the best. He also thought he might vomit soon and prayed he did not.

"Are we going?" Candace muttered.

"No," Granger replied and shut his ears to sounds of sucking and contented chewing. "We're waiting for the rest of your family."

She nodded as if she had expected nothing else. Then:

"We are going to kill your friends."

Granger managed a smile. "I know you'll try."

Softening the landscape of half-dead woodlands and the snaking road, the fog pressed its soundless weight on the world.

Chapter Fifty-Two

They clambered over a damaged wall, its highest point no higher than Mary's waist. The broken bricks scattered into the weeds and scrubby grass; ahead, a flat brown field eventually reached tall trees. From the east, the fog that had formed several hours earlier was matching their pace and drifting closer in white branches.

"Wait."

Lazarus stopped and let out a quick whistle as Mary walked on another step. The child turned around. Although scarves obscured much of her face, enough skin remained visible to reveal her exhaustion and unhealthy pallor. With any luck, there was no blood poisoning from the wound to her hand, but she needed rest and something stronger than the pills they'd taken from the police station.

"You have a choice," Roe said.

"What choice?" Lazarus replied with little interest and Roe had to wonder if that was down to tiredness or a genuine lack of caring.

It had to be said; had to be if they were to avoid any more bloodshed.

"You can't do it like this. Not injured. Not without. . .your weapons."

"He has our sisters."

"I know, but you. . .you can't fight him. Not like this. You're tired and hurt. He. . .he's more dangerous than you think."

"He has our sisters."

Lazarus said the same words in the same tone as seconds before.

"I know he does, but if you just go after him with barely any weapons and no real plan, you'll—"

Roe shut up when Mary took a few paces to her brother and placed gentle fingers on his hand holding the gun. Lazarus looked at the weapon, then at his sister.

"We are going for the others," he said. "You set us free. You can help."

He tossed the gun to Roe's feet where it fell among the weeds.

"We will kill him. We will kill you if you stop us. If you stay with us, we will keep you alive."

"You're giving me the gun?" Roe murmured.

"Your choice. Your brother or us."

Roe crouched; his knees cracked. Scooping the gun up, he stood again and wiped a sweaty hand on his thin leg.

"Granger is not my brother," he said.

"Then you are with us. If not, kill us now," Lazarus said.

Closer and thicker, the fog swallowed the grass. Roe fancied he could feel the dank chill soaking through his clothes and coming for his skin that felt much older than it should.

"Granger is not my brother," he whispered and marched ahead of Lazarus and Mary.

When they reached the treeline, Lazarus and Roe looked back while Mary focused on the route ahead and pushed low-hanging branches away from her face.

The route they'd taken was lost behind a drifting wall of white while finally free of the weighted clouds, the sun was a weak yellow turning patches of the fog into a sickly shade. For some reason he couldn't identify, Roe wanted to weep.

The group entered the woods, leaves crumbling muffled by the fog.

Less than five minutes passed before Roe realised he was at the mercy of Lazarus and Mary in a new way. Not only could they kill him whenever they chose to, they could also leave him in the woods with its trails only they seemed to find and the fog slipping between branches.

Left to die. And was that worse than being killed and eaten by cannibals?

Roe didn't know.

Not too keen on finding out.

That was true. While he was as resigned to death as he thought it possible to be, that didn't mean he fancied being eaten alive or left alone to the elements in such a desolate place. All he could do instead was to hope Lazarus and Mary kept him with them, and walk close to the boy while the girl led the way.

Visibility was next to nothing. All the same, Mary seemed to know the route they needed to take as if she'd taken it many times. Through individual trunks nearly lost from view, and along a path sloping up and down, she steered them with little hesitation. Broken pieces of wood and foliage untouched by the sun in years broke apart under their feet, the fog crawling from behind and the sides acting as a blanket on the sound. The further they walked, the more Roe felt that he'd become disconnected from anything he knew and was now nothing more than a floating balloon let loose in the woods.

Get a grip, man. Keep calm and walk.

He ducked when he saw Lazarus do the same and branches misshapen like broken fingers brushed the hood of his coat.

How did he know to duck then?

If there was an answer, he wasn't sure he wanted to know it.

They squeezed between three sturdy oaks, each forced to turn so they shouldered through the narrow gap, and bark rubbed on Roe's cheek like cold ash.

He cringed.

The path brought them to an open space which wasn't the relief it might have been owing to the proximity of the fog. With no trees to shield the clearing, the white spread in from all sides. Peering down, Roe could no longer make out anything below his knees and his mind brought up images of hands reaching for his ankles, eager to yank him down into the soft and silky cloud.

"How far?" His throat was far too dry to speak at any volume. It was the first thing he'd said since they'd entered the woods.

"Not far," Mary said and that was all she would give him.

They passed the mid-section of the clearing, sweat and the air clinging to Roe's face and neck. Behind and close, the mouldering leaves of the woodland floor cracked.

Roe spun around, saw a brief discolouration to the fog before white took it back, and hissed Lazarus's name.

The boy turned again, axe ready. Mary did the same with her knife.

"What?" Lazarus said.

"Something's there. Following us."

"What?"

"I don't know." Panic made Roe's voice high and rushed. He fought for calm if only to slow his raging heart and stop the need to run as fast as he could.

They waited, listening to nothing but their own soft exhalations. A minute passed before Lazarus spoke again.

"We need to go now."

Roe listened for another moment, then nodded. "Okay. I. . .don't know. Maybe it was nothing."

But he didn't believe that. Not in the least.

Mary still leading, they left the clearing and walked into a section of the wood that felt older than anything before. Oaks and elms loomed from above; branches were entwined with their own and each other; the aroma of soggy earth and rotting vegetation mixed with the fog, and the path became more uneven. Inclines and slopes slowed their passage while encroaching shrubs pulled at their feet. Roe forced himself to stare at Lazarus, using the boy as a guide and an emotional anchor. A drop of sweat stung his eye; he blinked it away and a smudge swam over the fog to his left.

No.

Another smudge, moving with precise steps. There was no random darting or jerking around. It matched his pace and all it would take to see it clearly was a slight movement of his head.

No. I won't. I will not.

While he knew Lazarus and Mary were close in front, they could have been miles away because time, for him alone, had slowed. Every step took a year;

every inch of the woods he covered was a decade, and the movement creeping closer to the centre of his vision was purely his.

A sound emerged out of the fog and it was the only sensation passing at normal speed. He understood why. It meant he could hear it for so much longer than normal.

A voice, soft and rational even with what lived underneath its words. A suggestion of something animalistic, of hunger.

That was it. Murmurs slipping to his ears, seemingly not reaching Lazarus or Mary; murmurs of the need for ripped flesh and flowing blood in its mouth to fight off the gnawing, *chewing* hunger in its belly, and whatever food it found was never enough because it was a starving animal. The fires had set it free. They had turned the country into an oven and cooked people in cities, in towns, in villages. So it would eat and eat and eat but it would never be full. It brought others to its arms and it loved them because love meant a chance to open its mouth wider, to scoop more bodies between its teeth.

Roe. It crooned to him and he was still moving, somehow. Time remained at a crawl; the fog hid its secrets and all he had control over was his vision focused squarely at Lazarus's form. He still saw the stain on the white come closer to his side, its upper half turned to him so it could watch his face as they walked.

Roe. Are you hungry? Do you long for food? Do you dream of meat in your hands and in your mouth? Do you wish for children like mine? Do you, Roe?

The tone clearly of a refined, educated man; the faint rasp in the throat as if the speaker made it through dozens of cigarettes a day; the calmness to his every reply even though he was trapped in a cell with his little group.

It was Priest.

Once a priest, always a priest. Always. And now I worship in a new place. Your friend Granger sent me here. Into the dark. Into the cold.

The voice went on, words fading from it and leaving images in their place. They clung to Roe's skull and while he wanted to weep, there were no tears. He saw bodies hacked, their blood and insides washing over the freezing ground turned pale in moonlight; he saw ribs split and sternums hammered in half to reveal hearts which were then cradled in a child's hands while streams of red flowed down their skinny forearms to drip at their feet.

Teeth stripping skin from shattered bones.

Livers placed over fires and pierced to free the liquid inside while the flames cast wild patterns on cave walls.

Stomachs filled but not for long enough. Never for long enough.

Above every killing and every meal, the thing from the quiet places forgotten by life and the twentieth century; the thousands of square miles of woodlands and moors; the hills, mountains and caves in the earth hidden since the Ice Age; a godless being that existed solely to tear flesh and spill blood.

To eat and to eat and to eat.

Something of the wind and the rain, old before the Vikings and the Romans, watching in every lonely corner of the land, walking country lanes and new motorways.

Coming to eat.

Roe saw it brought out to the world of people and cities by the bombs; he saw it love its new children and keep them close to its bosom so they would again leave their home beside the sea and take their axes to the few survivors of the fire.

Their father, their Priest.

The hellish images sank into a pit underneath Roe's heart, swirling together while the muttering merged with his panting and the tread of his boots. It was only when he realised he had been weeping for a time that he also realised time flowed at its normal rate.

He managed to look directly at the spot where the shifting thing had kept pace with him. There was only fog in the trees. Roe swallowed a few times and tried to shake free from the scenes in his head and the sneaking whispers of whatever had spoken to him. Moments passed, the horrible sights fading with the ease of waking at dawn from a nightmare. At some level, he understood it was basic defence mechanism – jettison the creeping dread and terrible scenes to enable him to simply continue putting one foot in front of the other. Survival, defence, whatever it might be: he didn't care as long as it left him with the relative normality of the woods and their journey through it.

He shook his head and wiped his eyes with the back of a gloved hand, not taking his attention from Lazarus.

Just your head. Just the stress of all this.

He could almost believe the thought and *almost* was enough.

The path took them into a sharp right, then a second clearing. Some of the poor daylight fell through a gap in the branches forming the wood's ceiling. While it did little but make the fog brighter, it was a help.

"Through there," Mary said, pointing straight ahead. More trees, all much smaller and growing further apart than the others, grew in a straight line.

While it was hard to be sure, Roe had an idea a rolling field spread from the treeline. That could only be a good thing.

Promising himself he would not look back to whatever might walk in the woods, Roe marched forward, came close to overtaking Lazarus and the boy raised an arm to block him.

"Wait. Slow," he said.

Lazarus set out, following Mary, and Roe trotted to keep up. They entered the last cluster of trunks, the aroma of the air stronger now they were close to open land. He counted the paces until what passed for sunlight broke through the treeline. Thirty-three steps out of the woods and back to open space where he could run if need be.

He kept his mind blank for the last of their journey, refusing to let doubts or fear inside, concentrating solely on the earth crushed below his steps and the rasp in his lungs and throat. Moments later, they pushed through spiky branches and struck clear ground.

Never in his life had Roe been so glad to feel sky somewhere above even if the fog blanketed it. For a moment, he had the impression of the ground sloping down to meet a rising shape—something huge unseen beyond the fog. And there was another smell to the moisture.

Faint but there, he caught the scent of the sea. Here was Dover and here was the end of the country.

He knew what was ahead and felt no surprise. If Granger had been right with his obsessive plan to seek redemption with Dealey, it would make sense for any new government to set up base in Dover Castle.

Moving as smoothly as machinery, Lazarus and Mary walked side by side, neither paying him any attention. Even with their physical and emotional wounds, they managed to keep going.

At Roe's back, what was probably a branch breaking free from a trunk snapped, the sound like a crackling knuckle.

"No," he whispered and had no idea what he was negating.

There were no more falling branches behind him and that was good.

Wanting only to curl into a ball and forget he had ever existed, Roe followed Lazarus and Mary into the fog.

Chapter Fifty-Three

Martha watched for any discolouration in the white surrounding them that might suggest movement. The fog remained a mostly uniform shade. There was little in the way of noise to hear, either. The tired tread of their steps across the grass, earth sucking at their shoes and boots; the occasional harsh cry of a hungry bird was all that existed for her, and even those few sounds were made softer by the fog.

Despite their situation and the chill making her long for a fire, Martha felt a weak joy because there was other life in the in the fog.

They were coming. Lazarus and Mary.

Priest had whispered the truth to her once they were passed the woods, telling her to be ready for the others and to forget for the moment about any attempts to escape Granger. She would know what to do for them all when the time came; all she needed to do was love them as she always had, to be brave and to keep walking even if all she wanted was warmth and a rest from the horrible land that turned her into a speck below the sky.

One foot in front of the other, Candace at her side, and every swallow in her dry throat pulling more of the afternoon into her lungs.

They followed dips and rises, trudging on, visibility down to a matter of feet. Roads might remain nearby; there was no way of knowing for sure. Or maybe everything had become one massive piece of grassland coated in fog. She thought she could accept that if it meant keeping away from Granger's place. His Dover where more men like him waited for them with their guns and their judgement.

Martha stumbled, fell slowly and came close to hitting the soft earth before Candace shoved her hand out and caught Martha's chest. Everything spun; vision was a hot, trembling blur and the voices beyond the blur had slowed to a deep drone. She laughed at the idea they were coming from under the sea just beyond their caves, and her laugh sounded horrible and mocking to her ears. Frightened, Martha struggled to stand, to feel she was breaking through the waves and relaxed only when Candace's voice, slightly more normal, was right at her ear.

"It is all right, Martha. You are safe."

Granger spoke. She caught the word *head* and felt a calloused hand on her hair. Candace's hand so lovely and strong; black to her white and colours were only different lights. Priest had told them that long ago.

Candace pushed with gentle pressure and Martha let her head fall. Seconds or minutes passed. When Granger spoke again, he sounded almost normal.

"A faint. Nothing to worry about."

Candace replied with her frightening anger – the anger swimming below her own surface. "She needs food and rest."

"You ate at the farmhouse," Granger said, and Martha was not so far removed from her situation to stop her missing his smug mocking.

"Not enough."

"It'll have to be. We're close. Up, little girl. On your feet."

Martha hissed at him and tasted blood. She'd bit her lip when she fell. Eagerly, she ran her tongue over the tiny wound. It wasn't much but it was all she had. Martha understood that on an adult level and focused on her breathing for a moment until her head felt less like the fog and more like her own.

Candace extended her good, strong wrist and Martha used the thin forearm to help her stand. Hands on the shotgun, Granger watched.

"Believe me or don't. I'm not fussed. All I will say is I know how tired you are. Killers or not, you're still just skin and bones." He grinned fiercely. "Unfortunately, there's bugger all we can do about that. So, if you would."

Martha lifted a foot. Never in her short life had she wanted to see level ground of stone as much as she did at that point. She did her best to shake off whatever had happened a moment before and ignored the lingering effects as best she could.

Candace kept her hand low so Martha could keep her fingers on the scant flesh and stick-like wrist. They walked, Granger following. He waited no more than a minute before speaking in a low but carrying voice.

"No need to slow down. We're there soon."

Candace and Martha had fallen into step together, their pace matching the others without a single look passing between them, and that pace had slowed to a crawl.

Still in a friendly but firm tone, Granger spoke again. "Candace?"

While she didn't look back at him, he spoke as if she had.

"If you don't move faster, I will shoot the girl in the legs and leave her here. Do you understand?"

Candace might as well have not heard him for all the reaction she gave.

"Do you understand me, Candace?" Granger asked.

Again, she wouldn't face him, but she did reply.

"I understand."

"Glad to hear it," Granger replied.

They crossed grass, the route remaining uneven. The fog continued to muffle sound, and scents mixed into an unpleasant stew of their sweat, the grime coating their bodies, and the clinging dampness turning their clothing cold. The springiness of the grass and the changing gradient of the land was all they could go on to feel their way further south-east.

Movement overhead caught Martha's eye. The object streaked downwards, then back up. A hushed noise rained from above, the sound disturbed, and it took Martha a moment to realise it was birdsong—or had been in another time. Sickness or hunger had turned the once pretty sound into something ugly and broken. The bird, still out of sight, swooped erratically before letting out another jagged caw and vanishing further into the fog.

"Bird." Martha brushed her fingers on Candace's forearm. "Seabird."

As she said the word, she inhaled salt and brine; a faint suggestion of both, but enough to make her want to weep for their home and all they had lost since leaving it.

Candace smiled although Martha knew her sister was far from happy. Candace would have had the same thought and doubtless the same memory of the beach outside their caves as Martha recalled. Lots of birds there, all pecking at whatever the waves brought to the sand before making their noise and flying into their homes up in the cliffs.

No beach like their home here; no caves. All they had was the open land and the fog and the sky, far too large, just out of reach beyond the white.

"Move on," Granger said although it was with more gentleness than at any other point.

The ground dropped in a definite slope and there was a sense of the grass spreading much further – a sensation Martha loathed. Heat spread over her chest and up into her throat, rising higher. It wasn't like the *fainting*. It was more like wanting to drop her face to the chilly earth and hide in the long grass, cool and refreshed and protected by it.

All will be well, child.

She looked around for Priest, remembered he was dead and let her love for her father slip into the breeze.

They continued and alternating her attention between the route ahead and their surroundings, Martha was the first to see a weaker patch of fog. While it wasn't open enough to offer much, it did give a glimpse of what might have been Dover. She didn't know, and so could only see.

Another town of wrecks, of fire-damaged homes and shops. Like so many places the family had passed through or hunted in during their time together, what grew in the white after the grass was a grave.

The grave opened for her. Granger, his gun and his crimes flowed away like a retreating wave. Even her dear sister went with him along with the constrained terror of being so exposed below the sky. Martha saw the town because she knew dead places, and all its decaying secrets were hers alone.

As with London and a dozen other cities, the nuclear fire rains on Dover, a lone warhead detonating in the atmosphere somewhere high above the Channel instead of finding its target much further inland. Fires spread in seconds, raging from street to street, consuming buildings and pavements with a great hunger. Windows become jagged holes; glass coughs in or out, either turning floorboards into spikes or shattering on curled up grass and flowers now ash before melting. Cars, buses and vans, racing to escape the inevitable, are blasted by shockwaves and tossed to spin end over end on the roads upended or on their sides with broken chunks of their bodies hanging loose before the flames find them, turn each into an oven, cook the few survivors with their crushed bodies and blinded eyes and ruptured eardrums. In under a minute, bodies are stripped of their flesh and faces. And still the flames streak onwards, screaming winds propelling them further, licking over the falling houses, bursting through more windows where the people desperately seeking shelter and protection are either scorched into husks or blown against walls to break their limbs and their skulls. Entire bodies burst and limbs and organs are shredded before the inferno finds the remains or those few who were quick enough to flee into cellars – the doors and stairs no saviours against the blaze or collapsing ceilings and shattering bricks.

In the centre of the town with its scores of pubs and centuries-old buildings, a toppling hotel smashes into its neighbour, and the joined bricks and glass crash into a third. And so on while the conflagration grows higher, stronger, and the winds born from the detonations shove the flames through the rooms and corridors, finding running flesh, turning it from people into screams. Underground gas pipes rupture and smaller explosions erupt through windows and doors to join the fire turning the hub of the town into its own sun. Water pipes, split and twisted, are useless. The gallons inside each boils in a heartbeat; steam streaks through the rapidly growing cracks, and superheated water explodes to spray the ruptured pavements and shatter more windows before the blistering air turns the liquid into condensation hot enough to melt bone.

This is exactly what happens in an underground storeroom to a five-star hotel: pipes covering a wall crack, uttering sly creaks and groans at the weeping group who bolted the heavy doors against others equally desperate to take shelter. When each pipe splits, boiling steam adds its shrill whistle to the screams but the screams do not last for long.

Three pubs on a backstreet shelter their owners and customers in their cellars. The drinkers and the staff listen to the speeding flames and the din of collapsing buildings. In the gloom illuminated by a few old torches, they weep and watch the dust swirl while outside, Dover has become Hell. They huddle together for comfort while trying not to think of their families and what is happening to the world. They hammer on the connecting walls, trying to call through to the neighbouring pub, making out little more than panicked yells and muffled voices in return. They crouch in corners, between barrels and someone tries to make a joke about cracking one open so they can have a pint but the man's words decay into sobs.

The dust swirls a little more.

In each pub, they cough and sputter at it and those in the third pub—the oldest of the three and the one furthest in the line from the high street—have to listen to the people in the other pub shriek and plead for help when the flames find them.

Then when the smoke bleed through the fine cracks in the walls, their coughs became pleas to God, for help, for mercy.

Several workmen digging up Dover's main street to lay new water pipes manage to raise a manhole and clamber down into the sewer when the white flash blooms at the horizon, each man understanding at once what has occurred. Weeping, muttering their wives' names, they race through filthy water, stomping through muck and stink. Four minutes after the silent light turns the Channel and its pleasant blue into a white sheen, broken gaslines create an underground fire that chases the workmen, finds them and breaks out of the same opening they'd used as a supposed escape.

The few teachers who stay in one of Dover's primary schools and don't run for their cars or their nearby homes when the horizon flashes herd the children into storage cupboards and under their desks. Men and women hold the weeping children in their arms and tell them to close their eyes. The elderly head turns her back on the approaching shockwave and has time to lead three teachers and a dozen children into the opening lines of God Save The Queen.

And the fires and the winds and then the peace.

Martha closed her eyes, saw only blackness which was worse than any inferno, and opened them again.

She knew nothing of Dover's history, knew its name solely from Granger and his men and not a bit of mattered compared to what she had seen.

Dover had burned like the rest of the country. If there was any rule in the town, it was a rule over nothing but memories and dust.

Martha found she was still holding Candace's hand. Her sister had gone nowhere despite the terrible sensation of a fleeing wave holding her prisoner and leaving Martha alone with nothing but the ashen town beyond the white for company. She smelled salt water, the briny aroma stronger than the hint of it a few moments before.

"Straight on," Granger said. "The road should be close. We're better off approaching from there rather than across country. Give them chance to see us instead of looking like we're sneaking at them. Right through the main entrance. In full view." He smiled although to Martha, it looked like he was hurt.

"Where are we going?" she asked.

Granger blinked, plainly surprised Martha and not Candace had asked him. He covered the surprise as best he could while Martha pressed her head against Candace's side. Granger pointed straight ahead. Martha peered that way and made out a faint suggestion of a darker shade beyond the fog. As weak as it was, she had the impression of *bulk* stretching from side to side and up. Looking down, she had enough visibility to know the land ascended in a steep incline which meant they were at the foot of a hill.

"The road should be close. We're better off approaching from there rather than across country. Give them chance to see us instead of looking like we're sneaking at them. That wouldn't do at all."

Candace repeated Martha's question. "Where are we going?"

"To the rulers," Granger replied and shrugged off his backpack to drop it to the soft ground. The water bottles inside his bag were empty and it seemed he no longer cared about possessions here at the end of his journey. "The castle, of course."

Chapter Fifty-Four

"Wait."

Lazarus looked back, almost surprised to see Roe still with them. They'd descended the slopes at a good speed, the movement helped by the layout of the land. While he and Mary had managed to move relatively quietly, even with the occasional hiss Mary uttered owing to her wounded hand, Roe had been like a lumbering, panting beast. The fog would have done some good in keeping him hidden from anyone listening, but the rattle in his chest and voice would pinpoint him the closer they drew to the castle.

"What?" Lazarus replied. His thoughts about Roe and their approach to the huge pile of stone ahead had gone through his head in under a second; images, senses and instinct rather than actual thoughts.

"Nobody. . ." Roe had to spit. He tried again. "Nobody here. No lookouts?"

Lazarus didn't miss the man's point but thought it unimportant. There would be lookouts. Hidden men in the fog probably watching from the same hills they'd run down to level ground.

He sniffed; Mary did the same. There was little wind. Certainly not enough to carry the stink of their bodies in the air. Likewise, no smell of nearby men. Lazarus caught nothing but the aroma of his own dirty skin, his sister's and the tired sickness brought to life inside Roe.

Knowing they needed to hurry, Lazarus kept calm and studied what he could make out of their surroundings.

They'd seen the outline of the castle through the fog twenty minutes before while they crossed open land and listened to the muffled roar of the nearby sea hammering at a beach. The structure, without question the largest Lazarus had ever encountered, jutted from a raised section of the land – a hill big enough to make Lazarus feel smaller than a spider – and the approach to the shade like a piece of midnight in the fog rapidly became too steep to traverse. Roe had pointed to the north and the glimpse of burned buildings of all sizes. Before the town, a road cutting through the sickly green. It was where they stood now, the road narrow and made more so by the grass and shrubs spreading in from the edges. Another series of bumps and slopes were lost to the fog and the occasional cry of a gull while Dover was just the same as the towns Lazarus and his siblings had encountered. If any men like Granger lived there, they had nothing to rule or organise and nothing with which to protect themselves. Not down there among the streets filled with rubble and cars crushed and flattened. Not down in another dead place.

"They are hiding," he said eventually. "In your castle."

"Not my castle." Roe coughed for several moments. Blood splattered his chin when he finished, and he wiped his mouth, eyes dazed. Lazarus knew Roe would be dying on the ground soon and while he also knew he and Mary could kill Roe in less time than it would take the man to scream, he did not. A promise had been made in Priest's name.

Lazarus sticking to one side of the road, Mary on the other and Roe lurching down the centre, they followed it as it rose in twisting inclines, taking them back level with the steep slopes of the castle's edges.

"You know where he is taking them?" Lazarus called to Roe who was now holding his stomach as he walked. Colour had left his face, leaving his face resembling a nude skull.

"In the castle," Lazarus added.

Roe nodded. "Whatever they have there. . .Dealey. . .whatever's he got, they'll use the most secure place. Granger is scared of them. He's scared of all you." Roe snorted laughter that bubbled in his nose. "That's what it's all about for him. Fear. He's scared out of his mind by you and what you do. Fear is the only reason he's ever done anything. Fear of not knowing what's going on. Fear of differences. Fear of not being the man in charge." Roe laughed again, more gently than before. "It's what his whole life had been about and he doesn't know that."

It was the longest statement Roe had made in hours which meant little to Lazarus. If Roe wanted to use up his remaining time on such things, it was his business.

They reached level ground again. The fog made it impossible to tell the distance between them and the hulking stain marking the fog ahead. Rock, grass, the land become a streaming flow pushing the castle as high as the sky. The castle breaking the world in two: on one side, Lazarus and Mary and a man too foolish to know he was dead; on the other side, everything else with a space big enough to crush Lazarus's comprehension to nothing.

"Tunnels." Roe drew closer to Lazarus. "There are tunnels under the castle. A lot of them. They could hide down there for years if they had supplies or if they want us to never find them. If you walk through the gates, they could get underground just like that." He clicked his fingers, the snap weak and somehow sad.

"We follow them down," Lazarus said, not bothered by any tunnels. He and Mary knew caves and the secrets they held. Tunnels under a castle were no different.

"They'll kill you." Roe sounded closer to sleep than waking. "They have all the advantages. You have nothing."

Mary hissed at him and he jerked back to full consciousness, fright powering him.

"Or maybe you do," he muttered and attempted a sickly smile.

She hissed again although with less force and dismissed him to face their approach to the castle.

Lazarus tested the weight of his axe. While the metal was dull and not as sharp as it had been, the weapon would still do the job. If only Dumah was here to wield it with his strength. And if Priest was with them to guide and instruct. . .but then if Priest and Dumah remained by their side, there would be no need to go after Candace and Martha because his sisters would be nowhere near this silent place.

He held a sob inside, chest hot and pounding, and heard Priest speak from somewhere nearby.

Hurry, Lazarus.

The need to weep vanished. Steel encircled his heart and would not break. He puffed for a moment and turned, ready to tell Roe to keep up.

Roe had stopped several steps away. White fingers slipped over his legs and waist as if the fog was streaming up from the ground. His focus was an unblinking stare to the land spreading away from the road, becoming the hills and the route they'd taken. None of it was visible. In his mind's eye, Lazarus saw the earth descending in a slope before it merged with the woods they'd pushed through.

Hurry, boy. Time is almost done.

Roe turned to Lazarus, blinking, licking his bloody lips. He looked like he might scream at any second.

"Lazarus," Mary said, her little voice thick with urgency.

Somewhere in the fog, a hollow bang crashed down and it took Lazarus a second to identify the noise simply because he had not heard many gunshots in his life.

Then he and Mary were sprinting along the road to bear down on Dover Castle.

Chapter Fifty-Five

Size was first; smell was second.

Knowing they should walk apart, Candace remained close to Martha as Granger ushered them through the castle entrance and into an open space. She kept her body and head still, moving only her eyes to take in as much as was possible of the layout and land beyond the gates.

The fog was thicker than out in the fields and woods, perhaps because of the lack of wind pushing it on anywhere. Around them, white shielded much of the castle's buildings, walls and roads from view, leaving only the suggestion of the structures puncturing towards the sky, along with the sheer solidity of the place. Candace knew buildings despite spending so long in the open land and in the caves beside the beach at Whitstable; Dover Castle was a massive difference to any house or building they'd raided before now because of its immense physical weight. It seemed to Candace the ground should break under its pressure and spill each outbuilding, sloping grass and the giant castle itself to the sea where the water would never be strong enough or the waves high enough to swallow it. Cities were husks thanks to the bombs; everything of before was a memory belonging to people like her who didn't care to remember any of it, but Dover Castle had survived the fires because its size was impossible to break or burn.

Then the smell. She knew Martha had picked up on the same. Mixed with the salty tang of the sea somewhere beyond the fog and slipping below the wet rock and earth, a faint but still discernible stink. Something gone bad. Something spoiled. It was like a faint sheen on the ground or an animal decomposing miles distant, and its fetid aroma brought over the sea by the wind.

But there was no wind.

Her senses relaying all this in seconds, Candace listened for Granger's old friends to make themselves known, to challenge Granger or to order him to lower his weapon.

Nothing happened and that was no surprise.

"Casemates."

Granger croaked the word and tapped Candace on the shoulder with his shotgun.

"What is that?" she asked.

"Where we're going. Harris told me all about it before died." Granger trembled. "Was it your lot? I've never been sure about that."

Candace said nothing at first. Granger was clearly losing his mind. His thought processes were all over the place which could be good for her and Martha because it meant he had less focus.

"Sure about what?" she asked.

"Who killed him."

He stomped from behind her and shoved the shotgun under her chin. Martha made it a step towards him and managed to raise a fist before he reacted.

"Stop right there, little girl. I'm not in the mood."

Candace did not take her eyes from his. "Martha," she whispered and the girl relented.

"Did you do it?" Granger said. "Did you kill the boy like you killed my wife?"

"No. We did not."

He snorted and shifted the gun away from her face. "You wouldn't know if you had or not. Too much blood on your hands, Candace." Granger grinned, the expression utterly real. "Sorry. Hand."

He shifted position, standing at her side, weapon aimed loosely at both of them.

"He was bitten. All over. How the hell Harris made it back to us in that condition, I don't know. The lad was strong, though. Bleeding to death, skin shredded and almost dead, he made it back to me and told me about the castle. The tunnels. Casemates. The War Rooms. That's where my old friend is hiding. That's where we're going."

He waved the gun to the right. Side by side, Candace and Martha walked on a flat road, leaving the gates behind. A bird called, once, twice. Fog rolled up the slope, obscuring the sides of small buildings and walls. Still, the castle rose all around, looming at them even as its highest points were seemingly miles out of sight. The waves on a beach were faint hisses instead of booming claps, and the familiar aroma of salt water was offset by the wet earth. And whatever was rotting somewhere.

"Go right," Granger muttered when another road branched off from the main one. They passed a cracked sign with a few arrows jutting from it. While faded, the writing on the arrow aimed to the right was still legible. Knight's Road. Candace knew about knights, and Martha would, too. They were in the stories Priest had read to her and Mary. Not surprised to see Martha smile, Candace drew closer to the child. Granger would note her movement, but she was too tired to care. They were almost done one way or another. She would stick close to Martha while she could.

Following Granger's quiet directions, they passed towers and low walls with the town blocked from view beyond. Candace noted how the low cloud clinging to the ground dropping towards Dover could not be differentiated from the sky and dismissed it all. Dover was a nothing-place fit only for decaying into the earth.

"Your friends aren't here," Martha said, and Candace wondered if her sister had thought the same as she had about the town. "They're dead."

"Shut up," Granger murmured. He sounded too exhausted to be angry or threatening. "I told you I'm not in the mood."

Several minutes later, he told them to follow the descending route and stick to it instead of following any of the branching off lanes. They did so, each step sending jagged pain up Candace's legs. She needed rest and food. Neither were coming, though.

"Stop here," Granger said.

They'd come close to the lowest point of the road. Ahead, it looked as if it hugged a curve before rising around the other side of a mound.

Granger shone the torch to their left. "Over there."

They approached the mound. Secure in an alcove, a set of doors were almost indistinguishable from their surroundings. Faded green and secure with pieces of wood hammered over their centre, they could have been untouched since before the bombs.

Candace didn't believe that was true, and a quick glance down at Martha showed she also didn't believe it. The entrance was freshly sealed. She listened for a change in Granger's breathing, any indication he was paying less attention to her and Martha. The fierce desire to attack him, to try to escape had burned inside for hours without the slightest opportunity to make that attempt.

He spoke and she knew it was no different now.

"Casemates," Granger whispered. "Hello, Dealey."

"You'll die in there," Martha told him.

Granger fired once.

The shot exploded, deafeningly loud against the afternoon, and Candace went down.

Chapter Fifty-Six

Panting like a dog but not slowing, Roe sprinted after Lazarus and Mary, his feet finding sure purchase despite the wet and bumpy ground. Even with Mary's injury and Lazarus clearly being close to done in, Roe struggled to keep up. Next to frozen but still sweating under his heavy coat, he lumbered after them, free hand holding his chest.

There was no point in calling for them to stop or even slow. Candace and Martha were in the castle grounds; there'd been gunfire, and Lazarus and Mary would not stop until they found their sisters. Roe could either try to keep up or slink away to whatever else might be out there.

Waiting back in the woods and whispering in the fog.

He ran on. His death was probably waiting for him inside Dover Castle, but at least he would die for something. Better than he'd lived.

They passed through the entrance, much of the daylight blocked by the arch and the entrance remaining solid in contrast to the town below. Bursting through to the other side, they skidded on wet tarmac and Lazarus doubled over, panting hard. Roe swallowed blood, gagged and snorted more of the hot liquid.

"The government's here. They—"

"I don't care about your government," Lazarus replied to Roe without looking at him.

"You need to." Roe's voice broke apart into coughing and it took him another moment before he could speak again. "If they're open to Granger, if they don't shoot him on sight, they'll have no use for your sisters."

Dismissing Roe, Lazarus and Mary stood side by side, the girl holding her injured hand and seeming to not care about the red staining the dirty wrap around her fingers. They both sniffed, Mary tilting her head. Roe inhaled, doing his best to ignore the scent of blood sticking to his nose as he ignored the taste.

The predominant aroma was damp earth and rock. Also strong, the nasty reek of sweat and dirt clinging to bodies. He coughed again before he had chance to smell anything else, cradling his mouth and nose with his elbow while blood sprayed over his arm.

Mary crouched, peering at the ground.

"Feet," she muttered and stood upright.

For a ghastly moment, Roe thought she'd spotted severed feet before realising she meant tracks beside the road. The prints small but distinct as if whoever made them had deliberately pressed down hard, marking their passage. They vanished about ten feet away.

"Can you still walk?" Lazarus asked his sister.

She raised her bandaged hand. No fresh blood stained the wrappings but her face was much too pale and there was a distinct swaying to her body. Roe wondered if she was powered by the same raw anger that had kept Willis on his feet for so long.

"You're just going ahead?" Roe asked. "Full view. No cover?"

He realised as he spoke that the fog would be enough cover for them. But then they probably would have kept going if the day was bright and cloudless.

"Yes," Lazarus replied.

"Wonderful," Roe said.

They moved again, Mary sticking close to the tracks while Lazarus stayed on the opposite side and kept close to Lazarus despite wanting to be anywhere else in the world. Oddly, he felt less fear of the siblings than he did of whatever was ahead. They could kill him whenever they liked; he could have been torn apart at any moment but they were sparing his life. As soon as they knew he had killed the big man back at the school, that he and not Granger had shot their brother, Roe figured he could count the remainder of his life in seconds.

Throat on fire, he forced his aching body to keep up despite the urge to simply collapse.

While the fog remained thick in general, a fresh wind was blowing in from the sea, creating thin patches that offered glimpses of their route. Sloping grass on their left where Mary kept much of her focus on the ground and the tracks in the earth; on the right-hand side, a wall overlooking the descent to Dover and the town's seafront. There was the impression of patchy grass and bare rock before the buildings and shops smashed into pieces. Another town, another wasteground. Roe didn't want to know anything about Dover because he knew enough.

It wasn't the town Granger had promised them.

The taste of salt stabbed at Roe's dry throat as he trotted to keep up and they passed under a squat tower and then beyond the old stone. The road narrowed; the wall seemed to roll beside it, unfurling like a banner while the other side where Mary studied the ground was a steep hill, the grass and weeds soggy from years of poor light and sea-fog.

Lazarus moving his head in a rapid jerking movement caught Roe's attention along with his quick sniffing. The boy was searching for threats and signs of his sisters, watching for any movement and clearly ready to use his axe judging by his firm hold on the handle. More than ready. Eager. Watching Lazarus jog level with Mary in a strange cross between a shuffle and a gallop, Roe had some idea of how the family had survived so long.

Because they're willing to do whatever it takes.

They continued for another few minutes, passing buildings, always with the town and more of the sea at one side, the castle proper a giant's home somewhere in the soft grey, and the road spreading and closing in the further they went. Eventually, Mary had no more prints to follow. Presumably made by Martha, they ended abruptly, leaving the wet earth unmarked ahead. Roe swallowed fog, his teeth and tongue aching for water, and panted hard. Lazarus studied the ground, then their surroundings.

"Tunnels." He faced Roe.

His axe was high.

"Where are they?"

"I don't know," Roe replied and refused to look at the dull blade. "Underground. That's all I know."

Lazarus grunted and marched to Roe, axe ready.

"Where?" the boy growled.

"I told you. I don't know." Roe thought his entire body might be coated in sweat even with the cold. He couldn't be sure. He couldn't be sure of a single thing.

Lazarus flexed his fingers on the axe handle. Roe's lone thought was hope that he would not have time to feel the metal enter his forehead.

"You are lying," Lazarus said. "You know."

Mary said a single word, voice soft enough to almost be missed. "Brother."

Lazarus blinked.

"Down there," Mary said.

She pointed further along. Roe managed to take it in without shifting his attention from Lazarus. Rising inclines of brown faded green; the road meeting the fog; the faintest outline of a few buildings, one large and imposing, and each marking the white like a stain.

And a section of the slope with an overhang. An alcove, maybe. A natural curve growing out of another curve.

On the ground around it, shattered wood, the pieces snapped and scattered.

Lazarus lowered the axe and jogged to the mess on the ground, Mary following.

Congratulations. You've led them to where they wanted to go. And now you die. Either at their end or Granger's or Dealey's. Whatever happens, you die down there.

Roe ran after them, fighting not to cry out when Lazarus and Mary kicked the debris aside and then booted the remains of the tunnel entrance wide open.

Desperate not to be alone in the soft chill and left as a speck below the darkening sky, Roe found the strength to sprint to the tunnel entrance.

Chapter Fifty-Seven

Stone steps, all soaked with brackish water, took them down into not quite full darkness. Grunting, Granger managed to free a torch from his coat pocket without lowering the shotgun. The beam he cast shone over walls that had once been grey but were now green with fungi. Pipes criss-crossed the walls while motionless vents let warmer air from somewhere into the tunnels. They descended further, leaving the roads around the castle as well as the tunnel entrance as they eventually reached the bottom of the steps and Granger shone his torch on a brick-lined passageway. The ceiling curved, forming a semi-circular roof. Water dripped from it with regular taps. A shaft opened to a hole; rungs cut into the wall ascended into the shaft and anything further than twenty feet into the opening was lost in the black.

Desperate to move faster, Granger took a moment to study the immediate area. His impression was of entering a disused factory. There was a distinct industrial air to the tunnels, an atmosphere helped by the multitude of pipes and grated vents. While everything was lifeless, it didn't take much imagination to picture the shafts and passages thrumming with activity.

Granger told Candace and Martha to walk straight ahead, to follow the light of his torch as it bounced off the walls to the floor and revealed every few feet of the area as they went on.

The floor sloping and the air flowing through cracks in the brickwork, they squelched in puddles and over cracks. It remained warm even as they descended further underground, and along with the occasional scent of the sea, there was something else salty in the currents. Something familiar.

Granger ignored the aroma, theorising any number of competing smells would fill the tunnels the further they went. The urge to call out Dealey's name as well as the names of the other men he'd not seen in a decade beat in time with his heart. They were down here, somewhere. Hiding. Aware of him. Waiting.

He blinked away sweat and wished for the fresher taste of the fog above even if it was cold.

Granger's torchlight flowed over a new surface, a white ball reflected back at them. A window. Lots of window. He paused, told Candace and Martha to stop and traced the beam across the glass.

They'd come to several rooms and the doors to most were fully open. The spare furniture and equipment left to rust was decades old while the fittings and pipework were either torn from walls or twisted out of shape. Any flood out of water pipes had been brief and long since dried. Granger's torch ran over stains, presumably from moisture damage, then tracked the higher walls inside the rooms. Shelving units, a few cupboards with doors hanging loose, vents with the metal grilles dented and worn. There was nothing for them here. By the looks of the mess, there'd been nothing for anyone in years.

"Onwards." Granger looked behind for a moment. "Peters?" Immediately, he shook himself to clear his head. There had been no voice from the tunnel at their back, no greeting. Peters and all the men like him from his days in the Office, their bodies had been turned to nothing by the bombs, their legacy forgotten by everyone but Granger. They'd been good men in charge in the old days, men who knew how to make a hard decision and stuck with it in the face of doubters and backstabbers.

Granger's lip curled, the action unfelt. "Bastards," he muttered.

They most certainly had been, all those who'd leaked information to the press, who'd created panic when there'd been no bloody need for it. And who knew? The business with the Yanks and the Soviets, that could have been fixed if Granger and his colleagues had been left alone to get on with it. The plan had been a good one and would have solved a hell of a lot of problems. All right, getting the Americans and the Ruskies into a meeting was proving hard, but it *could* have worked. Get them talking in Paris, have a bomb go off and blame the Arabs. A war, brief and probably bloody, but *brief.* Control of the region, control of the oil and a Middle East finally ruled by men with some decency and some idea of what the hell to do.

It could have worked. It really could.

But, no. A leak to the press; misinformation whether deliberate or accidently getting only part of the story and the Americans thinking the sodding Russians were coming for them in Paris.

And then it was all over.

"It would have worked, Peters. We had the right idea."

Peters agreed, his reply a soft mutter from all sides while behind his always gentle and calm voice, a dozen other voices from people Granger had not spoken to in too long. Men he called friends; friends who worked their arses off to get the job done, and each one letting him know how glad they were to see him because it really had been too long and could they shake his hand once again? Could they have a short in his office before meeting with the PM to discuss the latest round of cock ups from the Yanks? A swift drink was most definitely required, and *Herself* wouldn't mind. Bloody hell, she'd practically insist because these were difficult days, Peters. Culver agreed; he knew the situation. Hard choices to make, one and all. Plenty of work to do, but they'd get through it. They always got through it as long as they stuck together and kept their word to themselves and to each other.

All for the best and all for the good of the country.

Always the country.

Sinuous movement at his back, the air parting as something streaked towards him while everyone in front, Peters, Culver, Herbert, Lucas, Brown, King and countless others along with even *Herself* on the phone to Ron, all of them who'd come to shake his hand and tell him to get the job done, all became a white flow of smoke blown away to skirt over the ground and the walls and leave the tunnel a silent cell again.

Granger whirled around, the shotgun pointing at the ground. A reflex jerked through his left hand and his finger clamped on the trigger. He came within a second of firing into the ground and saw Candace, hand an inch from his eyes, freeze on the spot. Reality came back and the ghosts of his past returned to their graves. She'd obviously seen her chance while he saw nothing and spoke under his breath, whispering to people only he saw; she'd gone for him, but luck or fate had kept him from her claws.

Granger spoke, dismissing the civility he'd pretended to feel since the moment they'd met back in South Calcott. Doing so was a relief.

"You are alive only because you need to see what lives here."

Candace lowered her hand. Behind her, Martha did the same. The girl had aimed for Granger's groin, her teeth and nails eager for his flesh.

"Move," Granger said in the same dead voice.

They left the kitchens and mess rooms behind; the passage took them past dormitories and dressing rooms, each as abandoned as the previous areas. More stains from water damage marked the floors while the steady drip from leaks followed their steps.

Not pleasant down here, is it, Culver? I'm willing to bet you're not a fan. Never liked being cold, did you?

A murmur, a gentle protest.

Hah. Don't lie, man. We all know you kept the heating on all year round in your office. Patterson says it's like walking into an oven in the middle of summer. Mind you, he's never had any meat on his bones so it's not surprising. Can't say I like it too much, either, but this is the last of it for all us, I think. We've done our work. We've kept our heads together, haven't we?

Mutters. Soft agreement.

Good to hear it. I know we don't say it; I know we don't need to say it, but it is true. I rely on all of you; you rely on each other and we do our jobs. This is everything our jobs and our work stands for. Once we do this, we can relax for a bit. The Americans will be straight in there and none of the mad Arabs will be able to stand in their way. And when the Russians join in, it's all done. Give two enemies a common foe and we clear up all this unpleasantness.

Right, Patterson?

Wonder of wonders, even sodding Patterson was cracking a tired smile.

Good stuff. Now let's get to work.

"All your friends are dead," Candace whispered and he rammed the shotgun against her back as if it was a dagger. She didn't even flinch.

"My friends?" Granger replied. "What do you know about them?"

"I know they were like you. I know they and others like them were responsible for what happened. I know they thought they were in charge of others and that they wouldn't be hurt when the bombs came." Candace's flat tone held nothing at all – not even judgement.

"I know how everything was before your friends ended it. I know what our lives were." She and the child had come to a stop at some point. He didn't know when. He didn't know a thing or so it felt. Candace turned and her face was shadowed by his small torch and the candles spluttering their last on the floor.

"I know what you are, Granger."

Was it the first time she'd uttered his name? And had he ever heard it spoken from a corpse's mouth? Because she may as well have been dead. She and the girl were reanimated cadavers come to lead him down and down and down to whatever waited below the earth.

For the first time in hours or days or weeks, Carolyn muttered to him. *Deep breaths, darling.*

You've almost found everything you want. Don't let this terrible woman change that.

Granger found his voice as well as the strength in his arms to push the shotgun deeper into Candace's scant breasts.

"Move," he said.

She and Martha turned on their heels without further comment and shuffled on for another moment before he barked for them to stop.

They'd reached the stairs that would take them down to the next level and closer to Granger's goal – where the boy Harris had told him Dealey waited. Told Granger he'd almost made it to the big room while Dealey shouted at him to come and see what waited for them, the tunnels mad with echoes of shouts and Harris's running feet as he fled.

Granger and Harris alone in the seconds before Granger had wept and put his hands around the lad's neck. A mercy. A kind act to stop Harris's suffering.

So thinking, Granger had sobbed over the boy and wept over his staring eyes.

And now here they were – coming for Dealey's throne.

"Down there." Granger indicated the stairs. The rail had been snapped free in places, leaving jagged chunks poking out of the walls like broken teeth. Each step was discoloured and treacherously wet. Water continued to drip, unseen and sly.

They descended, Granger resisting the urge to keep steady by running a hand on the wall. Instead, he held the shotgun and his torch on Martha and Candace, making their shadows march ahead to level ground.

On the next level, he illuminated ahead where tunnels ran parallel with each other and ventilation shafts were cut vertically into the rock. Silence ahead and the deeper belly of Dover Castle's tunnels. Half a dozen nearly burned out candles glowed on the ground.

Minutes later and after passing more snaking pipes unfurling to the unseen ceiling, they reached a wide room blocked from the corridor by windows, all surprisingly whole. Giving the interior a quick look, Granger theorised it had once been used as a dormitory. No bunk beds in there now; no sleeping soldiers ready to wake at a moment's notice. Instead, it had been cleared of all furniture, leaving a bare floor and several rusting vents ushering in trickling water and salty air.

Moving on, they passed a kitchen and several offices. Granger's torch shone on broken chairs and pieces of mouldering wood. No signs of life, though. He wondered if there'd ever been anything under the castle but a man-made factory fit for military needs, and the thought made him want to weep for some reason.

They drew alongside a second dormitory. Its entrance was a yawning mouth; its innards were identically barren to the first. Straight ahead, one of the many shafts offered the way further down and Granger tried not to let his dismay show. Leading them down stairs was one thing. Doing so in a shaft where he could not keep an aim on them was another. Behind was no use. Blinking, his body aching, Granger did his best to think and heard Candace's comment on his old colleagues. He spoke before he realised he was going to.

"They might all be dead, dear Candace, but Dealey is still here. My friend. He's down here. Hiding. He knows me. He knows we're coming."

Silence from the cannibal sisters. . .or mother and daughter. Or whatever in God's name they were.

"Dealey," Granger muttered, then inhaled a mighty breath which roared out a moment later.

"Dealey."

Behind and above, the unmistakeable bang of a door. Then splashing steps through puddles.

Then noises not close to human or animal, but somewhere between. Granger, staring at nothing he dared shine his torch towards, bit back a scream and fumbled to free the handgun he'd stashed in his coat pocket.

More feet splashing through puddles and over the bumpy ground and Granger's light finally beginning to rise, coming to illuminate whatever was coming out of the void.

In answer to the faint light, a volley of animal barks, yips and snarls.

Worse than any of the hellish sounds, Granger heard plaintive whines, the childish sound a recognisable word from far too many voices taking into a chorus.

Hungry.

Chapter Fifty-Eight

Candace shoved Martha to the floor; the girl went down, splashing into the grime, and Candace was moving again, going for Granger before Martha could rise and before the man had chance to register the attack she'd wanted to make for hours.

She struck Granger's wrist, knocking the shotgun from his grip, and immediately aimed for his eyes. He turned at the last second; her nails tore at his cheek. Screaming, Granger grappled for a hold on the handgun. Candace slammed an elbow into his nose. Granger screamed again and managed to lift the weapon.

Candace tried to knee his forearm, hoping to knock his hand higher as he went for the trigger a second time. He found it and a deafening bang exploded in Candace's ears. At the same time, stone burst from the wall where the round had struck it, turning old stone into flying daggers. A bonfire roared into life in

Candace's side near her hip, and the gun spilled from Granger's fingers.

Martha howled. The child was a flying beast, streaking for Granger's stomach as Candace collapsed. Martha clung to the man, teeth worrying at his belly while he pounded at her head and shoulders, shrieking for her to *get off me.*

Splashing above, *hurrying.* Things unseen sped for the stairs and they could only be seconds away, seconds from spilling into the winking glow of the candles and shaking light cast by Granger's torch rolling back and forth.

Martha's wail battered at Candace as she reached for the burning wound in her side. *"Candace."*

She broke free from Granger, dashed a few steps further into the tunnel and the screaming man lunged for her. Ducking, Martha shot between his legs, turning as she went under and using all her slight weight to shove the backs of his knees. Crying out unintelligible noise, Granger went down, rolled over and fell into the shaft.

He made no sound.

"Candace," Martha whispered and ran to her.

Groans merged with the thud and squelch of running feet. Eager groans.

"Up." Martha pulled at Candace's shoulders.

Trying not to weep, Candace lifted her head and faced whatever was staggering down the tunnel towards them.

He shot you. You are dying.

It wasn't a gunshot wound. Flying chunks of the wall had pierced her flesh and opened a hole in her body. Perhaps no better than a gunshot. Perhaps not life-threatening now but it would be with the infection crawling through the filthy ground and streaming walls. And in the stink that could only be decaying flesh.

"Gun," Candace croaked.

Lunging over the ground and splashing through freezing water, Martha found the shotgun and Browning. Without hesitation, she gave Candace the handgun, then reversed the shotgun to use as a club.

"Good girl," Candace said. "My sister."

"My sister," Martha echoed.

"Kill them all."

Screaming, her lifeblood soaking into her crotch and legs, Candace made it to her feet.

Side by side, they went for the groaning things in the dark.

Chapter Fifty-Nine

"Wait." Marty already held her knife high, the blade aimed straight up, and any slight tremor in her fingers froze at the same instant she spoke.

Lazarus listened, barely breathing while watching Roe who'd also frozen.

He heard nothing but didn't relax. They'd left the damaged entrance and outside world minutes behind, Mary and Lazarus sticking close to either wall while Roe alternated between who he followed. Holding his axe with one hand and keeping the other free and ready, Lazarus had led them alongside rusting pipes decorating the high walls. While the illumination cast by the occasional candle failed to shine much higher than their heads, Lazarus had the impression the ceiling was a wide curve and had been since they'd reached flat ground at the foot of the entrance steps and turned to the left. Standing close to Mary, tongue swollen with thirst, belly empty and his feet rich with blisters from their cross-country walk, he rejected all distractions and listened.

Wafting from the nearest vent, voices: echoing, jumbled. Female. Distance and acoustics turned the words into soup, and the speakers' location could have been miles distant. Even so, Lazarus was convinced they'd heard Martha and Candace.

The sisters were clearly not in the same tunnel as the one he, Mary and Roe had taken; it wasn't going to be as simple as just following them step by step. Frustrated, Lazarus fought the temptation to take his panic and exhaustion out on Roe by tearing into his throat. A promise had been made. Roe was safe with them.

"Where are they?"

What might have been a soft thud sounded somewhere, making Lazarus think of collapsing rocks in the cliffs of their home. Then another sound. A beat turned loose again by acoustics. Shouting, the sound as if underwater. Seconds later, a gunshot.

Mary voiced a hurt cry as if she had been wounded and Lazarus reached helplessly for the nearest vent. The grid was unpleasant to the touch – years' worth of rust clinging to the metal – and he tried shaking it loose. The vent held, giving him nothing but air slightly warmed by the innards of the tunnels.

"Lazarus." Mary sounded near tears and he wanted to bellow his frustration. He wanted to smash and break, to bite, chew, to kill.

High-pitched and warbling laughter flowed to them. Someone hysterical and utterly out of control was in another tunnel, their mad glee flowing from the pipes. Before they had chance to react, a screeched followed the laughter.

"Where the hell are you, Dealey?"

"My God." Roe's hands opened and closed in the same powerlessness Lazarus felt. "Granger."

"Herbert, I know you're down here, too. And what about Culver? Drunk again?"

"Damn you, Granger," Roe shouted.

Granger's shrill laughter continued, fading for a moment before coming back strong. He was passing vents. He was on the move. And still the rhythmic thuds pounded from another tunnel. Lazarus named the sound.

People. Running.

"We can't wait." Lazarus shook his axe. "We kill them."

"Yes," Mary agreed.

"What are you going—" Roe began.

"Candace. Martha." Lazarus howled the names like a dog desperate for their master, calling into the same vent he'd shaken.

The reply was another gunshot and female voices bellowing. Even with the blanketing effects of the tunnel walls, it was obvious one of the voices belonged to a child which could only mean the other was Candace.

As one, Mary and Lazarus sprinted ahead, the candles sending fluttering shadows rolling in all directions. Roe raced after them, coughing hard, plainly running out of strength but somehow keeping close to Lazarus's back.

They raced down the sloping tunnel, fewer candles lighting the way, the passage reeking on all sides, their slapping feet sending water splashing up their legs and Lazarus repeating his sisters' names. Reaching a slight curve, they came to a few more candles and the little lights showed the end of the tunnel.

Rungs built into the wall dropped into an unlit mouth. Above, they reached another hole.

"They're above," Mary said without hesitation.

"How can you be sure?" Roe panted and choked for a second on his blood. Wiping his mouth with a shaking hand, he fell on the wall, upright for probably just another few seconds.

"Our family is above. *He* is below," Mary replied.

Somewhere, another shot rang out. In the echo of the crash, new sounds spun around.

"What the hell is that?" Roe squealed.

Animal barking; shrieks of rage; howling like the wolves Priest had told them of; more gunfire, and discordant screeching: noise from a nightmare, and each sound losing itself in the collective storm.

"We go up. You go down," Lazarus shouted and stepped towards the shaft.

"You want to me to go alone?" Roe fought for breath. "You're letting me go?"

Lazarus glanced back. He wanted Roe to suffer for what he had been part of; he wanted to get his sisters away from this place.

The internal conflict died. He had promised Priest.

"Go," he said.

Mary ran to his side, then also looked back at Roe.

"Kill him," she said.

Roe attempted a smile. "I'll try."

Lazarus wasted no time with hesitation or debate. The gunshots and unfamiliar screams from above had ceased and that didn't have to be a bad thing, but it might be. He wouldn't argue with Roe.

"Take it." He all but threw the gun at Roe who managed to catch it. Swinging his face and upper half away from the weapon, he said:

"You need it up there."

"No." Lazarus kissed the dirty head of his axe. "We don't."

Roe nodded.

Lazarus pushed on his sister's shoulder. "Climb."

The girl had already clambered up three of the rungs, injured hand hanging close to her side and the thin muscles in her other arm shaking. She'd slid the long knife into the rope around her back. Its handle rested against the thick cushion of her hair.

"Save your family. I am sorry," Roe said.

They left him without a word, both scuttling up the rungs into the shaft and heading into the unknown.

Chapter Sixty

Aware anything might exist in the shadows cast by the occasional candle, Roe tried to put the thought out of his head and walked as quickly as the uneven floor allowed. He covered his mouth and nose with one hand, gun held limply in the other. He needed to take in fresher air but there was a terrible aroma on all sides and he cringed at the thought of swallowing any of it. Plus, the deep hurt in his chest and throat had grown much worse in recent hours. The sickness, whatever its name, was pushing into his mouth and nose, ready to burst free in a spray that would be the last sensation he'd feel. Fighting his growing panic, he splashed through puddles, stumbled on a loose piece of the floor and went down on one knee. Savage pain from the impact turned his lower half boiling hot and he groaned against his clenched teeth. A little more suffering wouldn't hurt in the long run.

There is no long run.

Gagging at the stink assaulting his nose, he stood. Another step and he stopped.

His shoe had come down on something soft, mushy.

Roe heard the instinctive voice of alarm in his head that said not to look. He overrode it and, still shielding his mouth, lowered his face towards the ground.

What he'd taken for broken pieces of the tunnel floor and puddles from several years' worth of rain soaking into the brickwork and foundations through the earth was lumpy chunks of flesh, and the puddles were more internal organ fluid than rain water. Roe's staring eyes took in the discarded pieces thrown without any care to either side of the tunnel and the short line of what could only be amputated legs dropped directly in the centre of the floor. Brown splashes marked the lower halves of the curving walls and it did not take much imagination to know the brown had once been red. Probably not long before given the stink.

Roe's stomach contracted, flooding his tongue and teeth with sour bile. Gagging, he spat until his mouth was clear and a wall came up in his mind. He lived behind the barrier and any horror of the hacked limbs and lumps of flesh and organs would not reach him. Not before he found Granger.

He marched forward, shoe snapping a broken bone denuded of skin. He kicked it away to a clump of rags; shredded clothing, he realised. Whatever had killed people down here had stripped them at some point.

Presumably to get at their bodies.

He had to spit again but refused to stop while he did so especially when he caught a distant laugh.

Granger was ahead, still laughing and enjoying his time with the dead.

"Granger." Roe gagged again. Vomit dribbled down his chin. "You bastard."

Granger cackled again and whooped his joy. Echoes stormed through the tunnel, making it hard to guess how far away Granger was. Roe increased his speed and ignored his aching knee as he ignored the cemetery he was passing through. Passing sealed rooms, he gave them only a cursory once over. Offices for the most part and all ransacked. Once upon a time, the military had made their plans down here in the Admiralty Tunnels; they'd received their intelligence and formulated plans and worked in utter secrecy to help end the war. And long before them, prisoners had been garrisoned here. Soldiers had slept and the darkness of underground had kept them secure.

Centuries of lives and battles and people turned to ash and dust and here came Roe to fight his own battle.

He wanted to laugh although it seemed that anything humorous in his life had long since faded away along with the hope Dover Castle represented a new chance. It was all gone. Not that it had ever been true. From the moment Harris staggered back into South Calcott Police Station, the boy riddled with wounds, their lives had been over because of Granger's lies.

No government. No hope. There was only whatever had set up home in the belly of Dover Castle. Whatever ate down here. And whatever Granger wanted to find.

Dim but still audible, Roe heard Granger shout more names in happy greeting. He knew all of them and could put a face to each. Why shouldn't he? Like Granger and Patterson, he'd worked with all those men. They'd argued together and joined in public unity when required to. They'd eaten and drunk side by side; they'd been the buffering diplomats between leaders too proud or stupid to sit down with each other, and they'd seen the way the world was going long before the first of the bombs fell from the sky.

They'd done all they could to change the inevitable outcome and every single one of those men was dead either in the nuclear fires or in the violence afterwards when Granger had appointed himself Lord Protector of the underground bunkers. Dead or not, Granger was happy to see them again and be back in their world.

Roe was following a madman deeper into the tunnels while the ruins of bodies lay scattered on the floor and the reek of the open wounds assaulted his nose.

Let him go. He's finished down here.

He couldn't. For what had been done to Patterson's daughter Lisa and for his cowardice in letting it happen, he had to find Granger and demand explanation. And then they could die together.

Somewhere close by, a quavering groan sounded. Wet steps followed it.

His internal temperature dropping several degrees and his mouth suddenly bone dry even with warm sick stuck to his teeth, Roe peered back the way he'd come. He saw nothing but heard plenty.

More steps, more splashing through the puddles infused with internal fluid.

The fire of his ruined lungs becoming a burning star, Roe sprinted deeper into the tunnels, kicking through the broken bodies and pieces of the broken walls in equal measure.

Behind, the moaning things came after him.

Chapter Sixty-One

Mary blinked sweat from her eyes and sensed Lazarus's movement change. He'd reached an opening. The child waited until she heard the faint splash of his boots, and sped up the rest of the way. The wall opened into a cavity and a tunnel floor soaked with at least half a foot of water. On level ground, the scent of blood was much stronger. The tunnel reeked of it and more. She knew the smell of bodies opened; they were both familiar with split organs and life fluid spilling from axe and stab wounds. In the enclosed space, it saturated every inch of the walls and Mary peered in their direction. She wanted to reach out and run her fingers over them to see if they were as splashed and tainted with blood as they felt. She didn't dare because the blood might belong to Martha and Candace and if that was the case, then the knowledge of what Willis had done to her hand would be nothing compared to the hurt in her heart.

"Come," Lazarus whispered.

There was nothing to be done about noise now. They kicked up ice-cold water as they walked with their weapons ready, and the water level sank into wide puddles within a few feet. Walking close to blind, Mary pulled her knife free from the rope strap on her back and crept beside Lazarus. The tunnel widened; a weak orange light glowed from low down where a few candles had fallen but managed to stay alight. Abruptly, the ancient stone wall became glass.

Not a window to the outside, not underground. A window to a room. Large, judging by the size of the glass. Furniture had been knocked in all directions. Beyond the overturned bunks and chairs, several more candles burned on shelves and sent monstrous shadows crawling up the wall.

Someone was coming.

Shuffling steps; clumsy and slow through the puddles—a person making no attempt to hide their approach.

Lazarus sucked in the stinking air and wrapped his fingers tight around the axe handle.

"Candace; Martha."

The boom of his yell stormed ahead, struck the walls and bounced back. Before it had chance to die, the approaching person broke into a lumbering run and Mary knew it was neither of her sisters before Lazarus advanced.

She pounded behind him, skidded and ran along the curving wall for a second. They drew level with the gentle illumination of the candlelight and the figure emerged from the murk, revealing its skeletal form clad in rags, dirt and shit staining its translucent skin.

For the briefest of moments, Mary hesitated as her mind uttered a word.

Child.

It swung its head towards them, tilting it and giving a profile view of its features. The sloping forehead. The mucous dribbling from its nostrils. The tongue hanging limp from its mouth, and the spittle coating its lips. The eyes, dull yet aware.

Lazarus's hesitation passed before his sister's.

He brought the axe down onto its skull, cracking bone. The genderless child shrieked, tried to pull away and Lazarus yanked it closer with the axe. Brain matter splattered over all three of them. The foul reek of waste followed as the emaciated thing soiled itself. Grunting, Lazarus tugged the axe free and the child squealed. It fell, clearly desperate to escape. Through its own muck and the puddles of blood and dirty water, it tried to do so.

Crying, Mary splashed after it, knife in hand. She dropped to her knees, shoved her knife to the child's throat and cut as Lazarus brought his axe down squarely on its back.

It sprawled flat, close enough to death to make no difference.

Mary stood, still weeping. Shaking, Lazarus kicked at the thing with its stick legs and twig arms and distended belly, booting it until it flopped over and the weak orange of the candles did little to brighten the shadows staining its face.

"What is it?" Mary whispered.

"A monster. A monster from a story. It isn't real."

The remains littering the tunnel now made sense while still making no sense at all. Whatever they were, Candace and Martha had killed them and hopefully fled towards the way out. A dozen bodies with their stomachs, chests and heads split wide open. Creatures with misshapen heads, with faces swollen by growths, with stunted arms and legs, with lumps jutting out of their flesh. Creatures that could have been human once but were now surely creatures from the stories Mary and Martha had always wanted Priest to read to them.

Because Mary knew *human*. She and the family were human even if others hated them for how they ate. *Human* was a recognisable state, a face, a thinking mind. The torn corpses cooling in the stench of their shit and internal liquid were not human and they were not animal. They were something caught between the two states, trapped there and made into beasts because of it.

In front and coming fast, graceless steps crashed over the tunnel floor and the storming approach was much louder than the lone thing making its way to them in the dark.

"Lazarus?" It might have been the first time Mary had ever said his name as a question.

They couldn't fight that many of the things. They couldn't retreat.

"In here," Lazarus yelled.

They went for the door to the candle room, kicking through overturned furniture, disturbing dust, frantically shoving whatever they could against the door. In seconds, they'd formed a makeshift barrier of desks, office chairs and a small cabinet. Soaked with freezing sweat, Mary wiped her forehead and let Lazarus push her to his back. She peered around his side, everything inside dropping to a tight focus and rejecting all superfluous thought.

They were out in the tunnel.

The deformed children halted, a few voicing querulous moans while others were seemingly mute. While the light in tunnel and the room was not strong, there was enough illumination to play over their faces and to show their eyes – those that were not swallowed by growths or distended skin.

Mary was crying again.

They wouldn't get to her. She knew that much. Lazarus would not allow it. She wondered if she would have time to feel the blow from his axe.

The first of the malformed creatures slapped a hand on the glass, fingers splayed. Too few fingers. With dim horror, Mary saw that three of its digits had fused into one.

Another did the same. Then another.

In seconds, each one was pounding on the glass with monotonous beats, and it took another ten seconds for the window to crack.

Chapter Sixty-Two

The occasional gunshot and scream reached Granger through the network of vents and damaged walls but the noise didn't register as more than background. Nearly all his attention was focused on old colleagues who crept alongside him, each shadowy figure keeping close to the walls or remaining a few steps behind. They spoke to him as he raced through the rolling mixture of yellow light cast by his weakening torch and the almost solid darkness. There were no candles down in the Admiralty Tunnels, only the wet ground and his colleagues.

Keep going. Almost there. You're close now. Very close.

That was Brennan – one of the spooks from MI5. He was at Granger's back, somehow keeping up without making any noise. And there was Culver slipping over the wall, his form merging with the pipes and the vents as if he was made of fresh glue.

Everything you want is down here, Culver said. *Remember what Harris told you before the boy died.*

Told you about the tunnels and the screams he heard, didn't he? Told you about Dealey making the castle his home. His rule.

Culver went on, whispers like hissing gas, and the others babbled over him, the merging voices losing all sense. Not that he cared. Two hundred feet below the ground and with his friends for company, Granger was glad simply not to be approaching the end of his journey from London on his own.

He slipped on a groove dug into the floor, the puddle shin-high and his trousers soaked in an instant. Cursing, Granger righted himself and shone the torch at his feet.

The ground was a mess: rents, cracks, loose stone and piled rubble. It appeared as if something huge had pushed its way from the tunnels below. Panting, Granger tracked the flickering beam to all sides. More grooves and wounds lined the walls, and while the way ahead was passable, the damaged ground would slow him.

No, it won't. No time for that.

He continued, men he'd known in the old days at his side and back. A fresh round of gunfire, clearer when he passed a wide vent spilling the scent of sea air, broke through to his conscious mind and he spun around. Aiming the shotgun at the unseen tunnel behind, he swallowed repeatedly and finally registered the impact from his fall down the shaft. Denial had kept it at bay for long minutes; it held his lower half in a vice, shins and knees aching, hips feeling like cracked glass. He'd been lucky not to be severely injured by those clever girls. Despite what they were and what they'd done to him, Granger couldn't feel too much hate for them. He no longer had the energy, not while he was so close to taking back his old life.

He closed his ears to the crack of gunfire and screams made distant by the layers of rock, and continued. Concentrating on not slipping or treading on an uneven surface, he realised several seconds later that a new sound had come for him.

Shuffling steps, each one wet and somehow clumsy as if whoever walked didn't quite know how to operate their legs.

Insides turned cold for reasons he couldn't identify, Granger increased his speed, crushing loose ground, stumbling on pits and holes while doing his best to shine the torch ahead.

The steps, soggy and stupid, also increased their speed.

Warbling noise, *voices,* became a jangled song. There was nothing human there, no thought, only instinct.

Run for it, Brennan said right beside Granger's ear. *They are coming.*

"Who?" Granger demanded and none of his colleagues wanted to answer.

Losing the last of his cool, rational thinking, Granger ran deeper into the Admiralty Tunnels while whatever followed him kept pace.

He didn't stop until he came, panting and close to collapse, to the doors of his destination: Admiralty Casemate.

When he saw what and who waited for him inside the massive room, he screamed.

Chapter Sixty-Three

The first of the children clambered through the hole in the glass while the others pushed at it. Lazarus counted three more weakening spots in the windows where they had split it.

"With me," he shouted at Mary and ran for the window.

He smashed his axe into the face of the first withered child—perhaps a six-year-old boy. Tugging it free as the child dropped, its blood raining to the floor, he brought the blade down towards the head of a second boy. It twisted at the last moment and Lazarus's axe split its neck. It screeched, attempting to pull away but blocked by the hole in the window and the other abominations. As Lazarus freed the axe and split the boy's skull, Mary's knifed blurred from face to neck to chest, cutting and tearing through deformed flesh with ease. Blood turned her face and head red, the liquid splashing into her mouth. Lazarus roared at her to duck as fingernails raked the air half an inch from her face. She did so, knife spinning and stabbing into eyes to blind a girl trying to claw her, blade turning the skin overhanging its forehead into shreds, then split two throats.

Blood exploded from the severed arteries, gore spraying. Pints of it saturated their clothing and the floor, turning the dust a lurid shade and drenching the window. Still, they hacked, cut, opened heads and chests with their weapons and still the creatures pushed at the bodies blocking their approach. Skidding, Mary ducked under a swinging fist and shoved her blade up. It pierced a flailing hand. The thing withdrew its arm and the girl lost her hold on the wet handle. Weaponless for a second until Lazarus spun around and handed her his blade, she kept her head down and then renewed her attack.

At the far end of the room, another piece of window split. Glass cracked, then caved in to smash on the floor. The first of the attackers shoved through. A naked girl no older than nine or ten crashed down on the broken glass, cutting her face and forearms before staggering upright to lurch across the floor. Behind, a second girl followed. Both resembled a pile of animal bones brought back to life.

"Kill them," Lazarus bellowed.

Mary raced to their new threat, small feet tracking blood while Lazarus hammered the axe into more faces, not pausing to attempt a clean kill before taking down another one.

Mary swung to the side as she reached the first girl, an arm like a stem of grass stretching for the spot she'd occupied a second before. The knife struck the side of the child's neck, came free as it fell to its knees and then found the second one's mouth. Choking, throat a gaping wound, it also fell.

A third girl was climbing through the hole in the window with a fourth right behind it, the remains of its clothing become strips catching on jagged glass and tearing further.

The middle section of the glass gave away, leaving the window little more than a few hanging pieces of glass and shards jutting out of the frame. In the mammoth crash, Mary screamed for Lazarus and ran at him.

Side by side, they backed away from the opening and the bodies spilling into the room.

They won't take her.

"Behind me," Lazarus shouted.

A wall of twisted flesh rose. Twenty, twenty-five monsters from one of Priest's old stories come to life underground.

The advancing children sobbed and barked and snarled.

Once again, Lazarus lifted his axe. He made no move to wipe the gore from his face or mouth.

"Kill you all."

The children closed in.

Chapter Sixty-Four

Her stomach and legs awash with the blood spilling from the wound in her stomach, Candace pushed her back against the soggy tunnel wall and saw Martha peering up at her, waiting for instruction.

There was only a single command she could give. "Kill them."

Candace a step ahead of her sister, they raced to the milling bodies of the things too ruined and withered to be called children and opened fire.

Bullets struck body, tore muscle and sinew, opened wounds to send blood splashing across the floor and spraying over the window. Screeching their agony and fear, the children tried to flee, bashing into one another as they scattered, falling to be crushed below feet. No longer feeling her own blood pumping from her stomach, the wound a memory, Candace fired again, the shot blowing off a tiny boy's head and sending his body crashing into others who were knocked aside.

Air reeking of gunfire, shit, piss and destroyed bodies, Candace sucked it all in and let it go in a tribal bellow – her impotent rage at the hurt brought to her family, her disgust at the children less than human, her grief for what her life had become all spilling from her mouth and not doing a single thing to help. She reversed her hold on the shotgun, caught a brief glimpse of a waving axe beyond the broken window and heard only the rapid crack of Martha's shooting. She swung the shotgun, smashing it into a girl's face, breaking nose and stunted teeth, and the child dropped without another sound.

Fire burst into life down Candace's leg, the flames streaking out of her upper thigh.

A child barely older than three had fastened their mouth to her leg and sunk teeth into her skin, tearing, biting and snarling as they chewed.

Candace brought the shotgun down to the child's skull. Bone snapped. Still, the child—boy or girl, Candace didn't know and could make out little in the poor light other than what looked like a pile of bones topped with thick, matted hair—wouldn't let go. Candace realised she was screaming, the sound lost in the cacophony of other screams and Martha's final shot that blew a hole in the child attacking Candace. Trying to speak or at least make a noise, the toddler fell back against the tunnel wall, tiny chest a bloody pit.

Fighting for breath as she fought against the need to simply collapse, Candace faced the few children who hadn't fled. Injured, growling, clustered together like a malignant growth, they crowded in the centre of the tunnel. The ground below their bare feet was awash with bodies and waste. They made no sound.

"Go," Candace shouted to them. "Leave."

If they understood, they ignored her. Two crouched at the bodies and poked their fingers into the bullet wounds.

Behind them, others did the same, squatting, reaching, pulling and chewing. Those who weren't blind did not blink when Lazarus's axe smashed into the last of the glass, scattering shards to the broken limbs and blown out stomachs.

"Lazarus?" Martha cried. "Mary?"

Lazarus appeared in the smashed window frame. His entire face was black, smeared with what Candace at first thought was dirt. Blood, she realised a moment later. And not black. Utterly red. His eyes were white holes.

Groaning, he lifted Mary to the window and the child pushed her way free to embrace Martha, both children weeping, saying each other's name over and over. Skinny arms wrapped together, faces pressed into one, hot tears slipping through the muck and the blood.

Unable to speak, Candace limped to the sisters and kissed Mary's hair. Lazarus crawled through the opening and dropped at their side, his axe stuck to his fingers by torn flesh and muscle.

"Sisters," he croaked and they were joined again in the fluttering candle light, their reunion silent save for the contented grinding of broken teeth on raw meat.

Chapter Sixty-Five

Limping, weeping, Roe bounced off the soaking wall, kicked through the loose rubble and rounded a corner to see a set of large doors flung wide open. Beyond, a tiny beam of light, fading and sad, glowed like a beacon.

He tried to listen for anyone following through the series of tunnels even as he attempted to hear anything that might be in the room and failed on both counts. There was no strength left in him for focus.

Moving on legs that might have been broken for all the support they provided, Roe staggered through the doors and swung the light of his torch.

Granger.

Roe tried to say Granger's name and managed a croak. He bought the gun to bear on Granger's head; his aim shook horribly and he lowered his arm to Granger's back before focusing his torch further into the room.

He saw it.

On the sole item of furniture left—an oak table spanning at least twenty feet—a metal tube lay with its innards of wiring and tubing exposed. Its cover had been removed – plates snatched off to get to the internal workings. The object covered nearly the entire table and the light from the two torches revealed lettering down the side, the inscription too faint to be clear. Smears of dirt coated it along with a thick layer of dust. A growth sprouted from the centre of the open section, something like an old branch growing into or out of the metal. Something grey like old stone growing diagonally, tatty cloth wrapped around the branch.

It wasn't a branch.

It was an arm.

Roe's shaking torch shone on the elbow, higher to the shoulder and neck, the body surely too wasted to keep itself upright. Then the face.

A grinning mouth, the lips split in a dozen places and no blood in the tears. A few teeth left in the smiling mouth, and those remaining stained an unpleasant black. A flicker of a tongue as the figure drew breath, its lungs rattling like Roe's. A nose falling in on itself, a pit where one nostril had been, then the torch tracking over an eye obviously blind but the other. . .the other staring, cold, fully aware.

"Hello, Roe." It was the grate of a coffin lid coming free.

Even with his body ready to give up and the soggy tread of whoever was running through the tunnels drawing closer with each second, Roe found his voice.

"Dealey."

The thing that had once been Dealey nodded, revealing the few patches of his hair.

"Long time. Waiting for you. Willis. Patterson." Dealey smiled and the worst thing in the world was the genuine warmth in the smile. "Granger."

"Willis and Patterson are dead," Roe replied. The words made no sense. *Nothing* made any sense.

"I know," Dealey replied. "Granger told me."

Roe inched closer to Granger's back and fought the crippling need to cough and splutter. His lungs were fire; his throat was a pinhole. "Granger?"

"Don't move, Roe," Granger said. "Bomb."

Bomb?

Roe looked again at the object on the table. What he'd taken for as a tube was actually a case.

Dealey's hand rested in the workings of a nuclear bomb.

"Jesus Christ."

Roe tried to back away and heard the things outside kicking through puddles and broken bricks. They'd be at the door in under a minute.

"They'll stop when I tell them to," Dealey whispered. "Don't worry about them. Children."

Roe wanted to close his eyes. Dared not.

"Dealey? What the hell is this?"

"I told Granger." Dealey's voice shrank further. Roe knew enough of radiation poisoning to know what constant exposure to an unguarded nuclear device was doing to Dealey. God alone knew how he was still on his feet.

"You kicked us out, Roe. Remember? We went back to the ground and we walked straight into Hell. The City. . .the world. . .it was burned to nothing. No government or police or law and order. We had *nothing.*"

The approaching steps were simultaneously growing louder and softer: louder because they were almost right outside the doors, softer because they were slowing.

"We died. Infection. Starvation. Disease. Attacked by survivors. The women. . .we lost most. Saved three. We kept them safe whatever the cost because without women. . ." Dealey sighed and it was like falling pebbles. "We ran from the cities. We ate whatever we could. We killed people for sticks, for minutes' worth of kindling. We made it to Dover."

"You are an abomination," Granger roared and Roe knew the man he'd known for close to twenty-five years was gone. In his place, this broken shell with nothing left to believe.

Dealey spoke as if Granger hadn't said a word. "It was winter, always winter. We were freezing to death. Starving in the castle so I took charge. I sent five men out to find anyone they could and bring them back to us and I made sure the women were safe. We killed everyone we could." His tone remained the same when he said:

"We ate them."

"Holy God," Roe said.

Dealey nodded.

"Everyone we could. We killed them. Ate them. We had nothing else." Keeping a hand inside the bomb, he gestured with the other behind Roe where the steps had come to a stop.

"Our children," he said. "We made the women have them. Ten. More. They were always pregnant. We had no choice. Needed hunters. Needed food." Still no change of tone. It seemed there was no horror in the world terrible enough to affect his whispering, cracked voice. "We ate. We hunted. We had more children."

All the implications and bald statements of the depravity seared into Roe's mind and he cried out for it to stop. It did not.

"We did what we had to. They're all gone now. The women." He sighed, the noise rattling in his chest but still managing to sound close to genuine. "Dead in childbirth. Dead from blood loss. Their children. . .I know what they are, but we had no choice. We need the children to hunt in the countryside and the towns out there. Bring us others. Bring us food. We need the weaker ones for when the winter comes and we have nothing left. I know what they are. The children. I know they're hurting. I know they're wicked. . .but it's what we have left now."

Roe tried to speak; his mouth and throat too dry. He hissed out the words. "Where is everyone else, Dealey?"

Dealey frowned. Confusion. It was at Roe for not seeing the apparently obvious. "Here," Dealey replied and jerked his head to the empty shadows of the giant room. "With us."

The man honestly thought the other survivors of the bunker were with him, crouched in the corners, watching this madness play out. Roe wanted to weep but lacked the strength to find the emotion fully. Dover Castle was as devoid of life as the rest of the country. Dealey ruling it like a king changed nothing when all he ruled were his memories and the abominations he'd fathered.

Dealey dismissed the matter and shook his ravaged arm. "And when we found this." He nodded at the bomb. "Down in the tunnels below this one, I had it brought up here. When Harris arrived and met the children, I knew you'd come. I waited for you, Granger. Always for you. The man who threw us out into world turned into ash."

Roe heard snuffling and snorts behind him. Grunts. Mewling. There were demons close to his back. Moronic demons poisoned by their proximity to a nuclear weapon, none with any idea of love or family or a life that did not involve the stinking dark of the castle's bowels or hacking and stabbing bodies to turn them into food.

"Why here?" Granger murmured. "Why keep a bomb here, Dealey?"

"Defence, of course." Dealey wheezed laughter. "There are others. All underground. Defence. Stop invasion. We lose a city or a town; we kill some of our own, but we save the country. Here. The train tunnel they were building under the Channel; there's one down there under the sea. Others along the coast. They closed off tunnels down here years ago and said they were weren't safe. But the bomb was down there. We found it. Damaged. The casing cracked, but I knew what to do."

Making no attempt to hide his movement, Granger aimed his shotgun at Dealey's decaying face.

"Don't." Dealey sounded close to regretful. "It's armed, Granger. Ready. You understand?" He sighed – pebbles rattling in a can, again. "There's an arming key in here. One turn. . ."

"Dealey, please," Roe began and had no idea what else to say. Dealey paid him no attention; all the man's focus was on Granger. Roe could have been dead already. Perhaps he was. He could have died hours before – back in the lonely woods with the shadowy thing coming behind to take him to all the bleak and forgotten corners of the broken country.

No.

He'd made it to Dover. A dead man walking, maybe, but he'd come this far. All he had to do was go a bit further.

Roe stood utterly still, caught between monsters he dared not face and the choice of shooting Granger or Dealey.

Making his decision required no thought.

Chapter Sixty-Six

*A*re you here, sweetheart? Are you coming with me?

Carolyn somewhere close. He can't see her which makes no difference. His wife back at his side, her hand linking with his and while he might expect the touch to be as cold as a freezer, it's warm. It's welcome. Soft. Clean. He links his fingers with hers and she tightens her grip on him. She forgives him, the hold says. He's done terrible things and he's wasted so much time; he's destroyed lives in his quest to return to government and his power, but she has let that go. Dear Carolyn, always so kind, understanding. Always the woman who supports him even during the most difficult times and choices.

There is pain in his back, has been for what might be hours or days or weeks, but he no longer cares about the pain – if he ever did. It belongs to his old life and old days. The future is here and he will walk into it with Carolyn's hand in his and that white light will wipe away all his many mistakes. He will be made clean again in the white.

Someone behind. Someone he used to know centuries before the white light. And someone who was ahead but is now just as behind as the first person even though they have not moved. Two men with names lost to memory and time. Their injuries and their spilling blood have faded along with their names.

Carolyn mutters their names, but *Roe* and *Dealey* mean nothing to him now as the surroundings he knew once upon a time mean nothing. The spacious room and all the power and decisions it held: the men who had changed the course of wars and subsequently altered the world for the better; the influence, the rule and the law contained in one single room below.

Below what?

He no longer knows. It probably doesn't matter.

The castle, Carolyn says in his ear. *Remember, dear?*

It's coming back, a speeding bullet bursting through memory and time and all the white in front of his eyes. He's opening his mouth to scream, to protest and deny truth, but it's still streaking down on him, *at* him, and all the idiot truth is coming with it.

Dealey, Roe; Admiralty and Casemate. The castle, the tunnels. The children bred from a few captive women forced to bear them, existing only to exist, to hunt the surrounding countryside and eat whatever and whoever they find. Then to feed on each other while their father rules from down here. While their father watches over the cold inner workings of his bomb, their god, and their father waits for the man who turned him away.

And all of it whispered from his dear wife in her mocking, furious judgement, everything hissed in his ear and held in his hand before Carolyn is gone from his side because she is a frozen corpse miles distant as she is also something terrible: the judge at his trial. His crimes. His wicked violation of a young woman justified in the secret passages and locked rooms of his soul as taking charge of a destroyed world and life. All lies. All bullshit, and Carolyn is her unforgiving verdict. It is given to him in the streaking bullet fired from Roe's gun and in the twitch of his own finger to fire at Dealey.

Who's smiling.

And twisting his hand inside the bomb.

And in the white, someone far ahead but coming closer with each moment of time turned into something beyond slow, taking her sweet time to draw towards him and ready to take his hand into the fire that comes after the white, a pretty teenage girl. A shy thing, she'd been. Quiet.

Made no sound when he hurt her so long ago.

Granger begins to scream.

As the white grows warmer, he thinks he might be screaming for a long time.

Chapter Sixty-Seven

The fog had cleared.

Lazarus in the lead, they burst through the smashed entrance to the Casemate Tunnels, hit level ground and had a clear view of the Castle for the first time, the remains turned cold by the slight pink hue to the air that passed for sunset. The inner walls were split and crumbling; piles of rock grew a dozen feet tall, some had tipped over to spread rubble across the slopes and grass. Flames had cooked the earth and wrecked many of the outer buildings while towards the cliffs, the roof of a church had fallen in, turning the centre of the building into so much stone and exploded glass. Sections of the outer wall, bordering the castle from the expanse of open land on two sides, were broken in huge chunks and revealed staring sections of sky and green.

"Together," Lazarus panted. Not a single piece of his body was free from hurt or exhaustion. Sweat dribbling through his thick hair fell into his eyes and down the sides of his nose. He had picked up Martha the instant they cleared the trapdoor to the tunnels and slid a shard of glass free from her thigh. Fresh blood soaked from the wound splattered her leg and the ground and she kept her wrapped hand over the sliced flesh.

"Woods," Candace gasped. "Safety."

None looking back to the ruined entrance to the tunnels, they ran, swallowing the mixed stink of their blood and the salt of the sea. Mary stumbled; Candace ducked without slowing her pace and shoved her one arm under the child to halt her fall. The bite wound in her leg had opened wider; blood soaked her thigh and puddled on the ground as they ran.

"Your hand," Candace hissed, reaching for the ragged wrap around Mary's fingers.

"No pain," Mary said. Although it made her face shake, she managed to smile and Lazarus loved her in a bright and clear way.

Following the route they'd taken, they passed below archways, the low wall overlooking the town and the sea at their side. Lazarus's axe fell from his hand, the metal grating when it landed.

Groaning, he came close to falling while still holding Mary and grabbed the weapon.

"Gates," Candace said. "The road out."

She obviously no longer had the strength to speak clearly; the wound in her stomach was like a bloody mouth. The fleshy lips had spread further, and even keeping her hand against it failed to stop the pulsing red.

Trying not to think of it, Lazarus attempted to increase his speed as they reached the junction of the two roads and came into view of the huge gates.

As one, they halted.

Dozens of the children from underground filled the opening to the gates, their sickness and deformities clearer in the daylight. Some wore rags while most were naked, the ruins of their bodies, the sunken chests and the swollen bellies perfectly visible. Tumours and defects, wounds and broken limbs inexpertly mended, the day caressed them all and let every eye witness them.

Lazarus spun in a circle, seeing the only other available route. It was back behind them, far across the castle grounds to where the ruined church lay on its mound; the cliffs beyond the old building and the beach far below.

Standing still, he looked at Candace. She understood as he did. It was no way out. Even if they could outrun the children, there was nowhere to go beyond the cliffs.

Only a long jump down to the rocks and sea.

Kill them all.

A prayer; a motto and nothing about it any use to him or his family now. For the first time he could recall, their battle-cry would do them no good.

But it was all they had.

Without speaking, Lazarus lowered Mary to the grass where she leaned on his side and took her hand from her wounded leg. Blood pumped from the slash in her thigh. Mary held her and Candace slid her thin arm around both of them.

The first of the children crept out of the castle's entrance.

Mary and Martha linked hands. Neither wept and Lazarus knew their thoughts as well as he knew his own. They wanted to see the sky beyond the cliffs and listen to the waves exploding on the rocks as they had at home.

Backs to the front of the castle and the remains of Dover, Lazarus saw Candace through his tears. She was smiling.

"Brother."

"Sister," he replied.

Still with their backs to the advancing children, they raised their weapons and blood dripped from the rusty blades.

"Remember your stories," Candace shouted to Mary and Martha. "The fairy stories Priest told you. They were real. The places were real. Do you remember them?"

"Yes," Mary replied. Lazarus saw through Mary's eyes, listened to the good push and pull of the waves through Martha's ears, and rejected all the hurts of Candace's injures because they were no longer important. He felt Priest's arm around Mary and listened to the soft crackling of the fire as it made the shadows dance and Dumah prepared dinner.

She smiled and Lazarus smiled with her.

The land of the fairy tales somewhere beyond the sea. The story place where the stories were real and every adventure Priest had given to them lived and breathed just as they lived and breathed.

Still holding hands, Mary and Martha closed their eyes and saw the fields and beaches and woodlands of their land. They walked there, little feet kicking twigs and sand, toes caressed by warm grass while Dumah, Candace and Lazarus were at their backs and Priest waited for them ahead on the beach, in the trees, in the open fields.

Lazarus opened his eyes and saw the sky over the sea, so wide, so open. And, for the first time he could recall, not stained with a fading but ever present black.

From the Castle gates, the children began their shuffling advance.

"Together," he whispered. "We kill them all."

"Together." The word echoed by his sisters, and a gentle hoot from somewhere that might have been a lone bird perched on a crumbling tree branch.

You are their leader, my son. You will lead them

Lazarus made a promise to his father, to his family as they ran, their aching feet kicking up mud and pebbles, their battle-cry roar bursting from their mouths, their weapons raised and their hands ready to spill blood again and for the last time: he would not take his eyes from the sky or his heart from the sea.

Even when the dusk became a blinding white sheet that blanketed everything from ground to the top of the world, he did not look away.

Chapter Sixty-Eight

Pushed by strengthening winds, the radiation followed behind the shockwave that blasted across the Channel, drifting through the high miles of the atmosphere, ready to begin its slow descent to the fields, beaches and woodlands.

About Your Author

Luke Walker has been writing dark fiction for most of his life after getting hold of paperbacks belonging to his dad and brother and reading Poe, King, Herbert and Lovecraft when he was far too young. His books include the horrors The Unredeemed, Hometown and The Mirror Of The Nameless as well as the dark fantasy Dead Sun. Several of his short stories have been published online and in magazines and books.

When not writing, he can found watching bad films or reading good books. He has novels and short stories to be published soon and is currently working on new fiction.

Luke welcomes comments at his blog, which can be read at www.lukewalkerwriter.com and his Twitter page is @lukewalkerbooks. Sign up to his newsletter at www.tinyletter.com/LukeWalkerWriter.

He is forty-one and lives in England with his wife.

Kidnapped in broad daylight from a busy Edinburgh street, Hannah Wilson has no idea what her abductors want with her, as they chain her in the back of their van and speed out of the city. They tell her she's perfectly safe when she's terrified for her life.

Transported to the far north of Scotland with dozens of others, all yanked from their lives across Britain, Hannah is taken to an isolated compound they call Pandemonium, which is an ultra-secure prison ruled by creatures that should exist only in nightmares - a place no one has survived for more than a few months.

Hundreds of miles away from help, her family's lives at risk if she disobeys any order, Hannah knows the key to surviving her captivity is to bond with strangers and teach them all to refuse to be victims. But, she's running out of time to convince the other captives to take their fight to the black heart of the prison and its inhuman warden; Hannah is yet to discover she is not the only one about to start a war.

In Pandemonium, all Hell is going to break out.

The Dead Room

A week before Christmas, terrorists detonate dozens of dirty bombs throughout Britain and release a man-made contagion, leading Nicola Allen to begin a frantic hunt for her husband and daughter while a nation burns. Fleeing from a horrendous event she refuses to speak of and desperate to find shelter in a dying country, Nicola's sister-in-law, Cate, takes cover in a partly destroyed hospital. Terrorised by visions of mutilated bodies and the screams of phantom children, Cate joins a group of survivors, all of whom are under attack by ruthless scavengers and looters. If Nicola is to have any chance of finding her family and if Cate is to escape from the siege, they must reunite and then descend into the belly of the ruined hospital where the horrific truth of what truly connects the two women is waiting for them. Waiting for them down in the dead room.

The Unredeemed

Four hundred years ago, Benjamin Harwood butchered whoever he saw fit to kill, knowing that sacrificing his murder victims to a demon would keep him safe from eternal punishment.

But now, their agreement has been torn in half and the demon is coming for Harwood's soul, coming to set him to burn.

Preparing for war, Harwood gathers the worst of the worst, the monsters and murderers he calls friends. With this group of damned killers, Harwood must return to the crimes of his past and seek help from his most recent prey: a teenage girl whose family he destroyed, a girl with more reason to loathe him than anyone in his life or death.

Only then he can try for a redemption that may be impossible or face a universe of suffering.

But Harwood doesn't know there is a hole in the floor of the world. And something much worse than the dead is down there…

Ascent

When terrorists target an American air force base with a nuclear bomb, Kelly Wells races to find her sister in a nearby office block, desperate for them to be together in their final moments.

At the same time, a handful of others fight their way through a panicked city to reach the building-frantic to make it to loved ones before the device ignites less than fifty miles away. In the frozen instant of the detonation, Kelly, her sister and three strangers are locked in that moment and trapped in the offices.

But they are not alone. An ancient god from the deepest pits in the earth has woken and knows their most private secrets and guilt.

Now, horror takes the form of their darkest dreams to draw sustenance from their terror, and the beast stalking them will dine well.

Because everybody is afraid of something.

The Toilet Zone
RESTROOM READING AT ITS MOST FRIGHTENING!

Compiled and edited by the grand master of 80's schlock horror, Bret McCormick, each one of this collection of 32 terrifying tales is just the perfect length for a visit to the smallest room....

At the very boundaries of human imagination dwells one single, solitary place of solitude, of peace and quiet, a place in which your regular human being spends, on average, 10 to 15 minutes - at least once every single day of their lives.

Now, consider a typical, everyday reading speed of 200 to 250 words per minute - that means your average visitor has the time to read between 2,500 to 4,000 words, which makes each and every one of these 32 tales of terror - from some of the best contemporary independent authors - within this anthology of horror the perfect, meticulously calculated length. Dare you take a walk to the small room from where inky shadows creep out to smother the light and solitude's siren call beckons you?

Dare you take a quiet, lonely walk into… The Toilet Zone

**A HellBound Books LLC
Publication**

http://www.hellboundbookspublishing.com

Printed in the United States of America

9 781948 318945